PRAISE FOR ABIGAIL DRAKE

This book is written entirely from the point of view of a Labrador puppy. It could be overwhelmingly cute but it isn't. It's funny and sneaky and presents a wonderfully refreshing world view of a dog who only wants to do the right thing and help his mistress to find true love while earning himself a more appropriate name. Pure fun.

EILEEN HODGETTS, AUTHOR AND SCREENWRITER

This story left me with a warm, gushy feeling inside. Lifted my spirits and put me in such a good mood I feel like a happier person.

AMAZON REVIEWER

This is a heartwarming story that will stay with you, and make you smile for weeks to come.

PAT PERRIER, AUTHOR

HEARTS, FLOWERS, AND A DOG NAMED AL CAPONE

ABIGAIL DRAKE

To Uncle Clancy.
Rest in peace, good boy

And to Mistress Patti.
A fine human and an excellent dog whisperer.

ONE

A list of things not to do at a wedding:

1. Steal the boutonniere
2. Chew on the satin and lace ring pillow.
3. Eat the wedding bands.
4. Bark at the priest.

I liked making lists. Lists kept me focused. They stopped my scattered thoughts from veering off in unnecessary, and often unpredictable, directions.

Well, most of the time. Because even though I tried to pay attention, and I wanted to be good, I had several factors going against me.

First of all, I was a puppy—a Labrador Retriever puppy, to be precise. And we were not known for making smart decisions.

Secondly, my name created a problem as well. My breeder called me Al Capone as a joke, but it stuck, and naming a puppy something like that was just asking for trouble.

I blamed my breeder for other things, too, including my obsession with books, regency gentlemen, and public television. She had my best interests at heart, but I was a weird little doggie. Eventually, however, I'd learned to accept myself—warts, drool, and all.

I just hadn't learned how to control my baser instincts. Those still needed work.

When my new owner, Miss Josephine St. Clair of Bartleby's Books, agreed to marry Mr. Nathanial Murray of First Impressions Coffee, I knew they'd need my help to pull it off—especially since I was not the only animal in the wedding party. It also included two Pugs, a small Sheltie, and a cat.

What could possibly go wrong?

The other animals belonged to various people. One of the Pugs, an obese, older dog named Jackson, was Mr. Nate's sidekick. The other Pug, an evil genius of a puppy called Faraday, was the property of the matron of honor, Ms. Anne. Or maybe she was *his* property. I couldn't be certain.

Gracie, the high maintenance little Sheltie, also belonged to Ms. Anne. I loved Gracie. Although a total diva, she had great fashion sense, and she usually herded all of us in the right direction.

And, last but not least, the final animal in our wedding party was a cantankerous kitty cat called Rocco. I considered Rocco to be my brother-by-another-mother. He also belonged to Miss Josie, and we lived in the same house, but he may or may not have hated my guts. It really depended on the time of day, his mood, and how annoying I'd been. And today, because of the wedding, I guess I'd been super annoying.

"Please shut up and go away," said Rocco for the

hundredth time as I bounced happily around the room. We were in a special area next to the chapel, called the bridal suite, and Miss Josie was getting ready for the big event.

"I can't help it," I said. "I'm so excited. I've never been in a wedding before. This is the best day ever."

Rocco tugged angrily at his bowtie. "Or the worst day ever. Who thinks having four dogs and a cat as part of their wedding party is a good idea?"

"Come on, Rocco. What could possibly go wrong?"

I should never have asked that question. It felt like tempting fate, since there were a lot of things that could go wrong, but a wedding would not be a wedding unless it involved at least one minor disaster. A little snafu. A tiny oopsie. A small faux pas. And Miss Josie's special day had all those things and more.

Let me explain.

As Miss Josie and her matron of honor, Ms. Anne, got ready, I vowed to keep all my bad qualities under wraps. Those qualities included awful impulse control, poor decision-making skills, and a particular propensity for getting into peculiar predicaments.

Oh, and I also tended to eat things that weren't technically edible. Not a good habit at all.

I tried to control myself, but, unfortunately, it was hard not to get caught up in the general splendor of the event. Excitement filled the air. It was like a regency ball, but even better. Miss Josie glowed with happiness, and she looked even happier when the wedding flowers arrived.

"Oh, they are beautiful," she said, eying the fragrant assortment of white roses, camellia blossoms, and greenery —all non-toxic to pets. Miss Josie had thought this through. She didn't want to kill a member of her wedding party by adding something potentially poisonous in her bouquet. That would have been bad planning indeed.

As Miss Josie and the other ladies gushed over the bridal bouquet, I tried very hard to behave, but the bride and her entourage had left Mr. Nate's boutonniere resting on the kitchen table. Alone. Unsupervised. And smelling of roses, camellias, and wedded bliss.

Who does not enjoy the taste of wedded bliss?

Probably a lot of people, but as Emma Woodhouse once wisely said in Austen's book of the same name, "One half of the world cannot understand the pleasures of the others."

This applied to all things, including wedding flowers, and I blamed the roses. Why else would I feel compelled to rip the petals from the boutonniere and eat them in one gulp? I could not fault myself for that indiscretion. Something so tempting should not have been left alone.

Fortunately, I did not eat the giant, pearl-capped pin shoved into the sticky green tape that held the blossoms together. I'm not that stupid. I also very wisely avoided the stems, which I'd learned (through trial and error), could be potentially thorny.

Eating only a few of the lovely, fragrant rose petals seemed like a minor infraction in the grand scheme of things. Miss Josie, however, took a different view.

"What happened to the boutonniere?" she asked, searching the table.

Ms. Anne shuffled things around as she helped Miss Josie try to locate it. "That's strange. I saw it right here two minutes ago."

"Where could it have gone?"

I let out a nervous burp. They both turned and stared at me, comprehension dawning on their faces, and I knew I was busted.

Curse my inability to hide my guilty conscience and my excess gas.

Not that I had anything to feel guilty about. This was all the result of human error. I was basically an innocent bystander.

"What are we going to do?" wailed Miss Josie, holding up what remained of the sad-looking boutonniere. It basically consisted of a few limp petals, floral tape, and the giant, pearl-tipped pin.

Mr. Nate must have heard her wail because he tapped on the door. He couldn't see her before the wedding since it was bad luck. Instead, he stood outside the door as Ms. Anne explained the situation and gave him the half-eaten boutonniere.

Mr. Nate laughed. "If this is the worst thing that happens today, we're getting off easy."

I loved Mr. Nate. He'd proven himself time after time to be the best sort of human. And he adored Miss Josie. Nothing else really mattered.

I felt so relieved. Maybe I hadn't ruined things after all. But the wedding was not over yet.

A FEW HOURS LATER, as we entered the church, Mr. Nate beamed as he waited at the altar for Miss Josie. He looked so handsome—even with the mangled flowers hanging limply from his lapel. Normally, Mr. Nate was a jeans and T-shirts sort of guy, but today he looked like a proper gentleman in his perfectly tailored tux. It warmed my Austen-loving heart.

As the wind howled outside and snow fell, blanketing the town in white, I stood nervously next to Miss Josie at the entrance of the church. Because she'd lost both her parents in a car accident many years ago, she had no one else to escort her down the aisle, so I'd been given the honor. It was a proud moment for me indeed.

The organ music played, and Mr. Nate's whole face lit up. Miss Josie's did, too. She was a vision in antique lace. A delicate veil covered her face and flowed down to the floor, and she'd arranged her blond curls in a complicated updo. She'd never been so beautiful or looked so blissfully happy, which said a lot. She loved Mr. Nate, he loved her right back, and they were getting married at last.

"It's showtime," she said softly, patting me on the head.

But before we began our march down the aisle, Ms. Anne knelt to speak to me, using her sternest voice. I tried very hard to pay close attention, but paying attention was difficult, especially when I got momentarily distracted by her lovely, emerald-green gown. Made of silk, it matched her eyes and set off the color of her long, red hair. I wanted very badly to lick it but decided to do that later—after we posed for photos. No one wanted doggie drool marks on their dress in a picture that might sit on someone's mantle for eternity. Even I knew that much.

"Focus, Capone," she said, snapping her fingers to bring me out of my reverie. She held up a white satin pillow with two shiny platinum rings on it. "Remember what we practiced, and don't screw this up."

I wagged my tail. I would not screw up. No way. I took my job very seriously.

She narrowed her eyes at me as if assessing my ability to do this. I couldn't tell if I'd convinced her or not, but she gave me the pillow, shot me one last worried glance, and walked down the aisle on the arm of one of Mr. Nate's brothers.

I took in a deep, steadying breath. I knew what I had to do. I would carry the rings up to the front of the church and wait patiently until the priest said, "Do you have the rings?" Then I would walk over to Mr. Nate and give him the pillow.

Easy peasy.

Note to self: Nothing is ever easy peasy. It's usually hardy wardy.

But joy blossomed in my chest as I trotted happily down the aisle, with the satin pillow clutched in my mouth and Miss Josie by my side. Ms. Anne waited at the altar, across from Mr. Nate, and I marched right over to her, precisely as we'd practiced. Jackson, Gracie, and Faraday did the same. We were wedding ceremony rock stars.

Rocco, the cat, did not march. He slithered down the aisle, eyes wide, and a terrified expression on his smushed gray face as he tried to get the big, fancy bow tie off his neck. He also swore up a blue streak. Fortunately, the humans didn't understand. They heard, "Meow, meow, meow," when he actually said, "Get this (bleepity bleep) thing off my (bleepity bleep) neck right now. It's (bleepity bleep) strangling me."

I won't include the expletives, but, let me tell you, they were all very rude words. He obviously disapproved of the bow tie, but I loved mine. I never wanted to take it off. It was glorious. It made me seem like a hero from an Austen novel.

But even if I possessed the accouterments of any fine man about town, I still acted like a puppy. Therefore, after a few minutes, my mouth got tired of holding the pillow. I put it down so I could lick my privates, and, out of the blue, a question popped into my Labradorian brain.

What would the pillow taste like?

It smelled faintly of lavender and happiness. I've always wanted to taste happiness, so I decided a nibble wouldn't hurt.

"Capone don't do it," said Gracie. She nudged Jackson, who'd fallen asleep. "Tell him not to do it, Jackson."

Jackson snorted, not opening his eyes. He had drool hanging down his chin. "Do it, Capone. Do it," he said, his words slurred as he blew out a spit bubble.

Gracie huffed. "You were supposed to tell him *not* to do it, doofus." Jackson didn't respond. He rolled onto his back and farted. That caused Gracie to get more irritated. "You are disgusting. Maybe you can help, Faraday."

The tiny Pug shrugged, an evil gleam in his eye. Faraday always had an evil gleam in his eye. It was kind of his thing.

"He should do it," he said. "Haven't you always wanted to taste a satin pillow, Capone? It's probably delicious."

He was right. I *had* always wanted to taste a satin pillow, but I should have known better. Never, ever listen to a dog named after a famous physicist. It was wrong to give something that small so much power. It was also wrong to give something essential and valuable to a Labrador to carry. That was a colossal mistake as well.

To my great disappointment, the pillow did not taste delicious at all, although the ribbons tying the rings onto it reminded me of fettuccine. Not because of taste or texture, but in the way I slurped them up. I'd just swallowed the last bit, my stomach full of ribbons and lace, when I heard the priest utter the words that sent dread coursing through my entire furry body.

"Do you have the rings?"

Oh, calamity. The rings.

TWO

Why eating non-food items is a bad idea:

1. They have no nutritional value.
2. They sometimes hurt going in.
3. They always hurt going out.
4. They cause distress, both emotional and intestinal.

Everyone in the church turned and laid eyes on me. I put on my best and most innocent face and tried hard to maintain it. I glanced behind me, faking a sort of "Are you all looking at me?" expression. It failed miserably. There was a fine line between innocence and desperation, and I guess I crossed it.

Mr. Nate leaned close to me, his brown eyes worried. "Where's the pillow, Capone? Where are the rings?"

Oh, dear. My inability to say no to ribbons that reminded me of fettuccine might haunt me forever.

I gave a tentative wag of my tail as my stomach gurgled. Now I'd ruined everything. How could Miss Josie and Mr.

Nate become husband and wife without rings? It seemed impossible.

This was a big problem. The boutonniere had been the first strike of the day, and the rings strike two. My heart sank as I realized I'd nearly run out of strikes.

Since I currently stood in front of a man of God, Father O'Malley, I thought I'd better confess. "Bless me, Father, for I have sinned. It happened two minutes ago."

My confession may have sounded rather aggressive, mostly because I felt so flustered. To the people in the chapel, it probably sounded like I was barking my head off at Father O'Malley—an elderly priest with a heart condition.

Oh, calamity.

"Capone, stop it," said Miss Josie, but she was too late. The damage had been done, and Father O'Malley had to sit down for a moment due to nerves. What a catastrophe.

"I can't believe you ate the rings," said Gracie. "What were you thinking?"

"I never think," I said. "Isn't that obvious?"

"You are in so much trouble," said Faraday with a snicker. "I bet they give you away after this. I bet they send you to the pound. That's where all the bad dogs go."

Faraday was right. What a nightmare.

As Jackson continued to snore and Rocco continued to quiver and hiss, Miss Josie and Mr. Nate took care of poor old Father O'Malley. I wanted to help, too, so I poked my nose in and licked Father O'Malley's shoe. And his sock. And his leg. When my tongue hit the bare skin of his calf, he let out a squeak.

"He tried to bite me," he said, his eyes bugging out in fear.

Oh, my. Now I had to add "Frightened an elderly man of God" to my long list of accomplishments.

Ms. Anne grabbed me by the collar and pulled me away from Father O'Malley. They explained I kissed him by way of an apology, and he seemed to accept it, although he stared in disgust at the slobber marks on his shiny black leather shoes.

Ms. Anne pulled a ring off her finger and handed it to Mr. Nate. She'd been married and divorced three times, and she was also rich, so she had plenty of rings.

Mr. Nate's brother Mr. Billy had a ring engraved with his initials. He lent it to Miss Josie to put onto Mr. Nate's finger. So, with a used diamond solitaire and a signet ring engraved with the letters BM on it, Mr. Nate and Miss Josie became husband and wife.

Jackson chose this moment to wake up. "Is it time for cake yet?" he asked with a yawn.

I doubted I would get any cake this evening, not even Miss Josie's special doggie cake. To be honest, I wasn't sure I wanted any, since my stomach was currently full of fluff, satin, and matching platinum bands.

"Capone ate the rings," said Gracie.

Jackson, who'd grown a little gray around the snout, rubbed his eyes with one paw. "Capone did what?"

"He almost ruined the wedding," said Faraday

I glanced up at Miss Josie. She had her back to me as the priest said, "I now pronounce you husband and wife. You may kiss the bride."

Mr. Nate smiled down at her, his eyes misty with tears. He cupped her face in his hands, and when he leaned down to kiss her, the guests cheered. It was a super romantic moment.

The wedding didn't seem ruined. It seemed perfect.

"Miss Josie looks so happy," I said.

"It's *Ms.* Josie now," said Faraday. "And you almost ruined it. After all, you are the dog that ate their wedding rings."

He made a valid point. My humans were about to begin their lives together, and I'd consumed the symbol of their union. Not a promising sign.

But I told myself it would be fine. They adored each other, rings, or no rings. They'd even bought a home together, the beautiful old Broussard mansion on River Road. It needed extensive repairs and would take time to bring it back to its former glory, but everything would work its way out eventually.

I just hoped something else worked its way out—meaning the rings from my digestive tract. Sadly, I knew from personal experience that what goes in must come out.

The reception went off without a hitch. The guests dined and danced and toasted the happy couple. Ms. Anne caught the bouquet, which caused titters of amusement. She'd been down the aisle three times already, but she lifted the bouquet triumphantly above her head. Apparently, she was ready to give it another go.

I mean, after she finished poop watch. After all, someone had to keep an eye out for the rings while Ms. Josie and Mr. Nate went on their honeymoon.

"I'll take care of it," said Ms. Anne, as Ms. Josie and Mr. Nate prepared to leave. "Don't you worry. Go. Have fun. Enjoy yourselves."

They were headed to a tropical island somewhere, and Ms. Anne had promised to take care of us until they returned. She was an outstanding friend. We were not an easy job.

Ms. Josie, still in her beautiful gown, lowered herself to

stare me straight in the eye. "Be a good boy for Anne. I mean it."

I licked her face to reassure her, but she didn't seem convinced.

After Mr. Nate and Ms. Josie sped away, Ms. Anne loaded us into her shiny, new BMW. The first two letters, BM, reminded me of Mr. Nate's brother and the signet ring. It also reminded me of something else.

"Uh-oh. I have to poop," I said as I sat on the backseat next to Jackson. He used to be Mr. Nate's dog, but he'd officially become my doggie stepbrother, a fantastic development. I imagined us hanging out together, maybe getting bunk beds, and doing all sorts of fun activities, but for now, I could only concentrate on one thing—my need to defecate.

Gracie glanced back from the front seat. "You can't, Capone. Not until we get home. This is a new BMW. No one poops in a BMW."

Faraday, Ms. Anne's new puppy, glanced back at me as well. "Do it," he said. "You have to go, I can tell. You won't be able to hold it."

I started to whine. Faraday made things so much worse. Now my belly gurgled, full of fluff and satin and many other things. I'd snuck quite a few treats from guests at the reception, too. I had to poop so urgently I feared I might explode.

"He's right. I can't hold it," I said, grunting under the strain.

"You have to," said Gracie.

But I couldn't. I whined some more. Then I did several circles on the back seat, hoping to find the right angle in case I had to do an emergency squat.

Ms. Anne finally realized something had gone amiss. "Capone. What's wrong, puppy?"

I didn't answer, of course, because I couldn't. I'm a dog. If I could speak Human, we wouldn't have had this problem.

I tried hard to contain myself, and my excrement, but when Faraday chanted, "Do it, do it," from the front seat, I lost all hope. I let it out. I did the dirty deed in the back of Ms. Anne's beautiful, new car.

This was a bad thing, and not only because of the car. I'd also forgotten something very important. Rocco slept on the floor right next to me, and he woke up when I pooped on top of his head.

"What the—"

A series of choking noises cut off his words. Poor Rocco. It reminded me of when he had to cough up a furball, but worse, and with more gagging. And I didn't blame him one bit for vomiting. My excrement produced a dreadful stench, and no one wanted to be awoken by doggie poo falling on their head.

Being a dog with impeccable timing, Jackson chose that moment to pass gas. He did that a lot, but the combination of my poo, Rocco's puke, and Jackson's gaseousness made Ms. Anne gag as well. Despite the snow and chilly temperature, she rolled down all the windows and sped home as quickly as possible.

When we pulled up in front of her house, a pretty Victorian painted pale green with pink and dark green accents, Ms. Anne practically flew out of the car. So did Rocco. He jumped out the open window and rolled about in the snow, trying to get my poo off his fur. Gracie, Faraday, and Jackson exited through the open driver's side door, but I didn't leave. I burned with shame over what had happened and feared Ms. Anne might be mad at me. I remained in the back seat, shivering, with my head down until Ms. Anne opened the door.

She lifted a hand to her nose at the smell wafting from her vehicle. "Oh, puppy. What did you do?"

I gave her a hesitant wag of my tail, hoping she might suspect perhaps Jackson, or maybe Rocco, had done the deed. But they all stood staring at me from the sidewalk, witnesses to the mess I'd made inside the formerly pristine car.

"Come on, Capone," said Ms. Anne. "Let's get you inside so I can change out of this dress and clean up your mess."

My mess. She was right. This *was* my mess. It *always* seemed to be my mess.

As I stepped onto the sidewalk, she patted me on the head, indicating she didn't hate me, which made me feel the tiniest bit better.

"What's that?" she asked, leaning closer and squinting as she peeked inside her car. I followed her gaze. On top of my disgusting pile of excrement, I could just make out something sparkly and metallic. Something still tied with ribbons that resembled fettuccine.

She looked at me. I looked at her. Then, with a long sigh, she pulled out her phone. "Josie," she said, her phone on speaker. "I've got good news. Your rings have made it out safely."

Ms. Josie, probably still on her way to the airport, responded with a note of surprise in her voice, "They did? Already? Thank goodness."

"Yes. They're in my car."

A long pause ensued, during which I could almost hear the wheels clicking in Ms. Josie's head. "Oh, no, Anne. In your car? I'm so sorry."

"Please don't worry about it," she said. "It's far better than a bowel obstruction, right? Just relax and enjoy your trip, Josie. I've got this. Everything will be fine."

She turned off her phone, and said it again, as if trying to convince herself, as she stared at the stinky interior of her car. "I've got this. Everything will be fine."

I felt awful for Ms. Anne. I hoped she was right, but I knew one thing for certain.

This was not a promising start.

THREE

Things one should not do as a guest in someone's home:

1. Steal their stockings.
2. Drool in their shoes.
3. Romp in their bed.
4. Set their house on fire.

Ms. Anne always exuded an aura of calm, even under the worst circumstances. That, combined with her easygoing nature, explained why she agreed to act as the caregiver to three pets belonging to other people. She already had two pets of her own, and five animals could get into a lot of trouble. Oddly enough, I seemed to be the only one causing problems.

Grabbing a blanket from the trunk of the car, she carefully picked up Rocco, murmuring to him softly as she tried to soothe him. He was obviously distressed. He called me names I'd never heard before, but I guess I deserved them.

Curse my impulsive nature and my irritable bowels.

Placing Rocco on a bed of towels in the utility sink of

her laundry room, Ms. Anne quickly slipped out of her dress and heels and washed off Rocco wearing nothing but a pretty lace push-up bra and matching panties. She had excellent taste in lingerie and possessed a great deal of wisdom. If she'd washed Rocco while in her evening gown, the results could have been a disaster.

Well, more of a disaster. They already seemed rather disastrous.

Rocco swore at me the entire time she washed him. She used a sprayer attachment from the sink and took care not to get soap in his eyes. Bathing an angry cat was never a pleasant experience, but Rocco was so desperate not to smell like my poo anymore he took it like a champ.

"I hate you, Capone," he said, shouting to be heard over the sound of the water. "I'm going to get you for this. I'm going to make you pay. You have to sleep sometime, and when you do, I'll be there."

I shivered at the tone of his voice. He sounded serious. "Rocco. Buddy. I didn't mean to do it."

He popped his soggy head up over the side of the tub so he could glare down at me. "You never mean to do it, and yet you always do it. Do you see a pattern here? No matter how hard you try, you fail. You're a *bad* dog."

I gasped. "You don't mean that. Take it back."

He shook his head, spraying Ms. Anne with water, and I felt very sorry. It had not been an easy day for her. And now she stood in the laundry room in her skivvies, taking care of a poopy cat.

"Wow. Happy Valentine's Day to me," she muttered under her breath.

Oh, snap. I'd forgotten it was Valentine's Day.

Wiping her face, Ms. Anne used a clean towel to wrap up Rocco and lift him out of the tub, holding him close to her. All I could see were Rocco's angry green eyes. The rest of him remained covered in the towel.

"I *do* mean it," he said. "You're a bad dog, and the others all agree with me."

I shot a quick and desperate look at Jackson and Gracie. Neither of them could quite meet my eyes. It stabbed at my furry little heart because it meant they agreed with Rocco.

Faraday did meet my gaze, and the jerk had the nerve to laugh. "The feline is correct, Capone. You are a bad dog indeed. Possibly the worst I have ever encountered. And you're a bit dim as well."

Considering Faraday was roughly the size of the poop I'd made in Ms. Anne's car, standing up to me seemed like a bold move on his part. Then again, he knew I wouldn't hurt him. I was, after all, a gentleman. It annoyed me, however, that no matter how badly he misbehaved, he never got caught. I got caught every time.

It may have been a size thing. I outweighed Faraday by nearly seventy pounds. When I did something, it was kind of hard to miss.

After Ms. Anne washed Rocco, she got dressed and went outside alone in the cold to clean her vehicle. I'm sure that's not how she planned to end her evening. She went from wearing an evening gown to tromping to the car in snow boots.

We watched her from the window. "She's had a rough time," I said. "I'm going to have to be extra thoughtful to make up for this."

My friends laughed. Well, everyone except Rocco. He turned his back to us and slept on a chair next to the fireplace, still covered in a towel. Rocco may have been a bit traumatized.

"Don't laugh," I said. "I mean it. I want to do something considerate for Ms. Anne. What can I do?"

Gracie rolled her eyes. "There is nothing you can do to help Ms. Anne."

"I need to come up with something. What does she want most in the whole world?"

Gracie sighed. "What she wants most is to fall in love and find her happily ever after, but it never worked out for my unfortunate human. She's been married three times, and she's now searching for husband number four."

I frowned. "But if Ms. Anne married all those times, she must have been in love a lot."

The small Sheltie shook her head. "It's not like that, Capone. It's a sad story. Do you want to hear it?"

"Yes, I do."

As Ms. Anne went upstairs to shower, we sat with Gracie in front of the fire. "A long time ago, Ms. Anne fell madly in love. It happened back in high school, but I heard her talk to Josie about it once after they'd had several bottles of wine. He was her first love. Ms. Anne gave her whole heart to that guy, and now she has nothing left."

I rose to my feet, excited. "That's easy. I can fix this. We'll find her long-lost love and reconnect them. How hard could it be?"

"Impossible," said Gracie sadly. "Because he drowned, swimming in the river with some friends. The currents were strong, especially in the springtime, and he disappeared in seconds. My human never got over it. She never got over *him*." Jackson, Faraday, and I sniffed in unison.

"That's so sad," said Faraday. When we gaped at him in surprise, he scowled at us, changing his tone. "I mean, she needs to get over it—stupid human. There are lots of fish in the sea. She needs to find another fish."

I licked Faraday's head, even though I really didn't like him. I couldn't help it. He may have been evil, but his cuteness overwhelmed me. Also, I was a licker by nature.

"Faraday. You are a genius."

"Tell me something I don't know," he said, wiping my kiss from his head.

Jackson regarded me with a worried frown. "You aren't thinking what I believe you're thinking, are you, buddy?" he asked. "Because if you plan to find a Mr. Darcy for Ms. Anne, you'd better stop right now."

I shook my head. "No, no, no. Not a Mr. Darcy. Ms. Anne needs a *Mr. Knightley.*"

They all stared at me blankly. I opened my mouth to explain, but Rocco butted in. "Mr. Knightley is also a fictional character. He's the romantic hero in Jane Austen's book *Emma.* Dingbat has been watching that stupid movie non-stop for the last month, and he's obsessed, but Mr. Knightley isn't real, just like Mr. Darcy isn't real. You live in La La Land, Capone. Life is not a regency novel. It's real, and it's hard, and sometimes poop lands on your head, and there is nothing you can do about it."

Rocco typically didn't give such heart-felt speeches, and we stared at him in surprise. He let out a growly noise. "And I hate you all. Now shut up and leave me alone."

He didn't really hate me. He said that as a sort of endearment. Being snarky was the way Rocco hugged.

When Ms. Anne came back downstairs, she opened a bottle of wine, poured a big glass, and sat by the fire. Despite his bath, Rocco still smelled like poo, so Ms. Anne lit a candle. She turned on some soft music and curled up on the couch. Jackson, Faraday, and Gracie all snuggled together on Gracie's doggie bed by the fire. Being such small dogs, they could all fit. I could not. I had my nose on the bed, but the rest of me remained on the cold, hard floor. Ms. Anne took pity on me and patted the spot next to her on the couch.

"Come here, boy," she said. "Warm me up."

I jumped at the chance. I mean, literally. I loved nothing more than cuddles on the couch, so I curled up next to her, my head on her lap, and let out a blissful sigh. This was heaven.

"For all your faults, you are an excellent cuddler," she said, patting my head. "And I don't care what anyone says. You're a good dog. But you're a puppy. It's normal for you to make regrettable decisions now and then." She pointed to the rings now clean and sparkly on the coffee table. "Except eating those rings. Please don't do something like that again. And please don't poop in my car. Deal?"

When I let out a small bark of agreement, she smiled at me. Ms. Anne had to be one of the kindest humans I'd ever encountered. A real gem. And she seemed to like me, too.

"You're a great date, Capone. There is no one else I'd rather spend Valentine's Day with." Her eyes grew sad. "Well, one other person comes to mind, but..." She paused, swallowing hard. She must have been recalling her long-lost love. I snuggled closer, encouraging her to continue, and she stroked my head. This may have been better than watching a Nicholas Sparks movie on TV, and perhaps even more tear-inducing.

"I don't understand why I'm thinking about this tonight. Maybe it's because I spent my last truly romantic Valentine's Day with him. It's not all hearts, flowers, and chocolate, you know. Maybe seeing Josie and Nate so happy made me realize what I'm missing in my life. I once had a love like that, too. His name was Bennet O'Reilly. And he was trouble," she said, biting her lower lip. "Kind of like you, Capone."

I glanced up at her, affronted, and she laughed. "Good girls always go after the bad boys, don't they? That perfectly described Ben and me. I was the homecoming queen and the class president. He skipped school and got detention. We shouldn't have matched, but we did, and I fell crazy in love with him." Her expression grew pensive. "Do you believe in soulmates, Capone?"

I pondered her question, wishing I could tell her I did, indeed, believe in soulmates. Mr. Darcy and Miss Elizabeth served as prime examples, as did Ms. Josie and Mr. Nate. But I had the distinct impression she didn't seek an answer from me. In my limited experience, when women had too much wine, the subjects of soulmates and regret often reared their ugly heads. I'd been here before, since Labradors happened to be great listeners and the best sort of therapy.

"Bennet O'Reilly was my soulmate. When he died doing something stupid, part of me died with him, which is why I've been married and divorced three times. *Three.* And I've given up. I'm not hoping for love anymore, but I don't want to grow old alone, and the clock is ticking. If I want to find a decent guy, I'm running out of time."

I snuggled closer, attempting to comfort her. As she dozed off, the empty wine glass still in her hand, I felt unsettled, so I decided to investigate Ms. Anne's abode. I figured the better I understood her, the easier it would be for me to find Ms. Anne her own Mr. Knightley. Also, I'd never visited her home before, and I was nosy.

I found her pretty dress from the wedding hanging in the laundry room. On top of the hamper sat her lacy dainties and her stockings. I went up on my back legs and gave the stockings a yank. They were delightfully stretchy. I loved stockings, so I decided to bring them with me as I explored.

By the door, I found her high-heeled shoes. They had pointy toes and smelled so incredible I started to drool—a reflex with me. One whiff of something tempting, and the floodgates opened.

Remembering how much Ms. Josie disliked it when I drooled on and/or chewed on her shoes, I left the heels by the door, picked up the stockings again, and continued on my way.

Walking up the steps with stockings in my mouth proved trickier than expected. I tripped several times. But the effort was worth it when I found Ms. Anne's bed. It was huge, and so cozy. I jumped up, stockings still in my mouth, and hung out there a while. But after knocking all her throw pillows onto the floor, I got bored, so I trudged back down-stairs. I brought the stockings with me. I'd grown attached to them at this point.

Yawning, I realized I should probably rejoin Ms. Anne on the couch and go to sleep. As soon as I got there, some-thing crazy happened. A log fell on the fire. It made a big hissing noise, which startled me so badly I jumped. And when I jumped, my legs got tangled in the stockings.

Dang my puppy clumsiness and lack of decent balance.

After that, everything seemed to happen in slow motion. With the stockings still wrapped around my feet, I crashed into the end table near the couch. The candle flew off the table, hitting Ms. Anne's sheer and highly combustible curtains, and they went up in flames.

Oh, calamity.

FOUR

What to do in case of a fire:

1. Stay low to the floor to avoid inhaling poisonous gasses.
2. Make sure the doorknob isn't hot to the touch.
3. Stop, drop, and roll if clothing catches on fire.
4. Get out as quickly as possible.
5. No matter what, do not go back inside.

Ms. Anne woke with a start. Jackson, Faraday, Gracie, and Rocco woke up, too. Gracie screamed when she realized what had happened.

"Fire," Gracie yelled. Leaping to her feet, she herded all of us, including Ms. Anne, toward the door. Being a Sheltie, herding came naturally to her.

"Oh, my heavens," said Ms. Anne, coughing due to the thick, dense smoke. The rest of us coughed, too. We needed to get out of here. Now.

Ms. Anne grabbed her purse and picked up Rocco from the chair. He seemed frozen in fear, hissing at the flames.

Her coat hung by the door, and she got that on her way out. By the time we reached the front yard, all of us safe and accounted for, Ms. Anne's house was burning. We stood and watched in shocked silence.

The firetrucks arrived within minutes. An attentive neighbor must have seen the flames and called right away. But as we waited on the sidewalk, Rocco jumped out of Ms. Anne's arms and ran back into the house.

"Rocco, no," I screamed. I tried to run in after him, but Jackson held me back.

"Don't go in there," he said. "Remember what happened last time."

Jackson made a valid point. This was my second experience with the fire department. The first had been when I still lived in Ms. Josie's apartment, right above Bartleby's Books. A pair of senior citizens (Mrs. Steele and Mrs. Hurst) had been stealing from Bartleby's, with the help of Mrs. Hurst's much younger boyfriend, Bill Elliot. Mr. Elliot triggered the sprinklers in the shop with a bunch of cherry bombs tied together that he placed right under the sprinkler. We'd thought the shop had been on fire, but it was only smoke. The smoke itself nearly killed me, but I had little puppy lungs at the time.

"I have to go get him," I said, lunging forward, but Ms. Anne stopped me, tears rolling down her cheeks.

"No, Capone. Stay."

I plopped my bottom on the ground and let out a mournful wail. I couldn't lose my feline brother Rocco. He mostly hated me, but we'd still become friends and allies over the last few months. The whole "the enemy of my enemy is my friend" thing certainly applied in our situation.

As the firefighters entered the house, Ms. Anne put her

face in my fur and sobbed. I could feel the wet warmth of her tears on my skin. I'd caused this. It was all my fault.

Right then and there, I made a promise. If Rocco made it out alive, I swore I'd turn over a new leaf. I'd be a better, wiser version of myself.

If he made it out. Because I couldn't imagine what would happen if he didn't.

And I'd make it up to Ms. Anne, too. Despite what the others said, I'd find her Mr. Knightley. I could do it. All I needed was a sign.

A tall fireman emerged from the front door, smoke billowing around him. Like a scene in an action movie, he materialized out of nowhere and saved the day. The fireman certainly seemed like a hero, and I realized when he removed his mask that he was movie-star handsome. Dark eyes. Dark skin. A smile that was a flash of white. And he also had dimples. Dimples were always delightful. But what made him the most heroic of all had to be the fact that he'd been brave enough to rescue Rocco—a crabby, slightly charred, gray cat with an attitude.

I barked, which caught Ms. Anne's attention. When she saw what the fireman held in his brawny arms, she jumped to her feet. "Rocco," she said, running over to him.

Rocco coughed and spluttered. The fireman brought him over to the truck to give him oxygen, and that's when two shiny objects fell out of Rocco's mouth and onto the sidewalk. We stared at him in shock. Ms. Anne leaned down to pick them up.

"The rings," she said, crying harder. "You brave, stupid, wonderful kitty cat. I'm going to spoil you so much. You're going to live like a king, I swear."

"As I should." Rocco choked out the words, and

although Ms. Anne couldn't possibly understand him, she got the drift.

"And you'll have catnip," she said. "As far as the eye can see."

The fireman let out a laugh. "This is one lucky cat," he said, placing an oxygen mask over Rocco's face. Rocco still coughed, but it didn't sound as grave as it had only a few minutes ago.

"Thank you so much," said Ms. Anne, wiping away her tears with a shaking hand. In the other hand, she held the rings. Why hadn't I remembered the rings? Rocco had saved the day. He was a hero.

"Don't mention it," said the fireman, his dark eyes warm and kind. "My name is Fletcher. Nice to meet you."

"Fireman Fletch," I said softly. "Or maybe we should call him Fireman Fetch."

"Because he's so fetching?" asked Jackson with a snort.

I answered him quite seriously. "Yes, and also because he fetched Rocco from the flames and saved his life."

"I agree," said Gracie. She may have been drooling as she stared at Fireman Fetch. "He is fetching. And he's hotter than that fire."

The fire. When I thought about it, I let out a whine. How could this have happened? It may have been the worst thing I'd ever done.

Note to self: It's always darkest before it's pitch black.

But I saw a glimmer of hope hovering on the horizon. Despite Ms. Anne's house being in shambles, it now seemed like a stroke of luck. If Fireman Fetch turned into the perfect Mr. Knightley for our sweet Ms. Anne, I'd accomplished my goal already and found her one true love. And I'd done it in record time to boot.

"I can't judge," said Faraday. "Humans all look pretty

much the same to me. But I have to tell you, Rocco—I'm impressed."

"Because I risked my life to save the wedding rings?" asked Rocco, who'd finally stopped coughing.

"No," said Faraday with an evil laugh. "Because you put those rings in your mouth. You do remember they came out of Capone's—"

"Stop," said Gracie, but she didn't speak soon enough. Rocco made a gagging noise and puked all over the handsome, young fireman.

Poor Fireman Fetch. Poor Ms. Anne. Poor us. And, especially, poor Rocco. We'd only been away from Ms. Josie and Mr. Nate for a few hours, and he'd already been pooped on, farted on, and nearly burned alive.

"I hate you all," said Rocco, his eyes closed. He opened them and glared right at me. "Especially you, Capone."

"Well, now that things are back to normal," said Jackson, plopping his chubby Pug butt down on the sidewalk. "Where are we going to stay?"

Gracie's eyes widened. "He's right. We're homeless." She let out of cry. "All of my collars were in that house. And my doggie bed. And my princess sweater. And my designer poop bags."

I wanted to question the last one, but we had bigger things to worry about. "Maybe we can stay in your old apartment?" suggested Jackson.

I shook my head. "Ms. Josie already rented it out. She hired two sisters, Miss Isabella and Miss Olivia Vargas, to help in the shop, and they're staying upstairs."

"And Nate moved out of his apartment," said Jackson. "All of his things and Ms. Josie's things are already at their new house, but it's still under construction."

"It's going to be okay," I said. "We'll figure it out. The most important thing is that we have each other."

A long moment of silence passed as we contemplated our current situation. Things did not look promising for our little band of adventurers, but every dawn brought a new day. A new chance. A fresh start.

"We're doomed," said Faraday.

And as we stared at the still-smoking mess of Ms. Anne's house, I had to consider that for once, Faraday might be right.

FIVE

The crimes of Al Capone the gangster:

1. Bootlegging.
2. Tax evasion.
3. Murder.

The crimes of Al Capone the Labrador:

1. Stealing treats.
2. Eating rings.
3. Burning down Ms. Anne's house with a
    lavender scented candle.

I truly was a menace. We were fortunate because a kind neighbor, Ms. Shelton, took us in for the night. Sadly, Ms. Shelton was allergic to both cats and dogs, so we had to find somewhere else to stay.

"I'm sorry," said Ms. Shelton between sneezes. "I wish I could help."

Ms. Shelton, a large lady with a warm smile, looked like

she might be close to tears. Or maybe her eyes watered because of the allergies. She was also breaking out in hives. We had to go. A well-mannered houseguest never over-stayed their welcome, especially when it might involve anaphylaxis.

Ms. Anne gathered us up and put on her coat. "Thank you for letting us crash here last night. You're an angel. Now go and take some antihistamine. Please."

Ms. Shelton pointed to her swollen face. "This is me after taking an antihistamine." When Ms. Anne gasped, she continued. "Don't worry. I have an Epi-Pen. It's fine."

That was enough to make Ms. Anne usher us quickly out the door and into the cold. She held Rocco in her arms. He smelled like smoke tinged with annoyance and a hint of poo. He kept giving me dirty looks and swearing at me under his breath. Rocco hadn't forgiven me yet for pooping on him. It might take a while.

Standing on Ms. Shelton's porch, we gazed around at the pretty, snowy landscape in front of us. It looked like a postcard. The Ohio River was visible in the distance, and the houses, eaves heavy with snow, had a magical quality.

There was nothing magical about Ms. Anne's house, though. It remained standing, but the firefighters had broken several of the front windows on the first and second floors to put out the flames, and the pretty green exterior had darkened in spots due to soot.

Ms. Anne let out a shaky breath as she stared at it, and I cringed. She'd been nothing but kind to me, and I'd repaid her by pooping in her car and setting her house on fire. I needed to fix this. I needed to fix all of it.

Curse my desire for boingy-boingy stockings.

Fireman Fetch promised someone would come help Ms. Anne gather a few things from the house. They'd blocked the door with yellow tape and some repairmen put up plywood to cover the broken windows. The sound of their hammering echoed in the silence of the peaceful Sunday morning. Most people still rested at home, having their breakfast, or sleeping in, or getting ready to go to church, but not us. We were hungry, cold, and homeless.

Oh, calamity. How did we end up homeless?

Ms. Anne pulled out her phone and dialed a number, her phone on speaker. A sleepy-sounding Ms. Josie answered on the second ring.

"Anne? Is everything okay?"

The connection seemed spotty. Ms. Josie and Mr. Nate were luxuriating on a lush tropical island. They'd be there for two whole weeks, and I missed them already. Upon hearing her voice, I let out a whine. Ms. Anne smiled at me.

"Capone says 'hello.' He misses you."

"I miss him, too," she said. "What happened? Is this about Capone? Is he okay?"

I heard the panic in Ms. Josie's voice. "No," said Ms. Anne. "It's nothing like that." She swallowed hard, glancing at her fire-damaged home. "I'm sorry to call you so early. Everyone is fine. We're all safe. But my house caught on fire last night."

"What?" Ms. Josie's voice came out as a loud squawk. I heard Mr. Nate in the background, but I couldn't quite make out what he said.

"That's why I'm calling. Do you mind if we crash at your house for a few days? I realize it's being renovated. I promise we'll stay out of the way."

"Of course." A loud crackle sounded over the line. "But I have to tell you...(crackle)...is there...(crackle)...no problem...(crackle)...as long as you'd like."

Ms. Anne frowned. "Josie, I can't hear you. Did you say it's okay?"

"Yes. Please stay...(crackle)...a bad connection...talk later." I heard another crackle, a much louder one this time, and the call ended.

Mr. Nate, the owner of a popular chain of coffee shops and a busy guy, had wanted to disconnect from the grid during their honeymoon. Apparently, he'd succeeded. They seemed to barely have telephone service.

Ms. Anne put her phone back into her purse. "That solves the first problem. As soon as the person from the fire department gets here, we'll gather our things and head over to Josie's house." She glanced at her watch. "And they should be here any minute."

She'd no sooner spoken when an SUV pulled up in front of Ms. Anne's house with the words Beaver Fire and Rescue on the side. To my surprise and delight, Fireman Fetch got out. He didn't have on his fireman gear. He wore a uniform with a black coat and pants, and his hotness rivaled that of any fire.

I ran over to greet him, my whole body erupting in wiggles. My plan for Fireman Fetch to be Ms. Anne's new beau appeared to be moving along right on schedule.

"Hey, buddy," he said, kneeling to pet me. "Are you staying out of trouble today?"

Trouble? Did he suspect I might be the cause of the fire? If so, I could be in some deep doo-doo.

Note to self: Find out how many years they give out for arson these days.

But Fireman Fetch didn't seem angry. He smiled, and that smile widened when he caught a glimpse of Ms. Anne.

At the wedding, in her fancy dress, with her red hair and green eyes, Ms. Anne had been both gorgeous and glamourous. But today, exhausted, and emotional, she was kind of a mess. Her hair, which she hadn't brushed, tumbled around her face, and without makeup, she didn't look her actual age, which had to be somewhere over thirty. I couldn't be sure since one never discussed a lady's age, but I remembered she'd mentioned being slightly older than Ms. Josie. Today, however, she seemed much younger and vulnerable. Fireman Fetch sensed it, too. He eyed her with concern.

"Are you okay?"

"Yes," she said, holding Rocco close. Doing that appeared to give her comfort, although I had no idea why. The last time I'd tried to snuggle with Rocco, he'd hissed and scratched my nose. But he behaved himself with Ms. Anne. "Thank you. And thanks for coming today. I appreciate it."

"Then let's go inside and get your things. Are you ready?"

She nodded, and he led her into the house. Tears welled in her eyes when she saw the blackened walls and the damaged furniture. "It's not as awful as I thought," she said, somehow managing not to cry. She was so brave.

"Most of the damage is superficial," said Fireman Fetch. He pointed to the newly boarded-up window and the remnants of a charcoaled curtain rod. "This is where it started. It could have been a candle that caused the blaze."

Ms. Anne put a hand over her mouth. "Oh, no. I lit a candle, and I must have dozed off."

"These things happen."

"I woke up as the table fell over, so maybe I knocked it over in my sleep."

Except she didn't knock it over. I did.

Thank goodness dogs couldn't blush. If so, I'd be

blushing up a storm right now. Trying not to appear guilty is especially hard when you are, in fact, guilty.

Fireman Fetch spoke to her kindly. "You really should be more careful with candles in the future." He pointed to the fireplace. "And you should always douse any fire before you go to sleep."

"You're right. I'm sorry—"

He held up a hand to stop her. "I'm not trying to make you feel worse, but education is part of my job." He gave her a sympathetic smile. "And now that the lecture on fire safety is over, what can I do to help?"

"Nothing, but may I go upstairs and grab a few things?"

He nodded. "Yes. The only damage is from smoke and water, but it could be icy. Watch your step, okay? I'll keep an eye on the menagerie until you get back."

Fireman Fetch held out his hands for Rocco. To my surprise, Rocco went to him.

We waited downstairs until Ms. Anne packed a suitcase and rejoined us. Then she fed us (thank heavens) and let us out in her backyard to go to the bathroom—also an excellent idea. I'd gotten rid of most of the pillow last night, but a few strands of ribbon and some stuffing remained. I was glad it came out in her yard and not in her car.

"Do you have somewhere to stay?" asked Fireman Fetch. "It's going to take at least a few weeks to make your house inhabitable again."

"My friends bought the old Boussard house. They're away on their honeymoon, and it's being renovated, but they said I could stay there."

"The Boussard place? I thought Nate, the coffee guy bought that house."

"He did—when he married my friend Josie."

Fireman Fetch's eyes lit up, and he shot me an appreciative glance. "Wait, are you telling me this is Capone? The dog that found all those rare books buried behind the bookstore in town last year?"

Ms. Anne laughed. "The one and only."

Fireman Fetch gave me another pat. "I had no idea I was hanging out with a local celebrity," he said with a grin. "You're one amazing pup, Capone."

I beamed at him. "It is tough for the prosperous to be humble, but I do appreciate the praise."

"Are you quoting Austen out of context again?" asked Rocco. "Because I think I recognize part of that from *Emma*."

Dang it. Why did Rocco always call me out on this stuff?

"I didn't mean to misquote. I simply wanted to say it was kind of him to mention my recent exploits."

Rocco rolled his eyes. "Give me a break. We all helped."

"Rocco is right," said Gracie, lifting her nose into the air. "You couldn't have done it without us, Capone."

I frowned at them. "I never tried to take credit. A gentleman doesn't do noble deeds because he seeks recognition or reward. He does them out of a sense of duty and chivalry."

Now Jackson rolled his eyes. "Yeah, whatever. Can we get this show on the road? It's time for my post-breakfast nap."

SIX

What you should always do before purchasing a new home:

1. Check out the neighborhood.
2. Decide how much renovating will need to be done.
3. Figure out if it's pet friendly and has a fenced in yard.
4. Make sure it isn't haunted.

Fireman Fetch helped Ms. Anne load the car. We waved goodbye and drove the short distance to the Boussard mansion. Located on a hill, it overlooked the confluence of the Beaver and Ohio Rivers. The manor house had columns, a large balcony, and a curved turret. A wrought iron fence encircled the yard, and it seemed like the perfect home for our new family.

Well, other than the chipping paint, the rickety front stairs, the uneven porch, and the general state of disrepair. Other than that? Perfect.

Time had not been kind to the Boussard mansion. It sat

abandoned for years before Ms. Josie and Mr. Nate purchased it and decided to renovate it to its former glory. They'd closed on it only a few days before they left for their honeymoon, so they'd done little except deposit the furniture, pack their suitcases, and leave. It would take a lot of work to get this place up to par, but I could see the immense potential. When they finished, it would be amazing.

Ms. Josie had given Ms. Anne a spare key, for emergencies. This certainly qualified. We waited as Ms. Anne fished the key out of her purse and unbolted the large, ornately carved front door. It slowly opened with a loud squeak.

"Welcome home," she said softly.

Large and empty and kind of creepy, this place did not seem in the least bit homey. Peeled paint dangled from the ceiling, ancient wallpaper hung in strips on the walls, and stains and dark patches dotted the hardwood floors. *Drip, drip, drip* came from the kitchen, and everything smelled musty, dusty, and old. We stared at the dilapidated interior in silence for a few minutes before I spoke.

"Wow," I said. "Is anyone else getting a weird vibe from this place?"

"What kind of vibe?" Jackson yawned, evidently ready for a nap.

"I'm not certain," I said. "But it's strange."

"Strange how?" asked Faraday, his Puggy eyes wide as his gaze darted around the room. He panted, too—a sure sign of distress.

"You feel it, don't you?"

He let out a non-committal snort. "I have no idea what you're talking about."

"You do realize this place is haunted, don't you?" asked Gracie. "That's why it's been abandoned so long."

"Haunted? You're kidding, right?" I asked.

She shook her head. "I never joke about haunted houses, Capone."

A tingle went over my skin, and I broke out in a cloud of white dandruff. That always happened when I got nervous, scared, upset, or deeply unhappy. My seborrheic dermatitis seemed psychologically motivated. Or maybe stress induced. Either way, I had issues.

Ms. Anne shivered as she entered the house, rubbing her arms with her hands to warm up. She lit a fire in the fireplace, careful to check the flue first, then placed a large, ornate grate in front of it to keep us out. Ms. Anne had listened to Fireman Fetch's instructions and didn't take any chances.

As she shuffled around, checking the hot water (it worked) and the furnace (it worked too), my friends and I curled up on the small area rug in front of the fireplace. The only furniture in the room was Ms. Josie's blue velvet couch. It had taken up so much space in her apartment but appeared tiny here. Some tools sat on a table in the corner, along with a machine for finishing hardwood floors.

"So, tell us," said Faraday, feigning nonchalance but shivering, nonetheless. "Is this place really haunted?"

Gracie glanced at each of us, making eye contact before clearing her throat. Well, she did it with everyone but Jackson. He'd already fallen fast asleep and snored like a freight train.

"It's haunted. And cursed."

Gracie told the best stories, and she had a flair for the dramatic. As she continued, her voice took on a spooky quality. "It started in 1904, with Mr. Ralph Boussard, the owner of the Boussard Brewery in Beaver. A lucky man, he was wealthy, successful, and happy. All that changed when his youngest son, Billy, died of a fever in his room upstairs."

Gracie lifted her head, gazing at the ceiling as if she could see little Billy Boussard dying up there. This coincided with the winds picking up outside as the sky darkened, and snow fell.

I shivered. "This is a horrible idea—"

Faraday interrupted me. "Shut up, kibble for brains. Let her continue." He nodded at Gracie, and she went on.

"Lost in his grief and perhaps drunk on too many beers from his brewery, Ralph Boussard took his own life. Right in this very spot."

I stared down at the carpet. "He died right here?" I asked.

"So the story goes," said Gracie, really getting into it. She knew how to tell a great ghost story.

"What happened next?" asked Faraday. "Is that all?"

She shook her head. "Nope. Ralph's wife, Melody, died of cancer a few years later. Then, in 1922, Ralph's son, Ralphie Jr., shot himself. Only one member of the family remained. Henry. The last surviving Boussard."

Ms. Anne dropped something upstairs. I let out a bark and we huddled together. Once we settled, Gracie spoke again. "The brewery had closed during prohibition, then went belly-up during the great depression. Around that time, Henry got married to his high school sweetheart. Sadly, she died a year later in childbirth."

I covered my ears with my paws. "Please don't say it happened upstairs."

"It did," said Gracie. "And it devastated Henry, of course, but he rallied for the sake of his son, Peter. According to local legend, Peter had been born a golden boy, a wonderful, happy child who grew into an outstanding young man. He gave Henry a reason to live, and they seemed happy for a time." She let out a sigh, and I braced myself for the worst. "Peter had a dog, a great big thing named Boo. People recognized them wherever they went and loved both the boy and the dog. Henry had improved as well. He rebuilt the family business and became nearly as successful as his father. And life was, at long last, good, until Peter enlisted in the army to fight in WWII when he turned eighteen. He died only weeks later. They never recovered his body."

"How heartbreaking for Henry," said Rocco. I hadn't realized he'd been listening to our conversation. When he caught my gaze, he rolled his eyes. "Why are you gawking at me like that, Capone? Do you think I have no compassion? That was the most horrible story I've ever heard."

"But there's more," said Gracie. I let out a wail, but my friends ignored me. "Henry lost his mind after Peter died. He went bankrupt. The brewery closed. And in 1949, he did the unimaginable. He killed himself—"

"In this house?" asked Faraday. He shook so violently, I thought he might wee himself, but he didn't.

"In this house," said Gracie. "Right after he killed Boo."

Faraday did wee himself this time, but we were all too shocked to care. "He killed the dog?" I asked.

Gracie nodded. "He took dear old Boo down into the basement, and..." She swallowed hard. "And shot Boo right before killing himself."

I got up and paced back and forth nervously. "That is awful. It's the worst story I've ever heard. Everyone dies a horrible death or commits suicide or murders the family pet. Why would you tell us this story, Gracie?"

"Because it's true." She let out a yawn. "And they say odd things happen here all the time, like doors slamming and footsteps and lights turning on and off. I've also heard someone died in the carriage house out back. A gardener or something." She tilted her head to indicate the large structure in the garden. "Anyway, it's all a bunch of nonsense. I don't believe in ghosts."

She curled up next to Jackson on the dry part of the rug. "But I will say one more thing," she said, pausing for dramatic effect. "If you hear the sad sound of a dog barking in the night, that's probably Boo. I'm going to take a nap now. Behave you two." She closed her eyes and then opened them again. "And never go into the basement alone. Trust me."

Gracie fell asleep, and so did Rocco, but Faraday and I stared at each other. "We're screwed," he said. "This place is haunted, and we're all going to die."

When he peed again on the carpet, I didn't judge him. Tiny dogs had tiny bladders, after all. But when I glanced at the door leading down to the basement, a shiver went over me.

I curled up next to Gracie, but I couldn't sleep. She might not believe in ghosts, but something was unsettling in this place. I felt it in my bones. Although the Boussards had died a long time ago, their memories lived on in this house. My house. And I realized Faraday was right.

We were screwed.

SEVEN

A list of the wonderful people who bring us deliveries:

1. The United States Postal Service (our mail carrier, Ms. Beth, is a letter-handling angel).
2. The United Parcel Service (brown trucks, brown suits, cool scanners).
3. FedEx (white trucks, blue suits, equally cool scanners).
4. Instacart. The food people.

I sometimes wondered if all the various delivery people talked about us. I was pretty sure they did.

When Ms. Josie first began ordering from Instacart, she included a note that read, *"Please leave by the front door and don't knock unless you want to be licked and body-slammed by an annoying dog."* Because of that note, I never got to see any of the Instacart people. They reminded me of the Tooth Fairy or Santa. The food simply arrived, as if by some miracle.

Ms. Josie must have told Ms. Anne about the instructions because I woke from my nap to the sound of someone dropping off groceries by the front door. It may have been the most exciting moment of my life.

I jumped to my feet and tripped over Jackson, barking my head off. The other dogs followed me, barking their heads off, too. They likely had no idea what we were barking at, but it caused quite the commotion.

"Settle down," said Ms. Anne, taking a peek out the window. When confident the delivery person had gotten a safe distance away, she opened the front door. And that's when it happened. That's when I went into zoomie mode.

Curse my Labradorian energy spurts.

A zoomie is when a dog runs full speed then spins around in a crazy circle. In my case, I usually did this repeatedly, getting more out of control with each spin. Today, as I gained speed, all my recent stress over the fire and pooping in the car and the wedding came out in a burst as my level of excitement increased exponentially. Soon my brain became nothing but a big swirl of zoomie craziness.

Gracie and Faraday were tiny dogs. When they did zoomies, it was cute. When I did them, it was like some force from hell had been unleashed, destroying everything in its path. And guess who crossed my path on this snowy, icy, cold February day?

Ms. Anne.

I didn't mean to body slam her as she picked up the groceries. I blamed it on a combination of zoomie energy and a slippery porch. And I'm not saying Ms. Anne has a big bottom, but she blocked the doorway as she leaned over, and it seemed impossible not to slam into her bum. I mean, it was right there.

Note to self: A gentleman never head-butts a woman from behind like a billy goat. It simply is not done.

Ms. Anne landed on her hands and knees in the foyer with one grocery bag twisted around her ankle and another around her wrist. When I licked her face to make sure she was okay, she pushed me away. "Capone. What were you thinking?"

I lowered my head because I had no idea how to respond to her question. I never thought things out. That may have been part of my problem.

She sighed. "At least no one saw—"

"Knock, knock," came a voice from the front porch. A handsome blond man stood there in a blue wool sweater that matched his eyes. He looked like a Viking. Well, if Vikings wore blue wool sweaters and jeans. "I'm Val. Valentine Snyder. I live next door. I heard the barking and saw what happened." He went down on one knee next to Ms. Anne. "Are you okay?"

Ms. Anne stared at him, not that I blamed her. Viking Val was breathtaking.

When she didn't respond, he frowned at her, concerned. "Did you hit your head? Don't worry. I'm a doctor. I can help."

"He's a doctor," said Gracie, staring up at him, eyes wide. "He can help."

"And so tall," said Faraday. Then again, Faraday was a small Pug. Everyone seemed tall compared to him.

"And he smells like bacon," said Jackson, taking a long whiff. "The thick-cut kind. With maple syrup. And a hint of brown sugar."

Jackson took his bacon seriously. He was a sort of sommelier, but with bacon instead of wine.

"I'm Anne." Ms. Anne slowly rose to her feet. Viking Val put a hand on her arm to steady her. "And I'm fine. It's not the first time Capone has knocked me over, but it is the first time someone witnessed it."

"Trust me, I understand. I have a black Lab, too. Her name is Molly. Now she's an old lady, but I remember that from her puppy days. It's always worse when there is a witness. Are you sure you didn't bruise anything?"

A doctor, a Viking, and a black Lab owner? Be still my heart.

Ms. Anne checked her hands. "Nothing except my ego."

He smiled, all dazzling white teeth and sparkling eyes. "We can't put ice on that, but you should probably ice your knees. You landed pretty hard."

For a long moment, they stared at each other, and the air positively crackled with something. Attraction? Desire? Static electricity? I couldn't tell, but it shimmered in the space between them. And I realized if Fireman Fetch didn't work out, Viking Val could turn into another great candidate as Ms. Anne's own personal Mr. Knightley, an excellent development. In two days, I'd already found two potential love interests for Ms. Anne. I seemed to be on a roll. This was already much, much easier than when I tried to find Ms. Josie's true love. At this rate, I'd have Ms. Anne finding her happily-ever-after in no time.

A gust of wind blew a whirl of snowflakes inside the house. "Shut the door, you losers," said Rocco, shivering from his spot on the arm of the blue couch. "It's freezing outside."

Viking Val must have realized the same thing. "You should sit down. Let me help you get these groceries inside."

Ms. Anne protested, but Viking Val insisted. He carried the bags to the kitchen and put them on the counter. Ms. Anne followed him.

"I'd offer you a cup of coffee, but I haven't found the coffee maker yet," she said.

"You moved in only recently. I'm sure it'll take some time to get settled."

"Oh, this isn't my house." Ms. Anne explained about the fire and told him how Ms. Josie and Mr. Nate were out of town.

"Gosh," he said. "You've had quite the weekend. Is there anything I can do to help?"

She shook her head. "No, but thank you for offering. The movers unpacked the necessities when they moved Josie and Nate in and set up the bedrooms and the furniture. I haven't located all the smaller items yet."

"Like the coffee maker."

"Exactly." She shot him a smile. "Fortunately, Nate owns the coffee shop in town, so I'll be okay."

"He owns First Impressions?" he asked, lifting one golden eyebrow in surprise. "I love that place." I watched as things clicked in his head. "Wait a second, I read about these animals in the newspaper. Didn't they help the police bust a rare books crime ring?"

"They did."

Gracie preened. "At least this guy acknowledged all of us played a part. Everyone else seems to remember only Capone."

I let out an annoyed huff. "Once again, not my fault, Gracie. If anything, you should be the one they're talking about. You're the most photogenic of all of us."

That seemed to make Gracie happy. But Faraday snorted. "Suck up," he said under his breath.

Faraday acted jealous. He hadn't been a part of our heroic escapades. Ms. Anne adopted him after we'd saved the bookstore and helped Ms. Josie.

Knowing Faraday, he probably would have helped the bad guys. He gave off an evil genius/villain vibe.

"It's nice to have someone living in this house again. It's been years since the last family moved out," said Val, shaking his head sadly. "I wanted to buy it, but the previous owner sold it to a developer. They tried to get it zoned commercial but ended up in a long legal battle instead. When they lost, I tried again, but your friend beat me to it. I've always thought it was such a beautiful home. I hated to see it sit abandoned and neglected. And it'll be wonderful to watch your friends restore it to its former glory."

"Why did it take so long to sell?"

He shrugged. "It's a big project, obviously, and a lot to tackle. And then there's the history of the house."

"Are you talking about the whole 'Curse of the Boussards' thing?" she asked with a dismissive wave of her hands. "Yeah, I don't believe in any of that stuff."

"What kind of stuff?"

"Ghosts. Curses. Malevolent spirits. It's all a bunch of nonsense." When he didn't respond, she eyed him curiously. "Wait a second. You don't believe in it, do you? I mean, you're a doctor. A man of science."

He shoved his hands into the pockets of his jeans. "I'm not sure if I believe in it or not, but there is a great deal science cannot explain. The last family that lived here, the Tamburris, had some strange experiences."

"Like what?"

Viking Val shrugged his broad shoulders. "Like things moving around. A chair would be in one room when the family went to bed, and it would be in another when they woke. Lights would go on and off. And sometimes, there were voices. People talking. Someone crying. The sound of a dog barking, but no dog lived in the house at the time."

A shiver went over me. "Boo. The ghost dog," I said. "I'm certain of it."

"Shut up, Capone," said Faraday. "I want to hear the rest of the story."

Viking Val continued. "Then one night, after Mr. Tamburri went on a business trip, something frightening happened. Mrs. Tamburri was home alone, asleep in the main bedroom upstairs. She awoke to the sound of her bedroom door opening and watched a man stroll in. She insisted it was Mr. Boussard. She recognized him from a portrait she'd seen online. To make matters worse, he had a rope around his neck. He's the one who hung himself from the top of that stairway."

He pointed to the elegant sweeping stairs leading to the house's second floor. At the top, several spindles were missing from the railing. We all gasped. Well, everyone except Ms. Anne. She crossed her arms over her chest and narrowed her eyes.

"I remember Betsy Tamburri. She wanted to move to Florida in the worst way, but her husband wouldn't consider it. I bet she made up half that stuff to get him to move."

"Maybe," said Viking Val. "But I saw her that night— when she ran out of the house screaming. I guess it happened about ten years ago, but I remember it like it was yesterday, mostly because I'd never seen someone so terrified."

Oh, calamity.

Why, oh why, had Ms. Josie and Mr. Nate chosen this house?

Ms. Anne didn't seem convinced, though. When she spoke, I could tell she struggled to remain patient. "Betsy has always been..." She waved one hand as she tried to find the right word. "A dramatic person. Maybe she didn't make the whole thing up. But it's more likely she had a nightmare and thought she'd woken up when she was still asleep. Doesn't that make more sense than the ghost of Mr. Boussard appearing at the foot of her bed?"

He gave her a sheepish smile. "I suppose you're right. I guess I'm kind of a sucker for the paranormal."

"And I am not," she said. "Ghost stories are fun, but they have no basis in fact. I do, however, find the history of the house fascinating."

"You might like to meet my friend, Tony Lavorgne," he said. "He researches local legends and wrote a book about them."

I perked up. "Hey, I met that guy. He told a ghost story at the gazebo during Beaver Tales last fall. Do you remember Jackson?"

"Of course, I remember," said Jackson. "That was the night you ate an entire bag of chocolate, and they had to rush you to the vet."

"Oh. I forgot about that part."

"You almost died, Capone," said Gracie, shaking her head in disbelief. "How could you have forgotten?"

"I've 'almost died' a few times. I make terrible choices, and most involve eating things that I shouldn't have eaten. It's kind of a thing with me."

"No kidding," Jackson deadpanned. "Like wedding rings?"

If I could have blushed, I would have, but instead, I ducked my head. "Exactly."

"I'd better get going," said Viking Val. "I'm sure you have a lot to do."

Ms. Anne nodded. "Between finding the coffee maker, keeping the animals out of trouble, and watching for stray ghosts, I have my hands full."

He laughed, but then his blue eyes grew serious. "Why don't I give you my phone number?" he asked. When she seemed confused, he rushed to explain. "In case you need anything."

She pulled her phone out of her pocket, unlocked the screen, and handed it to him so he could enter his number into her contacts. "You're planning to rescue me if the ghost of Mr. Boussard shows up?"

"Or if you're unable to find the coffee maker and things get desperate."

Ms. Anne's mouth quirked. "Are you asking me to call you if I'm desperate?"

He blushed and shook his head. "No. I meant—"

She held up a hand to stop him. "I'm messing with you. I appreciate the offer, and I'll call if I need anything."

"Excellent," he said with a nod, but he seemed disinclined to leave. "Would you like to come over for dinner tomorrow night? I love to cook."

"Uh, sure," she said and then glanced down at us. We were all listening attentively to their conversation. "Oh. I forgot about these guys. I can't leave them alone here."

"Bring them," he said. "I don't mind. My Molly loves company. She's a sweet old girl, and I'm sure she'd be a great mentor for Capone."

"A mentor, huh?" she asked with a laugh. "He certainly needs one of those."

"Hey—" I began, but the humans ignored me like always.

Viking Val grinned. "Wonderful. Would seven work?"

She nodded. "That's perfect. I'm helping at Bartleby's Books all day tomorrow, but I should be back by six at the latest."

"Then I'll see you tomorrow." With a wave, he walked

outside into the cold. We watched him go. Gracie voiced what we were all thinking.

"That man has a nice ass," she said with a sigh.

She didn't lie. His bottom was perfection itself, and Ms. Anne seemed to notice, too. I saw her watching as he walked down the path and to the sidewalk before turning toward his house. He caught her staring at him and gave her another wave. She waved back and then hurriedly shut the door.

"Wow," she said, leaning against it for a moment. When she noticed we were staring at her, she clapped her hands together. "Okay, guys. Time to get to work. No more dawdling. If I don't find that coffee maker soon, I could die. And that would be another ghost haunting the Boussard mansion."

She joked, of course, but her words sent a shiver over my body.

Ghosts were no laughing matter.

EIGHT

How to determine if your house is haunted or not:

1. Research the home's history.
2. Have a séance.
3. Call a priest for an exorcism.
4. Hear the pitiful cries and wails of a ghost dog named Boo.

After an exhausting day following Ms. Anne from room to room and watching her get her things in order, we finally went to bed. Being a helper was so tiring. When she went upstairs, I went upstairs. When she went downstairs, I went downstairs. When she cooked dinner, I stood right next to her. That ended up being a bit of a safety hazard since she nearly tripped over me several times. She may have called me a rude name, but I didn't mind, especially when she dropped a carrot on the floor by accident.

The other members of my animal posse didn't seem to feel the same need to be by Ms. Anne's side constantly. They came in when she cooked dinner but mostly slept on the rug in front of the fireplace. They didn't have my puppy energy. Faraday was also a puppy, but he lacked the usual characteristics. He spent most of his time plotting instead of playing. It made me nervous, mainly because he kept giving me weird looks—like maybe some of his evil plans involved me.

By the time we went up to bed for the night, we were all beat. It had been a long, eventful day. Ms. Anne took a bath then climbed into bed. We joined her there, and she didn't protest. Unlike Ms. Josie, Ms. Anne did not seem to have an issue with sharing her bed with members of the canine or feline persuasion.

Jackson passed out immediately in one corner of the bed. He rested on his back, his big belly in the air, and snored so loudly the walls nearly shook. Gracie curled up in a ball next to Ms. Anne, and Faraday slept next to her, too. Rocco somehow managed to snag a spot on Ms. Anne's pillow, which left the bottom of the bed for me.

I didn't mind. I got to snuggle with Ms. Anne's feet, and I rested my chin on her calves. Within seconds, my eyes grew heavy, but when I saw something move in the back-yard, I snapped awake in an instant. Squinting, I stared out the window at the carriage house. To my surprise, a light turned on.

I nudged Jackson to wake him up. "Jackson. There's someone in the carriage house."

He didn't answer. He turned over, farted, and went back to sleep. I gagged at the smell and tried to wake up Gracie. She growled at me, told me to shut up, and said she'd do me bodily harm if I woke Ms. Anne. I considered that a serious threat. Since no one would help me, I decided to figure it out myself.

I climbed out of bed and crept over to the window.

There were no curtains since no one had hung them yet. What I saw when I looked outside caused my heart to slam to a stop in my chest.

The back door to the carriage house appeared to be open. Light streamed out of it, and standing right in the middle of the yard, was a dog.

"Boo," I said softly to myself.

It took me a minute to register that not only did a ghost dog live in my backyard but also that he stared right up at me. He didn't move or bark, but he let out a long, ghostly howl. When a man appeared in the doorway of the carriage house, I changed my mind about dealing with this problem on my own. Instead, I flew back to the bed and climbed under the covers, shaking from head to toe.

Boo, the ghost dog, lived in our backyard. He'd seen me watching him. And one of the other Boussard ghosts hung out with him. This was a nightmare.

Curse my curious nature. I'd always known it would get me in trouble someday.

I hid under the covers, sure I'd never fall asleep, but I must have dozed off at some point in the night because I woke up to the sound of Jackson licking himself. A wet slapping, slurping sound, it went on long enough that Ms. Anne let out a groan.

"Jackson. You're disgusting," she said, attempting to pull the covers over her head. It didn't work. She occupied a bed with five animals. There was no way we'd allow her to go back to sleep.

Rocco let out a plaintive *meoooooowwww*. Jackson walked to the head of the bed and panted in Ms. Anne's face. Gracie nudged Ms. Anne's hand with her wet nose. Faraday climbed on top of her and started to whine. I thought about doing that, too, but feared I'd crush her. At seven and a half months old, I'd reached my grown-up doggie weight of eighty pounds. Instead, I remained under the covers and licked her pretty toes.

Who does not love a first-class toe-licking? And I performed such a thorough job. I ran my tongue around her toes, between her toes, over her foot, and across her arch. When I reached her calves, she groaned and got out of bed.

"For Pete's sake," she said, stomping to the bathroom. "The sun isn't even up yet."

She might be technically correct, but it was February in Western Pennsylvania, so the sun would not officially rise for hours. Animals did not wait for sunrise and had no qualms about requesting breakfast before the rooster crowed.

Did roosters crow when they saw the sun or did they wake up at the same time each day like doggies? If the latter ended up being correct, a rooster might work well as an alarm clock for my humans. It could potentially save me so much effort.

Maybe we needed a rooster.

Sadly, due to her early wake up, Ms. Anne got out of bed in a grumpy mood. She acted even grumpier as she tried to feed us breakfast. It was like a three-ring circus.

First, she fed me, which seemed wise. But instead of behaving, I pushed my friends out of the way, ate my food, and waited for my post-breakfast treat. She did not provide a post-breakfast treat, so when she tried to feed Jackson, I pushed everyone out of the way again and ate Jackson's food.

"Yo, buddy," said Jackson. "Not cool."

"Sorry," I said, my mouth full of kibble. "She forgot my treat."

When Ms. Anne tried to block me and feed Jackson

again, I pushed her out of the way, and (once again) ate the food.

Let me explain something here. I have a food addiction problem. I can't help myself. I am a food-motivated dog. All Labradors are food motivated, but I take it to a completely different level.

After I'd scarfed down my third breakfast for the day, Ms. Anne got annoyed. "Capone. Stop eating Jackson's food."

She may as well have been speaking Martian. I heard her words, but they made no impact on me at all. My friends tried to get through to me, too.

"You are being rude," said Gracie with a sniff, shaking out her long fur. "We're all hungry."

I understood that, but it made no difference to me. I'd entered the zone. I could only focus on food at this point— food, food, food. I almost forgot I had friends.

When Ms. Anne dug into the dog food bag for another cup, I sat prettily and waited.

"No way," she said, wagging a finger at me.

Next to the kitchen was a powder room. Next to the powder room sat a baby gate. Ms. Anne had a moment of inspiration. She put the bowl in the powder room and then tried to gate all the smaller dogs in there.

Things did not go as planned, mainly because the little dogs were confused. Every time she thought she had them in the powder room, I'd rush in, and they'd run out. Finally, she got them secured inside, but she'd forgotten the food. She climbed over the baby gate (not an easy task in a silk nightie), got the food, and tried to climb back. She tripped over the gate this time, knocking it over. The food fell onto the floor, and guess what? I ate it.

Huge surprise, right?

My friends all groaned at once. "Please stop it," said Faraday. "Or I will literally kill you in your sleep."

I thought it seemed harsh, but then Rocco chimed in. "And I'll help."

I gasped in surprise, hoping Jackson and Gracie would show some support. They didn't. They were both too hungry.

"You're being a selfish piggie of a puppy," said Gracie.

"And a horrible friend." Faraday always hit me where it hurt most. But I wasn't a horrible friend. I happened to be a wonderful friend. I was just very, very hungry—all the time.

When Jackson turned on me, however, it hurt my heart. "Faraday is right," he said. "You need to stop."

Jackson and Faraday shared a moment of Pug solidarity, and I thought I might weep. Rocco, of course, made it worse.

"Go away. No one wants you here."

This time, when Ms. Anne brought the food to the powder room, I didn't steal any. Not because I didn't try, but because she'd gotten more adept at leaping over a baby gate in her nightie. She fed Jackson, Gracie, and Faraday one by one. They were so well-behaved and polite, which made things even worse. To express my pain, I started barking.

"Not before I've had my coffee," said Ms. Anne, in a harsh voice. She never spoke to me like that. She must have reached her limit.

After feeding Rocco, she opened the kitchen door to let us out into the backyard. It was large and fenced in and provided a wonderful, safe place for us to play. As soon as I caught a glimpse of the carriage house, however, everything I'd witnessed last night came rushing back. I stood in the kitchen doorway, legs locked, refusing to go outside. There was no way I'd pee where Boo the Ghost Dog had been last night.

The other dogs had no such qualms. They stomped around in the snow, doing their business quite happily. I stayed in the house and whined, bladder full but too scared to move.

"What is your problem, Capone?" asked Ms. Anne, struggling to shove me out the door. I refused to budge, despite my need to go. After several attempts, she gave up.

"Fine. Have it your way."

The other dogs came in, shaking the snow from their fur. I tried to talk to them and explain what I'd seen the night before, but apparently, no one wanted to speak with me.

Curse my kibble addiction.

Ms. Anne found the coffee maker and drank a cup as she puttered around the kitchen. Thank goodness she'd located it; otherwise, this morning would have been even bleaker. But as I watched her, I realized eating triple breakfasts had taken its toll, and more than my bladder felt full. I had to go potty, and I had to do it now. But I could not face Boo the Ghost Dog. So, I sat in the kitchen, attempting to hold it, and wondered how long I'd last before my bladder exploded or my intestines burst.

Not an intriguing visual. And not a great way to die.

I wondered whether I should sneak off to another room and relieve myself, but then I heard a thump on the front porch. My ears perked up. It sounded like a newspaper being delivered. Huzzah! This might be my big chance.

I raced to the door, barking my head off. Ms. Anne followed me sluggishly, coffee in hand. As soon as she opened the door, I knocked her aside. She spilled coffee on her pretty nightgown and the floor, but I didn't care. I was a doggie on a mission.

Flying past the rolled-up newspaper on the porch, I ran down the steps, found the first available bit of grass, and squatted to poo. It had to be the best feeling in the whole wide world.

Ms. Anne stared down at her coffee-stained nightie, aghast. "Why, Capone? Why wouldn't you do this in the backyard like a normal dog?"

Alas, I am not a normal dog. I wish I could explain that to Ms. Anne, but (once again) our language barrier precluded it.

As soon as I finished doing my business, I marched back up the steps, tail wagging. Typically, after I went outside like a champ, Ms. Josie would give me a treat. I hoped Ms. Anne would do the same, but she adamantly refused.

Note to self: Never body slam someone in a nightgown, then demand a reward.

NINE

The ten Most Famous Bookstores in the World:

1. Shakespeare and Company, Paris
2. The Strand, New York City
3. City Lights Books, San Francisco
4. El Ateneo Grand Splendid, Buenos Aires
5. Libreria Acqua Alta, Venice
6. The Booksellers Bazaar, Istanbul
7. Selexyz Dominicanen, Maastricht, The Netherlands
8. Atlantis Books, Oía, Santorini, Greece
9. Honesty Bookshop, Hay-on-Wye, Wales
10. Bartleby's Books, Beaver, Pennsylvania

Although disappointed Ms. Anne was now withholding treats, I understood her reasoning. I had been a bit of a jerk this morning, but Ms. Anne didn't realize I'd seen Boo the Ghost Dog last night. Otherwise, she would have understood, but I owed her one for spilling her coffee this morning.

And burning her house down.

And pooping in her car.

I guess I owed her for several things. I vowed, again, to be a good boy for the rest of my stay with her.

That lasted about forty-five minutes. That was the amount of time it took her to get ready and take us to Bartleby's Books for the day.

I loved our bookstore. I loved the bright blue paint on its façade and the gold lettering that sparkled on this bright and clear winter morning. I loved the way it smelled—that unique combination of vanilla and almonds that only old books produced. I also loved the interior, the wood, the windows, and the shelves and shelves of books. I even loved the special vault that housed the rarest and most valuable books of all.

Sadly, I could never go inside that special vault. It was strictly forbidden. No dogs allowed.

I guess I could understand why Ms. Josie put that rule in place, but it still chafed. I had, after all, been the one to find a whole bunch of rare books buried in the garden under the late Mr. Bartleby's rose bushes. Surely that counted for something.

The bell above the door chimed as we walked in, all wet paws and happy energy. Four dogs and a hostile kitty cat might be a lot for a tiny bookstore, but we were used to being there, and out of the five of us, only one ever misbehaved.

Oh, calamity. It was me. I misbehaved. Not anyone else.

I used to blame it on my puppy energy, but Faraday was younger than me, and he behaved impeccably—in public, at least. Then again, Faraday had always been a strange dog. Part of me wondered if an alien inhabited his tiny Pug body.

Also, he was evil, and he hated me, no matter how hard I tried to be his friend.

The Vargas twins, Miss Isabella and Miss Olivia greeted us at the door to the shop. In their early twenties, and graduate students in museum studies and library science, respectively, they'd moved into Ms. Josie's apartment upstairs and assisted Ms. Josie in the bookstore. Both ladies were tiny with dark eyes and hair. Miss Bella, the elder twin by only a few minutes, had delicate features and a quiet nature. She usually styled her straight hair in a bun at the nape of her neck. She was the more serious one of the two and wanted to work in a museum someday. Miss Olivia had a big smile, deep dimples, and a heart-shaped face surrounded by a riot of dark, heavy curls that hung past her shoulders. Miss Olivia seemed like the firecracker of the family. She wanted to be a children's librarian, and I thought she'd be great for the job. Although she resembled her sister in appearance, they were nothing alike in personality. I loved them both, and they loved me, proven by the way they cooed and fussed over me as soon as I walked up to them, tail wagging. They also fussed over the other animals, but I held a special place in their hearts.

"Look who's here, Bella," said Olivia. "It's our boy, Capone."

My tail wagging became a full-body experience. "Hi, Capone," said Miss Bella, scratching me behind the ears. "Have you been a good boy for Anne?"

The wagging slowed as I glanced up at Ms. Anne warily. "Define 'good,'" she said to Miss Bella. The two sisters laughed, but I saw nothing remotely funny about the situation. I tried my best not to be a bother all morning. I'd gotten so little sleep the night before that I napped most of the time away, so maybe it wasn't a huge accomplishment.

I yawned as the women puttered around the shop. Since they were closed to customers on Mondays, they spent their hours filling online orders, shelving new books, and checking inventory. For such a small shop, it required a lot of effort to keep it running.

"Do you mind if I run out for a few minutes?" asked Ms. Anne, reaching for my leash. "I wanted to drop a thank you gift off at the fire station. I'll take Capone with me. He could use the exercise."

"No problem," said Miss Olivia. "If you see any hot firemen, send them my way. Or, better yet, get one for yourself. You deserve a nice man. You're overdue."

Ms. Anne's cheeks got pink, and I wondered if her thoughts had turned to Fireman Fetch. He seemed like a nice man. Dogs always sensed these things. No one could ever deceive us.

Well, except for the many times I picked all the wrong men for Ms. Josie to date before she ended up with her soulmate, Mr. Nate. Hey, what can I say? I'd been misguided. I'd searched for Mr. Darcy, but we'd been surrounded by Wickhams and Willoughbys at the time.

I learned from that whole experience, though, and now considered myself a matchmaking professional—the Emma Woodhouse of Beaver, Pennsylvania. Ms. Anne didn't have a clue, but she'd benefit from my new expertise. Lucky, lucky Ms. Anne. I'd find the perfect man for her, too.

We left the bookstore and walked down the main street. A picturesque town filled with intriguing shops and fun places to eat, Beaver always seemed to be bustling. We picked up a large basket full of yummy treats from a place called Café Kolache and headed to the fire station. Located only a block from the bookstore, we didn't have far to go.

Fireman Fetch met us at the entrance. "Anne," he said, giving her a big grin.

Tall, dark, and yummy, he smelled lovely, too. Like chili. I sniffed his leg. Had he been cooking lunch? Would he offer some to me? Sadly, he was too focused on Ms. Anne to notice me or anything else.

"How are you?'

"I'm fine," she said, handing him the basket. "I wanted to thank you for everything you did for us the other night. I appreciated it very much."

"Thanks," he said as he accepted her gift. "But you didn't have to do this. I was happy to help."

They chatted for a few minutes, and Fireman Fetch fawned over me and called me a good puppy. He was obviously an excellent judge of character, but, then again, he also had no idea I'd caused the fire at Ms. Anne's house, so maybe he *wasn't* such a great judge of character. But the important thing was he liked Ms. Anne and she liked him, too.

"I'd better get back to work," she said as we prepared to leave. "Thank you again."

"You're welcome," he said. "Again."

A moment of super awkward silence spread between them. I wanted to yell, "Will one of you please say something?" but all I could do was let out a loud bark.

Another fireman walking past laughed. "The dog is right. Ask her out already."

I stared at the fireman in shock. He'd somehow grasped precisely what I'd been thinking. I didn't understand how, but it worked. Fireman Fetch went for it.

"Uh, would you like to go out to dinner sometime?" he asked, rubbing the back of his neck nervously with one hand.

Ms. Anne bit her lip. "I'd love to," she said, and he grinned at her.

"Great."

They made plans for Saturday night, and as we walked back to the bookstore, Ms. Anne had a happy smile playing on the corners of her lips. "At least something went according to plan."

Had Ms. Anne planned this? Wow. She may have been even more intelligent than I'd realized.

TEN

Rules and regulations for the proper behavior of puppies in the bookstore:

1. No books shall be eaten.
2. No books shall be licked.
3. No books shall be chewed on.
4. No books shall be touched.
5. No books shall be (ahem) peed on.
6. No books (or humans) shall be drooled on.
7. No kissing.

I didn't intend to drool all over Ms. Anne, but a thick strand of slime, similar in consistency to a wad of mucus, now rested on her pretty skirt. She wiped it off with a frown.

"Capone. You are disgusting."

She wasn't wrong. Curse my excessive saliva.

Drool might be disgusting, but kisses were not. I was very skilled at giving doggie kisses, especially stealth doggie kisses. I decided to kiss Ms. Anne to make up for all the drooling. She hadn't experienced my special brand of kisses yet. She was in for such a wonderful surprise.

I waited for the right moment. When she bent over to study the names of the books on the lowest shelf, I saw my chance. I snuck up to her, the music from *Mission Impossible* going through my head.

I loved that music. To quote another line from *Emma*, "Without music, life would be a blank to me." The same applied to licking. Without licking, life would be a blank to me.

When Ms. Anne seemed fully engrossed in the task at hand, I sprang into action, licking as much of her face as possible. I also licked her neck. I loved licking necks. And since I managed to get my tongue in her mouth, too, I considered that a bonus. A French kiss from a Labrador was the best thing in the world.

Ms. Anne must not have gotten the memo.

"Capone," she said, wiping her mouth with the back of her hand. "Why did you do that?"

I had no idea. I do what I do. I don't question it. Perhaps that was part of the problem. I really ought to ask more, lick less.

Fortunately, Ms. Anne did not stay irritated with me for long. She was too busy shelving books and chatting with the twins about Fireman Fetch. The other dogs slept on a bed in the corner of the room, and Rocco napped on the front desk, right next to the cash register. I did not sleep. I wanted to hear about Ms. Anne's latest escapades.

"So, you brought that hot fireman a basket of carbs and ended up being asked on a date?" Miss Olivia sounded impressed. "You are amazing. I want to be you when I grow up. Teach me your ways."

Ms. Anne rolled her eyes. "I don't have ways, and I've

been divorced three times." She held up three fingers. "I'm the last person you should want to emulate."

"But you're so awesome. Why the heck have you gotten divorced so many times?" asked Miss Olivia. Miss Bella looked horrified.

"Olivia Vargas," she said. "That is none of your business."

Ms. Anne waved her hand. "It's okay. I don't mind." She let out a long breath. "I've had no luck with men. And I wanted to start a family, but I've had no luck with that either." A sad shadow crossed over her face.

"You're still young," said Ms. Olivia, patting her hand. "There is time."

"I'm not sure," said Ms. Anne. "My first husband and I saw a fertility specialist. They couldn't find anything wrong with either of us. Since I didn't get pregnant with husband number two or three, I had to assume the problem was with me. I guess it wasn't meant to be, but I haven't given up on finding a husband. This time, however, I'm approaching things differently."

"What do you mean?" asked Miss Bella, a worried frown on her face. Miss Bella always looked concerned, and Miss Olivia always seemed so happy and carefree. It must have been a twin thing—yin and yang.

"I'm looking for friendship," said Ms. Anne. "Companionship. Mutual respect. Nothing more."

"Wow," Miss Olivia deadpanned. "That's super romantic. But isn't that why you have dogs?"

Miss Bella elbowed her sharply then turned to Ms. Anne. "I hate to say this, but my sister has a point. Is there no room for love in that plan?"

Ms. Anne's eyes grew sad. "I had love once, but he died, and I've never found it again."

Miss Bella let out a sad gasp. "I'm so sorry, Anne. We had no idea."

"It happened a long time ago. When I lost him, I realized no one else could ever take his place. Instead, I tried to find..." She paused as if struggling to come up with the right word. "Someone to fill the hole in my heart he left behind, but that hole was way too big for any one person to fill."

"That is the saddest thing I've ever heard," said Miss Bella. "Everyone deserves love. Don't you believe in second chances?"

Ms. Anne considered the question before giving her head a definitive shake. "No, sweet Bella. Sadly, I don't."

WHEN IT CAME time to leave, Ms. Anne put on my leash and regarded me sternly. "No pooping in the car."

I couldn't believe she would say such a thing. The night of the wedding had been an anomaly, caused by the pillow, the wedding rings, and all the excitement. I'd never done it before, and I never planned to do it again.

Hopefully.

Oh, calamity. What if I did it again?

But it turned out I was worried for no reason. I acted like a total angel the whole ride. It only lasted a few minutes, so I guess it wasn't all that impressive, but it still seemed like progress.

When we arrived at the house, I peed, once again, in the front yard. Faraday, curious about what I might be doing, stuck his head under my leg. Sadly, that meant I tinkled right on his face.

"Capone—don't pee on the Pug," said Gracie with a huff. "Now he's going to stink for the rest of the night."

I had no idea why I got blamed for these things, but somehow it appeared to be my fault that Faraday needed a bath, which meant a delayed dinner. Which meant everyone got more annoyed at me.

Note to self: Always check your undercarriage before you urinate.

Fortunately, Ms. Anne fed us more successfully this time. She manipulated the baby gate with great skill and precision. As soon as we were clean, fed, and calm, she went upstairs to change for dinner at Viking Val's while the rest of us waited downstairs.

"Something is different," said Rocco with a frown. At least, I thought he frowned. It was hard to tell since he always seemed so miserable.

"What do you mean?" asked Jackson as he attempted to lick his behind. I offered to help him, but he declined. He may have still been mad at me over the breakfast debacle, or perhaps he preferred to lick his own butthole. I couldn't tell, but it made me sad.

"Someone moved my chair." Rocco indicated the wing-back chair near the fireplace with a tilt of his head. "It wasn't there when we left."

I had no idea what he meant, but Faraday agreed with him. "The feline creature is correct. The chair was much closer to the fireplace when we left this morning."

Jackson shrugged. "Maybe Ms. Anne moved it."

Gracie shook her head. "She didn't, and Rocco is right. My doggie bed is in a different place, too."

As we sniffed around the room, exploring, something became painfully obvious, and we seemed to sense it at the same time. "Do you smell what I smell?" asked Jackson.

Faraday nodded, sidling closer to the older Pug. "I smell

another dog. That means another dog must have been in our house today."

Rolling her eyes, Gracie let out a huff. "How could there be a dog here while we were away? How would they get in? We must be imagining things."

But she was wrong. "We are not imagining things," I said, pausing for dramatic effect. "It's Boo. The ghost dog. We're being haunted."

ELEVEN

What to do if a ghost inhabits your home:

1. Ask the spirit to leave.
2. Call a priest.
3. Perform an exorcism.
4. Burn some sage.
5. Help the ghost with unfinished business.
6. Guide the ghost to the light.

Although I felt confident we were facing issues of a spectral nature, my friends only laughed at the idea. It kind of hurt my feelings.

"Boo the Ghost Dog? That is the stupidest thing I've ever heard," said Jackson. "And I've heard a lot of stupid things in my day."

"It's not stupid. I saw Boo with my own eyes."

"Sure, you did," said Gracie with a snort.

"I'm telling the truth. And I'd rather be without sense than misapply it as you do," I said, getting worked up.

Jackson tilted his head. "Is Capone quoting Austen again?"

"Of course, he is," said Rocco, licking his paw. "Mr. Knightley, to be exact."

Gracie grunted. "That's priceless. The dog with zero common sense is lecturing us. Get over yourself, puppy."

Her words hit me like stabs to the heart. I tried to come up with a scathing response, but Rocco beat me to it.

"Don't be mean," said Rocco. "He can't help it if he's an imbecile."

I stared at Rocco in surprise. "Why, thank you, Rocco. That may be the kindest thing you've ever said to me."

Note to self: That could be a sad commentary on our relationship.

"You're welcome. Now leave me alone."

As Rocco walked upstairs to take a nap, Faraday turned to me. "There is one thing you aren't taking into consideration," he said. "A ghost dog would not leave a scent."

I had to admit he made a compelling point. "But I saw him—"

"Enough, Capone," said Jackson, with a sigh. "Why do you have to be so exhausting?"

Oh, calamity. Jackson found me exhausting. How could that be? He was my best friend in the whole world.

As Ms. Anne got ready for her evening with Viking Val, I pondered what had changed in my relationship with Jackson. I could think of one thing: Faraday had joined our family. From the moment he'd come, he'd ruined everything. He'd flushed my life down the toilet with his Puggy paw, and he'd stolen all my friends in the process. I'd never hated anyone in my life, but I may have hated Faraday. A lot.

I felt miserable as we walked over to Viking Val's. I had

a problem, but no way to solve it. I thought I might never feel happy again, but I perked up immediately when I caught a whiff of dinner.

Lasagna. Viking Val had made us lasagna. Oh, happy day.

As soon as we entered his domicile, I realized it was not just any lasagna. He'd made what smelled like the loveliest, cheesiest, most delicious-smelling lasagna ever. The rich scent of beef, tomatoes, sausage, oregano, and cheese wafted out the door. The smells immediately activated my saliva buds, and I started drooling like a fountain. It was precisely the thing to take my mind off my mean friends and Boo the Ghost Dog. And Viking Val had made something else— Jackson smelled it, too.

"Garlic bread?" he asked, lifting his snout into the air. "Ooooh. Come to papa, baby."

A voice came from behind us, startling me. "I doubt you could handle it, big boy."

I'd had my eyes closed to enjoy all the delicious smells better, but I opened them when I heard a new dog speak. A black Lab like me, she seemed older. I could tell because of the gray around her snout. But she was still beautiful, and when she smiled, her brown eyes seemed kind.

"I'm Molly," she said. "You must be Capone. I've heard all about you."

Molly led us into her house and showed us around. Compared to our house, which was a work in progress, Viking Val's house was beautiful. It reminded me of him. Elegant. Tasteful. Charming. And so, so clean. How on earth did he keep it this clean?

"He's a bit anal," said Molly, by way of explanation. "But a respectable guy. We've been together nearly a dozen years now."

She lowered herself slowly to a dog bed near the fire-place. I sat down next to her. "You've lived here a while?"

"Almost my whole life," she said.

I glanced around. My doggie friends were in the kitchen with Ms. Anne and Viking Val. I usually stayed in the kitchen, too, but I didn't want to be around my friends at the moment. Also, I had some things I wanted to ask Molly.

"Is our house haunted?"

"Definitely," she said, without any hesitation at all. "I've seen strange things going on over there all the time. Lights turn on and off when the house is empty. Noises that sound like gunshots. Screams."

I shivered. "Have you ever seen a ghost dog?"

She shook her head. "No, but I've heard him barking. It's the saddest sound in the world. The spirit of a lonely dog, howling at the moon. Searching for his long-dead master."

"The master who killed him."

"Exactly." She reached out a paw to touch me. "But don't worry about it, puppy. It's not like the ghost dog can hurt you. And if you're ever scared, at any time, bark in your biggest voice, and I'll come right over. I promise."

I licked her in gratitude. "Thank you, Molly."

"You're welcome," she said. "We black Labs have to stick together, right? Speaking of which, what is up with that guy?"

She tilted her snout to indicate Faraday, who sat in the doorway of the kitchen, watching us. "Oh, he's crazy."

"Definitely," said Molly. "But why does he hate you so much?"

I shrugged. "No idea. It might be because I'm kind of famous. My friends and I thwarted a band of book thieves."

"Thwarting is always fun."

"Isn't it? But somehow, I got most of the attention for it since it was my owner's bookstore. Jackson and Gracie act like I'm a fame hog, but it's not something I wanted. And it's not like I can explain it to the humans."

"It's small dog syndrome," said Molly. "Little dogs always seem to have a chip on their shoulder about something. Big dogs aren't the same. We're not compensating." She shook her head sadly. "Chihuahuas are the worst, but Pugs and Shelties are monsters, too. I'm not a breedist, but that's what I've observed. And there is something else, too."

"What?" I asked, almost afraid to hear her answer.

"When it comes right down to it, a dog will always choose its breed over others. A Lab will choose a Lab, and a Pug? He'll choose another Pug."

I knew it. Curse the powers of my intuition. I feared this might be the case all along, and it turned out I was right.

At that moment, Jackson strolled in from the kitchen, letting out an enormous belch. "Capone. You'd better get in there. Val dropped a piece of garlic bread. Holy cow, that man can cook."

"We'll be right in," said Molly as she got slowly to her feet. Then she turned to me. "But remember what I said, pup. Faraday's out to get you. Be careful who you trust, okay?"

I nodded but didn't want to think about it. Was it possible? Would my best buddy Jackson choose Faraday over me?

Gosh, I hoped not.

TWELVE

Why Viking Val would make a great Mr. Knightley:

1. He acts like a gentleman.
2. He'd look amazing in a cravat.
3. He's an excellent cook (not exactly a requirement, but more like a bonus).
4. He has a dog of his own (Molly).
5. He lives right next door.

After a lovely evening, during which Viking Val let all of us lick the plates (he's a wonderful host), we went home, stomachs full and hearts happy. Viking Val and Ms. Anne made plans for brunch on Sunday, and Viking Val once again offered to cook since Ms. Anne didn't have a pulled-together kitchen yet.

Ms. Anne seemed extremely happy, both with the promise of brunch and the meal they'd shared. When he walked us home, I fully expected him to smooch her on the front porch. I wish he had. If so, my work in finding Ms. Anne a suitable Mr. Knightley would have been done.

Viking Val fit all the requirements. He even had the house that abutted her estate.

Not Ms. Anne's house exactly, but she currently resided here. The real Mr. Knightley lived in the estate abutting Miss Emma Woodhouse's in Jane Austen's book. It seemed like an important fact at the moment. Abutting was abutting, right?

But Viking Val didn't kiss Ms. Anne. He walked her to the door, handed her a container of leftover lasagna for her lunch on Tuesday, and said goodbye. Ms. Anne waved, lasagna in hand. She seemed disappointed, but, in all honesty, if I had to choose between a kiss on a cold, snowy night and leftover lasagna, I'd go for the lasagna. It's always, always better the second day.

But Ms. Anne seemed happy, despite the kiss that didn't happen. She hummed to herself as she got ready for bed. It was wonderful seeing her like this. The woman had been through a lot.

She climbed into bed, smelling of rose-scented face cream and lilac laundry detergent. I inhaled deeply. No wonder I associated Ms. Anne with the scent of flowers. She always smelled so clean and fresh and beautiful.

Ms. Anne fell asleep as soon as her head hit the pillow. I stayed up much later, watching the backyard while the other dogs and Rocco snoozed in her bed. I didn't see any lights on in the carriage house, nor did I see any ghost dogs. All in all, it was a relatively uneventful night, but I still felt I ought to stand guard.

"What are you doing, numbskull?"

I glanced down in surprise to see Faraday standing right next to me. "I'm keeping watch."

He tried to glance out the window, but even when he lifted himself onto his back feet, he still wasn't tall enough.

That seemed to irritate him, and I remembered what Molly said about small dog syndrome. I thought this would be an excellent time to mention it.

"It's not your fault, Faraday. You can't help it if you're teensy-weensy."

He shot me a hostile glare, so I tried again.

"Itty-bitty?"

That didn't work either.

"Puggly-wugg—"

"Shut it, Capone. Being bigger does not make you better." Faraday came closer to me, so close I saw the anger in his bulbous eyes. "I am superior to you in every way. Even my name is better. Michael Faraday was a famous physicist. His discoveries included electromagnetic induction, diamagnetism, and electrolysis."

I frowned. "Electrolysis? Like hair removal? Because Mrs. Steele, the lady who used to work at Bartleby's, had that done to take care of her mustache. I mean before she got arrested for robbing Ms. Josie."

Faraday stared at me. "What I'm referring to is the chemical decomposition produced by passing an electric current through a liquid. Or through a solution containing ions."

"But it's also hair removal? Like Mrs. Steele's mustache?"

He made a noise of pure frustration. For such a tiny dog, Faraday carried a lot of anger. He might need therapy.

"My point is," he said, with a growl—cute coming from such a tiny dog. "I am named after a world-renowned scientist. Who are you named after?"

Oh, no. This again? If only I had a better name.

"Alphonse Capone," I said, wishing I could say something else, but alas. The truth was the truth.

He laughed, a mean sound. "Al Capone. They named me after a brilliant scientist. Your breeder named you after a mobster who went mad from syphilis and died a terrible death."

I straightened to my full height, which was about five times taller than Faraday would ever be. "My name does not define me or my actions. I am myself, not a corrupt guy who lived a hundred years ago."

He didn't seem intimidated by my height or my words. "Oh, really?" he asked, the nasty gleam in his eyes getting nastier. "Are you sure of that?"

The sad truth was that I could not be sure. Unbeknownst to everyone else, I'd set fire to Ms. Anne's house. It had been all my fault. Burning down a house indeed constituted a crime—first-degree arson. I could have killed all my friends.

Maybe I was more like my namesake than I cared to admit.

IT TOOK me a long time to go to sleep. Ms. Anne tossed and turned in the middle of the night, keeping me up. I heard her cry out in her sleep several times and murmur the name "Ben" over and over again.

Dear, sad Ms. Anne. She still mourned her long-lost love, and I needed to help her. Viking Val seemed like a worthy option. Fireman Fetch was also an excellent choice. Undoubtedly, one of them would do nicely as her future Mr. Knightley, but which one?

I finally fell asleep, and it seemed like only minutes later that her alarm clock went off, and Ms. Anne woke up. When she stumbled down the steps, I stumbled right along with her. She fed me first, eyes still half-closed, and let me out front to do my business. While I was thus occupied, she fed the others and led them out back. This worked a lot better than the baby gate in the bathroom fiasco. She pressed a button to make a cup of coffee, filled her mug, and stumbled back upstairs, followed by all four dogs. Rocco didn't bother following us. He perched on the arm of the chair closest to the fireplace and may or may not have made a rude gesture at me as we left the room. He was still mad at me for pooping on his head, but it seemed unfair to blame me for my irritable bowels.

We watched as Ms. Anne turned on the water, stripped out of her nightgown, and stepped into the shower. The show was over, however, when she pulled the curtain shut. I found it disturbing. I'd heard on PBS that nearly all bathroom-related injuries occurred in the shower and most of those involved women for some reason. Since Ms. Anne was both a woman and in the shower, I thought it prudent to keep a closer eye on her. I did so by sticking my nose between the shower curtain and the wall and nudging my face slowly inside.

The shower curtain closed, and the shower became like its own little room—delightful, warm, steamy, and smelling of Ms. Anne's lavender-scented soap. I licked the edge of the tub, where I found remnants of that soap. Sadly, it didn't taste as wonderful as it smelled. It tasted nasty. Now I faced a dilemma since I needed to find something else to lick to get the bitter taste off my tongue.

When Ms. Anne dropped the soap in the shower and leaned over to get it, she unknowingly presented me with a solution—the solution being her posterior.

Let me say, surprising a half-awake and slightly hungover woman by poking her naked bottom with a cold nose is never a courteous gesture. Nor is licking her bottom without permission. She made a noise that frightened me so badly I jumped backward, pulling the entire shower curtain with me. The rod came as well, and with it, Ms. Anne.

Note to self: PBS had been right, as usual. Most bathroom injuries *do* occur in the shower.

Thankfully, Ms. Anne didn't seem seriously hurt. Yes, she remained flat on the floor, staring up at the ceiling. Yes, she seemed stunned. Yes, the shower still ran, causing water to pool on top of the shower curtain and the floor. But that wasn't necessarily a terrible thing. It gave me the chance to get a much-needed drink of water.

I also lapped at Ms. Anne's skin. I kind of went to town, which may have been why I didn't notice everyone staring at me with horror in their eyes.

Oh, calamity. What had I done?

"Capone. How could you?" asked Gracie, shaking the water from her fur. "You broke my human."

We glanced at Ms. Anne, who remained on the floor but didn't seem broken. She looked like she was taking a moment to rest and reevaluate every choice she'd ever made, leading to this moment. She must have made a lot of appalling choices because she still hadn't gotten up.

Faraday panicked. "Should we call for help? Can anyone dial 911?" We stared at him blankly, and he huffed. "I'm surrounded by idiots. We need to get her off the floor and make sure she's okay. And we also need to get her to open the door. If not, we could be trapped in here forever, and we'll be reduced to eating each other to survive. If that is the case, I vote we eat Capone first since he caused this mess."

I gaped at him in surprise. "You went from a minor slip

in the tub to cannibalism?" I asked, looking at the others for support. "Isn't that a bit of a stretch?"

No one answered. Jackson wouldn't meet my eyes.

Oh, crap. They *were* planning to eat me first.

I gave Ms. Anne a gentle nudge with my nose. She didn't move, so I licked her face. Thank goodness that worked. She sat straight up and scanned the room as if confused about how she'd gotten here.

Curse my curious nature. Maybe she did have a head injury.

Muttering a word no lady on any PBS special had ever muttered, Ms. Anne got up and turned off the shower. She wrapped a fluffy white towel around her body and cleaned up the mess. When I tried to help (mostly by splashing in the water and planting my bum on top of the shower curtain), she pointed to a spot by the bathroom door.

"Place," she said, her tone hostile. "Sit right there, Capone, and don't you dare move. I mean it."

I did as she requested. It looked like I'd officially been named persona non grata of the bathroom set. It didn't seem fair, especially since this happened out of an abundance of concern for her safety and well-being.

As Ms. Anne struggled to hang the curtain rod back up, I heard a strange scratching sound at the door. "Capone," said Rocco, his voice a worried hiss coming from the other side. "Someone is in the house. You have to warn the human."

"A stranger?" I asked, getting excited. In my experience, a stranger was simply a friend I hadn't met yet, even if they may or may not have broken into our house.

Uh-oh. If that were the case, maybe this wasn't a positive thing. Perhaps this was a dangerous thing. And perhaps it would be up to me, Capone the Fearless, to save the day.

I did what any respectable guard dog would do. I barked like a maniac. This caused a chain reaction since the other doggies barked like maniacs, too.

Ms. Anne covered her ears. "What is wrong with you guys?" she asked, grabbing the doorknob. She opened the door and backed out of the bathroom, directing us to follow her out. She still had nothing on but the tiny white towel, her long, red hair wet and dripping down her back. Her hair flopped into her eyes, too, which may have been why she didn't notice the man standing in her bedroom until she bumped right into him.

She gasped and jumped away, nearly tripping over Jackson and Gracie. Faraday growled, which I found super cute, but I couldn't appreciate it fully since so much was going on.

The man, tall and attractive, had dark hair, gray eyes, and an expression of pure astonishment on his face. A strange dog stood behind him, hackles raised, and teeth bared. The dog, white and brown with freckles on his nose, did not seem happy to see us. I had to admit I wasn't exactly delighted to see him either, but I was too distracted by what the humans were doing to care.

Ms. Anne used one hand to keep her towel in place and the other to push her hair out of her eyes as she tried to regain her balance. The man reached out to steady her, grabbing her gently by the elbow.

"Annie?" he asked, his tone an odd mix of surprise laced with something else. Something I couldn't quite identify. Astonishment? Hope? Confusion? I really couldn't tell.

"Bennet?" The name burst from Ms. Anne's lips, and I realized it was the same name she'd been murmuring in her sleep all night.

Bennet O'Reilly. The name of her long-lost love.

I glanced up at her in surprise. We all did. And, for a moment, there was no barking or growling or snarling or talking. There was only a moment of stunned silence before the towel slipped from Ms. Anne's fingers, and she did what any regency lady would do in this sort of situation.

She swooned.

THIRTEEN

Ways not to greet your long-lost love:

1. Sneak up on her while she's coming out of the bathroom.
2. Scare the bejesus out of her.
3. Allow your dog to growl at her.
4. Forget to tell her you're still alive.

Mr. Ben carried Ms. Anne to her bed and placed her gently on top before covering her with a blanket. She'd regained consciousness but seemed to be in shock. Not that I blamed her. The woman had been through a lot. Falling out of the shower was awful enough. Finding out the person you thought was dead for the last fifteen years was alive and well, and in your bedroom qualified as a good reason for swooning.

And she'd done it so gracefully. Her eyes had closed, the towel had plopped onto the floor, and she'd fallen right into Mr. Ben's waiting arms. I wish I could have videoed it. It may have been better than the scene in *Sense and Sensi-*

bility when Willoughby carried Marianne across the moors after she turned her ankle. I mean, there were no moors in this situation, but he did carry her across the bedroom, so that should still count, right?

That's when I realized something with absolute certainty—Mr. Ben had to be her Mr. Knightley. I had found him already.

Oh, happy day!

Ms. Anne didn't act happy, though. She stared up at Mr. Ben, her eyes filled with unshed tears. "Ben? Is that you?" She grabbed his arm, almost as if to assure herself he was real.

"It's me, Annie."

It was the most romantic thing I'd ever seen, except for one small detail. Where had he been for the last fifteen years, and why had he let Ms. Anne believe he'd died?

Ms. Anne seemed to be thinking the same thing since she said it practically word for word. "Where have you been for the last fifteen years, and why did you let me believe you'd died?"

Note to self: I may be psychic, or that could simply be the most obvious question.

Ms. Anne sat up in bed, keeping the blanket tucked carefully around her, and frowned at him. Mr. Ben didn't respond right away. He opened his mouth, then closed it again. His dog stood by his side, hackles still raised, and teeth still bared (at us, not Ms. Anne).

Mr. Ben patted him on the head. "Easy, Luke," he said, his voice soft, before turning back to Ms. Anne. "It's a long story."

Ms. Anne's confusion morphed quickly into anger. "*A long story?* Well, you'd better start telling it."

"I... I can't." He glanced away. "I'm sorry."

"You've got to be kidding me." Taking the blanket with her, she got up, marched around to the side of the bed where he still sat and pointed a shaking finger at him. "I watched you get swept away in the river," she said, her voice thick with emotion. "I attended your funeral. I cried over you for years. You broke my heart, Bennet O'Reilly. And yet here you are, in my bedroom, as if none of that ever happened." She wrapped the blanket more tightly around her body as she glanced around the room. "Wait a second. Why are you in my bedroom? How did you get in here?"

"Wow. Lots of questions." He rubbed a hand over his head. "I'm not sure where to start." He rose to his feet and stood next to Ms. Anne, a pained expression on his face. "I didn't realize you were here. I never intended to surprise you like this. I never wanted to hurt you, Annie."

"And I'm supposed to believe that?" She shook her head in amazement, the wet strands sending sprinkles of water around her like spring rain, or maybe like a wet dog, and she shivered. Glancing down, she seemed suddenly aware she wore nothing other than a blanket, and Mr. Ben had likely seen her naked. She pulled the blanket tighter around her body. "I need to get dressed, and then we're going to talk. Sit." She pointed at a chair. "Stay." She flipped her wet hair over her shoulder. "And don't you dare move a muscle until I get back."

All the males in the room, both canine and human, followed her commands. We sat, and we stayed. Gracie did not. She followed Ms. Anne, nose in the air, back into the bathroom.

"Men," she said with a huff. "You are all the same."

"Baby, that's not true—" Jackson's words got cut off when the door slammed behind her.

I stared at Jackson in utter shock. "Baby?" I asked. "Are

you and Gracie a thing now?"

Jackson shot me a silencing glare. "I am not the kind to kiss and tell, puppy."

Rocco laughed at us. "Of course, they're a thing, numb-nuts. Jackson is doing her."

I gasped in surprise. There were several reasons why. First of all, Jackson no longer had cojones, so "doing" Gracie seemed entirely out of the question. Secondly, Jackson and Gracie didn't like each other. She found him disgusting. She said it all the time.

And last, but certainly not least, was the "ick" factor. The image of Jackson and Gracie somehow making love, against all odds, now seemed firmly planted into my head, and I couldn't shake it out no matter how hard I tried.

"Ew. Ew. Ew. How could you, Jackson? And how could you not tell me?"

"Because it's none of your business," said Faraday, plopping down next to Jackson. "But we figured it out. You were the only one in the dark. As usual."

He once again did that "Pugs united" thing I hated. It happened any time I had a discussion or an argument with Jackson these days. Faraday immediately took his side no matter what, making me the odd dog out and treating me like they didn't want me around. Acting like I was useless. And it hurt.

Ever since Ms. Anne adopted Faraday, he'd been nothing but trouble, but the worst thing he'd done was to create a wedge between my best buddy Jackson and me. It seemed like we hardly talked anymore.

Was Jackson still my best buddy? It certainly didn't feel like it. If I had been his best buddy, wouldn't I have known about Jackson and Gracie?

Jackson seemed follow my train of thought as soon as it

left the station. "Nothing to tell, Capone," said Jackson with a sad sigh. "Drop it. Please. I'd rather not discuss it."

"Drop it?"

Drop it—one of my favorite commands. Ms. Josie said it to me about a hundred times a day. She asked me to drop things all the time but hearing it from Jackson felt different. Hearing it from him hurt.

Since my so-called friends didn't want to talk to me, I turned to our newest canine companion, Luke, and extended my nose in friendship. That did not go over well. Luke turned into a snarling, growling mess again, and I immediately backed off.

Mr. Ben soothed him, then patted me on the head. "Sorry, pup. Luke has been through a lot. I rescued him only a few months ago. He's still a puppy, too."

Mr. Ben's eyes were kind, his voice soft, and he had a gentle touch. I realized I liked this guy instantly. But his pet was another story. Luke seemed to hate me on sight. Jackson tilted his head and studied Luke's face.

"You must be a shelter dog."

Luke didn't answer. Instead, he turned his head away.

"What's a shelter dog?" I asked.

The other dogs exchanged glances. "A shelter is where dogs have to go sometimes," said Jackson, his response oddly evasive. "It can be a scary place, but not as scary as being on your own. Were you on your own, Luke? Is that how you ended up in the shelter?"

Luke didn't say a word, but his big, brown eyes spoke volumes. I saw an opportunity to connect with him. "I also understand the pain of loneliness. After my brothers and sisters were all adopted, I was left alone, too."

My friends groaned. "You weren't left alone, pup," said Jackson. "You had a human taking care of you."

"But I had no canine companions."

"So what?" asked Rocco. "Who needs them? But humans? Well, that is another thing entirely. I could survive quite nicely on mice and other rodents. You guys wouldn't make it a day without people."

"The cat's right Capone," said Jackson. "You had it easy. We both did."

I stamped my foot. "No, I didn't. The barn cat, Mr. Collins, was rude to me. And the horses made fun of me all the time. And I only got to watch PBS with my breeder, Ms. Sue, at night. She made me play outside during the day. It was tiring."

Luke stared at me in confusion. "Hold on. Is this guy serious?" Those were the first words I'd heard him utter, and I could hardly call them complimentary. But I didn't blame him. My so-called friends painted me in an unflattering light.

"For your information, it wasn't all sunshine and good times. I had my struggles, too." No one seemed to agree with me.

"You have no idea what that means," said Faraday.

I let out a huff. "And you do? You grew up on a farm in the country, too."

Faraday shook his head, a slight shudder passing over his body. "It was not that kind of farm."

Before I could ask him what he meant, Ms. Anne and Gracie emerged from the bathroom. Ms. Anne had on a pair of black pants and an emerald-green turtleneck that matched her eyes. She'd pulled her damp hair up into a bun and wore no makeup at all. Without it, she seemed younger, paler, and a lot more vulnerable. And she'd been crying. Seeing her red nose and puffy eyes made my heart hurt. She shot Mr. Ben a hostile glare and pointed a finger at him.

"Downstairs. Now."

Ms. Anne seemed to be saving her words for later. When we got to the kitchen, she poured each of them a cup of coffee, sat down, and stared at Mr. Ben as if she still couldn't believe he was here. Then everything came out in a rush, all the pain and hurt and sorrow.

"Fifteen years ago, I watched you jump into the Ohio River, like a total idiot, showing off after graduation, and never come out. I can still see it. I still have nightmares about it. But what I couldn't see, what I imagined, was worse. I pictured you struggling against an undercurrent, getting caught in one of the dams, and somehow, with no logical explanation, never getting washed ashore. They searched for you for weeks."

Ms. Anne closed her eyes as if picturing the events from so long ago in her mind. "Do you have any idea what that felt like, waking up every morning and wondering if that would be the day they found you? Going to bed every night, realizing another day had passed, and I still didn't have a clue what happened to you?" She swallowed hard, and when she opened her eyes, they were twin pools of emerald-colored misery, like the algae growing on the pond in the park. Her eyes reminded me of that algae, green and so sad. "Your funeral turned into a total nightmare. Your mom was a mess. They had to sedate her."

He snorted. "I'm sure she did that quite nicely herself. She'd been 'sedating' herself for years."

"Yes, she drank, and she'd never been a decent mother to you. She had issues, but no one deserved to suffer that sort of pain. It was absolute agony, Ben. We had no idea what had happened to you. No body to bury. No closure. And also, no hope. It became clear that you would not be coming home as time passed. Or so we thought."

She stared into her coffee cup as if staring into a window to the past. "Oddly enough, I never stopped hoping. It seemed illogical, but no matter how hard I tried to convince myself you were gone, something inside me refused to accept it." She rubbed a spot in the middle of her chest like her pain was physical, not only emotional, and her expression softened. "What happened, Ben? Tell me. Please. I've waited so long for this. Too long."

For a moment, I thought Mr. Ben might not speak. He seemed like a man of few words in the first place, and I had to imagine these would be difficult words to get out. He cradled his coffee cup in his hands, and when he finally spoke, his voice was soft.

"I never wanted to hurt you."

"You've said that already, but you did hurt me. Terribly."

"I know." A muscle worked in his jaw. The man had a fine jaw, all chiseled and strong. He had a fine everything, to be honest—from the silky, dark hair that fell across his forehead to his broad shoulders and his lean, powerful frame. He looked like the kind of guy who gained his physique from working, not working out, but I had to guess the body currently enclosed in jeans and a blue flannel shirt rivaled that of all the versions of Mr. Darcy and Mr. Knightley I'd ever seen on PBS. They were handsome, sure, and quite dignified, but soft around the edges. As far as bodies went, Mr. Ben seemed more like Captain Wentworth or the book version of Colonel Brandon. Or at least that's what I imagined.

When he spoke again, Mr. Ben startled me out of my ruminations over his hot body. "I caused trouble wherever I went. I was wild back then and did some stupid stuff. I ended up involved with the wrong people, and things turned ugly. When I got swept down that river, it seemed like a sign. I managed to come out on the other side, but I thought it best for everyone if I disappeared."

She regarded him sternly, her eyes cold. "Oh, that clarifies everything. Rather than tell me, 'Hey, Anne. I need to get away for a while,' instead, you faked your death. That is definitely what normal people do."

His lips quirked. "I never pretended to be normal."

"But you did pretend to be dead." I heard the tears in her voice, but she held them back somehow. Sometimes being angry was the only way to hold back the sadsies, and Ms. Anne was furious. "It almost destroyed me. You realize that, right? I didn't know if I could go on for a long time. It hurt too much."

"You certainly found a way." He spoke so softly I thought I may have misheard him, but there was no mistaking the bitterness in his tone.

"Oh, no, he didn't," said Gracie, aghast. "Is he talking about my girl's romantic life right now? If so, I might have to bite his ankles."

Ms. Anne seemed to feel the same way. Her head snapped up, and she glared at her formerly dead love interest. "What do you mean by that?" she asked.

He shrugged, slumping in his seat. He may have realized he'd gone too far with the last comment. "Nothing. Forget I brought it up."

"No, tell me."

He sat up, his eyes flashing with pain and anger. "I did come back. But by then, you'd already married husband number one. The old guy."

Her eyes widened in surprise. "Nearly six years after I thought you died. And he wasn't that old."

"Oh, he was old. And wasn't he one of your college

professors or something?"

"Yes," she said with a frown. "How would you know that?"

Another shrug. "I asked around. You'd been married a few months at that point, and you seemed happy."

"I wasn't, but I made an effort to appear that way."

"My point is you got over me pretty quickly."

She narrowed her eyes at him. "Six years is not 'quickly,' and a side note, in case you've forgotten." She leaned forward in her seat, folding her hands in front of her as she enunciated each word carefully. "I thought you died. So, don't act like I was an evil person for moving on with my life."

"And move on you did," he said, ticking off his fingers, as I sensed the anger between them build. "Husband number one. The rich, old professor. Husband number two, the richer and even older stockbroker. Husband number three, the oldest and richest one of all. The guy with all the boats and airplanes. What did he do for a living?"

"Real estate. You've been keeping tabs on me?"

He slumped again. "I asked around. It wasn't hard to find out. You love posting about yourself on social media."

"You follow me on social media?" She eyed him with a frown. "Unbelievable. And this entire conversation is making me realize something important."

"What?"

"After you died..." She gave a shake of her head. "I mean, after you *left*, I idealized everything about you in my mind. I remembered the good things about you but forgot the bad parts. Like what a stubborn, prideful, arrogant ass you are sometimes."

"And I'd forgotten how you never seem to realize something might not be about you."

She let out a gasp. "You're seriously blaming me for being upset about the fact that you lied about your own death?"

"No," he said, sounding resigned. "Of course not."

"Because it sure seems like it."

"I'm not blaming you for anything." He leaned forward, copying her pose until there was little space between them on the small kitchen table. "I did you a favor when I disappeared. Trust me."

"Oh, thank you. That's so kind of you. So unselfish. And it's great to see you thought only of me when you nearly ruined my whole life."

He let out a noise of pure frustration, twin spots of color appearing on his cheeks. "Stop it. Please. You made out pretty well, with all your husband upgrades. Each one was better and more lucrative than the last. Because that's what you do, right?"

Oh, calamity. Had he just called her a gold digger?

For a moment, she stared at him in stunned silence. When she spoke, her words dripped with anger and pain. "I hate you."

"I don't blame you. But that doesn't change the fact that you were better off without me than you would have been with me."

"How dare you decide that for both of us? And how dare you show up now and give me no explanation at all? You are such a jerk."

She stood up, grabbed the closest thing she could find, and threw it at his head. Unfortunately, it was one of Rocco's cat toys, so it didn't make much of an impact when it bounced off his face. It landed in Mr. Ben's coffee with a plop. We stared at them a few moments in stunned silence, unsure what they might do or say next. Mr. Ben pulled the bedraggled mouse toy out of his coffee, wrinkling his nose in disgust.

"Rodents in my coffee. Well played, Annie. Well played."

When Ms. Anne giggled, it came as a pleasant surprise. It got better when Mr. Ben smiled at her in return.

"Gosh, he's handsome when he smiles," Gracie said, and she was right.

Faraday glanced from the giggling Ms. Anne to the grinning Mr. Ben and shook his head in confusion. "Humans are so odd."

"Truer words were never spoken, Puglet," said Jackson.

"What did they do to my toy?" asked Rocco, clearly upset. When he let out a meow of fury and snatched it out of Mr. Ben's hand, it made the humans laugh harder.

Once the giggling died down, Mr. Ben gave Ms. Anne an apologetic smile. "I deserved that, and I don't blame you for wanting me gone, but I've been hired to renovate this house." He waved a hand around to indicate the peeling wallpaper, the old carpet, and the leaking faucet. It punctuated the silence with a steady drip, drip, drip. "By your newest husband."

"My newest *what?*" Ms. Anne lifted an eyebrow. "I don't have a husband."

"You're living here, and the newly married owner hired me to fix up the house."

"Hold on. Josie hired you to renovate her house?"

He shook his head, confused. "Nate Murray hired me. I'm staying in the carriage house out back until the project finishes. Are you saying this is Josie St. Claire's house?"

"It's Josie Murray now. They got married a few days ago."

"And Nate isn't your husband?" His question hung in

the air. Ms. Anne blinked at him in surprise.

"Of course not. Why would you ask that?"

He shrugged. "Nate said he was getting married, but he didn't give me a name. I had no idea who it might be." His expression grew nostalgic. "Little Josie? That's hard to believe. She had to be eleven or twelve the last time I saw her."

Ms. Anne's eyes once again welled with tears, and she had to glance away. "Ten. She made flyers after you went missing," she said, her voice thick with emotion.

He rubbed a hand over his head. "She was a sweet kid."

"Still is."

They were silent a moment, Mr. Ben remained in his seat at the table, Ms. Anne, arms crossed, didn't sit back down. She leaned against the counter. She seemed unsure how to process everything, but as she glanced around the room then up at the ceiling to where a large stain covered one spot, something became abundantly clear. The house was a mess.

"I'll stay in a hotel," she said.

"With four dogs and a cat?" He gave her an incredulous shake of his head. "No, I'll stay in a hotel. It'll be fine."

"No," she said, giving a shake of her head. "You don't have to do that. I only need somewhere to stay until the contractor can repair the fire damage in my house. This isn't a long-term thing. I'll figure something out."

"Hold on. Fire damage?"

She explained what had happened. "And Josie told me I could stay here, but the connection was awful. I couldn't hear half of what she said, but she must have been trying to tell me someone was staying in the carriage house. I didn't catch it, though."

"Capone is Josie's dog?" he asked, scratching me behind

the ears.

"He is. And Rocco is her cat. Jackson belongs to Nate. The only two that are mine are Gracie and Faraday."

"I figured Gracie had to be yours," he said. "She's got that whole spoiled princess thing going. She's like you in canine form."

"He does have a point," said Faraday. When Gracie narrowed her eyes at him, he went on. "You're both beautiful. Two fine specimens of femininity."

"Good save, Puglet," said Jackson.

"I learned from the best," said Faraday.

Mr. Ben got up, poured more coffee into her mug, and handed it to her. "I don't blame you for hating me or for being angry. I deserve it. But that doesn't mean you have to leave. I'm staying there." He pointed at the carriage house. "I'll stay out of your way. I'll work while you're at work and leave you alone otherwise. You won't know I'm here."

She let out a snort. "As if."

"I'm serious. I won't bother you. And this place is a mess. Nate hoped I could at least do some of it before they got back from their honeymoon. Do you want them to come home to this?"

As if the house agreed, a chunk of plaster broke off the ceiling and landed at their feet. Mr. Ben pulled Ms. Anne out of the way and squinted up at the hole in the ceiling. "This place is falling apart around our ears. What do you say, Annie? Can you deal with living next door to me for a few weeks, or is that too much to bear?"

I heard the challenge in his voice, and Ms. Anne must have heard it, too. "I can handle it if you can," she said, walking away from the crumbling ceiling with a wary eye. "But don't call me Annie. The boy who used to call me that left a long time ago. It's Anne now. Don't forget it."

FOURTEEN

A list of new things I'm now afraid of:

1. The dark. It's scary.
2. Ghosts. Also, scary.
3. Wet grass. Not scary, but gross.
4. Frozen grass. Too crunchy.
5. Forks. Too pointy.
6. The carpet steamer. It's a monster.
7. Ghosts. Worth mentioning twice.
8. Mr. Ben.

I wasn't afraid of Mr. Ben. Not exactly. But I really feared I might be wrong about him.

What if he wasn't a swell guy after all? What if he didn't become Ms. Anne's Mr. Knightley? What if he hurt her again? It might be too much to bear.

I pondered over my list as we piled into Ms. Anne's car and headed to the bookstore. A fresh coating of snow had fallen the night before, and the homes on River Road took on an almost surreal quality, like gingerbread houses dusted with powdered sugar.

This was the first time I'd ever experienced February before, and it felt different than I expected. Colder. Grayer. Quieter. And yet somehow beautiful.

There was nothing beautiful about Ms. Anne's conversation with Ms. Josie, however. She dialed Ms. Josie's number as soon as she started the car. Thankfully, they had a decent connection this time because Ms. Anne had quite the story to tell.

"Wait a second. Ben O'Reilly is alive?" Ms. Josie's surprised voice rang out in the car, amplified by Ms. Anne's Bluetooth.

"He is."

"And Nate hired him to work on our house?" I heard a tin drum in the background and waves crashing against a shore. I also imagined the fancy drink she must be holding in her hands. It probably had an umbrella in it. Lucky Ms. Josie. Ms. Anne, however, was slightly less fortunate. She didn't have a rum punch. She had a haunted house, four dogs, an irritated cat, and her long-lost love living in the backyard. She let out a sigh.

"Yes, he did."

"Hold on a second. Let me tell Nate what's going on."

We listened to bits and pieces as Ms. Josie explained to Mr. Nate what had transpired. It seemed Mr. Nate had hired Mr. Ben to restore several properties now being used as coffee shops. He'd agreed to work on their house as a personal favor to Mr. Nate.

"He's the best there is," said Mr. Nate. "And I've worked with him for ages, but I didn't know any of this. I'm so sorry."

Ms. Anne sighed. "Nate, none of this is your fault. It's

entirely the fault of one person. Ben the Jerk Face O'Reilly."

Ben the Jerk Face? That seemed like an odd way to refer to the man destined to be Ms. Anne's own personal Mr. Knightley.

"That name suits him," said Ms. Josie, jumping on the Ben-bashing train.

"It does, doesn't it? I'd call him something worse, but there are puppies present."

Ms. Josie let out a snort. "I'm sure Capone and Faraday appreciate that, but where has Ben been all this time?"

Ms. Anne frowned. "Excellent question. I never got an answer, and I was too overwhelmed with the fact that he was still alive to deal with anything else."

There was a moment of silence. For a second, I thought the call had been dropped, but then Ms. Josie spoke again. "I'm so sorry. I realize how much you loved him. How much you grieved for him. And I remember how much he loved you, too."

"Not enough, apparently."

"He was crazy about you. I can't believe he'd do something like this. There must have been a reason."

"If there is, he isn't willing to share it."

Another long pause. "I'll have Nate call him and tell him to move out of the carriage house this minute. We'll find someone else to oversee the project and—"

"No." Ms. Anne's reply was adamant. "We can be grownups about this. He'll work while I'm at the bookstore, and we'll avoid each other as much as possible."

"Are you sure?" Ms. Josie was miles and miles away, but I heard the worry in her voice like she sat right next to me. I let out a long and loud sigh, which made Ms. Anne laugh.

"Yes, I'm sure, and did you hear that? Capone misses you."

"I miss him, too. How is he doing?"

Unsure how to respond over Bluetooth, I let out a tiny bark. That made Ms. Anne laugh once more. "He's perfectly fine. Other than being afraid to go to the bathroom in the backyard, he's been perfect."

"Wait. He's afraid to go out back? Why?"

Ms. Anne pulled into a parking place in front of Bartleby's Books. "No idea, but we'll figure it out. He's strange, but he's smart." Ms. Anne gave me a pat on the head, reaching back from the front seat. It made me feel better about her calling me weird. "I'm at the bookstore now, Josie. I'd better go. Have a great time, kiss Nate for us, and don't worry about a thing."

After she hung up, she said the same words again. "Don't worry about a thing." For a minute, I thought she spoke to us, but I soon realized she was talking to herself. She covered her face with her hands and let out a groan. "I can't believe he's alive. I can't believe he's been alive all these years."

"Is she going to cry?" asked Jackson. "I hate it when they cry."

"Me, too," I said. "I hope she doesn't."

Gracie let out a huff. "She is not going to cry. She cried enough over that man. She's too mad to cry right now."

GRACIE UNDERSTOOD HER HUMAN. Ms. Anne didn't cry. Instead, she composed herself and went into the shop. We followed behind, all behaving for once on our leashes. While the others were sent up to Miss Bella's and

Miss Olivia's apartment to hang out for the day, I remained downstairs—mostly because no one trusted me to behave upstairs on my own.

Curse my failure to control my baser impulses.

But at least being in the shop meant I could hear Ms. Anne tell Miss Bella and Miss Olivia all about the surprise appearance of Mr. Bennet O'Reilly.

"Are you kidding?" asked Miss Bella, her eyes wide. "You thought he was dead all this time?"

"Everyone did," said Ms. Anne. "It was all over the news. His mom and stepdad offered a reward for anyone with information about his disappearance." She frowned. "I always thought that part seemed weird. I mean, he drowned —supposedly. Why offer a reward?"

"That is strange." Miss Olivia tapped a pen against her chin, then her eyes widened. "Wait. I remember hearing about this. Wasn't his stepdad really wealthy or something?"

Ms. Anne nodded. "Sam Goodman. The richest man in Beaver. But the name is deceiving."

"Mr. Goodman wasn't a *good man*?" asked Miss Olivia.

"Exactly." Ms. Anne pointed a finger at her. "He was an evil man, in fact—a criminal. When I was in college, he went to jail for murder. He died while in prison."

"Wow. What about Ben's mom?" asked Miss Bella, her expression sad.

"She died not long after Ben's...disappearance." Ms. Anne shook her head. "That seems like an odd choice of words, but I'm not sure what else to call it. I'm so used to saying he died. Anyway, Ben and his mom lived on their own for a long time, and she always had major issues. Drugs. Alcohol. When she married Sam, it seemed like things got better. Sam owned a construction company, and although he had a reputation around Beaver for being a crook, he took Ben under his wing and treated him like the son he'd never had. Ben almost seemed happy, but for all the money his stepfather had, they didn't have a pleasant home life. Ben didn't talk about it much, but it was easy to see. And trouble followed Ben wherever he went. He attracted it like a magnet. I'm not sure if he sought it out or if it sought out him, but it was always, always there."

Ms. Anne glanced out the window, a faraway expression in her eyes. It broke my heart. Ben had a rough start, but he seemed like a decent guy. Well, a decent guy who faked his own death and lied to the woman who loved him. I mean, other than that small detail.

"But it doesn't matter," said Ms. Anne. "I'm glad he's okay, but it makes no difference to me, to be honest. We both moved on a long time ago."

Miss Olivia and Miss Bella exchanged a long look. As twins, they seemed able to communicate silently with each other. But because I was a dog, I could easily interpret their conversation. It was almost like being psychic.

Miss Bella: *"She is not over him. This is so sad."*

Miss Olivia: *"What are we going to do?"*

Miss Bella: *"Help her? She still has feelings for this guy, whether she wants to admit it or not."*

Miss Olivia: *"Agreed. Is Capone eavesdropping on us?"*

Miss Bella: *"Impossible. We aren't speaking out loud."*

Miss Olivia: *"I don't know. It seems like he's listening to every word."*

They both stared at me, and I tried to put on my best innocent expression. They didn't buy it.

Miss Bella: *"He's definitely listening to us. Stop eavesdropping, doggie. Nothing good ever comes of it. Trust me."*

She was right, but this felt important. How could I prove to Ms. Anne that Mr. Ben had to be her one true love if I didn't follow everything that went on? Eavesdropping may be behavior unbefitting of a gentleman, but in this case, it seemed to be for the greater good.

Also, I was nosey.

But I digress. The important thing here was not my choice of words or my impoliteness in jumping in on Miss Olivia and Miss Bella's private, telepathic twin conversation. The important thing here was getting Ms. Anne to fall back in love with Mr. Ben. How hard could it be?

Miss Olivia and Miss Bella left the shop to run errands. Miss Bella had to meet with a potential customer. Miss Olivia left for the post office. Ms. Anne had settled down to skim over a list of books available at auction when the bell above the door chimed, and in walked a policeman. A handsome policeman. He had dark hair and blue eyes, so light they reminded me of a husky I'd met at doggie daycare once. The dog, Frosty—a decidedly uncreative name for a husky —had irises so pale they almost seemed white. The policeman was the same way. But his pale eyes positively lit up at the sight of Ms. Anne.

"Annie Weston. My, how you have grown."

Ms. Anne's face broke out in a happy smile. "Pat?" She opened her arms to give him a hug. "What are you doing here? I thought you worked in Pittsburgh," she said, pointing at his badge. "When did you join the Beaver Police Department?"

He glanced down at the BPD badge on his jacket. "A few weeks ago, actually. I started right after the new year."

"That's great news," she said. "Can you stay for a few minutes? Let me get you a cup of tea."

He glanced at his watch. "I can stay for a bit, but I don't need tea. I had an overpriced coffee from the place next door."

My ears perked up. Had he called Mr. Nate's fabulous coffee shop overpriced? The nerve of this guy. I mean, yes, the coffee Mr. Nate served did seem expensive, but that was because he paid farmers a fair wage for the beans they grew. And it was also incredible coffee.

Or so I'd heard.

Ms. Anne guided him to a small table near the front window of the shop. "First Impressions?" she asked, lifting one eyebrow. "Josie is married to the guy who owns that shop."

He let out a laugh. "You're kidding me."

"I'm not, and she is also the owner of this place," said Ms. Anne, indicating the interior of Bartleby's Books with the wave of her hand.

"What about this handsome dog here?" he asked, scratching me behind the ears. "Who does he belong to?"

Due to the "handsome dog" comment, I decided to forgive Policeman Pat for the complaint about Mr. Nate's wonderful coffee. Policeman Pat may have been misguided when it came to caffeinated beverages, but he had great taste in doggies. I licked his hand, and he smiled at me. So did Ms. Anne.

"He's Josie's, too," she said. "I'm dog sitting for her. She's on her honeymoon as we speak. I'm staying at her house until she gets back."

"Good for her," he said. "After all she went through, losing her parents in that car accident and everything, I'm glad to hear she's doing so well." He eyed Ms. Anne carefully. "Speaking of which, there is something I need to tell you." He cleared his throat, his expression concerned. "It's about Ben."

"Are you referring to the fact that he's not actually dead?" she asked.

Policeman Pat blinked at her in surprise. "When did you find out?"

"Not long ago. He walked in on me as I was taking a shower." She frowned. "Or to be more precise, I bumped into him coming out of the shower."

Policeman Pat's expression darkened. "He broke into the house?"

She shook her head. "No. It was a misunderstanding. He had no idea I was staying there."

He frowned. "Are you sure? Because I can file a restraining order for you if he's harassing you, and I wouldn't hesitate to do it. That jerk deserves everything he gets."

She watched him speculatively. "I take it you didn't realize he was alive either?"

"I found out rather recently, too," he said. "I heard about it through the grapevine, but I haven't seen him. I'm not sure what I'll do when it happens. After what he did to you, what he put you through..."

He covered Ms. Anne's tiny hand with his big one. She gave him a grateful smile. "It's water under the bridge."

"But you were so close to him in high school."

"So were you, Pat. He was your best friend."

"That's what I thought. But a best friend doesn't fake his own death, does he? A best friend doesn't let you grieve over him for more than a decade. That's not a best friend. That's no kind of friend at all." He gazed at Ms. Anne with those pale, intense eyes. "And that's no kind of boyfriend either."

"I agree." They sat for a moment in silence, still holding hands. Ms. Anne was the first to break it. "Is that why you're here? Because of Ben?"

It seemed to almost hurt her to say his name. Policeman

Pat shot her a confused glance. "Do you mean 'here' as in Beaver?"

"No. As in the shop." She sat up straighter in her chair. "Did you come to warn me about him?"

"Yes," he said. "I didn't want you to have a shock if you saw him. But I guess I got here too late."

"I appreciate the sentiment."

He shifted in his seat. "But that isn't the only reason I stopped by," he said, cheeks coloring slightly. "I also wanted to see you. I've missed you, Annie."

"I've missed you, too. And whatever the reason, it's great to see you again."

He glanced down at their hands, still clasped on the table. "Would you like to get together sometime? For old time's sake? I'd love to take you out to dinner."

She paused only for a second. "That would be great."

Oh, calamity. Yet another candidate for Ms. Anne's affections? This was getting out of control. How could I possibly keep track?

I'd find a way. I had confidence. But at this point, you couldn't swing a stick in Beaver without hitting one of Ms. Anne's beaux.

They made plans to meet on Friday night. Ms. Anne was a quick worker. Friday with Policeman Pat, Saturday with Fireman Fetch, and Sunday with Viking Val. At this rate, she'd have a new boyfriend in no time, but would he be her Mr. Knightley? I had my doubts. Mr. Ben was still my number one choice, but Ms. Anne couldn't seem to see it.

FIFTEEN

A list of reasons why Mr. Ben was the perfect Mr. Knightley:

1. He's handsome.
2. They have a history.
3. He lives in an abutting estate (aka, the backyard).
4. She still has feelings for him, even if she won't admit it.
5. He's a dog person.

A list of reasons why Mr. Ben was not the perfect Mr. Knightley:

---

1. He makes Ms. Anne's face turn all angry and squinty.
2. Although he looks at her like he wants to kiss her, he doesn't kiss her.

3. He's a lying liar who lied.
4. He has secrets.

These were all valid reasons, but maybe they all linked back to number four on my list, the one about secrets. As my dear breeder Mistress Sue used to say, "Secrets, secrets are no fun. Secrets, secrets hurt someone." Mr. Ben's secrets certainly hurt Ms. Anne, but that didn't mean he wasn't perfect for her. If only I could figure out his secrets, I could help them find a happily ever after.

I mentioned it to my friends over lunch in Ms. Josie's old apartment above the bookstore, the one now occupied by the Vargas sisters. As soon as I explained my theories about Mr. Ben and Ms. Anne, they all stared at me in shock.

"You're kidding, right?" asked Jackson. "She hates that guy. I mean, I watched them this morning, and even I picked up on that much."

Gracie agreed with his assessment. "Jackson is right, Capone. The man faked his own death to get away from her. There is no way my human could ever forgive him for something like that, especially when he won't tell her why he did it."

"He's a horrible person," said Faraday, munching on a bully stick. "Big Bad Ben. I hate him."

I tried to pay attention, but all I could focus on was his bully stick. We'd been given the yummy, chewy, meaty delights as a special treat and an excellent way to keep four dogs occupied for an extended period. Rocco had a toy filled with catnip, and he was currently high on a bookshelf. Meaning, he was literally high. And he sat on top of a second edition copy of *Northanger Abbey*. At least he had first-class taste in literature.

"Big Bad Ben," said Rocco with a snort, rolling onto his

back and nearly falling off the shelf. "An adorable alliteration from the fabulous Faraday."

The Fabulous Faraday? What the f—?

I shook my head before I even thought such a naughty word. A gentleman never used such language, even if he was super upset and jealous. How dare Rocco call that runt of a Pug fabulous? It seemed like an insult to fabulous dogs everywhere.

I let out a sniff. Not only did Faraday receive praise from my curmudgeon of a cat, but he also still had a bully stick to nibble on. Unfortunately, I'd eaten mine in minutes, which was why I now stared at Faraday's longingly.

Boy, did he ever eat slowly. It must have been because of his tiny Pug mouth. And his tiny puppy teeth. And his smushed-up Pug face that everyone found adorable, but I didn't. I guess beauty truly was in the eye of the beholder, and maybe Pugs were slow eaters in general. Jackson, although older, wiser, and much fatter than Faraday, hadn't finished his bully stick either.

Why was I always the first one done? And why were my friends so oblivious to my suffering?

Gracie nibbled delicately on her own bully stick like she had all the time in the world. These little dogs seriously drove me crazy. Gracie, however, didn't act at all concerned about her bully stick, and it seemed she had a lot more to say on the matter of Mr. Ben and Ms. Anne.

"He's handsome, I'll give him that, but they are virtually strangers at this point. They haven't seen each other in over fifteen years. And I don't believe that man wants her forgiveness. Did you hear what he said about her moving on too quickly? What a jerk. Although his dog seemed quite delightful."

Now I stared at her in shock. "Are you kidding me? Luke hated us. He growled at me."

She shrugged. "I thought it was kind of hot."

Jackson dropped his bully stick, his Puggy eyes bugging out of his head even more than usual. "What do you mean by that, Gracie Lou?"

Jackson had a big wad of drool coming out of his mouth. Not his best look. I would have offered him a handkerchief from my pocket, but I sadly lacked a handkerchief. And pockets. Not that it mattered since Gracie refused to make eye contact with him.

"Nothing, Jackson. A girl can talk, can't she? And it's none of your business anyway. I thought I made that clear when I heard about you sniffing that Poodle's—"

The rest of the conversation was lost on me. I completely blocked it out because I focused on one thing alone. As Gracie and Jackson argued, I did the unthinkable.

I stole Jackson's bully stick.

Oh, calamity. Why was I such a thieving glutton?

I ate it up, lickity-split. I mean, I practically inhaled the thing. It's a miracle I didn't choke. But it had been Jackson's bully stick, not mine, and I felt terrible. I felt even worse when, moments later, a tiny lull occurred in the conversation, and Jackson searched for it.

"What happened to my bully stick?"

I let out a belch and ducked my head, pretending to be suddenly interested in my dewclaws. I glanced up to find everyone staring at me.

"Uh, lovely weather we're having, isn't it?"

It wasn't lovely weather. I said that because I always engaged in idle chatter when feeling incredibly guilty. The sky had turned gray and ominous, threatening another snowstorm, and the air blew in from the north, bitterly cold.

When Ms. Anne took me out to tinkle earlier, I nearly froze my Winnebago, but the atmosphere in this room seemed nearly as frosty as the temperature outside.

"I can't believe you did that, Capone," said Jackson, sounding sad, disappointed, and sort of resigned—like he expected me to let him down at this point. It broke my heart, and I wished at that moment I could yak up that bully stick and give it back to him, but, sadly, it wasn't possible.

Not without hydrogen peroxide and a willing human to administer it.

Note to self: Disappointing your best friend is worse than puking up a whole bag full of chocolate.

Sadly, I understood this happened to be true from personal experience.

"I hope you're proud of yourself," said Gracie with a scowl. "Now Jackson has nothing to nibble on."

I thought things couldn't get worse, but apparently, hell had a basement. And his name was Faraday.

"Here, Jackson," he said, pushing his own bully stick closer to the older Pug. "You can have mine."

The other dogs let out a collective sigh, basking in the glow of Faraday's adorableness. Personally, I considered it another way for Faraday to make me look bad, but I'd basically handed him the opportunity on a plate.

Curse my insatiable desire for a chewy bit of bull pizzle.

Faraday, it seemed, had no such pizzle problems. He gave up his bully stick without a single thought, but I saw the calculating expression in his eyes as he did it. He cared more about making me look bad than he did about having a special treat, and that said a lot. It said he really, really wanted to make me seem selfish—not that I hadn't done a fabulous job on my own.

Rocco, still high on the bookshelf, let out an evil cackle.

He smelled like catnip and unscrupulous choices, but his words stung me to my core.

"Way to go, bully breath. Who's the outsider now? You really are a douche canoe, aren't you?"

I had no idea what a douche canoe might be, but it sounded extremely unpleasant, and I suspected Rocco might be right. Jackson and Gracie were mad at me. Faraday had usurped me, taking my place as the cutest and sweetest puppy in the group, and even my cat thought I was a loser.

That last part wasn't technically anything new. Rocco had always called me a loser, but the rest felt new and hurtful. Sadly, I couldn't do anything to repair the damage. The deed had been done. The die had been cast. The ship had sailed. And it all happened when the bully stick had been eaten. As much as I loved bully sticks, this one left a bitter and unpleasant taste on my tongue.

When Ms. Anne came to bring me back downstairs for the afternoon, I turned and looked over my shoulder at my friends. I begged for forgiveness with my eyes, but none of them seemed to see it.

"I guess I'd better go."

Silence.

"I'll see all of you later."

More silence.

"Bye."

Not one of them responded, and it broke my heart. They all wanted me to leave. Even worse? They wanted Faraday to stay.

SIXTEEN

A list of things eaten by various dogs of my acquaintance:

1. Socks.
2. Ponytail holders (aka Boingy Circles of Delight).
3. Glass.
4. An entire box of Godiva chocolates.
5. A tray of uncooked City Chicken with wooden skewers.
6. Shoes.
7. A wallet.
8. A sofa.

The last one was rather impressive. Ms. Josie and Ms. Anne should consider themselves lucky. I'd never eaten a sofa or glass. I was a jewel. Unfortunately, no one else seemed to see it.

During the remainder of the week, we slipped into a pattern. We'd leave every morning for the bookstore. I'd hang out with Ms. Anne and the twins. The other dogs and

Rocco stayed upstairs because they were "good" and could be "trusted." I obviously could not.

Gosh, I wished Ms. Anne had heard about the dog eating broken glass. Then she'd realize I wasn't so terrible after all. And I'd never considered eating a sofa, no matter how yummy it appeared.

But she did not know those things, so I remained stuck downstairs. It may have been a kindness since none of my friends appeared to be speaking to me. They were still mad about the bully stick theft, the kibble theft, and all my other crimes and misdemeanors.

I tried to apologize to Jackson, but he let out a sad sigh. "Would you honestly be able to promise me you wouldn't do it again?"

Oh, calamity. I knew I couldn't make that sort of promise.

I stared at him, slack jawed. He understood, and I saw the sadness in his Puggy eyes.

"Mutual respect, not just general friendship, makes a doggie what he ought to be."

Jackson had just misquoted Mr. Knightley to me, and he'd done it on purpose. This was terrible. "What do you mean?" I asked. "Are you saying we aren't friends?"

"I'm saying an apology doesn't count if you didn't learn from what you did wrong, especially if you plan to be a repeat offender. Better save it for when you mean it, pup."

He made an excellent point, but I still felt sad about it. And Ms. Anne seemed sad, too. I caught her, once or twice, staring out the window at the carriage house. We hadn't seen Mr. Ben since the day he caught Ms. Anne coming out of the shower. He'd done as he promised. He worked on the house while we were at Bartleby's Books and left before we arrived back home. We saw his lights go on and off, and I heard Luke in the backyard once or twice, but they kept to themselves—exactly as Ms. Anne had requested. But she didn't seem happy about it. In fact, she acted positively gloomy.

On Friday, as Ms. Anne got ready for her date with Policeman Pat, she instructed us on how to behave. "I'm going to keep all of you upstairs, but Capone will be in the front room. It's where he can cause the least amount of damage."

I gulped. Alone? At night? All by myself? I let out a low whine, and Ms. Anne cupped my face with her hands.

"You'll be fine, buddy. I'm doing this for your own good. I want you to be safe."

Humans always say they are doing things for your own good when you've been a really naughty doggie. It's kind of a thing with them.

I hoped maybe she was joking, but no such luck. She closed me in the front room with nothing but a nightlight and a soft blanket for company. I could hear my friends in the room right above me, chatting and having a great time, but here I sat—all alone and so lonely. In a haunted house. Where Boo, the ghost dog, had died.

Curse all the decisions I'd ever made that led me to this point in my life.

I could end up being the next Boo. I might die here.

I heard the front door click and watched Ms. Anne walk down the sidewalk with Policeman Pat from my spot by the window. I stuck my nose through the blinds, bending them slightly as I did so, but I was too upset to care.

Ms. Anne got into Policeman Pat's car, and that's when I realized all hope was truly lost. I might be alone for hours —possibly days. And unlike Boo, whose death had probably been quick and painless, I'd likely die of something painful, like thirst. Or maybe hunger would get me first. I felt hungry already. Yes, I'd eaten my dinner and done my business in the front yard less than an hour ago but thinking about being hungry made me hungrier.

I eyed the blanket. I could eat that, but it didn't look particularly tasty. I thought it might be wise to ration it. Maybe I'd eat it a few bites at a time to keep my strength up, but for now, there was only one thing I could do.

Howl.

I'm an enthusiastic howler, even if what I produced sounded more like whining than howling. I heard a bloodhound howl once, and he'd been super impressive, but, for a Lab, I'm not half bad.

And so, I howled, singing the song of my people, expressing my misery and wretchedness and isolation. I was a lone wolf, baying at the moon and sharing my pain with the universe.

"Shut up, Capone."

I heard Jackson's voice coming from upstairs. It made me howl louder because not only did I feel lonely, but also, my best friend in the world hated me. And as much as I loved Ms. Anne, she wasn't my human. Ms. Josie was my human, and yet she'd deserted me. Maybe Ms. Josie had lied about the honeymoon. Maybe it had all been a ruse to get rid of me. Maybe she didn't love me. Maybe no one loved me.

That thought made me increase my volume. My life had become a living nightmare. I had no friends. No human. No love. No warmth. No joy. No happiness. And Ms. Anne had been gone at least ten minutes, but it seemed like hours. And I got more frantic when I saw something move in the room that had become my prison. It may have been my shadow, or it may have been the eerie presence of

Boo, the ghost dog, coming to drag me to the depths of hell. That's when I really freaked out.

Note to self: A pup with an overly active imagination should never consider living in a house haunted by a ghost dog.

SEVENTEEN

How to keep your pet safe at home when you're out on a date:

1. Leave them in a secure environment.
2. Find a good pet sitter.
3. Keep them busy with toys.
4. Let your neighbors know the pet will be alone.
5. Make sure your house isn't haunted.

I'm not sure how long I howled or how long the dogs upstairs barked at me, telling me to be quiet. I shivered and shook and wailed and saw Boo in every dark corner, in every shadow on the wall. Time had lost all meaning. But everything stopped when I heard footsteps on the front porch, and a key turn in the lock. This was soon followed by the sound of a human voice.

"Capone. Are you okay?"

Mr. Ben. The wonderful, incredible, one-in-a-million Mr. Ben. I barked, my voice hoarse until he opened the door to the front room. The lights went on, all the shadows disappeared, and I'd never been happier to see anyone in my whole life. I greeted him with wiggles and tail wags and lots and lots of kisses. He deserved it. He was my savior. And he'd brought Luke with him, too.

Mr. Ben knelt next to me, accepting my enthusiastic greeting with calm pats and soothing words. I had no idea what the words were at this point. I was too far gone to listen. But eventually, I settled down, and my heart slowed to an almost normal rhythm.

"You sweet boy. Did she lock you up in here?" asked Mr. Ben. He sat cross-legged on the carpet, and I perched on his lap. I weighed eighty pounds, but Mr. Ben didn't seem to mind. I nuzzled him, wanting to hold him in place so he'd never leave me ever again.

"What happened?" asked Luke, his brown eyes worried. "We heard you screaming and thought someone was torturing you or something."

"Someone was torturing me," I said. "Ms. Anne locked me in here all alone. In solitary confinement. Like the real Al Capone when he got sent to Alcatraz. This room is my Alcatraz."

Luke seemed confused. "You barked like that because you had to stay in this room for a few hours?" He glanced around, taking in the soft blanket, the assorted doggie toys (which I honestly hadn't noticed until this moment), and the butterfly nightlight.

"I was by myself—a cruel, horrible punishment. She may have violated the Geneva Convention. I'll have to look into it."

Luke frowned. "I understand about half of what you say, dude. You are definitely the weirdest dog I've ever met."

I sniffed. "I get that a lot. And did I mention this place is haunted?"

His eyes widened. "What?"

"It's true. A dog died here. He was murdered. And his ghost still roams these halls, searching for his lost owner."

Luke shivered. "That's some freaky stuff."

"It is," I said. I wasn't sure why Boo roamed the halls, to be honest, but it seemed like a decent theory.

After I'd calmed down enough to let Mr. Ben get up, he went upstairs to check on the other dogs. They followed him down the steps.

"What happened to you?" asked Jackson, licking my face. Had he been worried? Maybe my best friend didn't hate me after all.

"She locked me up down here. Alone."

Jackson stopped licking. "We thought someone hurt you."

"Ms. Anne did hurt me. She deserted me. She left me. And she kept me away from all of you."

"Because she didn't want you to hurt yourself, ding-a-ling," said Jackson with a roll of his eyes. "We stayed upstairs in her room because we've earned her trust. You have not."

This was about trust?

"No. You're wrong. Ms. Anne hates me. She wants me to die a slow, sad, lonely death, with nothing but a blanket standing between me and starvation."

"And doggie treats?" asked Gracie, indicating several biscuits in a bowl in the corner. "She killed you with doggie treats?"

I hadn't noticed the doggie treats either. As soon as I saw them, I ran over and ate them all. The other dogs stared at me. Maybe I should have offered to share my treats with them, but I was in dire straits. I'd been on the verge of starvation, after all.

"He'll never learn," said Faraday shaking his head sadly. "Capone, you are a selfish, pampered, whiny, bi—"

"Hey," said Luke. "Stop it. The puppy was scared. And I hear there may have been a ghost involved. Show some sympathy."

Luke, the former shelter doggie, had become my new best friend and my hero. I couldn't believe he stood up for me.

"Thanks, Luke," I said softly, overcome with emotion.

"Don't mention it, pup. You might be a weirdo, but I understand what fear sounds like, and you were scared."

Rocco sauntered into the room with a yawn, rubbed against Mr. Ben's leg, and laughed in Luke's face. "Oh, you silly canine. You have no idea what we put up with daily. Capone is more than weird. He's psychotic. And delusional. You'll see."

Luke snorted. "Like I'd listen to a cat? Please. I know better."

I loved Luke. At that moment, I honestly loved him.

Mr. Ben watched our interaction, a perplexed frown on his handsome face. "I'm not sure what to do with all of you," he said. "If I take you back to the carriage house with us, Annie will freak out when she gets home. Then again, if I'm here, she might freak out, too. Probably the second option is the wisest. She might be mad if she sees me, but she'll be scared if she doesn't see you, and I certainly don't want her to be scared."

That was how we ended up spending an enjoyable evening by the fireside with Mr. Ben and his canine companion Luke. Mr. Ben had a book of Pablo Neruda's poetry in the pocket of his jacket. Interesting and romantic. He pulled it out and sat on the couch to read, after giving all the other dogs treats, of course, and lighting a fire. He may have slipped me a few treats, too, even though I'd already had some, but who's counting?

The fire Mr. Ben made was warm and crackling, and I felt safe, contented, and at peace. My friends still weren't talking to me, but I had a new friend now, so I sat next to Luke and watched the flames.

He glanced over at the pile of three little dogs and one cat sitting on the couch next to Mr. Ben. Jackson snored—loudly. So loudly, the other dogs kicked him and muttered that he should be quiet, but he didn't notice. Jackson scratched his big belly, readjusted his position, and snored some more.

"What's up with the annoying miniatures?" asked Luke.

"Huh?"

He tilted his head to indicate Jackson, Gracie, and Faraday. "The other dogs. I mean, I understand why the cat hates you," he said, glancing up at Rocco, who currently sat on the chair closest to the fire, fast asleep and purring softly. "But why are those dogs so mean to you?"

I let out a sigh. "No idea. We used to be such bosom friends. Now it's like everything I do annoys them. It's awful."

"Don't overthink it, pup. I realize exactly what the problem is." I eyed him curiously, and he continued. "They're jealous. It's your size. It makes them all yippy and hostile. Have you ever met a big dog who acted like that?"

Most big dogs seemed pretty chill. Well, except for me. I'd never been chill in my life. Some may have called me a tiny bit neurotic.

Heck, I'll be honest here. Who was I kidding? I went

way past "a tiny bit neurotic" and bordered on all-out crazy, but I didn't need to share that with Luke.

"I guess you make a good point."

Smaller and shorter than me, Luke had to be about fifty pounds, but he still outweighed Faraday by close to forty pounds. I outweighed the tiny Pug by seventy pounds. I could crush him like a bug if I chose to do so, and the thought gave me pleasure to no end.

"Never trust a cat or a small dog," said Luke. "I learned that the hard way. I lived on the streets a while before some kind human brought me to the shelter. I know what I'm talking about."

I studied his face. He'd been through a lot, but he was still so kind. It said a great deal about his character. "I'm sorry that happened to you," I said. "It must have been rough."

"It was," he said. "But now I have Ben, and life is good. Actually, it's better than good. I've never been happier."

I fell asleep next to Luke on the carpet, and my dreams were plagued with visions of small, mean dogs (most of them Pugs) chasing me down dark alleys. Gangs of them, and they all acted super nasty, calling me names, and making fun of me. At one point, they surrounded me, chanting my name, but then something changed, and they said another name instead.

"Ben. Ben. Get up."

Disoriented and confused, I woke with a startled snort to find Ms. Anne standing by the couch and shaking Mr. Ben's shoulder. He must have fallen asleep reading. He'd stretched out his long legs, his book resting on his chest and his reading glasses still on his nose. He'd ended up covered in canines since Jackson, Faraday, and Gracie had somehow climbed on top of him. Rocco nestled next to him, curled up against his arm. He seemed quite cozy until he opened his eyes and blinked at Ms. Anne in surprise.

"Annie? What are you doing here, babe?"

Mr. Ben obviously wasn't fully awake yet. Otherwise, I doubt he'd ever call Ms. Anne "babe." She seemed surprised.

"I could ask you the same thing. Well, minus the 'babe' part."

Fully awake now, he sat up, being careful not to knock any of the sleeping animals off the couch. Gracie yawned. Jackson and Faraday continued to snooze. Mr. Ben placed them all gently on one cushion, gave Rocco a pat, and rose to his feet.

"Sorry. Capone had a meltdown. He sounded really upset. I let myself in to check on them and didn't have the heart to lock them up again, so I stayed. I'll go now." He ran a hand through his rumpled hair. Ms. Anne studied him closely.

"When did you start wearing glasses?"

He seemed confused by her question, then felt for the glasses on his face. "Oh. These are reading glasses. I started wearing them in college, I guess."

"College?"

He took off his glasses and put them in his shirt pocket. "Yes. I went to college, Annie. That must come as a shock."

"What did you study?"

"Architecture."

Ms. Anne's face softened. "You always wanted to be an architect. You loved building things, even when you were small. You used to build castles in the sandbox."

"You remember that?" he asked. "We were in elementary school."

"I remember everything."

A moment of silence hung between them, during which the two humans stared awkwardly at each other. They did that a lot. Luke broke the ice by staring up to Ms. Anne with adoring eyes as he pressed against her leg.

She beamed at him. "Hi, Luke," she said, crouching down to look at him eye to eye and giving him gentle pets. "Aren't you a beautiful boy?"

His tail wagged so hard his whole body shook. He licked her face, making Ms. Anne giggle. Mr. Ben watched their interaction, a small smile on his handsome face.

When Ms. Anne straightened, Luke kept his gaze fixed on her. "I'm in love," he said.

Studying Mr. Ben's face as he watched Ms. Anne, I realized he stared at her the same way Luke did—like he might be in love, too. "There seems to be a lot of that going around," I said wryly, wondering if Mr. Ben might start licking her face, too. Not that I blamed either one of them. Ms. Anne was a vision, with her red hair falling over her shoulders and her cheeks still pink from the cold.

She shrugged off her coat and hung it in the closet. "Thanks for checking on the dogs. Capone always overreacts. I'd only been gone a few hours. I went out to dinner. With Pat."

The smile vanished from Mr. Ben's face, and his expression darkened. "Pat Cavanaugh?"

"Yes," she said, a frown forming on her lips. "Why do you ask?"

He shrugged. "No reason. Have you been dating him long?"

Her frown deepened. "I'm not dating him. I went out to dinner with him. Once. And tomorrow, I'm going out to dinner with someone else. And Sunday, I'm having brunch with my next-door neighbor, Val."

"Busy weekend," said Mr. Ben. "Pat always did have a thing for you."

She stared at him in amazement. "You're an idiot. I haven't seen Pat since your funeral." She shook her head. "Gosh, it sounds weird to say that."

"But you're chummy now."

"He came to the bookstore to tell me you were still alive," she said through clenched teeth. "Kind of as a courtesy. He didn't want me to be shocked if I ran into you, but he was too late because I'd already run into you. Literally." She sent him a hostile glare. "And he asked me out for old time's sake. That's it."

He rolled his eyes. "Yeah, right. Is Pat aware you're seeing other people? Because I'm sure he's not asking you out for old time's sake. I know that much."

"What do you mean?"

Mr. Ben shoved his hands into the pockets of his jeans. "Nothing. Forget it."

"Like you forgot about all of us?" I heard the pain in Ms. Anne's voice. Mr. Ben's expression morphed from irritated to contrite in a single second.

"It wasn't like that."

"Then what was it like?"

She folded her arms across her chest and waited for an answer, but it never came. Finally, she let out a sound of pure disgust and turned to go up the stairs.

"No comment. It figures. Thanks for your help with the dogs, but I really prefer not to do this again."

"Do what again?" he asked.

She paused on the first step. "Any of this. The Ben I remember, the boy who built castles in the sand and made a filthy playground beautiful, died a long time ago. You're a stranger to me now." When she glanced at him, I thought I saw the glint of unshed tears in her eyes. "And I want to keep it that way. Good night, Ben. Lock the door on your way out."

EIGHTEEN

How to become a better friend and a better pet:

1. Stop stealing treats belonging to other dogs.
2. Eat fewer treats and take more walks.
3. Stop being such a jerk.
4. Stop scaring that deaf and senile beagle that lives down the street.
5. Learn to poop in one area of the front yard.
6. Snuggle more, bark less.
7. Appreciate the kindness of both my human and dog families.
8. Earn Ms. Anne's trust.

After some aggressive negotiating, Luke finally convinced me to poop in the backyard. "Come on, Capone," he said as I stood in the doorway of the kitchen and shivered in fear. "I won't let anything hurt you."

He shot the other dogs a sidelong glance, as if he thought they might be what I was afraid of, but that wasn't the case at all. "You don't understand. The first night I came here, the lights in the carriage house turned on mysteriously, and then Boo, the ghost dog, howled in the backyard. I don't want Boo to drag my soul to the depths of hell. I saw a movie about that once when I stayed up too late, and there was nothing on PBS. Biggest mistake of my life."

Luke frowned in confusion. "Once again, I'm following about half of what you said, but as far as Boo the Ghost Dog is concerned, are you sure you didn't see me?"

That never occurred to me. "Oh. Maybe you're right."

He rolled his eyes. "Then you have nothing to be afraid of, do you? Come out and hang with us."

And with that, objective number six had been met. I pooped, for the first time, in my new backyard.

"This is great," I said, looking around at my new space. Large for a yard in the middle of town, especially for one on River Road, it had a sturdy fence around its perimeter and a giant oak tree in the corner.

Molly called out to me from the other side of the fence. "Did you poop in the backyard, Capone?"

I couldn't see her, but I heard her, and I felt so proud. "Yes, I did."

"Good boy," she said.

Faraday called me a name I shall not repeat. It rhymed with "rum bass." Then he gave me a snarky sneer. "Huge accomplishment. Yay. What next? World peace? Invent the cure for cancer? Teach humans how to speak Dog?"

I might be a rum bass, but Faraday was a bass pole. "Maybe I will, Faraday," I said, lifting my nose in the air. "You never know."

The small dogs went off to do small dog things in the corner. Thank goodness for Luke and the soothing presence of Molly one yard over. It made me feel so much less alone.

"I dealt with dogs like that a lot when I lived on the

streets," said Luke, giving Faraday the stink eye. "All bark and no bite. You have to show him who's boss."

"How do I do that?"

He shrugged. "Every time he's mean to you, you have to say to yourself, 'I'm the alpha.' Can you do that?"

"Yes," I said with a nod. "I'm the alpha. I am the alpha. I am most definitely the alpha."

Five minutes later, when we went back inside the house, Faraday set me straight. "You are not the alpha, dork-face. You are a beta male if I ever met one, and the most metrosexual Labrador I've encountered."

Note to self: Look up the meaning of metrosexual. Faraday might be onto something.

I tried to stand my ground, but I couldn't. Faraday intimidated me. I had no idea why since he was roughly the size of my head. I shouldn't have been at all afraid of him.

Gracie noticed. "Don't let him bully you, Capone," she said when Faraday made me get off the couch and sit on the floor. "You have to be firm."

I felt so happy Gracie was talking to me again that I decided to follow her advice and hopped back onto the couch. It didn't last long, though. Faraday growled and showed me his teeth. I recognized a threat when I saw one, so I hopped back down.

Egads. I truly was a beta male.

But I wasn't the only one Faraday bullied. Jackson seemed to be dealing with the same issue. I realized that when Ms. Anne sat on the couch, and both Pugs tried to crawl onto her lap. Jackson was big for a Pug. He weighed over thirty pounds. Faraday was barely more than ten, but when Jackson tried to take his spot, Faraday showed his true colors. He stood on his hind legs and punched Jackson repeatedly with his paws until Jackson finally moved. Then Faraday took Ms. Anne's lap all for himself.

"He is definitely a bass pole," I said.

Gracie agreed. "But Jackson won't stand up to him," she said. "Due to the whole puppy mill thing."

"What are you talking about?"

"Faraday came from a puppy mill in Ohio."

"What is a puppy mill?"

Letting out an impatient sigh, Gracie explained. "They breed puppies for profit, and sometimes the conditions are horrendous. I came from a puppy mill, but a smaller operation and the conditions weren't that bad. My human rescued me after I'd been purchased by a family that couldn't handle a puppy of my delicate nature." She meant she was high maintenance, but she didn't have to spell it out for me. "Faraday, however, came from one of the worst ones —so awful, state inspectors shut it down. Every other puppy in his litter died. Faraday was the only survivor. It made him a little different."

"A little?" I asked, but now I had sympathy for Faraday. Oh, no. Why did I have such a kind and generous temperament?

No wonder he responded with disbelief when I said I'd grown up on a puppy farm. The person who owned my farm, Mistress Sue, had always been so kind and responsible, and my brothers and sisters all went to loving homes. I was the last of the litter to be adopted, and my beloved Mistress Sue read books to me and nurtured me. She introduced me to the wonders of public broadcasting and made me into the literature-loving gentleman of a Labrador I was today.

Faraday had apparently never had a Mistress Sue in his life. He must have been so scared and all alone. But Luke had been scared and alone, too, and yet he was courteous to me. Faraday chose to be a jerk, but I decided to treat him with more patience. Appreciating my dog family had been, after all, goal number eight.

A knock came at the back kitchen door. It had to be Mr. Ben, and we responded with happy barks and hops. Ms. Anne did neither. She opened the door with a frown on her face.

"What do you want?"

Mr. Ben's lips quirked as if he found her irritation amusing. "Nothing. I thought I ought to apologize for last night. I shouldn't have let myself in. And I shouldn't have said some of the things I did. It wasn't my place, and I'm sorry."

Ms. Anne studied him. She didn't smile, but she did seem somewhat neutral as she considered his words. "I understand why you did it, but you surprised me. Thank you for checking on Capone. I'm sure he made it sound like someone was killing him. He can be such a drama queen."

My eyes widened in surprise. A drama queen? Really? The woman left me in a haunted house all alone, and I was a drama queen?

Sadly, Mr. Ben agreed with her. "I realized that as soon as I opened the door, but he'd gotten so worked up, I didn't have the heart to make him go back into that room."

She nodded. "I appreciate that."

A moment of silence followed. It seemed like a temporary truce had been established. It was reinforced when Ms. Anne offered him coffee, and Mr. Ben accepted, leaning against the counter.

"If you want, I can watch the dogs tonight, too. You said you have a date."

She shot him a wary glance. "Are you sure you wouldn't mind?"

He shook his head. "Nope. I could get a bit more work done, and Luke loves the company. By the way, have you seen my keyring?"

"I haven't, but I'll keep an eye out for it. How many keys are on it?"

"At least ten. That's the thing about old houses. They come with a million keys, a different one for each door. And as much as you want to preserve the original hardware, it can be tricky at times."

Ms. Anne studied him. "Where did you learn to do this stuff? I remember you worked in construction part-time in high school. Wasn't it for your stepfather's company? Goodman Construction?"

"Yes," he said, and I saw a shadow pass over his eyes. It disappeared before I could figure out what it meant. Mr. Ben cleared his throat. "I worked my way through college. It paid the bills. It took me a few extra years to get my degree, but I loved it. A year after I graduated, I had the chance to do an apprenticeship in England with a master builder. He was wonderful, and I learned about carving, masonry, and how to restore older houses. It was something I'd never done before, and I'd found my calling. I thought I could play a part in preserving history with my work. If that makes sense."

"It does. How long were you in England?"

"Two years," he said. "I went to Italy for a while, too. And France."

She gave him a small smile. "You always dreamed of traveling. You've had quite the life, Ben. You got everything you ever wanted."

"Not everything," he said, his voice soft.

I wondered what he meant. Was he talking about Ms. Anne? Her cheeks got pink, and she changed the subject.

"Tell me more about your plans for the house."

Mr. Ben led us through each room, detailing his plans and showing us his drawings and blueprints. Ms. Anne seemed fascinated, both by what he wanted to do and with what he'd already accomplished. The fireplace mantle, which had been a mess when we first moved in, now looked quite beautiful, with intricate carvings of flowers and animals. When I noticed a dog resembling me, something clicked in my mind.

"Holy guacamole," I said, nudging Jackson. "Does that remind you of someone?"

Jackson squinted his eyes at the carving. "I thought that was a duck."

"You need glasses, dude. Climb on the chair so you can get a closer look."

Jackson did as I said and stared at the carving a moment. "You're right. It reminds me of you. That's weird."

A chill went over me. "I think it's Boo. He must have been a Lab."

NINETEEN

Labs are:

1. Always ready to play.
2. Easy to train.
3. Selfless and kind.
4. Good with children.
5. Skilled at tracking with scent.
6. Very agile.
7. Simple to groom.
8. An exceptionally handsome breed and much cuter than Pugs.

The humans noticed the similarities of the dog on the mantle as well. Mr. Ben ran a hand over the carving, then smiled down at me. "It's definitely a Lab, and it looks like you, buddy."

Ms. Anne laughed. "Maybe it's a sign. Josie and Nate were meant to be here. What do you plan to work on next?"

"After I finish the mantle and the other detailed work, I'll do the rest of the interior. Repairing and refinishing the hardwood and fixing any damage to the plaster walls. I have a team to take care of the painting, plumbing, and electricity. They'll be here in a few days. But I like to do most of the tricky stuff myself. The outside work will have to wait, unfortunately. I wish I could start, but it's too cold. Other guys will take care of the roof, the exterior, and the windows once the weather warms up. It'll be a beautiful space soon, but the full project won't be completed until summer. I'll be gone by then, of course."

There was a tiny pause. "Where will you go?"

He ran a careful finger over the carvings on the mantle. "I have a job in New York, and then I'm moving back to England. The man who gave me the apprenticeship is retiring. He asked if I wanted to take over. It's a once in a lifetime opportunity."

"I see," said Ms. Anne, the brightness in her voice held an artificial note. "I'd better go get dressed." She pulled her robe tighter around her slim body. "I have some errands to run."

"You can leave the animals with me if you'd like."

"Are you sure?"

He nodded. "They aren't any trouble."

She let out a laugh. "Have you met Capone? Trouble is his middle name."

That was a lie. I didn't have a middle name. But I was interested in this whole going to England thing. If Mr. Ben went to England (the land of Jane Austen and all things perfect and wonderful), what would happen to Ms. Anne?

It created a conundrum. Mr. Ben seemed like her Mr. Knightley, but could I be wrong? I decided to play it safe by entertaining the possibility that it might be Policeman Pat, Fireman Fetch, Viking Val, or maybe someone else.

If Ms. Anne married Viking Val, she'd live right next

door, and we could always be together. That might be the perfect situation. Far preferable to her being in England, but I didn't have much time left to work on this. Ms. Josie and Mr. Nate planned to return a week from today, on the last day of February. If I wanted to succeed, I had to work quickly.

Fortunately, Ms. Anne seemed to be working quickly as well. Three dates in three days? It must be a new record.

As she dressed, the four of us sat on the floor and watched her. Rocco curled up by the window. He didn't seem at all interested in what Ms. Anne was doing, but I caught him gazing at her every once in a while. He liked her as much as we did, even if he didn't care to admit it. Rocco reminded me of an overcooked campfire marshmallow—dark, crusty, and bitter on the outside but with a sweet, mushy, soft center.

When he noticed me staring at him, he muttered a profanity and turned his back to me, but kept his face pointed toward Ms. Anne.

Crusty marshmallow. Soft center.

"You all need to behave while I'm gone," she said, pulling on a tight sweater dress and some high-heeled boots. "Especially you, Capone."

She singled me out. Great.

I glanced out the window. The snow swirled and danced in big, fat flakes that already covered the roads and sidewalks. I had questions about her choice of footwear—her boots seemed potentially hazardous—but I'm hardly one to judge when it came to fashion, and she looked lovely, as always.

Mr. Ben seemed to agree. As Ms. Anne walked down the steps, I caught him staring at her, his heart in his eyes. Or it could have been dust. Hard to tell, but it reminded me of the way Rocco stared at her—sneaking glances at her when he thought no one noticed. That made me realize something important: Mr. Ben was a crusty marshmallow, too.

WE SPENT a pleasant morning with Mr. Ben as Ms. Anne did her errands. She came back with food from a delightful place called Don's Deli. Ms. Anne had ordered a turkey Rueben for herself, and something called "The Don" for Mr. Ben. It was a delightful mix of all things Italian—prosciutto, capocollo, soppressata, and mozzarella. Yum.

I sniffed hopefully at his sandwich, and Mr. Ben sent Ms. Anne a questioning look. She shook her head. "No way. It'll make him sick."

Curse my irritable bowels and my inability to process human foods.

Ms. Anne patted my head. "Don't worry, Capone. Kristin from the deli would never forget you." She pulled out a bag of cheese cubes and doled them out to all of us. "Here you go."

Oh, happy day!

"Have you seen the original plans for the house anywhere?" asked Mr. Ben, as we nibbled on cheese, and they nibbled on sandwiches. "I had them with my blueprints, but they're missing."

Ms. Anne shook her head. "I haven't, sorry."

"First the keys and now the house plans. I don't understand it."

"It's a big house. I keep losing things, too. One of my slippers is missing, for example."

I ducked my head. When I glanced up, the humans were both staring at me.

Oh, calamity. If only I could control myself around ladies' footwear.

The slipper, or rather what remained of it, was currently tucked into one of the couch cushions. I'd tried to ignore it, but there was only so much a puppy could take. Slippers were so satisfying.

"It's pretty obvious what happened to your slipper," said Mr. Ben, eyes twinkling. "Someone seems guilty."

"Someone certainly does," said Ms. Anne, shaking her head. She turned back to Mr. Ben. "Why do you need the original plans?"

"It's always helpful to have them. You can never be certain what might pop up in a house this old."

"Like secret rooms? A sex dungeon? A walk-in closet?"

He grinned. "I'm not sure how you went from a sex dungeon to a walk-in closet, but yes, there are sometimes secret rooms. Places boarded over and then forgotten. It's important to have the old plans so you can compare them with the current plans, but there is something else as well. I like framing them and giving them to the new owners. As a sort of homecoming gift. Like the house itself is welcoming them."

"That is sweet. And thoughtful. Josie and Nate will love it."

"If I can find them."

I watched Mr. Ben and Ms. Anne carefully. They acted comfortable around each other for once, and they conversed in a way that did not seem like arguing. I considered that progress. Luke agreed. But things got weird when Mr. Ben asked about Ms. Anne's upcoming date.

"So, who is the lucky guy tonight?"

He had a bit of a smirk on his face as he posed the question. Ms. Anne paused, and for a moment, I wondered if she might not answer him, but she did. "His name is Fletcher. He's a fireman. I met him when my house caught on fire last week."

Mr. Ben nodded, the smirk disappearing. "How are things going with the repairs?"

She shrugged. "I heard back from the insurance company yesterday. Everything is on track, but the snow and cold are causing a delay. The house will be habitable soon, and I hope to be back in it before Josie and Nate return."

"Aren't they coming back in a week?"

"Yes."

He considered this. "Do you want me to take a peek at your house? I might be able to help."

"That would be kind of you." She still sounded stiff and awkward, but she often sounded that way around Mr. Ben. Not that I blamed her. What could be classified as "normal" in a situation like this? He'd been dead, and now he wasn't. It would confuse anyone.

Things got stranger when Fireman Fetch arrived, carrying flowers. A handsome guy, he even had on a suit, which earned him gentleman credits. But when Mr. Ben answered the door, Fireman Fetch squinted at the house number.

"Sorry. I thought I had the wrong house for a second. Is Anne here?"

"She's upstairs getting ready. Come on in."

Mr. Ben was finishing the fireplace, painstakingly slow work. The carvings were quite elaborate, and there had been significant damage over the years. He indicated a chair where Fireman Fetch could sit. It was Rocco's chair, which meant it was covered in cat fur. Fireman Fetch took one peek at it and declined the offer.

"I'll stand," he said.

"Suit yourself."

Had Mr. Ben hoped Fireman Fetch would end up covered in cat fur? It sure seemed that way.

"I'm Fletcher, by the way," said Fireman Fetch, extending his hand. Mr. Ben took it grudgingly.

"Ben O'Reilly."

Fireman Fetch's eyes widened in surprise. "The same Ben O'Reilly who..."

He seemed at a loss for words. Mr. Ben filled them in for him. "Supposedly died fifteen years ago? Yep, that's me."

The fireman ran a hand over his head. "Wow. I heard you'd come back—what a shocker. I was in middle school when everyone thought you drowned. You were an urban legend, dude."

"Middle school?" asked Mr. Ben raising an eyebrow. "If that's the case, aren't you a little young for Anne?"

"Age is only a number," said Fireman Fetch with a grin.

Mr. Ben eyed him carefully. "Why do you seem so familiar to me?"

Fireman Fetch's grin widened. "You were friends with my older brother, Rob."

"Rob Hart?" asked Mr. Ben, returning Fireman Fetch's grin with one of his own. "Gosh. You're the spitting image of him. How's he doing?"

"He's happy you're alive, that's for sure. He heard it through the grapevine and called a few days ago to tell me about it. He lives in New York now. I'll tell him I saw you. I'm sure he'll be in touch."

They chatted about Fireman Fetch's brother until Ms.

Anne came down the stairs, elegant in a black dress and heels. "Sorry to keep you waiting."

"No problem," said Fireman Fetch, handing her the flowers. "And definitely worth it. You look amazing."

"Oh, smooth," said Jackson. I hadn't realized he'd been listening. He let out a snort. "I need to remember that line. It's a good one."

Fireman Fetch was smooth. And polite. And handsome. And Ms. Anne seemed to like him, but it still didn't convince me he was the right man for her. Maybe it had something to do with the expression I saw on Mr. Ben's face as he watched them leave to go on their date.

"He still has feelings for her," I said.

"No kidding. And she still has feelings for him," said Gracie, tilting her head. "But it doesn't matter."

"Why would you say that? Love conquers all."

Gracie shook her head. "Love conquers most. Not all." She glanced at Jackson, who pretended not to be listening, but kept shooting us stealthy looks. It seemed to make her more annoyed. "But some things cannot be forgiven. Or forgotten. And certain males would be wise to remember that."

TWENTY

Ode to a Metallic Ballet Flat

You are alone now.
You used to be a pair,
but your partner is long gone.
I blame myself for that,
mostly because I ate it.
Oh, calamity.

"Where are my ballet flats?" asked Ms. Anne, digging through her closet. She shot me a squinty-eyed glare. "They were imported from Italy. And expensive. Do you know anything about it, Capone?"

Uh-oh. Here we go again.

I turned away, attempting to appear both innocent and confused. She didn't buy it, clever woman. In truth, I vaguely remembered stashing one of her ballet flats under a cushion in the sofa. The other one currently worked its way slowly through my intestinal tract.

I had to eat it. I couldn't stop myself. It had been so pretty and so shiny.

Note to self: Stop acting like a squirrel.

"It's a good thing it's snowing," she said, with an angry huff. "I'll wear boots instead."

Her boots. Oh, no. I drooled all over those. Maybe she wouldn't notice.

I listened as she made her way downstairs and heard her squeal when she stuck her foot into her soggy boot.

"Capone. You're disgusting." She shouted the words up the stairs. "Why would you slobber on my new boots? They're even wet inside."

I cringed. "How did she know it was me?" I asked, keeping my voice low.

The other dogs stared at me in disbelief. "Because it's always you," said Faraday.

"And we're not tall enough to drool in her boots," added Jackson, attempting to wiggle out of his collar. Ms. Anne had dressed us up for our visit to Viking Val's. Gracie had on a flouncy skirt. Jackson, Faraday, and I wore spiffy bow ties. I was the only one who actually liked the bow tie, but Gracie seemed to enjoy her skirt. Or maybe it should be classified as a tutu. I couldn't be certain, but it was sparkly and pink and perfect, and she looked amazing, so I told her so.

"Gracie, you look amazing."

She preened. "I do, don't I?"

She shot Jackson a questioning glance, but he ignored her. "Let's get this show on the road," he said. "I'm starving, and I'm sure that Val guy will have bacon. He seems like a bacon eater, doesn't he?"

Ms. Anne, in her drool-stained boots, stood by the door. She put on her coat as Mr. Ben came in. He eyed her from head to toe, pausing briefly on her unfortunate and very moist boots.

"Capone?" he asked, pointing at them.

"Capone," she said, displaying the boots from different angles. I really had done a number on them.

Curse my loose jowls and lack of control over my oral secretions.

Mr. Ben leaned against the wall, hands in the pockets of his pants. "I'm going to start on the kitchen today if that works for you. The cabinets and appliances are being delivered Tuesday, so you'll be without a kitchen for a couple of days, but I have to get it done. We're on a pretty tight schedule."

"Oh. Okay."

"I have a small kitchen in the carriage house," he tilted his head to indicate the backyard. "You can use it if you want. Or I could, uh, make you a meal or whatever."

Ms. Anne folded her arms across her chest. "You can cook?"

"I'm not a high school kid anymore, Annie."

She smiled, almost like she couldn't help it. "That's excellent news."

He smiled back at her. "What do you say? Can I make you dinner tomorrow night?"

I stared at him in surprise. It sounded almost like Mr. Ben was asking Ms. Anne on a date. This could be it. Maybe she'd realize he was her Mr. Knightley, and they could finally walk off into the sunset together.

Or not.

I couldn't be sure because Ms. Anne still hadn't answered. We waited for her response with bated breath.

Well, my breath was bated. Jackson's breathing sounded

like an obscene phone call. He couldn't help it, though. It was a Pug thing.

"That would be lovely." Suddenly, Ms. Anne didn't seem like her usual super-polished and confident self. She acted oddly nervous, and Mr. Ben wasn't much better. His cheeks turned red, and he ran a hand through his hair, a habit of his. It made him appear rumpled but in an adorable sort of way.

"Good. Great. Do you still like Italian food? Or I can make a mean Indian curry. I learned how when I lived in England. Do you like tikka masala?"

"I love tikka masala."

"Perfect." He stepped away from the door. "I won't hold you up. You're going to brunch next door, right?"

"Yes," she said but didn't move. They stared at each other for a long moment before she finally spoke again. "I'm glad you're back, Ben."

"Me, too."

BRUNCH AT VIKING VAL'S was, indeed, lovely. He made quiche with bacon inside and sadly did not share any with those of the canine persuasion, but Ms. Anne seemed to enjoy it, and he gave all of us special homemade doggie treats. I had a great time hanging out with Molly. We chatted about Lab-related topics, and, for once, I didn't feel left out of the conversation, like I usually did with the Pugs.

Viking Val was a charming host, but I got the sense Ms. Anne's mind was elsewhere. Like back at the house. With Mr. Ben. I said as much to the other dogs when Molly and Faraday got up to search for a toy.

"You're right," said Gracie, keeping her voice soft. "But

it worries me. That man hurt her once before. I don't want to see it happen again. And he seems like the type."

"What type?"

She shot Jackson a pointed glare. "The love them and leave them type."

Jackson's eyes widened. "Come on, baby—"

"Stop calling me that," said Gracie, hackles going up. "I mean it, Jackson."

He flopped down on the floor, appearing miserable. "Fine. But you should at least listen to my side of the story."

"I already know what happened. Every dirty detail. And I don't want to speak about it ever again."

She flounced off, and Jackson huffed, more miserable than ever. "Love is a battlefield," he said to no one in particular.

I frowned. "I thought it was a many splendored thing."

"That too," said Jackson. "But it's mostly a battlefield. Especially with a girl like Gracie."

"Do you want to talk?" I asked. "I'm an excellent listener."

That was not exactly true. I'd always been a bad listener, but I cared enough about Jackson that I endeavored to focus for once.

"It's a tale as old as time. Boy meets girl. Girl has a nice..." He glanced at Gracie's retreating bottom. "...personality. Boy falls for girl. Girl accuses him of cheating with the Poodle at doggie daycare. Boy explains he didn't realize they were exclusive and didn't understand there was a no-humping rule in place. Girl calls him some names not fit to repeat. Boy promises never to hump another Poodle again. Girl tells him it's too late. Boy realizes he lost his chance at the best thing that ever happened to him."

I gasped. "It's like Romeo and Juliet, but with less death and more humping."

"Exactly," said Jackson, scratching his chin. "The thing I don't get is this—who told Gracie about the Poodle in the first place?"

I gasped again. "Wait. Are you telling me Gracie is the girl in this story?"

"Uh, yes."

"And you are the boy?"

"Yes, Capone."

"That changes everything. You need to apologize."

He let out a sigh. "I've tried. Trust me. She won't listen."

"Maybe I can talk with her."

"Would you?" he asked, giving a head tilt. Even for an old Pug like Jackson, there was nothing cuter than a head tilt.

"Definitely." I snuggled closer to him, happy we were friends again. "But who told Gracie about the Poodle?"

Jackson frowned. "I have my suspicions, but whoever it was is no friend of mine."

"And no friend of mine either," I said with a firm nod of my head. "I'll help you figure it out. There is nothing I like more than a compelling mystery."

"Thanks, buddy, but I already have an idea who the culprit might be." His gaze went to Faraday, who currently dragged a giant bone off to the corner to chew. The bone seemed bigger than the puppy himself, so it was comical to watch. Jackson didn't laugh, though. Jackson didn't seem to find Faraday comical at all.

WHEN WE GOT BACK to the house, part of the kitchen had disappeared. We'd only been gone a few hours, but Mr. Ben had obviously been quite busy. He currently hammered away, tearing up the tile floor.

"You're a fast worker," said Ms. Anne, glancing around at the bare walls that once held cupboards.

"So I've heard," he replied with a teasing smile.

"Can I help?" asked Ms. Anne. "I love doing this type of stuff."

"Demolition?"

"Exactly." She returned his teasing smile with one of her own. "But I actually meant restoring old houses. However, my forte is interior design. That's what I studied in college. I had my own business for a while but had to close it."

"Why?"

She couldn't seem to meet his eye. "I wanted to have a baby, but it never worked out. It ended my first marriage. Well, that and other things."

"Other things?"

She shrugged. "It's usually not one moment that ends a marriage. It's a million tiny moments. Not that I blame my ex-husbands. Not entirely. I was looking for something specific and never found it."

"What were you looking for, Annie?"

She lifted her eyes to finally meet his. "Do you seriously have to ask, Ben?"

He took a step closer to her as if he couldn't stop himself. "Annie, I'm so—"

A knock sounded at the door. Ms. Anne and Mr. Ben stepped apart. I ran to the door, barking my head off, and the other dogs followed. To my surprise, Policeman Pat stood on our front porch. Ms. Anne pushed us all aside, opened the door, and let him in. Mr. Ben slipped out the back door with Luke. I heard the door open and close, even though he did it softly. Ms. Anne and Policeman Pat didn't seem to notice.

"Hi, Annie," he said.

He wore civilian clothing, not his uniform, and he looked handsome. He also looked delighted to see me.

"Hey, Capone. Have you been staying out of trouble lately?"

I hadn't but wasn't about to admit it to an officer of the law. Instead, I licked him and tried to appear innocent. Unfortunately, appearing innocent is harder than it might seem.

"How are you, Pat?" asked Ms. Anne, sneaking a glance over her shoulder as if searching for Mr. Ben.

"Fine. It seems like you're in the middle of something." He indicated the partially torn-up house. In addition to the kitchen being a mess, Mr. Ben had been working on the hardwood floors as well. Some could be restored, but others were so damaged they had to be replaced.

"Josie and Nate are renovating. I'm here until my house is finished being repaired."

He nodded. "It's a good thing no one got hurt in that fire."

"Yes. We were lucky."

An awkward pause ensued. Ms. Anne didn't invite him to sit down, nor did she mention Mr. Ben was the one doing the renovation. I found both of those things odd.

Policeman Pat cleared his throat. "I don't want to bother you. I wanted to stop by and check on you. A big storm is coming this week. Do you have salt and everything you'll need?"

Ms. Anne bit her lip. "I'm not sure we even have a shovel."

His face brightened. "I can bring you one. I'll bring some salt, too."

"I don't want to trouble you—"

"It's no bother."

"Thank you. I appreciate it. You're a good friend, Pat." Glancing over her shoulder, she turned back and shot him a rueful smile. "I'd offer you a cup of coffee, but I have no kitchen at the moment."

"No worries," he said, stepping out the front door. He hesitated a moment on the landing. "Out of curiosity, who is doing the renovation?"

"It's Ben, actually."

Something strange flashed across Policeman Pat's face. "That's what I thought. Be careful, Annie," he said, lowering his voice. "He isn't what he seems. Not by a long shot."

She closed the door after he left and leaned against it, a worried frown on her pretty face.

What had he meant by that exactly?

TWENTY-ONE

A list of things Mr. Ben seems to have missed about Beaver:

1. Kretchmar's famous toasted almond torte.
2. Chili-cheese fries from the Hot Dog Shoppe.
3. Old friends.
4. Having a place to belong.
5. Ms. Anne.
6. Ms. Anne.
7. Ms. Anne.

We went to Mr. Ben's carriage house promptly at six pm. A small space, it had a couch and a coffee table on one side of the room, a tiny kitchen on the other, and a table and two chairs set up near the only window. A steep staircase led to a loft, and I imagined that's where Mr. Ben slept.

"This is amazing," said Ms. Anne, gazing around. She'd brought dessert, a toasted almond torte from Kretchmar's Bakery. It was a white cake with custard filling and covered with fresh creamy icing and sweet, crunchy, toasted almonds.

Yes, I have eaten it before. No, I wasn't supposed to eat it, but I did anyway. No, I am not proud, but what is past is past. I have no regrets, mostly because that cake tasted amazing.

Apparently, Mr. Ben thought so, too. His face cracked into a wide grin. "Is this what I think it is?"

She returned his grin with a shy smile. "It used to be your favorite."

"It'll always be my favorite. It's the best cake in the world. Thanks, Annie."

He put the box into the fridge and stirred a pot on the stove. It smelled amazing, like rich spices and things I'd never smelled before. I asked Luke about it.

"What is that heavenly aroma?"

"I have no idea, puppy. Dogs aren't allowed to have curry."

Distressing news indeed. "But why?"

Luke eyed me worriedly, probably noticing how I'd lifted my nose and moved closer to the food. "Because it'll rip your stomach to shreds. Don't even think about it, Capone."

But I did think about it. A lot. And it proved to be a conundrum. Eating something that smelled delicious versus maintaining the lining of my stomach? It was a hard call.

"Can I do anything to help?" asked Ms. Anne.

"No," said Mr. Ben, shaking his dark head. "Have a seat. It's almost ready."

His hair looked slightly damp, like he'd taken a shower, and he smelled lovely. Almost as delectable as his curry. Ms. Anne had taken a shower, too, and spent extra time on her appearance. Her red hair shone in the dim overhead lighting, and she had on her favorite jeans.

"They make her butt look really good," said Gracie

knowingly. "She only brings them out on special occasions. The sweater is for special occasions, too."

Her sweater had a wide neck that slid down a bit, exposing one of her shoulders. I couldn't really understand the point of it. Ms. Anne might catch a cold, baring her shoulder like that. I also caught more than one peek of her bra, which seemed risqué.

Or maybe that was the point.

Note to self: Women are a mystery.

When the meal was ready, Mr. Ben lit two long tapered candles on the table. He served the tikka masala next to fresh naan bread and then poured them each a glass of sparkling white wine. After he took his seat, he glanced up and noticed her staring at him.

"Why are you looking at me like that?" he asked, with a puzzled frown.

"No reason," she said, her cheeks turning delightfully pink. She paused, swallowing hard, before meeting his eyes. "It's just that I wondered so many times what you would have been like as a grown man, and now I know."

He gave her a sad smile. "And now you know." A long moment of silence hung between them, but it didn't feel uncomfortable this time. It simply seemed contemplative. Like they both had a lot to ponder. Mr. Ben broke it first, clearing his throat and raising his wine glass. "I'd like to make a toast to you, my oldest and dearest friend. You always were, and always will be, far too good for me, but I'm grateful I was able to be at least a small part of your life."

It was a nice toast, but Ms. Anne stopped him before he could take a sip. "No," she said, her voice unsteady. "You've got everything wrong, Bennet O'Reilly. I'm the one who is grateful—grateful that you're here right now. Grateful that you didn't die."

There was a pause, the light from the flickering candles playing on both their faces. Mr. Ben broke the spell, giving her a crooked smile, but his eyes were sad. "Then cheers to us, I guess," he said, with a crooked smile.

They clinked glasses and took a long sip. Ms. Anne let out a sigh. "This is amazing."

The wine probably was tasty, but it seemed like she wanted to change the subject. I didn't blame her. Things had gotten emotionally charged

He handed her some naan bread. "It's a Crémant d'Alsace. I got it in France. I lived in the Alsace region for a while, near Switzerland."

After Mr. Ben told her about his travels, she updated him on their mutual friends and all the things he'd missed while he'd been gone. Later, they helped themselves to generous slices of the almond cake and sat side by side on the couch with their feet up. They'd indulged in more than one bottle of wine at dinner and seemed relaxed and happy.

"Do you remember when we went to the winter dance freshman year?" asked Ms. Anne. "And you had to borrow my grandfather's tie?"

He nodded. "Your grandparents always treated me so kindly."

"But that tie was atrocious. I can't believe you wore it."

"It was pretty ghastly." He bit his lower lip to keep from laughing.

"It had lights."

"It did."

"And dancing reindeer."

"Yes," he said. "But I didn't mind. Especially when you taught me how to tie it. You learned how from a book in the library. Do you remember that part?"

"I do," she said, her cheeks growing pinker. "Our first kiss."

His gaze when straight to her lips. "Yes."

As he gazed at her lips, we gazed at both of them. "Oh, boy," said Luke. "He's going to do it. He's going to kiss her."

"Really?" I tilted my head and studied them carefully. "Gosh, Luke. You're right."

"He'd better not," said Gracie with a yawn. "My girl isn't ready for this. She might never be ready. Once bitten, twice shy."

Gracie gave Jackson a dirty glare. He rolled his eyes. "I did not bite you, Gracie. It was a love nibble. Nothing more."

"Hmph." She lifted her nose in the air.

Gracie may have been right about her owner. Ms. Anne didn't seem ready for canoodling of any sort. She pulled away from Mr. Ben on the couch and stood up. "It's getting late. I'd better go."

He rose to his feet, too, running a hand through his hair. "It's not that late, is it?"

She bit her lip, sadder than I'd ever seen her. "It is. It's way too late, Ben."

They were talking about more than just tonight. Ms. Anne glanced at the kitchen. "Let me help you with the dishes."

He shoved his hands deep into the pockets of his jeans. "Nah, I've got it. Thanks for coming over."

"Thanks for having me." I nudged her knee. She nearly lost her balance, but she got the message. "I mean, us."

He steadied her by reaching for her elbow. "My pleasure."

As Mr. Ben helped her put on her coat, we waited patiently, but they took a long time. Goodbyes didn't usually take this long. They stood by the door of the carriage house, only inches apart, and did nothing.

"Let's get this show on the road," I said, lunging forward, but Luke blocked me.

"Give them a minute. They might kiss."

We sat and watched them expectantly. When Mr. Ben and Ms. Anne noticed, they both laughed. "What are they doing?" she asked.

"No idea. They seem interested in our conversation, though."

She wrinkled her nose. "Or maybe they want an after-dinner treat."

I let out a howl. I did want an after-dinner treat. So much.

"I guess we got our answer," said Mr. Ben.

"I guess we did." She glanced up at him, her expression shy as she opened the door. "Good night, Ben."

"Good night, Annie. Should we walk you home?"

She laughed. "I can make it across the yard."

The snow came down hard, and Mr. Ben squinted up at the sky. "Conditions are looking pretty treacherous. I could carry you."

She waved at him, still laughing. "No, you couldn't."

He put a hand to his chest. "I'm stronger than you think."

Her laughter died. She stood in the middle of the yard, snow swirling around her and landing on her hair and face. "I know you're strong. That was never in question. See you tomorrow, Ben."

And with that, she turned and walked back to the house without glancing back. Although she didn't turn, I did and saw Mr. Ben standing there, his expression so wistful my heart ached for him.

"We've got to do something to help them," I said as we entered the house.

"Like what?" asked Gracie.

"I'm not sure. We need to make them realize they still love each other." The other dogs went to get a drink of water, and I saw an opportunity. "Like you and Jackson."

Gracie sniffed. "Stay out of it, Capone. You don't understand what you're talking about."

"Come on, Gracie. Give him another chance."

"Nope. No way." She blew out a breath. "Let me explain it in terms you'll understand. If a girl doubts as to whether she should accept a guy or not, she certainly ought to refuse him."

My eyes widened. "You just semi-quoted Austen to me."

"I did."

"You hate Austen."

"I do, but I had to get through to you. Do you get it now?"

"Yes, but can you at least tell me one thing?" I asked. "Who told you about Jackson and the Poodle at doggie daycare?"

She narrowed her eyes at me. "He put you up to this, didn't he?"

"No. I mean, yes. I mean, maybe...?"

Oh, calamity. I was the worst liar in the world.

Curse my honest and generous disposition.

Gracie didn't seem mad at me, though. She acted sad. "It doesn't matter who told me. The point is he did it. Once a cheater, always a cheater. And the same goes for lying, puppy. Look at my human and Ben. Will she ever truly be able to trust him again?"

I frowned. "I hope so."

She shook her head. "Once it's ruined, it's ruined forever."

"You don't honestly believe that, do you? What about forgiveness? What about turning the other cheek?"

She watched as Jackson belched, water dripping from his round face. "Sometimes, it's not worth it."

And when I saw the hurt in her eyes, I wondered if she might be right.

***

THAT NIGHT I dreamed of almond tortes and broken promises. Once, a long time ago, Ms. Josie had said I'd get a treat after dinner, and then she completely forgot to give it to me. I understood how Ms. Anne and Gracie felt. I, too, had suffered the sting of betrayal.

I woke up grumpy, but my mood improved when we got to the shop. We had a special, surprise guest.

"Uncle Clancy." I barked as soon as I saw the elderly brown dog come into Bartleby's Books. His owner, Mistress Patti, was friends with Ms. Anne. Even though the shop was closed on Mondays, they came to visit.

Uncle Clancy sat down slowly as if everything hurt. It was hard to watch. "What's going on? Are you okay?"

Ms. Anne asked Mistress Patti the same question. "Is Clancy okay?"

Mistress Patti shook her head sadly, eyes filling with tears. "He's not doing well," she said. "At all."

Normally, Uncle Clancy came to visit with Elliot, Mistress Patti's goofy yellow Lab. Today, however, he was on his own. The other dogs and Rocco remained upstairs. Only Uncle Clancy and I sat in the shop together, and I was glad to have this time alone together.

As Mistress Patti and Ms. Anne spoke softly to each other, I laid down next to the old, brown dog. He was my actual uncle. We came from the same breeder and everything.

Uncle Clancy took a deep breath. It made a strange huffing sound when it came out like it hurt him. "I've got some upsetting news, pup," he wheezed. "Time is running out. I don't know how much of it I have left, but I'm sure I'll be crossing over the Rainbow Bridge soon."

"The Rainbow Bridge?" I asked, panic swelling inside me. "What are you talking about?"

He let out another wheeze and I saw the pain in his big, brown eyes. "I've had a respectable run of it, and Mistress Patti is the best human I've ever encountered, but my life is coming to an end. It's time for me to move on."

I stood up, legs shaking. "No. You can't. Are you talking about dying?"

"Hush, puppy. It's okay. It's the natural order of things. We all have an expiration date. I'm old and tired. I'm at peace with it." He glanced over at Mistress Patti, who wept as she spoke to Ms. Anne, and Ms. Anne wept, too. And I'm sure Miss Olivia and Miss Bella would also be weeping, but they were at lunch right now.

"I know this really excellent vet. His name is Doc McHottie and—"

"Stop, Capone. What's broken in me cannot be fixed. I came here for one last goodbye."

I snuggled up next to him on the floor and let out a tiny whine. "But I don't want you to die. I love you, Uncle Clancy."

"I love you, too, which is why I wanted to see you today. There has been something I've wanted to say to you but never got the chance."

"Oh, no. What did I do now?"

I thought back on it. There were quite a few possibilities, but none of them involved Uncle Clancy.

"That's exactly what I wanted to discuss. You are way too hard on yourself. You're a first-rate puppy, Capone."

"I am?"

"Yes."

"Are you sure?"

He let out a soft chuckle. "Definitely." He took another breath, almost as if that tiny laugh had cost him too much. "All Labs are crazy as puppies. Take me, for example. I used to be worse than you."

"I don't believe it." I gasped. "You're so good."

"I'm old, Capone. I wasn't always like this. I've eaten my share of shoes and stolen my share of treats, but I learned something along the way. Do you want me to tell you what it is?" I nodded, and he continued. "Goodness isn't defined by who you are at your best. It's about who you are at your worst."

"I don't understand."

He let out a long sigh. "Even when you were naughty, your intentions were noble. Everyone makes mistakes. What matters is how we fix them. What matters is what is in your heart. And you, sweet puppy, have a heart of gold. I recognize a good dog when I see one, and you are a good dog. Remember that, okay?"

When it came time for Uncle Clancy and Mistress Patti to leave, I watched them go. She matched her steps to his slow ones and stopped twice to let him rest between the shop door and the car. After she carefully lifted him inside, his eyes met mine through the window, and I realized this would be the last time I'd see my uncle Clancy.

"This is what a broken heart feels like," I said softly to myself.

Ms. Anne knelt on the floor next to me and wept, putting her face in my fur. "It's hard, Capone. It's so hard."

As she mourned Uncle Clancy, I realized I now understood Ms. Anne so much better. She had a broken heart, too. Hers had been broken fifteen years ago when she thought she saw Mr. Ben die, and it hadn't healed since.

I lifted my nose and licked her tears away. She laughed, even though she still cried.

"You're a sweet doggie, Capone. Do you understand how special you are to all of us?"

I do now, Ms. Anne. I do now.

TWENTY-TWO

Ways I will improve the lives of others:

1. Convince Ms. Anne that Mr. Ben is her Mr.
   Knightley.
2. Help Jackson and Gracie find a peaceful
   solution to their problems.
3. Earn Rocco's forgiveness for pooping on his
   head and nearly killing him in the fire.
4. Make Luke feel safe and help him understand
   he's part of the family now.
5. Gain Faraday's trust and show him how to be a
   true friend because he has no clue.
6. Find a way to put the soul of Boo the Ghost
   Dog to rest at last.

Uncle Clancy died the next day. I never got to ask him about the Rainbow Bridge, but his final words to me made an impact. All along, I'd been striving to fix myself. To be more of a gentleman. To be a better dog. But now, I wanted to do something entirely different. Instead of fixing myself, since, according to Uncle Clancy, I wasn't broken, I would devote my time and energy to helping others.

And I had my work cut out for me, but I felt determined. The question was, where should I start? I had no idea. Perhaps when Ms. Josie and Mr. Nate came back, things would be easier, but until then, I had another pressing issue.

Mistress Patti.

Poor Mistress Patti. She was devastated by the loss of her dog. We all were. Uncle Clancy had been a special guy.

On Wednesday morning, she and Elliot stopped by the shop to visit. They were both a mess. While Ms. Anne focused on Mistress Patti, I spent some quality time with Elliot.

"I keep looking for him," said Elliot, his eyes full of pain. "He's really gone, isn't he?"

I licked the yellow Lab on the head in a gesture of condolence. When Uncle Clancy had been alive, we'd been a complete set: one chocolate Lab (Uncle Clancy), one yellow Lab (Elliot), and one black Lab (me). Now we were incomplete. And Mistress Patti was a mess. She held Uncle Clancy's collar in her hands as she cried.

"He was such a good boy. I'm gutted, Anne. It hurts so much."

Ms. Anne patted her arm in her own gesture of comfort. I wanted to tell her licking was more effective, but it didn't seem like a thing humans did. They really ought to try it. It worked.

"He's not suffering anymore. That's what's important," said Ms. Anne.

He's not suffering anymore.

Her words made Boo come to mind. That dog still suffered even after death. Maybe I should reverse the order of my list and start with the number six. It seemed like an excellent plan. I decided to ask Elliot about it, because I wanted to take his mind off his loss for a few minutes, and I needed help.

"You think you're being haunted by a ghost dog?" he asked after I explained the whole story to him.

"Definitely."

He pondered it a moment. "I don't know about ghosts, but when Mistress Patti had a mole infestation, she had a heck of a time."

I stared at Elliot. I had to admit I felt confused. Elliot had never been the sharpest tool in the shed, and I struggled to see a connection between moles and ghosts.

"A mole infestation?"

"Exactly. But before you say anything, I get it. Some of the methods they use to get rid of moles are pretty inhumane, right? Mistress Patti would never do something like that. Do you know what she used instead?" When I stared at him blankly, he continued. "Tabasco sauce. She mixed up water, castor oil, peppermint, and tabasco sauce, soaked some cotton balls in it, and put the cotton balls into the mole holes. Problem solved. Kind of."

"What do you mean?"

"After the moles were gone, I dug up a few of those cotton balls and ate them. They were yummy, but it had been an unfortunate decision. Castor oil makes you poo, and tabasco makes your poo...well, let me say, my rear door felt like it was on fire for a few days. It turned me off tabasco sauce for good." He shuddered, and I frowned at him.

"So, what you're saying is...?"

"It's simple. You need ghost repellent. Maybe they have an issue with tabasco sauce, too."

ALTHOUGH ELLIOT'S advice seemed questionable, I gave it some thought the whole way home. I was so distracted by his mole story that I didn't notice something very important when I entered the kitchen.

Our entire floor had disappeared. And I stood directly on top of the subfloor.

Egads.

I gazed around in shock. It must have happened while we were out. The old, cracked linoleum was completely gone, and all that remained was a thin, rough particle board. It felt very disconcerting.

"What happened in here?" I asked, legs shaking. I did not like change, and this was a big one.

The other dogs seemed confused. Rocco was the only one who answered me. "Ben is fixing the floor, dummy. He took out the old stuff so he could lay new tile."

Oh, calamity. I didn't want new stuff. I wanted our old stuff back.

The kitchen had been gutted by Mr. Ben the same way my heart had been gutted by the loss of my uncle Clancy. I was distraught, which was why I did the unthinkable. When Ms. Anne went upstairs to change out of her work clothes, I peed on the subfloor.

That was a bad, bad thing. Something I hadn't done in a long time. Something that caused me great embarrassment since all the other dogs and Rocco the cat saw me do it.

Curse my weak bladder and sensitive nerves.

It upset me terribly. Since the main part of the floor happened to be missing, it went from a minor faux pas to a major disaster.

Note to self: The subfloor was not like a regular floor. It leaked—a lot.

What had I done?

Ms. Anne came back downstairs, humming a happy tune. She walked into the kitchen, so preoccupied that she didn't watch where she was going and stepped right into my puddle in her bare feet. She gasped, gazing down at the mess on the floor and then back at us.

"What happened in here?"

I wish I could say my friends stuck up for me, but they didn't. In fact, Faraday totally threw me under the bus.

"Capone peed!" he yelled. "He peed on the floor."

I tried to appear innocent. It didn't work. And when Mr. Ben and Luke showed up a few minutes later at the back door, things got worse.

"Whoa," he said. "What's that?

Ms. Anne dried off her foot with a paper towel. "Guess."

She held up the now-yellow paper towel. Mr. Ben winced. "Uh-oh. We'd better check the basement."

"You're kidding." Ms. Anne scrambled to find slippers. Since I kept stealing them, it took her a few minutes, and the pair she put on didn't match. She called out to Mr. Ben, and she stuck them on her feet. "There is no way it could be in the basement. It happened five minutes ago—"

"It's in the basement!" Mr. Ben yelled from downstairs. "It came through the floor, and it's in the basement."

Oh, no. Not in the basement.

I worried it might be dangerous down there, but when Ms. Anne went downstairs, wearing her silly, unmatched slippers, I followed. I couldn't let her face the ghosts and monsters alone.

But it turned out ghosts and monsters weren't the problem. *I* was the problem. Well, me and my tinkle.

Ms. Anne stared at the giant puddle in disbelief. Then they both turned and gaped at me. I wagged my tail, but it was a tentative wag. Things did not look promising for me at that moment.

"Capone is the only dog big enough to hold this much pee," said Ms. Anne. "But I don't understand. I took him out to pee right before we left the shop."

"There's one way to prove it," he said, turning to me and pointing to the puddle on the floor of the basement. "Did you do this, Capone?"

Busted. I turned away, hoping if I didn't make eye contact, I'd look more innocent.

I did not look more innocent.

Mr. Ben bit his lip as if to stop himself from laughing. "We have our culprit. But, in his defense, at least he didn't go on the hardwood."

"Silver linings. And it didn't drip on anything valuable," said Ms. Anne, staring up at the damp ceiling in disgust. I'd narrowly missed peeing on all of Ms. Josie's Christmas decorations. She'd stored them in the basement, and they were in cardboard boxes. Experience had taught me that moisture and cardboard did not mix.

Also, Christmas should smell like cinnamon and happiness, not dog pee, so I guessed Ms. Anne was right about the silver linings, but I felt sorry and ashamed. I'd made a rookie mistake. Only little puppies peed inside the house. I had no excuse.

Ms. Anne patted my head. "He's probably upset by all the changes. Josie is gone, he's confused, he's been in a fire, and now this. Poor doggie."

"It is a lot," said Mr. Ben, but he didn't look at her. He

studied the floor instead. Raising a hand, he knocked on it, resulting in a hollow, echoing sound.

I started barking. Yes, I realized Mr. Ben knocked on the floor right in front of me, but I'd been programmed to bark at all knocking sounds. Better safe than sorry.

Ms. Anne rolled her eyes and told me to hush. "You saw him knock. You know it's not the door." She turned to Mr. Ben. "What is it?"

He still stared at the floor. "This doesn't make sense. Why does it sound hollow? I need to take a peek at the original plans for the house again. Something is off here."

"You haven't found the plans yet?"

He shook his head. "And I'm missing a bunch of other stuff, too. It's weird. It's like every single day, something new goes missing. It makes it that much harder to get things done."

"What's going on?"

Mr. Ben shrugged his broad shoulders. "I have no idea."

"Maybe it's Boo the Ghost Dog," I said under my breath.

Jackson groaned. "Not that again. Ghosts aren't real, Capone. When are you going to believe me?"

The words had no sooner left his mouth when the room went completely dark. Ms. Anne screamed, and so did Gracie. Heck, I may have screamed, too. It scared me.

"It's okay," said Mr. Ben, fumbling in the dark. I heard a click, and suddenly, we had light again. Mr. Ben held a tiny flashlight, shaped like a pen, in his hand. His other arm was wrapped around Ms. Anne's waist. He must have reached for her when the lights went out. Her green eyes were huge in her face.

"What happened?" she asked.

Mr. Ben glanced upward. "I'm not sure."

"Pat said a storm might be brewing. Is this it?"

"No, the storm isn't supposed to hit until tomorrow. What else did Pat say?"

"Nothing. He brought me a shovel and some salt. He was worried I might not be prepared."

"How thoughtful, but don't trust him, Annie," he said, something strange in his tone. "He isn't what he seems."

She frowned. "Funny, he said the same thing about you."

The lights came back on as suddenly as they'd gone off. Both Ms. Anne and Mr. Ben blinked in surprise. She stepped out of his embrace. He put the flashlight back into his pocket.

"We should clean this up," he said, reaching for a roll of paper towels on a storage shelf against one of the walls. Thankfully, I hadn't peed on the paper towels either.

Ms. Anne tried to take the towels from him. "I'll do it."

He refused to give them to her. "Let me help. You don't have to do everything on your own."

She reached for the paper towels again and, this time, took them from his hands. "But I do. I've had to for the last fifteen years, and that's the only beneficial thing that came from what happened. I learned to be independent. It's a gift, and I have you to thank for it."

"But I'm back now—"

"It doesn't change anything."

He sighed, running a hand through his hair. "I've told you I'm sorry. What else can I do?"

"Tell me what happened. Tell me why you left and why you lied and why you let me believe you were dead."

Mr. Ben's mouth opened and then closed again. He shook his head, his eyes sad and yet resigned.

Ms. Anne blinked away tears. "That's what I thought.

Until you can trust me, really trust me, there is no point in discussing any of this. I'm not being mean. I'm being honest."

"I realize that, and I am sorry, Annie. I'm so sorry."

"But not sorry enough. And please, stop calling me Annie."

TWENTY-THREE

Like Mr. Ben, I was sorry for an assortment of misdeeds and unfortunate decisions:

1. Eating the rings.
2. Pooping in the car.
3. Setting her house on fire.
4. Peeing through the subfloor.
5. Turning the yard into a minefield with my poo.
6. Nibbling on her slippers and eating her socks.
7. Shedding all over the furniture and her clothes.
8. Drooling on everything (and in everything), including her tea.
9. Costing her a small fortune in dog food and treats.
10. Waking her up way too early.
11. Destroying part of the garden shed.

She hadn't seen it yet, but I wanted her to understand in advance that I did it in pursuit of rabbits.

I hate rabbits.

Note to self: I had a lot to apologize for, maybe more than Mr. Ben.

That was on my mind when I woke up the next morning and toddled downstairs after Ms. Anne. She made her coffee and turned on the television, just in time to hear the weather report from my favorite Pittsburgh newsman, Scott Harbaugh.

"We have a storm coming, and we're expecting at least ten inches. The snow will come down quickly, folks, and it'll start later tonight. Stay tuned to find out how it might impact your Friday evening commute."

It wouldn't impact our evening commute since we could technically walk home from the bookstore, but I worried about Ms. Josie and Mr. Nate. They were due home from their honeymoon in a few days. What if the airport closed? What if they couldn't land?

Also, Ms. Anne had heard back from the people fixing her house. The repairs had been delayed in anticipation of the storm, and they weren't sure when they'd be able to finish. Also, Fireman Fetch had to cancel their date. They were going to go out to dinner, but, due to the storm, he couldn't make it.

Things were going poorly for Ms. Anne. I had to wonder if the reason Fireman Fetch cancelled had anything to do with seeing Mr. Ben in Ms. Anne's house. He seemed to like Mr. Ben. Maybe bowing out gracefully was the gentlemanly thing to do. I asked Jackson about it.

"Or maybe it is what it is. He had to cancel because of the snowstorm. It's going to be a doozy. Sometimes people are telling the truth." He shot a pointed glance at Gracie. She ignored him.

Rocco, who sat on the couch above us, chimed in. "Or

maybe he knows Anne has been sniffing other butts. I'm putting this in dog terms, so you can understand."

"Sniffing other butts is definitely a no-no," said Gracie. "Especially if the butt belongs to a Poodle named Fifi."

Jackson groaned. "It's not all about you, Gracie."

"Yes, it is."

Gracie sniffed and walked away. We watched her go.

"She always deserves the best treatment because she never puts up with any other," I said. They stared at me, and I waited for one of them to say something mean.

"Austen?" asked Jackson. When I nodded, hesitant, he continued. "In this case, it actually fits. Good job, puppy."

"Thank you, Jackson."

"Back to the sniffing other butts' stuff," said Rocco. "I like the fireman. He saved my life. But Anne is confused right now. She needs to get her head on straight. I, for one, will be delighted when she figures things out. I'll also be delighted when she takes both of you back to her house." He eyed Faraday. "Gracie the princess and you—the backstabber."

"Backstabber?" asked Faraday, his expression confused. I could tell he faked the confusion, though. His tail remained down, and he shivered in fear.

"We know you're the one who told Gracie about me and the Poodle, pup," said Jackson.

"I didn't, I swear." He lifted one tiny paw. "Pugs united...?"

He did that irresistible head tilt thing, but somehow Jackson resisted. "Give it up, Faraday. We know the truth."

Jackson and Rocco followed Gracie into the other room. I remained with Faraday. "If it's any consolation—" I began, but the tiny Pug turned to me with a growl.

"Shut up. This is all your fault."

"How is it my fault?"

Faraday's Puggy eyes got Puggier, and he snarled at me, baring his teeth. "Because everyone has someone who loves them best. You have Josie. Jackson has Nate. I have to share Anne with Gracie, and that's awful enough, but now I have to share her with you, too, and it sucks. I hate it. And I hate you."

I'd never realized how Faraday felt. He was the youngest and newest member of our group, but we'd all tried to welcome him—kind of.

Oh, calamity. When I looked back on it, I realized I hadn't done much at all.

But it really wasn't my fault. Faraday was a pain in the booty.

"I have to share Ms. Josie with a cat."

I'd thought my statement would have more impact, but —alas—it did not.

"You're joking, right?" Faraday rolled his eyes. "Give me a freaking break."

I was about to argue further, but Ms. Anne's phone rang. She answered it on the second ring and put it on speaker.

"Josie?"

"Hi, Anne."

Rather than the sounds of crashing waves and tin drums, I now heard beeping machines and the whine of an ambulance. Ms. Anne must have heard it, too.

"Is everything okay?"

"We're fine," she said, but she didn't sound fine to me. I nudged Ms. Anne with my nose, and she gave me a pat as Ms. Josie continued. "Nate broke his ankle. He slipped on the steps near the pool. I'm so sorry, but can you watch our pets for a few more days?"

"Of course. Don't worry about that at all. I'm sorry for Nate."

"Me, too," said Ms. Josie with a sniff. "I'd better go. The doctor needs to talk with me. Thanks, Anne."

She hung up, and Ms. Anne stared at the phone a long moment before glancing back at the carriage house. This meant Ms. Anne would be spending more time in close proximity to Mr. Ben but was it a good thing or a potentially awful thing? I had no idea.

The rest of the day felt strange. With the skies gray and the snow expected to fall all night, I was filled with a sense of excitement. I wasn't the only one who experienced it. Miss Olivia sensed it, too. She stared out the window of the bookstore, a smile playing on her ruby red lips.

"It's coming. I feel it in my bones."

Miss Bella rolled her eyes. The shop was quiet since most people were at the supermarket buying milk and bread in anticipation of the coming storm. Ms. Anne joined Miss Olivia by the window.

"I feel it, too," she said. "Whenever a big storm is predicted, it's like I'm a kid again. I even feel like doing all the rituals to ensure tomorrow is a snow day."

"Rituals?" asked Ms. Bella, glancing up from the copy of *Sense and Sensibility* that she'd been reading.

"Oh, you know. Like wearing your underpants backward and flushing ice down the toilet."

The Vargas twins stared at her blankly. "Anne, we grew up in Miami," said Miss Bella. "We only came north for college. We never had a snow day when we were small."

"That's so sad. Growing up near a beach with no snow or ice. However did you manage?" asked Ms. Anne with a snort.

"It was rough," said Miss Olivia. "All that sunscreen."

"The weather works out well for Josie and Nate," said Miss Bella. "By the time they make it home, the worst of it will be over. When will they arrive?"

"They aren't sure yet, but probably next week."

"That's not too long," said Ms. Olivia. "Will you stay at their house the whole time?"

"I may not have a choice. My house isn't ready yet, and the storm is delaying stuff all over the country. It's like the universe is conspiring against me."

Miss Olivia let out a laugh. "Or conspiring for you."

"What do you mean by that?"

She shrugged. "To keep you close to Ben O'Reilly a bit longer."

"That's not it at all," Ms. Anne spluttered. "This has nothing to do with him. It has to do with fires and broken limbs and missing tools and snow delays and..." She paused, frowning, then gazing skyward. "This has nothing to do with Ben O'Reilly, does it?"

As if on cue, the sound of thunder shook the shop. Everyone in the shop, including me, jumped.

Curse my high-strung mental state. I may need medication.

"Thunder snow," said Miss Bella, making the sign of the cross.

"Oh, Anne," said Miss Olivia, her eyes twinkling. "You're in for it now."

BECAUSE OF THE IMPENDING STORM, the ladies decided to close the shop early and head home—a wise decision. The roads had already gotten dicey. Thankfully, we didn't have far to go. We grabbed dinner on the way home, two orders of vodka penne from Mario's, along with garlic knots, salad, and tiramisu for dessert. I wondered why Ms. Anne bought two orders of pasta but soon understood the reason.

The lights were on when we pulled up to the house. When we went inside, we found Mr. Ben working in the kitchen. He'd painted it a pretty, pale blue and had speckles of paint on his hands and face. He glanced at his watch when we came in.

"Sorry," he said. "I meant to be finished before you got home."

"No worries. We left early because of the storm." She glanced around the room. "This looks beautiful. I love the color."

"Me, too. The new fridge and oven are delayed due to the weather, but I have the cabinets, the backsplash, and the flooring, so I can start putting all that in tomorrow." He wiped a hand over his brow. "Let me grab the ladder, and I'll finish up in here. I'll be out of your hair shortly. I promise."

"I brought you dinner." She nearly blurted out the words. "I mean, you always liked Mario's, and..."

"Thanks, Annie," he said, a slow smile spreading across his handsome face.

She gave him a quick nod. "We still have the microwave, so we can heat up our dinner."

"Thank goodness. I know how much you hate cold pasta," he said, letting out a laugh.

"You remember that?"

His laughter died, and his expression grew serious. "I remember everything."

"So do I, Ben." She said it with a sigh and left the

kitchen to change her clothes. We watched her go, then turned to Mr. Ben expectantly.

"What?" he asked, glancing down at us. "You're judging me now, too?"

With a huff, he grabbed the ladder and set it in the middle of the room. The ceilings were high in this house—it was over a hundred years old after all—so Mr. Ben needed a rather tall ladder to reach the light fixture.

We continued to watch him as he climbed to the top of the ladder and removed the old light. "I don't like this," said Luke with a whine. "Something is off."

He'd no sooner uttered those words when the entire ladder collapsed, sending Mr. Ben to the floor with a crash. I jumped back in alarm. Mr. Ben remained on the floor, a bit dazed.

"What happened?" he asked. Since none of us could answer, I assumed he asked himself that question.

Luke and I sprang into action, licking Mr. Ben's face furiously. It seemed like the right thing to do. I'm handy in an emergency.

"Ugh. Stop it, guys. I'm okay." He brushed us away, but when Ms. Anne came running down the steps seconds later, he didn't brush her away. She knelt next to him, eyes frantic.

"Are you hurt? What happened?"

She ran her hands over him as if assessing him for injuries. He grabbed her hands and gave them a squeeze. "I'm okay. Don't worry, Annie. I'm fine."

She rocked back onto her heels, and to my great surprise, she burst into tears. "I can't handle this," she said, putting her face in her hands.

Mr. Ben sat up with a groan. He must have been hurting, but he focused his attention on Ms. Anne. "Can't handle what?" he asked, pulling her hands away from her eyes.

With a sob, she threw her arms around his neck. "Worrying about you and caring about you and hurting over you. It's too much. And not knowing what happened to you and why you left is eating me from the inside out. It's not fair."

He held her close, patting her back as she wept, her face tucked into the curve of his neck. He swallowed hard and glanced skyward as if he too struggled not to cry. "I'm so sorry," he said, kissing the side of her head. "And you're right. It's not fair."

She leaned back to stare at his face. "You agree with me?"

He pushed her hair away from her eyes. "It's time that I told you everything."

"Really?"

"Yes. But we need wine first." He glanced down at her legs. "And you need pants."

She perched on Mr. Ben's lap, wearing nothing but a T-shirt and panties. "Oh. You're right."

She got to her feet, a little unsteady, and reached out a hand to help him up, too. After he got to his feet, her gaze went to the ladder on the floor. "Did you slip?"

He put his hands on his hips, a frown on his handsome face. "Nope." He pointed to a broken section of the ladder. "Someone unscrewed the spreader. It's the hinged part of the ladder that normally locks into place when the rails are extended."

She frowned. "And someone did it on purpose?"

Mr. Ben pointed to the bent metal pieces on the floor. "There should be eight screws. Someone removed six of them, so, yes, it seems to be on purpose." He let out a sigh.

"Which means it's even more important that we have a talk."

She gave him a slow nod. "I'll get my pants. You get the wine." He grabbed his coat and reached for the ladder. Ms. Anne stopped him as he hauled it outside. "And Ben, maybe bring a few bottles. We're going to need it."

TWENTY-FOUR

A list of reasons why honesty is the best policy:

1. Remembering what you said when you lied is tricky.
2. Keeping up a lie is stressful.
3. Lying about one thing always leads to lying about another.
4. Telling the truth is simpler.
5. They always find out in the end.

While Mr. Ben changed, Ms. Anne set the small table in the kitchen and waited for Mr. Ben's return, watching anxiously from the back door. Maybe she thought he'd change his mind, but he came back exactly fifteen minutes later. He'd left the broken ladder outside, and he'd washed up as well. No longer speckled with paint, he smelled clean and yet quite manly, like a sexy mix of soap and testosterone. And he brought wine, too. Three bottles.

Note to self: Mr. Ben is a wise man.

"He's not messing around," said Jackson with a snort.

"Armed and dangerous," said Luke, laughing.

Jackson eyed Luke speculatively. "I like you, Luke."

"Ditto, Pug."

"I'm glad we're all friends now," said Gracie. "But what is going on here? Is this a date?"

I watched as Mr. Ben opened the wine and poured it into two crystal glasses. "It certainly seems like a date, but I'm confused. What about Firemen Fetch and Viking Val and Policeman Pat?"

"Easy," said Jackson. "The cop never had a chance. Our girl didn't like him that way."

"The fireman was cute, but he seemed way too young for her," said Gracie.

"And Viking Val?"

"She was only interested in him for his lasagna." Faraday spoke from across the room. He'd been keeping his distance from all of us since his argument with Jackson. He looked sad and small and lonely.

Oh, calamity. I kind of felt sorry for the little guy. When did that happen?

"You've made an excellent point," I said, attempting to include Faraday in the conversation. "He did make really tasty lasagna."

Rocco watched all of us with an annoyed expression on his face before turning to Jackson. "Can you forgive the Puglet and move on? I'm tired of all this tension between you idiotic canines. It's exhausting."

My gaze met Jackson's. I tried to mentally convey to him that Rocco was right. He should make his peace with Faraday. He let out a huff.

"Come here, Puglet. I forgive you for stabbing me in the

back and destroying my chances with the doggie of my dreams."

"The doggie of your dreams?" I asked.

Gracie seemed as shocked by his words as I did. Her eyes widened in surprise, but her expression morphed from stunned to suspicious.

"If I'm the doggie of your dreams, why were you with Fifi?"

We swung our heads to stare at Jackson. It felt like watching a tennis match. Back and forth. Back and forth.

"I made a mistake," he said, his voice rough.

"A mistake? You hurt me."

"And I'm so sorry. Can you find a way to forgive me, Gracie? I swear I'll never do anything that stupid again."

We waited for her reply as the microwaved dinged. Dinner was ready. And as Ms. Anne carried the plates laden with food to the table, the lights flickered once. Then twice. Then everything went dark. I let out a frightened bark.

Curse my various phobias and insecurities. But at least I wasn't alone.

"Holy moly," said Luke, coming closer to me. "What's going on?"

"I'm not sure."

"Is it the ghost dog again?"

"Maybe," I said. "And Mr. Ben's ladder...maybe the ghosts did that, too."

Faraday shivered. "The storm knocked the power out. This is natural, not spectral."

Luke panted lightly next to me. "What are we going to do?"

"Wait for the humans," said Faraday. "They'll figure it out."

And they did. Mr. Ben pulled out his handy dandy flashlight. They found candles, lit a roaring fire, and sat on the floor next to a small coffee table to eat. Somehow, despite the circumstances, the evening had taken an unexpectedly romantic turn.

We curled up in front of the fire, both for warmth and in the hopes that someone might drop something for us to eat.

"This is delicious," said Mr. Ben. "Thank you."

"Thanks for the wine," said Ms. Anne. They clinked glasses.

"I'm really happy I'm here. I don't have a fireplace in the carriage house. I'd have to rely on Luke to keep me warm."

Luke let out a groan, and they both laughed. "He's not in favor of that idea," said Ms. Anne. She dabbed her lips with a napkin, her voice a bit unsteady. "Why don't you stay here tonight? You could sleep on the couch. It might be better. I mean, for Luke's sake. It doesn't sound like he wants to be your space heater."

"You're probably right." Mr. Ben narrowed his eyes at Luke. "Ungrateful mutt."

"Hey—" Luke began, and the humans laughed again. It sounded like a whine to their ears.

"Luke has a lot to say this evening," said Ms. Anne.

Mr. Ben laughed. "He does."

"How about you?" She eyed him over the rim of her glass. "Do you have a lot to say?"

He put down his glass with a sigh. "I do. But you'll have to be patient with me. It'll be hard to get this all out."

"Oh, I've been patient with you, Ben. Tell me what happened. Please."

I heard the pleading note in her voice. He must have heard it, too. He rubbed his hands over his jeans.

"The problem is where to start." He let out a long breath. "You remember how I worked for my stepfather, Sam Goodman? He and his brothers Chuck and Carl owned a construction company."

"I do remember. Your mom married him our freshman year of high school."

"Yeah. He was the only father I'd ever known, and he treated my mother decently. For a while, at least. She seemed to be drinking less, or maybe she got better at hiding it." He shot Ms. Anne a crooked smile. "Hiding the truth seems to be a genetic trait."

"I guess so."

He sighed. "Things were going well. I learned a lot from him. Sam did some shady stuff, but he kept me out of it. He protected me. He cared about me...or so I thought."

"What happened to change that?"

"At the end of our senior year, I went to one of Sam's warehouses. It was late. I'd forgotten my backpack there after school, and we had our AP American History test the next morning. I wanted to study."

Her brow wrinkled in confusion. "You missed that test. You didn't show up for it."

"I didn't," he said, swirling the wine in his glass. "Because the night before, at that warehouse, I saw something I shouldn't."

"What?" she asked, her voice soft. "Did you catch Sam stealing?"

"No, I caught him murdering someone."

She dropped her fork. It clattered to the table unnoticed. "Are you kidding?"

"Sadly, I'm not. I walked in on him as he shot someone

—a guy who cheated him on a big construction project." Mr. Ben's eyes flashed in the light of the fire. "No one messed with Sam Goodman."

"What did you do?"

"At first, I just stood there, in shock. Sam looked up and saw me, and something ugly passed over his face. For a few minutes, I thought he might shoot me, too. But then his logical brain took over. He recognized he had a sure way to keep me in line." Mr. Ben's eyes met Ms. Anne's, and he gave her a sad smile. "You. He knew I'd do anything to keep you safe, and he promised as long as I remained quiet, you'd be okay. He swore he wouldn't hurt you, and I believed him. But then things started happening, and they made me nervous."

"What kinds of things?" she asked.

"Like your tires being slashed in the school parking lot the night of prom."

"I thought that was the work of some random vandal."

"So did I, but then I found photos of you in my locker. Photos of you sleeping." Mr. Ben's voice sounded hollow and sad. "He sent me a clear message. He wanted me to understand how easily he could reach you. That he could kill you, and I wouldn't be able to stop him. And that's when I decided I had to find a way to take care of Sam."

"Take care of him?" She put a hand to her chest. "You thought about killing him?"

"No. But I had to do something."

"So you faked your own death?" she asked.

"The opportunity presented itself, and I thought I had no other option."

She closed her eyes. "You could have come to me. We could have gone to the police together."

He shook his head. "Not worth the risk. Better for Sam to think I'd died and go to the police in secret."

She blinked in surprise. "You were in protective custody?"

"Yes, and then the witness protection program. Sam's crimes weren't just local. The feds were after him, too."

Ms. Anne nibbled on her lower lip as she took in this information. "But Sam went to jail. Why didn't you come back?"

Mr. Ben stretched out his long legs as he leaned back against the couch. "Even though Sam was in prison, he still had a lot of people on the outside. If they had any idea I'd been the one to put him away, if they realized I was still alive, they would have gone after you. I had no choice. Annie, I wish things could have been different, but those were the cards I'd been dealt, and your safety meant more to me than anything else."

"Why are you back now?" she asked, unable to meet his eyes.

"Sam Goodman is dead. He died in jail last year. When that happened, I took a chance, and got permission to come back here. I figured it was probably too late, and I realized you'd hate me, but I had to come and see you. That's why I took this job. I didn't expect to be staying in your backyard." He let out a wry laugh. "But I'd hoped to maybe catch one last glimpse of you before I packed up and headed back to England. It seemed like my only chance to say goodbye. I never had the opportunity before."

She sat there, stunned. "This is goodbye?"

"It has to be, I'm afraid."

"But why?"

He tilted his head to indicate the kitchen. "The ladder isn't the first weird thing that has happened. Missing blueprints. Missing tools. Someone is sending me a message. Again. It's exactly the same."

For a moment, she sat there, stunned. Then she blinked. "No."

"No, what?"

"It's not the same." She put her elbows on the coffee table. "You aren't a scared kid anymore, and you aren't alone. I'll help you this time. We'll go to the police together. I have contacts. Lawyers. I can be of use. I truly can."

He leaned forward and tucked a lock of her long, red hair behind her ear. She had on yoga pants and a sweater, not a bit of makeup on her face, but Ben stared at her like she was the most beautiful thing he'd ever seen.

"I can't let you do that, Annie. I won't let you do it. I sacrificed everything to keep you safe. I'm not going to mess it up now. I'll leave, head to England, and this will seem like it was nothing but a bad dream."

Her eyes filled with unshed tears. "Being without you was the bad dream, Ben."

He shook his head. "You don't have any idea what you're saying. I'm not worth—"

She put her fingers on his lips to silence him. "Stop. You are worth it." Tears rolled down her cheeks now, unchecked, and her expression was open and vulnerable. "Do you understand why I got divorced three times?"

He shook his head. "No," he said, his voice husky and low. "I don't."

"Because they weren't you. I was always searching for you, Ben. Always. Even when I thought there was no hope. Even when I thought you were dead."

For a moment, he stared at her in stunned silence. Then he got up onto his knees, leaned over the coffee table, cupped her face in his hands, and kissed her. She rose onto her knees and kissed him back.

Gracie sniffed. "It's like the ending scene in the movie *Sixteen Candles* when Jake kisses Sam, and they're both sitting on his dining room table."

Jackson shook his head. "It's like that old movie with Doris Day. The man believes his wife died, but she's been stuck on a deserted island. She comes back as he's about to get remarried to someone else. It's hilarious. A classic."

Although it sounded like a great film, Jackson was completely wrong. "No," I said. "It's *Emma*. He's her Mr. Knightley."

As if to prove my point, Ben spoke, his voice husky. "I'm no good at speeches, Annie. You know that. But there's a reason why this is so hard for me." They were both still leaning over the coffee table. "If I loved you less, it would be easier. I'd be able to talk about it more. And it wouldn't hurt as much every time I had to leave you."

I nearly fell over. "That's the line," I spluttered. "From *Emma*. At the end of the movie, Mr. Knightley says, 'If I loved you less, I might be able to talk about it more.' Oh, my gosh. Ms. Anne is going to get her happily ever after."

"She's going to get something," said Jackson, as Mr. Ben pushed the coffee table out of the way. He pulled her close, still on his knees, his body flush with hers, and kissed the heck out of her.

"Oh, my heart," said Gracie. "This is so romantic."

It was super romantic, and lucky for me. In his haste to embrace Ms. Anne, Mr. Ben left their plates unattended. I helped by cleaning off all the dishes for them. Yummy. Puppy prewash.

When I glanced up again, Mr. Ben and Ms. Anne no

longer rested on their knees. They now lay on the rug in front of the fireplace, and they were...oh, my.

"Okay, kids," said Jackson. "Let's give them some privacy."

Gracie, always the excellent herding dog, rounded all of us up and led us upstairs. With the heat off, and no electricity, it was kind of cold up there, but I had my friends to snuggle with for warmth. Jackson, Gracie, Faraday, Luke, and Rocco, although Rocco didn't seem too pleased with the situation.

"I hope they finish quickly," he said, curling up next to me. He sounded crabby, but I heard him purr as he fell asleep. He felt happy for Ms. Anne and Mr. Ben, too.

The moon was full, and I watched from the bed as the snow fell outside in big, fat flakes, swirling and dancing in the wind. No matter what anyone said, I'd done it again. I'd found the perfect man for Ms. Anne, and she would now get her happily ever after at last.

I turned in surprise to see Faraday watching the snow with me. "That seemed too easy," he said.

"What do you mean?" I asked, keeping my voice low so I wouldn't wake the others.

Faraday tilted his head to indicate the couple downstairs. "They're happy. In my experience, as soon as you're happy, as soon as you let your guard down, that's when something really awful happens."

I heard the pain in his voice and wanted to comfort him. Faraday could be a real jerk sometimes, but I recognized genuine emotion and genuine fear when I saw it.

"No, Faraday. I've watched every Jane Austen movie possible, including all the remakes. I know what I'm talking about, pup. This is the happy ending."

Faraday shook his head. "Life isn't like the movies, and

it's certainly not a Jane Austen novel. Happy endings are not guaranteed. For anyone. Ever."

He yawned and closed his eyes. And as the storm outside picked up in intensity, leaving mountains of snow on the ground, I shivered, but not from the cold.

Although I didn't want to admit it, Faraday might be right. Something terrible was going to happen. I sensed it in my bones.

TWENTY-FIVE

How to tell if someone is truly in love:

1. They're uncomfortable.
2. They experience an odd tightness in their chest.
3. Their heart flutters.
4. Their breathing is strange.
5. They're sweating for no reason.
6. They feel like they might throw up.

Wait. I listed the symptoms of a heart attack. My bad.

Note to self: Love was oddly similar to angina, which meant there was a fine line between something romantic and something deadly.

As I wracked my brain, I realized that maybe Emma Woodhouse herself said it best. "They must be in love; they should be the oddest creatures in the world if they were not."

Ms. Anne and Mr. Ben were odd but definitely enamored with each other—I only hoped they'd remain on the romantic side of love and not the deadly one. It certainly seemed that way.

Sometime in the middle of the night, Ms. Anne and Mr. Ben came upstairs. Mr. Ben lit a fire in her room since the electricity still hadn't come back on, and then they kicked all of us out of the bed. Not cool, but I understood. There wasn't enough space in their bed for four dogs, a cat, and two humans, especially when the humans were engaged in... let me just say they weren't playing pinochle.

So, we gathered in front of the blazing fire instead. Due to the age of the house, it had fireplaces in nearly every room.

"What are they doing?" asked Faraday, too small to see anything and obviously concerned. "Is he hurting her?"

He barred his teeth in a super cute way like he wanted to protect Ms. Anne. We all laughed. For once, I was in on the joke.

"No, puppy," said Gracie, turning around in a circle before curling up on the carpet in front of the fire. "They were apart for many sad, lonely years. They're making up for lost time."

"They're making something. That's for sure," said Jackson, lying down next to her with a plop. "And it ain't bacon."

At the thought of bacon, my stomach growled, and my friends all laughed, even Rocco. It was kind of funny. But as we snuggled closer, I felt safe and cozy and happy. Maybe the odd sense of impending doom I'd experienced earlier had been nothing but indigestion. It had certainly happened before.

My mind kept churning, though, as the others fell into a deep sleep. Extracting myself as quietly as possible from the pile of dogs on the rug, I tiptoed to the window. The snow was high, and the town so dark it took on a surreal quality. Adding to that, the bright, full moon bathed everything in its glorious light, making the snow sparkle like diamonds from reflecting off the white.

As I stared, I thought I saw something move in the shadows, but between the heavy snow and all the shrubbery in the backyard, I couldn't quite make it out. And as I squinted at it, the dark shape seemed to disappear. Strange, and maybe a trick of the light, but I didn't think so.

I decided to remain vigilant. Although the chilly air made me shiver, I hunkered down next to the window. I wanted to keep my family safe. Someone had taken apart that ladder on purpose, and Mr. Ben could have been hurt. What would they try next?

Hearing the soft mummer of conversation from the bed, I turned toward them. Ms. Anne and Mr. Ben no longer, uh, played pinochle. They were wrapped in each other's arms, her back to his front, happy and content as they watched the snowfall.

"Capone is standing guard," he said. "Good boy."

I wagged my tail. I was a good boy. A very good boy.

Ms. Anne agreed. "We need all the help we can get. I don't understand what could have happened to that ladder. Could someone be playing a prank?"

He shrugged. "No idea. I'd planned to take a look around and see if anything else had been tampered with, but I got distracted."

She turned her face and fluttered her eyelashes at him. "Distracted, huh?"

"This has been an interesting night," he said.

She let out a laugh. "You always were the master of understatement, Bennet O'Reilly."

"Hyperbole is for losers," he said with a grin, kissing her hair. "I missed you, Annie."

"I missed you, too." She bit her lip, and I heard the emotion in her voice when she spoke. "It's like half of me left with you when you went away. Do you understand what I mean?"

She reached up to place her hand on his cheek. He turned his face so he could kiss her palm. "Oh, I understand it only too well. My life felt so empty without you, Annie—until you came barreling out of the bathroom wearing nothing but a towel, and everything changed. It was like I really had drowned that day in the river, but then I saw your face, and suddenly I could breathe again."

"You saw more than my face," she said with a snort.

"That I did." He bit his lip, giving her a sexy half-smile as he pulled her close. "In all the times I imagined what I'd say or do if we ever saw each other again, having you fall into a dead faint at the sight of me had never even been on the table."

She laughed, turning to face him. "I like to keep it fresh," she said. But then her tone changed, and she sounded suddenly serious. "I missed you, Ben. I don't know what I'd do if you left again."

He stared into her eyes, shadows from the fire playing on his face. "If it's up to me, you'll never have to find out. I love you, Annie. I always have, and I always will."

A log fell in the fireplace, making me jump, but Ms. Anne and Mr. Ben didn't seem to notice. They'd had a busy night and were soon fast asleep. It seemed like hours later, I dozed off at last.

EARLY THE NEXT MORNING, the sound of pounding woke me as soft morning sunlight streamed in through the window. The fire burned low in the grate, and the room had grown cold overnight. Jumping to my feet and still disoriented, I ran toward the door of the bedroom, barking my head off. I tripped over Jackson in the process, but I couldn't help it. What could be more exciting than an early morning visitor?

Mr. Ben groaned. "Who could that be?" he asked, glancing at his watch. "It's barely eight in the morning."

"No idea," said Ms. Anne, grabbing her robe and putting on her slippers. Mr. Ben reached for her hand.

"Hi, Annie," he said, all rumpled and sexy and delicious.

Ms. Anne blushed. "Hi, Ben." She leaned down and gave him a kiss. It was quite romantic, except I still barked in my biggest voice, and I'd gotten the other dogs in on the action. She let out a groan. "I'd better go and see who that is. Give me a second."

She slipped out the door and went to the stairs, a happy smile on her lips, despite the rude awakening. I'd never seen her look so happy, to tell the truth. There had always been a sort of sadness lingering in her eyes, but not today. Today, she practically radiated joy. Although happy for her, I was also in a hurry, so I pushed past her on the steps, nearly knocking her over.

Curse my lack of restraint. I could have done her bodily harm. Again.

The other dogs followed suit, which meant I'd basically started a Labalanche. Ms. Anne swore, grabbing onto the railing for dear life. "What is wrong with you guys?"

We ran to the door, barking and hopping up and down. Someone stood on the porch. I couldn't see who, but what an exciting way to start the morning. It got even more exciting once Ms. Anne regained her footing (we'd knocked her off balance with the Labalanche) and opened the door. We ran outside and greeted Policeman Pat with loud barks and wiggles. He tried to quiet us down since it was a lot of noise for the time of day, but we couldn't help it. The other dogs barked because I'd barked, and then I barked because they barked—a vicious cycle.

I flew off the porch and into the snow. It was so deep it came up to my undercarriage.

Oh, calamity. This would make peeing interesting.

I glanced over my shoulder at the other dogs. Luke joined me, jumping up and down and frolicking in the snow, but the others disappeared in a sea of white. I started to panic until Gracie popped out of the snow and headed back up the steps.

"Ew. Ew. Ew," she said, shaking the snow from her fur. "I am not doing that again."

Jackson followed her. He had a pile of snow on his head. "That was interesting," he said as the snow slid down his face and onto the step. He backed away from it and turned around with a frown. "Oh, no. Where is the Puglet?"

Luke and I sprang into action. It took only a few minutes since I had an excellent sniffer, and we located Faraday in a deep pile of snow. He shivered and seemed terrified.

"Come on, buddy," I said. "I'll get you out of here."

Together, Luke and I plowed through the snow, making a path for Faraday. He let out a sigh of relief when he made it back to the porch.

"You saved my life," he said, staring at us with something akin to awe.

I puffed out my chest. "All in a day's work."

Luke rolled his eyes. "Little dogs. Let's go play some more, Capone."

"I'll be with you in a second." I wanted to hear what Policeman Pat had to say to Ms. Anne. I ran up onto the porch and slid right into the smaller dogs like I was bowling for puppies. Rocco remained inside.

"You're all a bunch of idiots," he said, with a dismissive swish of his tail.

Ms. Anne picked up Rocco and frowned at Policeman Pat. "Sorry, Pat. The dogs were going crazy. How can I help you?"

"Uh, I actually came to help you," he said, holding up a shovel. A bag of salt sat on the porch next to him. "I figured you'd be snowed in, and since you're on your own—"

"She's not on her own." Mr. Ben stood behind Ms. Anne, wearing nothing but a towel. He probably had few options since his clothing was on the floor in front of the fireplace, but Policeman Pat blinked at him in surprise.

"Ben O'Reilly. Back from the dead."

"Hello, Pat. Long time no see."

Policeman Pat laughed, but I heard no humor in it. "You could say that. You appear..." He took in Mr. Ben's half-naked form and the protective arm Mr. Ben had around Ms. Anne's shoulders. "To be very much alive."

"I am." He kissed the top of Ms. Anne's head. "I'll get dressed, Annie. Pat's right. We should take care of the snow."

Mr. Ben went back into the house. Policeman Pat's pale eyes shot to Ms. Anne's face. "And I take it you're okay with this?" Ms. Anne's face turned red, but she didn't respond. He shook his head with a laugh. "You always could forgive him for anything."

"And I always will." She gave him a sad smile. "I'm

sorry you're upset, Pat. I realize he hurt you, too. Maybe you should talk with Ben about it."

"I'm not upset. I'm surprised. And I don't need to talk with Ben. It's water under the bridge."

"Is it?"

"Yeah. I missed him, too. But I didn't expect to see him here this morning."

"Understandable. You're a wonderful friend, Pat."

Policeman Pat gave her a crooked smile. "I try to be." He lifted his shovel. "I'll get started. It's supposed to snow again this afternoon. Do you have enough food and other supplies?"

"I do. Thanks."

Mr. Ben joined them, buttoning up his coat. "I'll grab a shovel from the shed and join you, but it seems like this is turning into quite the party."

I glanced up in surprise to see Viking Val approach. He pushed a snowblower. And Fireman Fetch came up the path right behind him. He had a shovel, too, but they all seemed confused. Well, all of them except Mr. Ben.

"You always were a popular girl, Annie," he said. He cupped her face in his hands and gave her a brief, sweet kiss. "Let the games begin."

I couldn't be certain what he meant by "games," but the snow shoveling did look fun. At one point, the men engaged in a friendly snowball fight. It was a blast. Luke and I joined in, catching snowballs with our mouths. The other dogs watched from the safety of the porch. Mr. Ben had kindly made a path into the grass for them so that they could pee without getting trapped in the snow, but it made Faraday so nervous he tinkled on the porch.

Jackson glanced skyward as if praying for patience.

"Puglet. You cannot pee everywhere, all willy-nilly. There are rules."

Faraday seemed totally embarrassed. "I can't help it. I've never seen snow before. Not snow like this. It's up to Capone's butthole."

I looked down. He'd called it. The snow did, indeed, come up to my butthole. "Go easy on him, Jackson. He's still so young."

Jackson let out a harrumphing sound. "That's no excuse. He should know better."

Faraday did know better, but since his pee was roughly the quantity of a tablespoon, I really didn't see the issue. When Jackson wasn't listening, I nudged Faraday. "It's okay," I said softly. "It happens to all of us. You saw what I did in the kitchen, right? It leaked down into the basement."

The small Pug sniffed. "You peed a lake."

I smiled at him. "Exactly. But yours isn't a lake. It's not even a pond. Don't be so hard on yourself, okay?"

"Thanks, Capone. You're an excellent friend." He gazed at me, his Puggy eyes not as evil as usual. "I've never had an excellent friend before."

I licked the top of his head. "You have one now."

The power came on as the guys finished shoveling, so Ms. Anne made everyone hot cocoa. They came inside to warm up by the fire. Viking Val studied Ms. Anne and Mr. Ben carefully. When Mr. Ben sat next to her, his arm around her shoulders, Viking Val cleared his throat.

"Excuse me, but you're the one overseeing the restoration, right?"

Mr. Ben nodded. "Guilty as charged."

Viking Val glanced at Ms. Anne. "How do the two of you know each other?"

"We dated in high school," said Ms. Anne.

"Until Ben died." Policeman Pat put down his mug and folded his arms over his chest. "He drowned in the Ohio River the night of graduation. I was there."

"My brother was there, too," said Fireman Fetch.

Viking Val frowned. "I'm confused."

"So am I," said Policeman Pat. "You owe us an explanation, Ben. And Anne deserves it more than anyone."

Ms. Anne shook her head. She had on a turtleneck sweater and jeans, with her hair pulled up into a loose bun. "He doesn't owe us anything, Pat. He's here now, and nothing else matters. Not to me, at least."

"It matters to me."

"Come on, Pat. I was a kid," said Mr. Ben, a muscle working in his jaw. "In a hopeless situation and way out of my depth, I ran away. My mom seemed to be drinking herself into an early grave, and I felt like I was on my own. I never intended for things to happen the way they did. I nearly drowned in the river that day, and when I found out everyone thought I'd died, it seemed like a good thing. Like all of you would be better off without me."

Ms. Anne reached for his hand, tears in her eyes. "Never. None of us were better off without you. Especially me. But if I can forgive you, so can everyone else."

He lifted her hand to his lips. "Thank you, Annie."

Things grew awkward, and Viking Val lifted his hands. "Sorry. I didn't mean to make anyone uncomfortable. I am curious about your plans for the house, Ben."

Since Viking Val seemed sincerely interested, Ben offered to show him around. Policeman Pat rose to his feet. "I've got to go," he said. He paused for a minute, staring at Ben. "Although I don't understand why you did what you did, I'm glad you're back. I'm glad you're alive." He seemed to get choked up on those last words. "For Anne's sake especially. Whether you realize it or not, your 'death' defined our lives. It's why I became a cop. It's why Fletch's brother became a journalist. It's why Anne..." He paused, shifting uncomfortably on his feet. Ms. Anne filled in the words for him.

"It's why I got divorced three times. You can say it, Pat. It's no secret." Ms. Anne gazed at Mr. Ben, her heart in her eyes. "But he's back now. That's all that matters."

Policeman Pat said goodbye and left, his shoulders hunched against the cold. He was hurting. I sensed it. And he felt angry. I sensed that, too.

Viking Val shifted uncomfortably. "It seems I've walked into a personal conversation."

Fireman Fetch raised his hand. "Me, too. However, I cannot wait to tell my brother everything that happened. He's already planning to come see you. He wants to interview you." Mr. Ben and Ms. Anne exchanged a look, and Fireman Fetch shrugged. "Or maybe not. Either way, he'll be glad to see you. We all are."

Mr. Ben shook his hand and took Viking Val on his tour. Ms. Anne walked Fireman Fetch to the door. "So, I guess we won't be going out to dinner again?" he asked with a wink and a smile.

Ms. Anne blushed. "It's nothing personal. You're a great guy. It's just—"

"It's just your long-lost love came back from the dead?" he asked. "Don't worry. It happens."

"It does?" She let out a laugh.

He laughed, too. "Nope. It never happens. That's why it does not hurt my feelings one bit." He glanced up at Policeman Pat's retreating car. "He's hurting, though. But I guess you caught onto that."

"I did."

"It's not all about you or about Ben. He's had a rough time of it. His wife left him the same week his mother got diagnosed with cancer, and his uncle died in jail. That's why he moved back here. He lost everything in the divorce, and his mom needed him. His wife even took his dog."

"Yikes."

"Also, according to my brother, Pat had a crush on you back in the day. Maybe he hoped the two of you might get together."

Ms. Anne shook her head. "I always thought of Pat as the brother I never had."

He let out a laugh. "He certainly doesn't see you as a sister, but his anger at Ben isn't only about Ben—if you understand my meaning. Could you tell Ben about Pat's mom? Pat could really use a friend right now."

"I will. Thanks, Fletch."

He walked down the steps, then turned and spoke once more, his words sending a chill over my furry body. "And Anne, be careful. You've been away for a while, so you may have forgotten something important."

"What?"

"We're interconnected here. We know each other's secrets. And nothing is ever quite what it seems."

TWENTY-SIX

My favorite things to eat in the town of Beaver in no
particular order:

1. The marvelously meaty sandwiches from Don's
   Deli.
2. Delicious and drippy doggie cones from Witch
   Flavor Ice Cream.
3. The perfect pepperoni pizza from Mario's.
4. Tantalizing tapas from Biba's.
5. Savory buns of joy and happiness from Café
   Kolache.

On Monday, three days after the big storm, it was time
to get back to work. After a weekend of cleaning up snow,
watching Mr. Ben and Ms. Anne canoodle, and guarding
the house, I was exhausted. Ms. Josie and Mr. Nate planned
to fly home in less than a week. Ms. Anne had circled it in
red on the calendar on the wall. I think she may have been
looking forward to it.

She looked forward to something else as well. The

repairmen had nearly completed the work on her house. It came as a relief but still seemed bittersweet. As far as I knew, she and Mr. Ben hadn't talked about the next steps. Would he move in with her? Would he stay? Was he still planning to go to England? I understood Ms. Anne well enough to realize she had a lot of questions swirling in her head. She didn't ask any of them, though. Maybe she didn't want to know the answers. But she did want breakfast, so she picked up Café Kolache Monday morning for Mr. Ben.

Kolaches are yummy, and she bought a ton. She came home with a big white box filled with them. Sausage and cheese. Bacon. Something with jalapeños. Big ones filled with scrambled eggs and other things.

Wasn't that thoughtful of her? But do you know what Ms. Anne got for me?

Nothing. Nada. Zilch.

And I was not at all happy about it. The only positive news was that a few crumbles of bacon fell out of the box like manna from heaven.

It seemed a bit more aggressive than manna. As Ms. Anne folded the box to put it in the garbage, those bacon bits flew right into my face. But I didn't complain. Not about the bacon bits. I did complain, however, about the lack of kolache in my life.

Sigh. I needed to learn how to make kolache.

A man was scheduled to arrive soon to measure for the countertops. He'd use a laser. I thought that would be great fun, but it turned out the laser guy was afraid of dogs. Such a disappointment. So, Ms. Anne decided to take all of us to the bookstore instead. Only Rocco got to stay home—mostly because he hissed and hid when Ms. Anne suggested he come.

Cats. They were very different from dogs. They were different from any other animal on earth.

As Mr. Ben and Ms. Anne said goodbye on the porch, Viking Val strolled over with Molly. I hadn't seen her in days. The old girl looked great. She had on a pretty, red sweater and smiled when she saw me.

"Hi, Capone. Have you been staying out of trouble?"

Oh, calamity. I had to consider her question.

"Define 'trouble,'" I said.

She laughed. She thought I was joking. I laughed, too, even though I hadn't been joking.

When Ms. Anne noticed Molly's sweater, she paused. "Uh-oh. I'd better grab a sweater for Faraday. He's not built for cold weather."

As she went back inside to grab it, Viking Val chatted with Mr. Ben. "How are things going?" he asked. "Will you finish the kitchen today?"

I listened attentively. I wanted to hear more because the kitchen seemed very important. Snacks came from the kitchen.

"I'll get the cabinets in this morning. The countertops will be here on Friday."

"You're getting close," said Viking Val with a smile. "Are you still planning to drywall the basement this week?"

Mr. Ben rubbed the back of his neck. "That's the plan, but this snowstorm is throwing everything off."

"So you might not get to the drywalling until later?"

"Possibly," said Mr. Ben, perplexed. "Why do you ask?"

Viking Val cleared his throat. "No reason. I'm planning on drywalling my basement. I thought, if you don't mind, maybe I could watch."

"Sure. Why don't you come over later? I can show you what we plan to do." He lifted a finger. "Speaking of plans, the original plans to the house went missing. You're on the board for the historical society, right?"

"I am."

"Any idea where I might be able to find copies of the original plans? I checked the library and the courthouse."

Viking Val considered it. "I'll ask the people in the historical society. They might have a copy."

"Thanks."

"How did the plans go missing?" He shot me a curious glance. "Was it Capone?"

Mr. Ben laughed. "That's possible."

I stared at them, aghast. They thought I may have stolen a bunch of smelly old blueprints? It hardly seemed fair. I realized Mr. Ben had experienced quite a few issues recently, but as Mr. Weston said in *Emma*, "If things are going untowardly one month, they are sure to mend the next."

Of course, I couldn't tell Mr. Ben that nugget of wisdom. It just seemed very odd Viking Val would point a finger at me.

Ms. Anne came back out and kissed Mr. Ben goodbye. She had five dog leashes with her, and Viking Val eyed her curiously. "Are you planning to walk all five of them at once?"

"The bookstore is only a few blocks away," she said. "How difficult could it be?"

Viking Val and Mr. Ben laughed. "With Capone, it could be challenging," said Viking Val.

I frowned at him. "What's with all the Capone bashing this morning?"

"You do cause most of the problems, Capone," said Gracie. "Let's be honest."

"That's not true," said Faraday, standing up for me. "He's been perfectly good lately."

"Define 'good,'" said Gracie and Jackson in unison. As they laughed, Luke came to stand next to me, too.

"Stop picking on Capone," said Luke, with a growl. "It's not polite."

Jackson and Gracie both stared at him in surprise. "We were joking," said Jackson. "Ease up, Luke."

"It's not funny if it hurts his feelings," said Luke. "Capone might be naughty sometimes, but weren't we all naughty as puppies? I mean, except for you, Faraday, but you're weird. No offense."

"None taken," said Faraday. "I am weird."

"But Capone is different now. He's growing up. The two of you need to stop treating him like he's a loser because he isn't. He's a good dog."

I experienced a wave of love for Luke. He was so considerate to defend me like that. "Yeah," I said, glaring at Jackson and Gracie.

"Is that it?" asked Jackson. "Luke gives that great speech, and all you have is 'yeah,' Capone?"

"Luke said it all," said Faraday. "Capone doesn't have to say anything else."

"Yeah," I said again.

Curse my inability to come up with a decent comeback. It embarrassed me.

Gracie rolled her eyes. "Fine. We're sorry for laughing at you, Capone. But you do bring it on yourself."

Jackson turned away, but I realized he agreed with her, which hurt. He was my best friend. My mentor. My brother-from-another-mother. But I didn't say anything. Once again, I had no comeback. I was, however, grateful for Luke and Faraday. At least they had my back.

Note to self: First impressions aren't always accurate. Especially where evil, genius, tiny dogs and grumpy, former strays are concerned.

Viking Val offered to help Ms. Anne walk all of us to Bartleby's Books, and she accepted. Molly came, too, but she didn't need a leash. Molly was an angel.

Viking Val asked Ms. Anne many questions about the house as we walked. He seemed disappointed that Ms. Anne didn't know much about the construction schedule.

"So have you heard or seen anything unusual in the house?" he asked. "Any ghosts?"

She laughed. "Not one. I must repel supernatural beings."

Molly glanced at me. "What about you, Capone? Have you seen anything?"

"I have," I said. "At least I think I did."

"What did you see?" asked Luke.

"Boo."

Luke seemed confused. "What?"

"I mean, I saw Boo. The ghost dog."

"When?" asked Gracie, with a skeptical narrowing of her eyes.

"Several times, but the last was the night of the big snowstorm. All of you fell asleep in front of the fireplace in the bedroom. I couldn't sleep, so I kept watch, staring out the window at the snow. I saw Boo moving near the hedges that separate Molly's yard from ours. And I saw the ghost of one of the Boussards."

"Are you sure?" asked Gracie.

"I'm pretty sure. It was dark, and there were shadows. Also, the snow was falling pretty hard at that point."

"Maybe you saw a random dog," said Gracie. "Did you check for paw prints the next day?"

"Uh, no."

"Then you have no proof."

"I saw what I saw, Gracie," I said, getting upset about her attitude.

"Hmph. Whatever."

She pranced on ahead. Molly gave me a comforting nudge. "I believe you, Capone. I've lived next door to that house most of my life, and I've seen and heard lots of strange things."

A shiver went over me. "What did you do?"

She shrugged. "What could I do? When I was younger, I barked at it a lot. Now that I'm older, I'm calmer. About everything."

"I wish I could be calmer."

She laughed. "It'll happen. Eventually. They say Labs act like puppies for at least seven years. I think it's longer. I'm nearly thirteen, and I'm still like a puppy sometimes."

"Me, too."

"You're a puppy, Capone. Don't be so hard on yourself, okay?"

I loved Molly. She was so wise, and her words reminded me of my dear uncle Clancy. May he rest in peace.

"Thank you, Molly. You're an outstanding friend." I glanced over my shoulder at Viking Val and Ms. Anne. They were still talking about the house. "Your owner seems really into ghost stories."

She followed my gaze, her expression unreadable. "Not particularly. He's interested in the Boussards and the mansion."

"Because of the hauntings?"

She shook her head. "Because of the treasure."

I came to a dead stop. "Treasure?"

She frowned as if confused. "You don't know? I thought

everyone did. Before the last Mr. Boussard took his own life, legend has it that he hid something of incredible value somewhere in the house. My owner isn't interested in the hauntings. He's interested in the treasure. The lost treasure of Henry Boussard."

TWENTY-SEVEN

Good and bad ways to get close to humans:

1. Good: Snuggling Ms. Anne when she curls up for a nap.
2. Bad: Jumping up to snuggle Ms. Anne on the couch, sticking my butt in her face, and slapping her cheeks with my wagging tail.
3. Good: Licking Ms. Anne's feet to show appreciation.
4. Bad: Barging in as Ms. Anne takes a bubble bath and licking all the bubbles.
5. Good: Sitting on her feet to keep them warm.
6. Bad: Sitting on other things, like the laundry as she's shoving it into the washer, the sheets as she's folding them, and her shoes as she's sticking them on her feet.
7. Good: Curling up under Ms. Anne's desk while she works.
8. Bad: Hearing the UPS truck while under her desk at Bartleby's, knocking her out of the way

to get to the window, and making her spill her coffee down the front of her dress.

Oh, calamity. If only I could exercise more self-control.

Thankfully, no one was harmed in the coffee-spilling incident. I learned more every single day, but it was a process. One thing, however, had become glaringly apparent.

I should have been more careful.

Sadly, the siren's song of the delivery truck proved irresistible to me every single time. Unfortunately, Ms. Anne did not appreciate my conundrum.

"Capone. Get away from me," she said, dabbing at her gray wool dress with a paper towel as she gave me a dirty look. I felt even worse when I realized it wasn't a delivery truck after all. It was a snowplow.

Curse my curiosity and my obsession with delivery trucks.

Ms. Anne sighed. "It's okay, puppy. I realize you can't help it, and I'm too happy to care, to be honest."

Miss Olivia lifted a dark eyebrow. "And why are you in such a great mood, Annie Weston?" She clapped a hand over her mouth. "Oh, my gosh. You got laid."

Miss Bella poked her in the arm. "Olivia. That's rude."

"Rude, but true. Take a gander at that face. She's glowing. I've never seen you look this happy, Anne. Was it the fireman?"

Ms. Anne shook her head. "Nope."

"The policeman?"

"Nope."

"Your sexy hunk of a next-door neighbor, Dr. Dreamy?"

Dr. Dreamy? An excellent name, but I still preferred Viking Val. And what was this getting "laid" stuff? She and

Mr. Ben had made mad, passionate love—many times. But I didn't remember anything about her getting "laid." Had I missed it somehow?

Ms. Anne laughed at Miss Olivia's question. "No. It's not Val."

"The UPS guy—?"

Miss Bella cut in. "It was Ben O'Reilly. It had to be."

Ms. Anne nodded, a sweet smile playing on her lips. "Yes. It was Ben."

Miss Olivia let out a loud hoot. "What happens now? Your long-lost love comes back from the dead. You jump his bones—"

"Olivia Vargas, your mouth," said Miss Bella, her cheeks tinged bright pink.

I, for one, was curious about this bone jumping stuff. First, Ms. Anne got laid, like sod. Then she jumped on bones. What else had I missed?

Note to self: I needed to learn more current vernacular.

Miss Olivia waved away her sister's admonishment. "Stop being so prim and proper, Bella. I want Annie to spill the tea."

I gulped. Wasn't spilling the coffee enough? Had Ms. Olivia lost her mind?

"The tea, huh?" asked Ms. Anne. "There is no tea to spill. Ben and I are together. For now, at least."

Miss Bella's pretty face wrinkled into a frown. "What does that mean? He's the love of your life. Your soulmate. Your destiny."

"I have to agree with Bella here," said Miss Olivia, with a frown matching her sister's. "If you don't walk off into the sunset together, I'm going to be pissed."

Ms. Anne smiled, but I saw a tiny bit of sadness in her eyes. "We made no promises to each other. We haven't talked about the future. Ben is supposed to go to England. As far as I'm aware, that plan hasn't changed. Nor has he asked me to accompany him. I'm enjoying this for what it is."

"And what is it, exactly?" asked Miss Bella.

"Stolen moments," said Ms. Anne. "Time I never expected to have with Ben, and I'm grateful for each second."

They stared at each other for a long moment. "That's depressing," said Miss Olivia, tugging on one of her dark curls.

Ms. Anne grabbed her hand. "No. It's a gift. And I'm taking it for what it is."

I told my friends about it over lunch. They were still allowed to hang out in the apartment upstairs, while Ms. Anne deemed me "incapable of being left to my own devices." But if being unreliable meant I got to hang out with the ladies and hear all the gossip, maybe it wasn't so awful.

"I have news," I said, gnawing on a bone filled with peanut butter. We each had one, but mine seemed the biggest. They must have based it on weight because Luke's came in second. Faraday's was tiny and cute—like him. But the bones reminded me of something both important and confusing. "Ms. Anne has bones somewhere in the house because she's been jumping them."

Jackson gaped at me. "Excuse me?"

I continued nibbling. "Miss Olivia said Ms. Anne has been jumping bones and getting laid, but that last part is confusing and probably inaccurate. There is no way anyone can lay sod in this weather. Not with all the snow we've been having."

There was a moment of stunned silence before Jackson,

Gracie, and Luke burst out into gales of laughter. Faraday and I stared at them in confusion. "What's so funny?" I asked. That, unfortunately, caused them to laugh harder. Finally, Jackson explained it to me.

"Those are both euphemisms for having sexual intercourse."

I stared at him, wide-eyed. "Oh, my. I'm seeing that whole conversation in a completely new light now."

Jackson snorted. "As long as they're happy, I don't care what they're doing. They're two consenting adults. What they do in bed is no one else's business but their own. I mean if they're honest and faithful with each other. That's important, too."

He shot Gracie a look so filled with longing it surprised me. Gracie didn't respond, but I noticed she edged closer to his bulky form. Perhaps they'd ironed out their differences after all, but would the same hold true for my beloved humans?

"Speaking of which, Ms. Anne believes Mr. Ben might leave again. Is that true, Luke?"

Luke tilted his head and stared at me for a long moment. "I sure hope not. I like you guys. I want to stay."

"And we want you to stay, too. Why did she say that, Capone?" asked Gracie, confused. "She loves him."

"I'm not sure. They made no promises to each other. It's so wrong, though. After all, he is her Mr. Knightley."

Jackson and Gracie groaned. "When are you going to stop doing that, Capone? Life is not a Jane Austen novel. You need to face reality," said Gracie.

I frowned. "What is fiction if not a better, kinder, and gentler blueprint of how to live our lives? I mean, some fiction. I'm not talking about *Animal Farm*, although I get that vibe sometimes from Rocco. But don't tell him, okay?"

As much as Rocco and I had made our peace and become friends, he still scared me a little. Actually, he scared me a lot. Cats were so unpredictable.

"We won't tell him," said Luke. "Dogs united."

We lifted our snouts in response. "But you're wrong about fiction, pup," said Jackson. "It's not a blueprint. It's a fantasy. A dream. And not something that can happen in real life. Ever."

"Hmph. Agree to disagree," said Gracie, delicately gnawing on her bone. "Sometimes life does imitate art."

Jackson gazed hopefully at her, and I understood exactly what went through my friend's mind. Had she forgiven him after all for the incident with the Poodle at doggie daycare? It sure seemed that way.

"If that's true," said Jackson, his voice low. "If dreams do come true, does that mean I still have a chance at my dream, Gracie? Because my dream is you. It always has been."

"Oh, Jackson," she said. "Are you saying what I think you're saying?"

"Yes. You're everything to me. What do you say, princess? Can a beautiful girl like you ever fall for a schlump of a dog like me?"

She glanced at him from under her lashes. "Maybe. Today might be your lucky day."

They toddled off together in the direction of the bedroom. Luke, Faraday, and I stared after them in shock.

"They're both neutered, right?" asked Luke.

"As far as I know," I said. The sounds of heavy panting came from the bedroom. I cringed. "Is that Jackson breathing, or are they, uh...?"

I had no idea what to say next. Faraday helped. "Yep. I don't understand how they managed it, but she's jumping his bones. It's a hump fest in there." He tilted his head to indicate the bones Jackson and Gracie had left behind. "Speaking of which, go for it, Capone. You know you want them."

My stomach grumbled. "Maybe not. Last time Jackson got mad at me." I pushed the bones aside. "But there is something else I need to tell you. Molly told me something important. You remember the story of Henry Boussard, right?"

"The guy who killed his dog?" asked Faraday, his Puggy eyes more prominent than usual.

"Exactly. Molly told me that he hid a treasure somewhere in the house before he died. We should try to find it. We located all those books buried in the back garden of the bookstore. We're excellent at solving mysteries and finding treasures. I'm sure we can find this one, too."

Jackson and Gracie came back into the room, disheveled but happy. And I couldn't be sure, but it seemed like Jackson had a hickey on his neck. Could dogs give hickeys?

I really ought to learn more about the mating habits of canines. They were vital since I happened to be a dog.

And as Jane herself said, "It's a truth, universally acknowledged, that a single dog in possession of his testicles must be in want of a lady dog of his own."

Or something like that. I'm paraphrasing.

"What were you talking about?" asked Jackson, plopping onto the floor in an exhausted heap, one paw resting on Gracie's back.

"Treasure," I said. "The treasure of the Boussards. It's in our house somewhere, and I want to find it."

TWENTY-EIGHT

A list of Jane Austen's heroes from worst to best:

1. Edward Ferrars (*Sense and Sensibility*).
   Agreeable and loyal. Completely spineless.
2. Charles Bingley (*Pride and Prejudice*). Great
   guy. Emotional depth of a teaspoon. Too
   influenced by his sisters.
3. Colonel Brandon (*Sense and Sensibility*). Way
   too old for Marianne, and yet wonderful.
4. Captain Wentworth (*Persuasion*). Bitter. Also,
   loyal, and very hot.
5. Mr. Darcy (*Pride and Prejudice*). Broody, but
   otherwise perfect.
6. Mr. Knightley (*Emma*). Swooooon. The
   ideal man.

As I explained this to Faraday, I glanced out the bookstore window and saw Mr. Ben standing on the sidewalk in front of Bartleby's. He'd come to meet us after work. He had his hands in his pockets and the wind ruffled his dark hair.

A big smile lit up his face as soon as he saw Ms. Anne. I heard Miss Bella and Miss Olivia sigh when they noticed him. Gracie sighed, too.

"*That* is a man in love," she said.

I agreed with her. "I knew it would be him," I said. "He had to be her Mr. Knightley."

Ms. Anne tossed on her coat and flew out the door. She went straight into Mr. Ben's waiting arms. "I missed you," she said as she kissed him.

"Yo. Chapped lips," said Jackson. "It's a thing, humans. Be careful."

They didn't seem to notice of the possibility of chapped lips or notice the cold. They indeed acted like two people in love. They practically glowed with it.

Ms. Anne pulled him into the shop and introduced him to Miss Bella and Miss Olivia. He ducked his head shyly. Mr. Ben was a quiet man—one of the many things I liked about him.

"I thought I'd walk you home," he said, buttoning her coat for her. "Five dogs are a lot to manage."

She laughed. "Four of them are fine. Only Capone gives me issues."

"Hey," I said. They heard it as a bark and laughed at my outrage.

Curse my unjust reputation.

Well, mostly unjust.

"He disagrees," said Mr. Ben.

Ms. Anne patted my head. "Faraday is a problem, too. I keep worrying I'm going to lose him in a snowdrift. If I did, he wouldn't last long. He doesn't have Gracie's fluff or Jackson's bulk."

"Did she call me fat?" asked Jackson with a frown. "I think she called me fat."

"She definitely called you fat," I said. "Bulk is a code word."

"Great," said Jackson, sucking in his belly.

Gracie laughed. "I like a male with some meat on his bones. You're perfect just the way you are, Jackson."

They started licking each other. Luke, Faraday, and I looked away. "Too much PDA," said Faraday, gagging. "Ew."

They ignored us and kept licking. Even the humans noticed it. "I guess we aren't the only ones," said Mr. Ben. "It seems like Jackson and Gracie have something going on, too."

As the snow swirled around them, he pulled her into his arms for another kiss. Mr. Ben had my leash and Luke's in his hands. Ms. Anne had Gracie's, Jackson's, and Faraday's. I stood for a moment, admiring the scene. It was so beautiful.

"It's all fun and games until someone gets frostbite," said Faraday with a shiver.

Ms. Anne noticed. She picked him up and tucked him into her coat, holding him close. "There you go, little guy," she said.

He let out a sigh of pure pleasure. "This is the life," he said.

There is something oddly quiet and mysterious about a walk in the snow, even when five members of the canine persuasion accompany you. The shop was only a few blocks away from the house, but the journey proved delightful. Trees dripping with icicles. Snow sparkling in the light of the moon. Everything covered in a blanket of white.

"I love winter," I said, sticking my nose into the snow. "This is the best."

Faraday, his voice coming from the confines of Ms.

Anne's coat, disagreed. "Speak for yourself. I want to move to Florida. Pronto."

"They have big bugs in Florida," said Gracie.

"And snakes," said Jackson. "Those snakes could eat you alive."

"Well, here we have coyotes," I said, striving to be helpful. A howl echoed through the night, and I gasped. "Oh, crap. Did it hear me?"

We huddled together for warmth and protection. "I hope not," said Luke, eyes wide. "I had a run-in with a coyote once. Those things are scary."

I wanted to ask him more, but we'd arrived at the house. To our surprise, Viking Val, Policeman Pat, and Fireman Fetch stood on the porch with another guy I didn't recognize. Mr. Ben grinned when he saw him.

"Rob Hart. Is that you?"

"In the flesh." A tall man, he looked like a slightly older version of Fireman Fetch. Black hair, warm brown eyes, dark skin. And he had the same mischievous twinkle in his eyes.

He walked down the steps and pulled Mr. Ben into a hug. After a few minutes, they stood back to study each other. "I hear you're a reporter now," said Mr. Ben. "It's what you always wanted."

"And you're fixing up old houses," Reporter Rob said with a smile. "That's what you always wanted, too. I missed you, Ben."

"I missed you, too. It's been too long," said Mr. Ben, his voice thick with emotion.

"It has," said Reporter Rob. "But you were dead, so..."

Mr. Ben winced. "Yeah. I'm sorry, Rob."

Reporter Rob shook his head. "Don't apologize. I'm happy to see your face again."

The two men struggled to compose themselves, but Policeman Pat lightened the mood. "I just came to get my shovel," he said.

Everyone laughed. "It's in the shed. I'll get it for you," said Mr. Ben.

"No rush." Policeman Pat tucked his hands into his pockets. "The shovel was an excuse. I wanted to apologize. I was more hurt than angry when we first spoke, but it didn't sound that way."

Mr. Ben clapped a hand on his shoulder. "I understand. Really, I do."

After a moment of bro-love between Mr. Ben and his two high school friends, Viking Val interrupted by holding up a tray covered with foil. He had a bunch of grocery bags with him as well. Molly stood by his side, and she seemed unenthusiastic to be out in the cold.

"I hate to interrupt, but I brought dinner. Enchiladas. Perhaps Anne forgot we'd made plans for tonight."

Ms. Anne frowned. "We did? I don't remember planning anything. Sorry about that, Val."

"No worries," he said, and he seemed to mean it. "I brought plenty. I always cook for an army. Is anyone else hungry?"

It turned out everyone was hungry, especially me. Not a surprise.

We went inside together—Mr. Ben, Reporter Rob, Ms. Anne, and Ms. Anne's three additional boyfriends. Mr. Ben raised his eyebrows at her, and she shrugged. It wasn't her fault that her callers had come calling. She hadn't invited them over. Or at least she didn't remember doing so.

"I did not have plans with Val," she said, speaking to him softly as he took her coat. The others were in the kitchen. Molly had gone straight to the fireplace, curled up, and fell asleep. The old girl looked tired. Jackson joined her, so he must have been tired, too.

I stood by the humans and watched as Mr. Ben kissed Ms. Anne's nose. "I believe you. Want to see something surprising?"

She narrowed her eyes at him. "The last time you said that to me, you'd found a snake by the river, and you threw it at me. I still have nightmares."

He laughed. "Not a snake. Not this time."

He took her hand and led her into the kitchen. She gasped because he'd installed the cupboards, and they looked bright and white. An island painted a beautiful shade of blue sat in the middle of the room. The only thing missing was the countertops.

"We'll have them tomorrow. White quartzite. It'll look amazing."

"It already does. Ben. This is outstanding. Josie will love it."

Viking Val set the enchiladas on top of the new stove and pulled a salad and a large container full of rice from his bag. While the men stayed in the kitchen, chatting with Viking Val, Mr. Ben led Ms. Anne to the front room.

"I'm nearly done with this area, too," he said.

She gazed around in astonishment. "Everything came together so fast," she said, her eyes going from the floors to the new light fixtures to the fresh paint on the wall. "And that mantle looks incredible, Ben."

He studied the mantle with her. "Yeah, I'm happy with how it turned out. The bit with the dog on it is wonky, though. It sticks out more than the rest of the carving."

"The dog that's Capone's twin?" she asked with a laugh. "I'd expect it to be wonky."

"Hey—" I said, but she cut me off.

"I see what you mean, though." She walked over and ran her finger across the carving of the dog. "It's almost like this is a separate piece of wood."

"It is. Maybe there was damage to the original, and they had to replace it."

She shrugged, resting her head on his shoulder. "It still looks great. You know your stuff, Ben. I'm impressed."

He raised his eyebrows. "With my woodworking skills?"

"With all your skills."

"Oh, no," said Luke. "They're going to kiss again."

He was right. Reporter Rob entered the room as they locked lips. He had to clear his throat twice to get their attention.

"Sorry to interrupt. Could I speak with you a minute, Ben?"

Ms. Anne stepped away from him. "I'll go help Val. I bought paper plates and disposable silverware to use this week, but he'll never be able to find them."

After she went into the kitchen, Reporter Rob joined Mr. Ben by the fireplace, his expression serious. "The newspaper wants to do a story on you." Mr. Ben groaned, but Reporter Rob continued. "It's a big story, Ben. I've already heard about three other reporters who are onto it. Someone will do it eventually. Wouldn't you rather it was me?"

"Yes, but it's complicated."

Reporter Rob studied Mr. Ben's face. "I'll be in town until Friday. Do you want to get together Wednesday and talk?"

Mr. Ben nodded. "But I'm not making any promises, okay?"

"Okay."

"Dinner is ready," said Policeman Pat, sticking his head

through the doorway. He gave Mr. Ben and Reporter Rob a funny look, and I wondered how much he'd overheard.

He acted jovial enough once they sat down, though. They ate in the kitchen. The house had a grand dining room with a sparkling crystal chandelier, but we had no furniture in that room yet. The kitchen table was small for half a dozen humans, but it worked, and they seemed to have a pleasant time. Viking Val had the foresight to make margaritas as well as enchiladas. He was a clever man. After several margaritas, everyone seemed more relaxed, except Mr. Ben. He didn't drink much and acted even quieter and more reserved than usual.

Viking Val made up for it, though. He asked Mr. Ben tons of questions about the remodel. A safe subject, it seemed to put everyone at ease.

"Val is a genius," said Gracie. "And such a great cook."

She eyed him wistfully. Luke's hackles went up. "My human is a great cook, too. And he's handy around the house."

Gracie gave Luke a nudge. "And my human is in love with your human. That's the most important part. Also, there is nothing sexier than a man who can fix things. Trust me on that. I've heard the ladies talking, and they all agreed on that one."

Exciting news, since I felt pretty confident Mr. Darcy was not good with a hammer. "Are you sure? Wouldn't they prefer a gentleman with a cravat, an estate, and a brooding nature?"

"The estate might be a useful thing, but the cravat seems unimportant, and the brooding would get old after a while." Gracie gave me a skeptical frown. "You're thinking of Mr. Darcy again, aren't you?"

"Uh, maybe."

She rolled her eyes. "He's a fictional character, Capone. When will you understand that? Real women want real men, flaws and all."

Jackson fell asleep on the floor next to her. She gave him a lick. He smiled, eyes still closed. "Yeah, Gracie. You know what I like, baby." Then he turned over and farted.

Gracie wrinkled her nose. "I take that back. Manners are an important quality. Skip the cravat and the brooding. When a man is broody, it can worry a gal. She worries it's about her, although it might not be about her at all. And that can create a whole host of trouble."

Broody. Mr. Ben acted a bit broodier than usual tonight, and he seemed stressed out about the interview with Reporter Rob. Could he tell a reporter about seeing a murder and being in the witness protection program? Probably not.

I suspected Mr. Ben came back to Beaver without really planning it through. He'd wanted to see Ms. Anne, and I got it, but he didn't have a believable story to cover what had happened fifteen years ago. And now it seemed like he'd have to come up with one quickly.

A wise man would have asked Ms. Anne for help with that. Mr. Ben seemed smart, but I guessed he'd been on his own so long that the idea of asking for help never occurred to him. Or at least that was my hypothesis.

I thought about asking Molly, but she seemed tired, and I didn't want to wake her. I decided to ask Rocco about it instead. Rocco understood a lot, but he was not a helpful sort of kitty. He called me a rude name and told me to leave him alone. That's when I went with my third choice. Faraday. Mainly because he was a genius.

"Your hypothesis is correct, Capone," he said, studying Mr. Ben closely. "He seems worried this evening. And rather preoccupied. This will require further observation on our part, but I do believe something is rotten in the state of Denmark. Or in the state of Pennsylvania, as the case may be."

I had no idea what Faraday meant precisely, but he sounded super bright. "Then let us observe," I said.

"Wise call."

It wasn't that wise. Since the humans were eating, we would have been observing anyway. After they finished cleaning up, Viking Val shared that he'd also made a tres leches cake for dessert. The humans were all too full to eat it right away, so they sat around chatting instead.

When Viking Val asked again about the drywall in the basement, Mr. Ben brought the group downstairs to show them the area. It was vast and dark and creepy.

"This is the perfect place for treasure," I said.

"But we'll have to look for it later," said Faraday. "We'll never be able to find it with all the humans around."

He was right. We'd have to postpone the treasure hunt. And the humans were discussing something so dull, I thought I might fall asleep.

Drywall.

Mr. Ben appeared to be an authority on the subject, and Viking Val hung on every word.

Note to self: Too much HGTV is not necessarily a healthy thing.

"The drywall guys will be here next week," said Mr. Ben. "I tried to get them in sooner, but the storm put our schedule back a few days. I guess that's a good thing. I requested the plans from the historical society as you suggested, Val. I should have them by Wednesday morning. That'll help because I hate to finish anything, especially a basement, without referencing the original plans. I'd only had them a couple of days before they went missing, so I barely got to look at them."

"It's cold down here," said Ms. Anne with a shiver.

Mr. Ben put an arm around her. "We updated the heating system for the house," he said, pointing to a shiny new furnace. "But we can't do the ducts down here until the drywall guys come. I left the basement for last since I figured Josie and Nate would need the kitchen and bathrooms first. We'll be done with everything above ground before they get back. It's kind of lucky for us Nate broke his leg. That gave us extra time," he said with a crooked smile.

"And with construction, you always need extra time," said Viking Val. "It goes with the territory."

We went back upstairs, and the humans ate their cake. Molly didn't wake up until it was time to go home, and even then, she barely spoke to us. It worried me. I asked Jackson about it later, once the humans fell asleep in their bed and the other dogs and Rocco had passed out in front of the fireplace.

"Is Molly sick?" I asked. "She didn't talk to us and slept the whole time Viking Val was here."

"She's old," said Jackson with a yawn. "Old dogs need to sleep more. Speaking of which, good night, Capone."

He flopped onto his back and started snoring loudly, but there was no way I could sleep. I had a lot of worries floating around my Labradorian brain. Things got worse when I heard noises, and they sounded like they came from the basement.

I got up and went to the window. I thought I may have imagined things, but Mr. Ben got up, too.

"Did you hear that boy?" he asked, putting on his slippers.

Ms. Anne, who'd had quite a few margaritas, didn't get

up. She slept soundly. Mr. Ben grabbed a flashlight, and together we went downstairs.

"It sounded like it came from the basement," he said softly. "Let's go check it out." He let out a tiny laugh. "Which is exactly what people say in horror movies right before they get killed. But I have you to protect me. I'll be fine."

Oh, calamity. I let out a whine. Was he sure about this?

He smiled and patted my head. "I have faith in you. You're a wonderful dog, Capone. And, anyway, I'm not too worried. It's probably a rat or some animal coming in from the cold. Nothing you can't handle."

While I admired Mr. Ben's trust in me, I had doubts. Those doubts increased exponentially when we went down to the basement. It seemed darker and creepier than before, and something made a banging sound—so loud it caused me to jump in surprise. It took Mr. Ben a few minutes to locate the noise source, and when he did, he laughed.

"It's a window," he said. "It must have blown open in the storm. I'm surprised we didn't notice it earlier."

The window, small and low to the ground, looked big enough for several rats or an average-sized human to slip through. As the wind blew, it opened and closed, making a slamming noise, and bringing in snow with it. Mr. Ben closed it, and we went back upstairs, but something still felt off to me.

Later, I realized what bothered me. Something I'd noticed, but Mr. Ben had not.

Snow had landed on the cold floor of the basement, directly under the window. Mr. Ben saw the snow, but he hadn't spotted the one thing that sent chills up my spine.

I saw a footprint in the snow. A human footprint. And it didn't belong to Mr. Ben.

The first step in addiction recovery is admitting I had a problem, so here it goes.

1. Always be honest with yourself and others: "My name is Capone, and I am a bra snatcher."
2. Understand how your problem began: "It started with sock stealing. Socks were my gateway garment."
3. Describe how your problem escalated: "It happened this morning before work, when Ms. Anne dropped a sports bra on the floor."
4. Remember the point when everything changed: "The sports bra was made of the boingy-boingy fabric I loved, and it was blue. Electric blue. I was hooked."
5. Explain when you first realized your addiction was getting out of control: "I thought sports bras would be enough to keep me happy forever, but then I discovered a secret. *Victoria's* Secret."
6. Account for how you rationalized your

addiction: "I don't know Victoria, but her secret is out. Her bras are the best. I have expensive taste."

7. Give details on how you justified your addiction: "When I shook my head back and forth, part of the bra landed on my nose. That made it special—like a padded bra hat."

8. Describe your lowest point: "Ms. Anne caught me nosing my way through her lingerie drawer."

9. Explain how those around you reacted: "Ms. Anne did not like this new hobby."

10. State the truth as plainly as possible: "I have a problem. I think I need a support group."

"Capone. Leave my bras alone," said Ms. Anne with a frustrated groan.

Mr. Ben smiled when he saw me. I guess I did seem ridiculous with a bra on top of my head and another in my mouth. I couldn't help it. They smelled like Ms. Anne and were so fun to chew.

"A little help?" she asked, as she chased me around the room.

Mr. Ben knew exactly what to do. He reached into his pocket. "Treat?"

As soon as he said that magic word, I dropped the bras and plopped my butt down on the floor in front of him. I was very skilled at sitting. I did it quite prettily, too.

He patted my head and gave me a dog biscuit. Mr. Ben was the best.

"I should take him for a walk today," said Ms. Anne. "I planned to go to work late this morning anyway. We have a shipment arriving after five. I said I'd stay for it."

"That works out well," he said. "My team is starting

today, and Capone needs to burn some energy. I'll keep the rest of the dogs and Rocco up here. Luke can be with me. He knows how to stay out of the way."

Luke wagged his tail, and Mr. Ben gave him a treat too. Ms. Anne patted Luke's head.

"He's a great dog," she said. "I wonder how he ended up as a stray."

"No idea," said Mr. Ben. "But the people at the shelter said he'd been on the streets a while. That's why he's so skittish. It's taken him time to trust that people aren't out to hurt him."

Ms. Anne leaned down to hug Luke. "Poor baby," she said. "And he's so sweet."

"Yeah, dogs are the most forgiving creatures on Earth, aren't they?"

The doorbell rang, and I lost my mind. It was Mr. Ben's work crew. They greeted me with smiles and laughter, appearing to enjoy my enthusiasm, but Ms. Anne did not laugh.

"I'd better get him out of here," she said, giving Mr. Ben a quick kiss on the cheek. She had on her snow boots and parka. This would be fun. She was about to leave, but Mr. Ben pulled her close for one final hug.

"Be careful," he said.

Something in his voice made her pause. "Are you okay?"

"Yes. Of course," he said and smiled at her, but the smile didn't quite reach his eyes. "Bye, Annie."

She frowned. "Are you sure you're alright?"

He nodded. "I had trouble sleeping last night. There was a window open in the basement. I heard it banging. Capone helped me take care of it."

I wagged my tail because I'd helped him. I was an excellent helper.

"And you have a lot going on today."

"I do. I'm the project manager, but the local contractor and his team will arrive soon. I haven't met him yet. Nate hired him. So, we'll have a lot to go over."

I tugged on the leash. Were we leaving or not? But Ms. Anne still hesitated.

"I love you, Ben."

He gave her one last kiss on the forehead. "I love you, too."

At last, she seemed ready to leave. Thank goodness. I nearly lost my mind. We'd only been stuck in the house a few days, but I was a puppy. If I didn't get rid of my excess energy, unfortunate things could happen—like bra thefts. And stolen slippers. And other forms of vandalism and criminal mischief.

I needed this walk in the park, and so did Ms. Anne. The quiet peacefulness of the forest soothed both of us. We walked on the scenic path above the lake in Brady's Run Park, and I realized nothing could be as relaxing as a walk in a snowy forest.

Well, unless you walked with a hyperactive dog who barked at everything. Even I had to admit the barking was getting annoying, but I couldn't help it.

Curse my overly enthusiastic and psychotically friendly demeanor.

We were walking on the path in the woods, minding our own business, when Ms. Anne heard people approaching. She started chanting, "Please don't have a dog, please don't have a dog, please."

It didn't work. Three human ladies came up the path toward us, and they had not one dog but two. Not good.

They were quite a distance away, but I'd already begun

barking and acting like a douche canoe. It was jarring—a definite tranquility killer.

One of the dogs did not seem to be on a leash, something we often saw in the park, even though it violated the rules. However, since this dog did not act like a douche canoe, it didn't matter. Also, the owner put the dog (a young black Lab) on a leash as soon as they heard me barking like an asshat.

Excuse my language—Ms. Anne's word, not mine.

As they came up the hill toward us, Ms. Anne took precautionary measures and held me off to the side. She tried to get me to sit and not bark, but it seemed hopeless. And things got worse as soon as they got close to us on the path.

What happened next was a disaster. I'm unsure how it occurred, but somehow Ms. Anne accidentally unsnapped my choke collar, the only thing holding me to my leash. Suddenly, I was the Labradorian version of *Free Willy*.

Oh, calamity. This would not end well.

The collar popped off, which left Ms. Anne holding the leash, and me running like a hell hound toward those unlucky women and their dogs.

They screamed. Ms. Anne screamed. One lady scooped up the smaller dog in her arms. The one with the Lab backed up so far, she almost fell off a cliff, but it did not deter me. I charged toward them, eyes crazy, drool hanging, tail wagging, and my body practically vibrating with excitement.

Best. Day. Ever.

For me. But not for Ms. Anne. It may have been the worst day ever for her.

"He doesn't bite. I swear he doesn't bite," she yelled as I lunged at the other dogs. "I'm so sorry."

Ms. Anne leaped on me, wrestling me like Crocodile Dundee wrestled crocodiles. With a great deal of maneuvering, she finally managed to get me locked in my choke collar again, still apologizing to the women on the path.

"It's okay," they said. "As long as he doesn't bite. He's just friendly."

They were kind women. One of them worked at the post office in Beaver. She recognized Ms. Anne, which meant Ms. Anne could never go into the post office again. She'd be too embarrassed.

We made it back to the car without further incident, but Ms. Anne had bruises in weird places and a cut on her thumb from my leash.

"I can't believe you," she said, pulling a twig out of her hair. "I'm going to have to go home and change. You were a bad dog."

I slouched in my seat. She may have been right. In fact, I knew she was right. I had trouble controlling my primal urges.

Note to self: Work on primal urges.

She opened the door of the house. Workers came in and out and acted very busy, and it was complete chaos. She waved at one of the men.

"Have you seen Ben?"

He shook his head. "Do you need something? Carl is the man in charge. He's over there."

He pointed to a big man in the kitchen who appeared to be installing the countertops. Ms. Anne didn't want me anywhere near the countertops.

"No. That's okay."

We went upstairs. The other dogs seemed happy to see me.

"Where have you been?" asked Faraday. "And why does Ms. Anne look so angry?"

"It's a long story," I said, ducking my head. "She called me an asshat. I'm not sure what that means, but she also called me a bad dog."

They all gasped. Well, all of them except Gracie. "Were you a bad dog, Capone?"

"Maybe?"

"There is no 'maybe.' If you were naughty, own up to it. It's better that way," said Jackson.

"Words from the wise philanderer," said Rocco with a sneer.

"Shut up, fuzzball," said Jackson.

"Make me," said Rocco with a hiss.

Ms. Anne covered her ears with her hands. She'd changed into a dress and boots and looked pretty but stressed out. "I cannot handle you guys today. Especially you, Capone."

I let out a whine. She was right. I might be the worst dog ever. But at least I'd found her Mr. Knightley for her. That should count as something, shouldn't it?

Except she didn't realize how much I'd helped.

She took out her phone and dialed a number, frowning when no one picked up. "Hi, Ben. Call me when you get a chance. Nothing urgent. I just wanted to complain about Capone."

I stared at her in shock. Had it seriously come to this?

She tapped her phone on her chin as she gazed out the window, then glanced back at us. "I should probably take all of you to the shop today. Ben seems busy, and I don't want to come home to puddles of pee."

This time she stared right at Faraday. "Busted," he said. "But I have a small bladder. It's not my fault."

"Rocco, you can stay here," she said, patting him. "Because you're a well-behaved kitty."

Rocco purred, a victorious gleam in his green eyes. "Take that, dimwit."

I'd thought I'd made progress with Rocco, but ever since I pooped on his head, he'd been mean to me. He needed to get over it since it had been a total accident, and it hurt when Ms. Anne called me a bad dog. Also, calling Rocco a well-behaved kitty moments later stung.

She leashed us up and took us to her car, pausing to watch the workers as she searched for Mr. Ben. She found Contractor Carl and introduced herself.

"Hi, I'm Anne. I'm housesitting right now. Have you seen Ben?"

Contractor Carl rubbed his stubbly chin. "I haven't seen him for an hour or so," he said. "Do you need something?"

She shook her head, but I noticed she had a worried frown on her face. It remained there all day. It was a busy day at Bartleby's Books, but Ms. Anne kept sneaking glances at her phone. She called Mr. Ben several times, but he never called her back. Strange, and by the end of the day, Ms. Anne was a nervous wreck.

"Something is wrong," said Gracie. "I feel it in my bones."

I had to agree with her. And when Ms. Anne finally accepted the late delivery and closed the shop, we were all eager to get back home, no one more than Ms. Anne.

But as we drove through the dark, snowy town, my dread only increased. I had no idea what we were going to find when we made it home, but every bit of intuition I had told me one thing.

It was going to be bad.

THIRTY

Advice on starting a new relationship or rekindling an old one:

1. Be yourself.
2. Don't move too fast.
3. Try not to be clingy.
4. Don't compare your new beau to your ex.
5. Be honest.
6. Watch out for red flags.
7. Try not to worry.
8. Don't play mind games.
9. Enjoy each moment.
10. Don't disappear.

We pulled up in front of a dark house. The door was locked. We stepped inside, and Ms. Anne had to use her cell phone to find the light switch. She turned it on and gazed around in surprise. The house looked amazing, but it was also empty.

Where had Mr. Ben gone? And where was Luke?

Ms. Anne took her phone out of her purse. She called him again. "I'm back home, and I'm worried. Please call me. I need to know you're okay."

She hung up, dropping her purse onto the table near the front door. She picked up a piece of paper lying there. "It's a note from Carl," she said. "Ben hasn't been here all day."

With her coat and boots still on, she went out the backdoor to the carriage house. She twisted the knob, but the door was locked, and no light shone from the windows. A noise came from next door as Viking Val let Molly out, and Ms. Anne walked over to the fence to speak with him.

"Val, have you seen Ben?"

He waved at her from his back porch. "Hi, Anne. I saw him this morning when I left for work. Is everything okay?"

"Yes. I mean, I hope so. Did you notice anything unusual when you saw him?"

Viking Val rubbed his chin. "Now that you mention it, he did seem kind of upset about something. I was in a rush, so we didn't speak, but I saw him get into his truck and leave."

"But you have no idea where he went?"

"Sorry. I don't," he said. "Is there anything I can do to help?

"No. I'm sure it's nothing. He had a lot on his schedule today. I'm certain he's..." Ms. Anne paused, unable to come up with any reason for Mr. Ben's absence. "I'm certain he's fine. Thanks, Val."

"Don't mention it."

We went back into the house. Ms. Anne was deep in thought, a worried frown on her pretty face. She fed us dinner but ate nothing herself. She paced back and forth for hours, checking the windows. Jumping every time she heard a car approach. Finally, she pulled out her phone again and called Policeman Pat.

"Hey, Pat. I hate to bother you, but have you heard from Ben today?"

She had the phone on speaker, so we listened to her conversation. "No, I haven't. Is everything okay?"

"I'm not sure. He's not here. He's not answering my calls or texts. I'm getting worried."

There was a long pause. "Well, you know Ben."

"What do you mean?"

"It's not like he hasn't done this sort of thing before. When we were kids, he used to take off all the time."

"That was different."

"Was it?" He let out a long sigh. "I'm sure he'll show up, Annie. Do you want me to come over?"

"No. I'm fine. You're right. I'm overreacting."

It didn't seem like she overreacted, though. "I don't like this," said Jackson. "And Luke is gone, too."

That night we didn't go upstairs to bed. Ms. Anne sat on the couch, wrapped in a blanket, unable to sleep. The other dogs passed out on the carpet. I was the only other one awake besides Rocco. He came downstairs, padding silently toward me, every muscle in his furry body tense.

"Something's wrong," he said, glancing nervously over his shoulder. "I feel it. Can you feel it, too?"

"I do," I said, my heart heavy. "Mr. Ben is missing. He left, and no one can figure out where he went."

"He left?" asked Rocco with a frown. "When?"

"Sometime this morning."

"That's odd."

"Why?"

"Because I saw that fleabag Luke outside, right before you came home."

I sat up. "What?"

Rocco tilted his head to indicate the front of the house. "He stood in the bushes across the street. It seemed kind of weird."

"Oh, Rocco. This is awful. Really awful. It's cold outside, Mr. Ben is missing, and Luke is alone. What are we going to do?"

He sighed. "There is nothing we can do right now, pup, but you're right. It looks dire. We must remember Luke lived as a stray for quite a while. He knows how to survive outside, unlike us. I'm sure he'll be fine tonight, and we'll find him first thing in the morning."

"Are you serious? You'll help? But you don't like Luke."

"I don't like you either, but I still wouldn't want you to be stuck outside in the cold. I wouldn't wish that on my worst enemy."

I gave Rocco a big lick to thank him. "You're the best, Rocco."

He scowled at me, wiping away my kiss. "Keep your tongue where it belongs, weirdo." He hopped onto the chair and curled up next to a pillow. "And I am the best. You're correct. Now get some sleep. It's going to be a busy day tomorrow. We have to save Luke and do that hero stuff again. It's exhausting," he said with a yawn.

He passed out in seconds, but I sat there staring at the fire. Something strange was going on. Mr. Ben would never have left Ms. Anne, and he definitely would not have left Luke.

Poor Luke. I imagined him outside, cold, hungry, and alone, and shivering. Rocco was right. I wouldn't wish that on my worst enemy.

"Are you cold, puppy?" asked Ms. Anne, patting the spot next to her on the couch. "Come sit with me. I need snuggles right now."

She didn't have to ask me twice. I hopped up and started licking her face. She'd been crying, so it tasted salty. "Thanks, Capone," she said with a sniff, holding me close and burying her face in my fur as she wept. "I should have known better. He left me again. I am such a fool. He never made me any promises. Why did I think this time would be different?"

Oh, calamity. This was tragic.

I stayed with her and let her cry. I wanted to cry, too.

Curse my inability to speak Human. I wished to tell her so many things.

I wanted to say Mr. Ben didn't leave. How could he? He was her Mr. Knightley. I sensed it to the depths of my soul. I'd been wrong about many things in my short life, but I could not be wrong about this. He loved her. It was an irrefutable fact.

But something else bothered me, too. Luke. Even if Mr. Ben had a completely random reason for leaving Ms. Anne, he would never have left Luke to fend for himself outside in the cold. No way. He'd never do that to any dog, let alone his dog.

Something was wrong here. Very wrong.

Ms. Anne wiped her tears, patting me. "Thanks, buddy. I needed that. You're an excellent shoulder to cry on," she said, and I snuggled closer, lying down on the couch, and resting my head on her lap. "The good news is my house is ready. We can go back there tomorrow. And Josie and Nate will be back on Friday. I bet you'll be glad to see them."

I licked her hand. I would be glad to see Ms. Josie and

Mr. Nate, but my work here was not done. Ms. Anne still needed me, and I had to find a way to make things right.

Exhausted from crying, she finally dozed off sometime in the middle of the night. I slept, too, never leaving her side. In the morning, we both felt awful, but I was a puppy on a mission. I had to fix this, but I couldn't do it alone. I needed my friends.

While Ms. Anne packed upstairs, I told them my plan. "We need to find Luke and bring him home. Once Ms. Anne sees him, she'll realize Mr. Ben didn't leave her."

Jackson tilted his head to study me. "If he didn't leave her, where did he go?"

Excellent question. "I have no idea," I said. "But there is more to it than that. Rocco saw Luke outside. In the cold. Alone. And he's probably hungry. We have to help him."

"Is that true, Rocco? You saw Luke outside?" asked Gracie.

"I did," he said. "As much as I hate to admit it, Capone is right. There is something odd going on here, and since the humans can't seem to figure it out, it's up to us. We need to save Luke and find Ben, and we need to do it quickly. The temperatures are dropping by the minute. Luke might not survive another night on his own, and I'm worried Ben is in danger, too. Call it feline intuition, but I sense it. Impending doom. Either that or I'm about to yak up a furball."

For a moment, we were silent, processing Rocco's words. Impending doom? That sounded even worse than a furball.

"I'm in," said Jackson.

"Me, too," said Gracie.

We turned our attention to Faraday. He ducked his head. "I'm too little to be of assistance. I can't even walk in the snow."

I nudged him. "We need you, buddy."

"Why?"

"I know how we can get outside," I said. "The workers will be here soon. Ms. Anne will be distracted. We can slip out when she isn't watching. That part is easy. The tricky part is how do we find Luke? We need a plan, and you're the smartest of all of us."

"Speak for yourself," said Rocco. But when I sent him a pleading look, he rolled his eyes. "But Capone is right. We need all the help we can get. And since brainpower is seriously lacking in this group..." He glanced at Jackson, who seemed very focused on licking his private parts at the moment. "We need all the help we can get."

"That's it," I said. "Operation Save Luke will commence at 0800 hours."

They all stared at me in confusion. "When is that?" asked Jackson.

I frowned. "No idea. But it sounded official, right?"

Note to self: Learn to tell time.

"Ignore the pup," said Rocco. "We'll leave as soon as the time is right."

It happened more quickly than we anticipated. Ms. Anne gave us our breakfast and let us out back for our morning potty time. Unbeknownst to her, someone had left the gate on the back fence slightly ajar. It took some pushing because of the snow, but we managed to get it open enough for us to fit through, then we snuck out into the alley.

"What should we do first?" asked Gracie, tiptoeing around a pile of garbage. "Ew. Was that a needle? I think I saw a needle."

There was no needle. Gracie had been watching too

many crime shows on TV. "You really should stick to PBS," I said. "Educational and enlightening."

"And boring," said Gracie under her breath.

I pretended not to hear her. We had more important things to discuss because Rocco happened to be correct. It was getting colder, and Faraday wouldn't last long in this weather. He already shivered so hard he vibrated.

"Where should we start?" I asked, hoping to distract him from the cold.

"At the most obvious place," Faraday said. "Where Rocco saw Luke last."

"Wonderful idea. Let's go," I said. "And we'd better be quick about it. Ms. Anne will realize we've absconded. She'll be searching for us soon."

"Absconded?" asked Jackson.

"Fled," I said. "Made off. Escaped. Ran away."

"Why didn't you say, 'ran away' in the first place?" he asked.

"Because 'absconded' sounds better?"

We heard Ms. Anne calling for us, and she seemed like she was already in a panic. That provided all the impetus we needed to hurry.

It was early enough in the morning that not many people were out. We snuck around the corner at the end of the alley and turned right to head to the river. It also meant going in front of the house, which would be tricky, but judging by the sound of Ms. Anne's voice, she currently searched the area around the alley.

"This is going remarkably well," I said as we crossed River Road. "We're almost there."

Then I heard a noise that made my blood run cold. A school bus. It was close, and Faraday remained on the road.

"Oh, no," said Gracie with a scream as we watched the

bus barrel closer. Faraday stood in the middle of the street, eyes huge, and he seemed frozen in fear.

Terrified and sure I was about to watch my buddy die, I did the only thing I could. I ran in front of the bus, grabbed him by the neck, and flew back to the sidewalk. When I got there, and the bus rolled past, I nearly collapsed in relief. Faraday was still in my mouth.

"You can drop me now," he said, his voice a bit muffled.

"Sorry," I said, opening my jaws. Thank goodness he was so tiny. He landed on the sidewalk with a plop. "You need to look both ways before crossing the street, Faraday. That's important."

"You're right. Thanks for saving me. But I was focused on something else."

"What?"

"That," he said, pointing at one of the bushes. Luke stood there, shivering from the cold, his eyes full of fear.

"Luke!"

I cried out his name in relief, but Luke did something unexpected. He took off.

"What is he doing?" asked Gracie as we chased after him. "Luke. Stop. We want to help."

"He's scared," said Rocco. "We have to follow him but be careful not to frighten him away."

"How?" I asked, keeping my eye on Luke as he ran ahead of us.

"Stay close, but not too close," said Faraday, struggling to keep up in the high snow. "He needs to feel safe. Don't freak him out. That'll make things worse."

I went first, plowing through the snow so the smaller dogs wouldn't have a problem, especially Faraday. Jackson brought up the rear. He wanted to make sure neither Faraday nor Gracie ended up getting lost or stuck in a snowdrift. Rocco walked behind me, complaining the whole time.

"Ew. Snow. Wet. Cold. Hate."

When Rocco got stressed, he communicated using single words, no phrases. It may have been a cat thing.

"We're all cold, Rocco," said Gracie. "Keep moving."

When Luke disappeared into a hole in the ground, I came to a stop. "What should I do?"

"Maybe Rocco can climb that tree," said Faraday. "And tell us what's going on."

"Always give the cat the dangerous jobs," said Rocco, muttering as he climbed the tree and went out onto a limb hanging over the place where Luke had disappeared.

"You have claws and the ability to scale great heights. It's a blessing, not a curse. Be grateful," said Faraday. "If I could climb, I'd be up a tree all day long."

"So would I," said Jackson, staring dreamily up at the branches. "But then I would probably fall, and it would be raining Pugs, and that would be no good at all."

Rocco stared at both of them in astonishment before shaking his head. "Do you want to know what I see or not?"

"We want to know," I said, getting frustrated. "Please ignore the Pugs and their dreams of grandeur and tell us."

"You aren't going to believe this," said Rocco. "But Luke has an igloo."

"A what?" asked Gracie.

"It's an Inuit word for a shelter made of snow," said Faraday. "And if you watched PBS as Capone suggested, you might realize that, Gracie."

I stared at him in surprise. "You watch PBS, too?"

"Of course. All geniuses do. Even evil ones."

Rocco hissed at us from up in the tree. "Are you done talking about the merits of public television? Because I have something to tell you." He waited until he seemed confident he had our attention. "Luke wagged his tail at me. He wants us to join him. But there is something you need to do first."

"What?" I asked.

"I can climb up, but I never learned how to climb down. Get me out of this freaking tree. Now."

THIRTY-ONE

How to get a grumpy cat out of a tree:

1. Stay calm.
2. Coax the cat down using a soothing voice and treats.
3. Lean a ladder or a big branch against the tree.
4. Guide the cat to safety with a laser pointer.
5. Physically attempt to retrieve the cat as soon as it's close enough.
6. Keep all dogs and other animals away.
7. If all else fails, call for help.

"Where is Fireman Fetch when we need him?" I asked, grunting as I tried to push a fallen branch close to the tree with my head. We had no laser pointers or treats. The branch seemed like our only option. Cats could climb a tree effortlessly, but unlike squirrels, who climb back down head-first, cats could only climb down butt first—like a human climbing down a ladder.

"Go on without me," said Rocco, eyes filled with terror. "I'll be fine. I'm super comfortable up here."

"You are not comfortable," I said. "Stop being such a scaredy-cat."

"Climb down the branch Capone set up for you," said Faraday. "Use it as a ladder."

"I can't."

"You can and you will."

Faraday started walking up the branch I'd placed against the tree trunk, to my surprise. "What are you doing?" I asked. It was a large branch, set at a steep angle.

"Rocco needs help, and I'm the only one small enough to climb this."

It wobbled, even under Faraday's slight weight. "This is dangerous."

"We don't have any other choices."

"You are so brave," said Gracie, fluttering her eyes at him.

Jackson coughed. "I would have done it, too. If I were a few years younger."

"You would have broken the branch," said Gracie, rolling her eyes.

"Hey. Stop fat-shaming me—"

"Shhh," said Gracie. "Faraday is almost there. Be quiet, so you don't distract him. If he falls, he could get hurt."

She was right. We watched in tense silence as Faraday slowly crawled up the branch. "Okay, Rocco. You can do this. Follow the sound of my voice. Ease your way down one step at a time."

"I can't."

"You can, and you will."

Faraday had a lot of authority for a dog roughly the size

of my head. He was small but mighty, and, to our surprise and relief, Rocco listened to him.

"Okay. I'm coming. Don't leave me."

"Never. I'm here for you."

Rocco slipped and let out a loud meow. For a second, he dangled by a single paw. I rushed to stand under the tree, hoping to catch him somehow if he fell, but he didn't. He managed to right himself, but now he looked even more terrified.

"That was the hardest part," said Faraday. "You did it. You're almost there."

Rocco took a deep breath. "Okay. I can do this."

When Rocco reached the branch I'd set by the tree, I let out a sigh of relief, but we weren't out of the woods quite yet. I couldn't tell if the branch would support both Rocco and Faraday, so I stood underneath and used my back to hold it in place.

"You come down first, Faraday," I said, worried about him.

"Sure," he said, turning around and prancing down the branch like it was nothing.

Rocco took much longer. "I hate this," he said, edging his way slowly down. "I hate being outside. I hate trees. I hate snow. I hate cold weather. I hate everything. I hate you, Capone."

"I know. Keep moving, kitty."

To my surprise, he listened to me.

Note to self: Perhaps I have more authority than I realized.

He made it to where I stood, holding up the branch, then slid off, falling onto my head, and rolling down into the snow. He lay there a moment on his back, dazed and breathing hard as he stared at the sky.

"I almost died," he said.

"It's a good thing you have nine lives," said Jackson, with a throaty chuckle. "You're down to eight now."

"Seven," I said. "Don't forget the fire."

We nodded in agreement. Rocco continued to stare at the sky. "Six. Capone once made me walk on a branch over a raging river to get someone's purse."

I rolled my eyes. "That's not exactly what happened. The purse had evidence in it that someone had stolen things from Ms. Josie's shop. And I didn't make you walk on the branch. You volunteered."

"Not how I remember it," he said, slowly rolling over and getting to his feet. He shook the snow out of his long, gray fur and shivered. "Let's see what's wrong with Luke. I want to go home as soon as possible. I've had enough. I'm an indoor cat for a reason."

We made it to Luke's shelter, but it was slow going. The snow seemed much deeper here, and I had to dig my way through at some points. The little dogs were useless, too small to help, so it was up to me. When we finally made it to the hole Luke had jumped into, I stared at it in shock.

"Is this a cave?" I asked. "I've never been in a cave before, but I saw one on—"

"PBS," said Gracie. "We know, Capone. Now move out of the way so we can all get inside. I want to make sure Luke is okay."

The space was small, but we fit, and it felt surprisingly cozy. Although not a true cave-like the ones I saw on PBS, the area provided excellent shelter. Located under a large rock that jutted out from the hillside, I couldn't see a single stalagmite or stalactite, but Luke sat in the corner, staring at us with big eyes.

"I can't believe you guys came for me."

I licked his head. "Of course, we came for you. You're family. But why are you here? Why did you run away?"

He whimpered. "Something awful happened. My human was in trouble. He told me to run, but I should have stayed. I should have helped him." He lowered his head. "I'm the worst dog."

Oh, calamity. This might be more serious than I anticipated.

"What kind of trouble?" asked Jackson.

Luke began to shake so badly he couldn't speak. Gracie shot him a worried look. "It's okay," she said. "You did the right thing. We'll figure it out."

I had no idea what may have happened to make Luke so frightened, but I didn't want to make him more upset by asking about it. "Gracie is correct. You did the right thing, Luke. You listened to your master. But where is Mr. Ben now?" I asked, snuggling close to the shivering doggie.

"I have no idea," he said, his voice sad. "I'm afraid something terrible must have happened to him."

We sat a long moment in silence, absorbing this information. "We won't help him by hanging out here," said Faraday. "Although I am impressed. This is a lovely shelter. How did you find it?"

"I got lucky," said Luke. "When I ran away, I went down to the river to get a drink. You can't see this space from above, but I noticed it from below. I'm glad I did. Last night it got pretty cold. Have you ever known the pleasure and triumph of a lucky guess?'

I blinked at him in surprise. "You just quoted—"

"*Emma*," said Luke with a smile. "My human made me watch it. He knows Anne likes it, and he wants to please her. I thought about it as I tried to stay warm and found it oddly soothing. There is something reassuring about Austen. It's so un-scary. So safe."

"You poor thing," said Gracie, moving close to him. Rocco did, too. They were both the furriest, so they sandwiched him in a fuzzy blanket. It reminded me of another time we'd sheltered all together outside. We'd been running away from evil people and saving Ms. Josie's business, so I'd been terrified.

I'd been quite different then. So small. Now I weighed twice as much and was also twice as bright and brave. But since we'd found Luke, today hadn't been anywhere near as scary. Our home was up the hill, but we had to convince Luke to come back with us. But how?

Curse my lack of preparation. I should have thought of this ahead of time.

I needn't have worried. A few seconds later, I heard the sweetest sound in the world. Ms. Anne, calling my name.

"Capone. Where are you?"

I popped my head out of the cave and saw Ms. Anne approaching. She had on boots and a puffy coat, and she seemed to be following the path I'd plowed through the snow. When she caught sight of me, relief washed over her face.

"Oh, puppy. What are you doing? Are your friends with you? Gracie and Faraday and Jackson and Rocco?"

I let out a happy bark. All would be well now.

"She didn't mention me," said Luke, sinking back further into the cave. "She must think I'm disobedient. She doesn't want me to come back."

"Dude, she has no idea you're here," said Jackson, giving Luke an incredulous shake of his head. "Of course, she wants you to come back. I guarantee it. She's been worried sick about you and your human."

"She has?"

Jackson nodded. "She cried all night. It got ugly. It's going to make her day when she sees you."

"Jackson is right," I said. "And there is no way any of us are leaving you behind."

Ms. Anne had several leashes in her hand. I kept barking until she got close enough to peek inside Luke's humble abode. When she did, her pretty green eyes widened in surprise.

"What are all of you doing here?" When she spotted Luke, she gasped. "Luke? Sweetheart? What happened? Oh, baby. Were you out here all night?"

We bounded out of the cave, climbing on Ms. Anne's lap to lick her and love her. In my enthusiasm, I knocked her over. I couldn't help it. But she got up right away and climbed partially into the cave to get Luke. He still cowered in the corner.

"Come on, Luke. Don't be scared. Everything is going to be alright. I've got you now." She reached for him, and he gave her hand a tentative lick. "Good boy," she said, patting his head. "Let's go home, okay?"

With a bit more encouragement, she managed to get him out of the cave. As soon as he was clear, she pulled him into her arms and held him close while kneeling in the snow.

"Thank goodness you're okay." She gazed at all of us in amazement. "How did you plan this? How did you know Luke was out here?" She kissed the top of Luke's head, realization dawning in her eyes. "And where is Ben?"

Attaching one leash to Luke's collar and another to mine, Ms. Anne scooped up Faraday. Unzipping her jacket, she stuck him in the pocket of her hoodie.

"Ooooh. I like it in here," said Faraday, his voice

muffled. "I'm like a baby kangaroo. This might be my new favorite spot."

Once Faraday was secured, Ms. Anne picked up Rocco and cradled him in one arm. He put his paws on her shoulder and nuzzled her neck, and she smiled. "This is no place for kitty cats," she said, rubbing her nose in his thick fur.

He purred. "You're right. Take me home, human woman. I need to dry off. I'm soggy and miserable and cold, and I'm never going outside again."

She laughed. Although she did not speak Cat, she understood that he was complaining. "Yes. We'll get you home, and you can sit in front of the fire all day long. I'll give you catnip. You've earned it, buddy."

We trudged back up the hill slowly. Going up proved much more challenging than going down. We followed the path I'd created, though, making things a bit easier. Once we reached River Road, we were all breathing hard.

Luke was a wreck—skittish and nervous. He jumped at the sound of a passing car, barked at a woman out for a run, snarled at a man shoveling snow, and even growled at Viking Val and Molly. They stood on their front porch and waved as we walked by.

"Out for a walk?" asked Viking Val.

"Not exactly," said Ms. Anne, struggling to control all of us. Jackson and Gracie trotted along nicely off-leash, but Luke and I hauled her to the house like a pair of oxen.

Viking Val stepped down from his porch. "You've got your hands full. Can I help?"

Luke increased his growling and pulling. Ms. Anne eyed the brown dog curiously. "No. We're fine. We need to warm up. Thanks, though."

"Why are you growling at everyone, Luke?" I asked.

"He's growling because he's scared," said Faraday, his voice sounding strange since he remained inside Ms. Anne's pocket. "It's a trauma thing. Trust me. I've been there myself."

When we got inside, Ms. Anne made a fire. She wrapped us in blankets, fed Luke, and brought treats for all of us. She also came through with the catnip for Rocco, and he was high as a kite in minutes.

"Whoa. Is the room spinning, or is it just me?" he asked, falling onto his side. Rocco had a low tolerance for catnip. It was kind of embarrassing.

The workers were upstairs, finishing the bathrooms. When Contractor Carl came downstairs, he smiled at us.

"This seems cozy. And there's Lucky Luke."

Luke snarled at him, a low growl, as I tried to reassure him. "Don't be scared," I said. "You're safe now."

But Luke kept his eyes on Contractor Carl. The burly construction manager frowned at him. "Calm down, buddy. I'm not going to hurt you."

"He's had a long day," said Ms. Anne, sitting next to Luke and gathering him close. "Can I help you with something?"

He scratched his head. "I hope you can. I've been calling Ben since yesterday. I can't find his notes for today, my toolbox went missing, and three of the guys got food poisoning. It's one thing after another. Do you have any idea where he is?"

"I'm not sure," said Ms. Anne. "I've been calling him, too."

"You haven't heard from him either?" asked Contractor Carl. His normally cheery face turned somber. "Oh, my. That's not good." When he saw the stricken expression on

Ms. Anne's face, he backtracked. "I mean, I'm sure he's fine. I bet his battery died on his phone or something. He'll call soon."

Ms. Anne nodded, unconvinced. Contractor Carl cleared his throat. "Despite everything, we're almost done with the bathrooms. This floor is done, too. The only thing we have left to do is the drywall, but we can't start that until the supplies get here. I'm guessing it'll be next week. But at least we'll be out of your way soon," he said, giving her a smile that didn't quite reach his eyes. He seemed worried. I didn't blame him.

Contractor Carl returned to work, his heavy boots clunking on the steps. Ms. Anne sat for a moment deep in thought, staring into the fire. When her phone rang, she jumped and nearly dropped it in her haste to answer it. She had it on speaker.

"Ben?" she asked.

"No, it's Josie." I barked at my lovely human's voice, and she laughed. "And I can hear Capone is there. Hi, puppy."

"How are you?" asked Ms. Anne.

"We're fine. Nate is doing much better. We'll be home Friday. Can you handle my crazy dog for another 48 hours?"

"Definitely."

Ms. Josie must have heard something in Ms. Anne's voice. "Is everything okay?"

"No," she said, her voice unsteady. "It isn't."

She explained what had been going on, and Ms. Josie listened. "Oh, Anne. I'm sorry."

Ms. Anne wiped away a tear that trickled down her cheek. "I'm so worried about him. I thought he left me again, but now I'm not so sure."

"He didn't leave," said Ms. Josie, her voice firm. "First of all, Ben loves you. He always has, and he always will. Secondly, he is in the middle of a construction project. He wouldn't do that. And thirdly, he would never leave Luke. No way. Something is wrong."

"What should I do?"

I heard Mr. Nate's voice in the background. "Nate said there is a spare key to the carriage house under the mat by the back door. Why don't you go and have a quick look? Maybe he has the flu or something. That would explain a lot."

"Okay. I'll call you back."

Ms. Anne rushed out the back door and grabbed the key from under the mat. We followed her, barking excitedly, but our excitement turned to dismay when we got inside the carriage house. Mr. Ben wasn't there.

"Ben?" Ms. Anne called out his name, glancing around. She searched his room, more puzzled than ever, and gasped in surprise when she saw Mr. Ben's wallet and keys lying on the table by the door.

"He wouldn't have left without these," she said. "And Val said he drove away in his truck. He must have come back."

We stepped outside, and Ms. Anne clicked the unlock button for Mr. Ben's truck. We heard a beeping noise, and when we followed the sound, it led us to the backside of the carriage house. Mr. Ben's truck was there, covered with snow.

"This is getting stranger by the minute," she said, taking her phone out of her pocket. She called Ms. Josie and told her what happened. "And it seems like he hasn't moved his truck since we got all that snow last weekend. Which makes no sense at all."

Ms. Josie had a hushed conversation with Mr. Nate. "Listen, Annie. We're jumping on an earlier flight. We'll be home as soon as possible, but you need to call the police. Now. Something is wrong. I think Ben is in trouble."

Ms. Anne sniffled, pushing her hair out of her eyes. "So do I, Josie. So do I."

THIRTY-TWO

How to tell if someone is your friend:

1. They've got your back. Always.
2. They comfort you when you're sad.
3. They give you treats.
4. They tell you the truth, even when you don't want to hear it.
5. They keep your secrets.

As soon as Ms. Anne hung up with Ms. Josie, she called Policeman Pat. He promised he'd be over soon. Five minutes later, we heard a knock on our door.

"That was quick," said Ms. Anne, but it wasn't Policeman Pat. Reporter Rob, the hunky journalist, stood in the doorway. Ms. Anne seemed surprised to see him. "Hi, Rob. What's up?"

"I came to talk to Ben about letting me interview him for the paper." Reporter Rob studied Ms. Anne's face, his eyes concerned. "Is everything okay?"

"No," she said, bursting into tears.

Reporter Rob pulled her into a hug. He led her inside to the sofa, plopped her down on it, and kneeled in front of her. "What is it? What's going on?"

"It's Ben. He's missing. I'm not sure what to do." She explained the situation to him, telling him about Luke. "I called Pat—"

Reporter Rob frowned. "Pat?"

"He's a policeman. I thought he could help."

Reporter Rob sat on the couch next to her with a sigh. "Annie. We need to talk, and we'd better do it quickly. Is Pat on his way over here right now?"

"Yes." She frowned at him in confusion. "Why do you ask?"

Reporter Rob blew out a breath. "Ben could be in danger. I wanted to talk with him about it today. It's one of the reasons I came." He turned to face Ms. Anne, his expression grave. "Now, listen. I'm going to take a few educated guesses. You don't have to say anything, but if you could tell me if I'm right or wrong, it might help us find Ben."

"Okay," she said. Her voice sounded unsteady, but she straightened her shoulders and wiped her tears away with an irritated swipe of her hand.

"I believe Ben disappeared all those years ago because he saw something—something terrible. And I believe it involved his stepfather, Sam Goodman."

Ms. Anne gave him a tentative nod. Reporter Rob continued.

"I also uncovered some evidence to indicate Ben must have been in witness protection all this time. Is that also correct?" Ms. Anne nodded again. "And the reason he got out of witness protection was because Sam died in jail."

"Yes, but how did you find out all of this?"

He tapped the side of his head. "Brains as well as beauty, my dear."

She let out a laugh, but I thought Reporter Rob made an excellent point. Gracie agreed. "He's so smart and funny and hot," she said, her expression dreamy. "If I were human, I would do him."

"Hey," said Jackson. "What's that supposed to mean?"

She hushed him. "Be quiet, Jackson. I'm not a human, so it's irrelevant. I want to hear what he's going to say next."

Reporter Rob spoke again, "And that brings me to my next point. Sam Goodman. Sam was a dangerous and ruthless guy, but he didn't work alone. He had people on the outside running his businesses, legal and otherwise, while he was locked up. And he had family out here, too. Including his nephew."

Ms. Anne slapped a hand over her mouth. "Pat is Sam's nephew. I totally forgot."

"They were close, Annie. Pat lost his father when he was small, and Sam treated him like a son."

"He treated Ben like a son, too."

"And Pat didn't like that much. He has always been jealous of Ben for so many reasons. When Sam went to jail, Pat was furious. He called it a setup, and he may have suspected Ben's involvement. Sam must have known, too. But there is something interesting that Ben might not realize."

"What?"

"Sam died a wealthy man, but he never updated his will. It was the same one he'd written when he married Ben's mom years ago. In it, he left everything he had to her. But in the event of Ben's mother's death, it would all go to Ben."

"Oh, my. Where did you hear that?"

"I have my sources," he said. "And those sources told me something else. If Ben dies, do you know who stands to inherit Sam's millions?"

She gasped, realization dawning on her face. "Pat."

Oh, calamity. Had Policeman Pat possibly put us in peril?

"Yes. Well, Pat and his cousins. He has two of them. They're the children of Sam's youngest brother," he said. "But even splitting it three ways...it's a lot of money. People have grown desperate over far less."

A knock sounded at the door. Policeman Pat stood on the porch, and he wasn't in uniform. As he peeked through the glass of the door, he must have seen Reporter Rob on the couch with Ms. Anne because he shook his head as if annoyed. We started barking like crazy, but Ms. Anne didn't move.

"What should I do?" she asked.

"Let him in," said Reporter Rob, pulling out his cell phone. "I'll call my friend. He's a federal agent. This is tricky since Pat is a cop. I'll go out back. Keep him in here."

"Okay," said Ms. Anne, her jaw set in a determined line.

"And Annie...?"

"Yes?"

"Be careful, okay?"

"I will."

Reporter Rob left through the kitchen. Ms. Anne opened the door to Policeman Pat.

"Hey, Annie. What's up?"

"I'm not sure. Ben's not responding to my texts. I'm probably overreacting."

Policeman Pat leaned against the door frame, his pale

eyes as cold as ice. Or at least they seemed that way to me. Jackson agreed.

"He has eyes like a husky," said Jackson. "Never trust a husky."

With Policeman Pat's dark hair and light eyes, he did remind me of a husky, but I didn't understand Jackson's advice. "Why shouldn't we trust a husky?"

"Because of their freaky eyes," said Jackson.

"That's rich, coming from a Pug," said Gracie with a laugh.

"And what do you mean by that?" asked Jackson, his Puggy eyes buggier than usual.

Luke snorted. "Have you ever glimpsed your reflection in a mirror, dude? Pugs have crazy eyes. Everyone says so."

Faraday agreed. "That is true. I have heard the same. But can we quit discussing the physical attributes of other dogs and focus on what the humans are doing? It's important."

Policeman Pat glanced over Ms. Anne's shoulder. "What's Rob doing here?"

"He came to see Ben, but Ben isn't here. Obviously."

"Why did he leave as soon as I arrived?"

She folded her arms over her chest. "He got a call from work and had to take it."

"I didn't hear the phone ring."

"It was on vibrate."

Policeman Pat studied her face. "I've known you since you were a girl, Annie Weston. I can tell when you're lying."

"Why would I lie, Pat?"

"I have no idea, but I'm going to find out. And I'm going to find Ben, too. Because Nate Murray called the police about five minutes after you called me, and he reported Ben missing."

Jackson groaned. "There goes my human. Why does he always have to be so helpful?"

Mr. Nate was helpful. But now, Ms. Anne faced a dilemma. She stood there, obviously weighing her options. Policeman Pat rolled his eyes.

"I'm here to help, Annie. Why don't you let me, and we'll find him together?"

"I don't need your help—"

"Yes, you do." Policeman Pat held up his phone. On it was a map with a red dot. I couldn't read maps, so I had no idea what it meant, but Ms. Anne seemed interested. "I tracked Ben's phone. Let's figure out where it's located."

Reporter Rob appeared in the doorway to the kitchen. He gave Ms. Anne an encouraging nod. "Hi, Pat. That sounds like a great plan."

"Fine," said Ms. Anne. "Come inside and we'll look for it."

"The phone isn't inside," said Policeman Pat. He pointed to the side of the house. "It's pinging from over there."

"I'll grab my coat," said Ms. Anne. When Policeman Pat stepped off the porch, she narrowed her eyes at Reporter Rob. "Are you sure this is wise?"

"My friend is running a check on him. He promised to contact me as soon as he hears anything. Let's keep him close, but be on your guard, okay? If he knows where Ben is, we need to figure it out as soon as possible. The temperature is going to drop again tonight."

He shivered, and Luke shivered, too. "What if my human is outside alone and cold?" He let out a howl. Reporter Rob leaned down to pet him.

"Don't worry, doggie. We'll figure this out. Leave it up to us."

"That's what they always say," muttered Rocco from his chair near the fireplace. "And yet it's always the cat who helps."

"Says who?" asked Jackson.

"Says everyone," said Rocco. "Have you never read a cozy mystery? It's always a cat."

He made a great point, but we didn't have time to discuss that now. We had a phone to find and a human to save—an extraordinary human. We had to save Ms. Anne's Mr. Knightley.

We followed Policeman Pat outside. It took a few minutes for him to realize the phone wasn't in our yard. "Where is it?" asked Ms. Anne.

"In your neighbor's yard," he said with a frown. "Although, I can't pinpoint it exactly. This shows its last location. Let's go over. Bring the dogs. Capone has the best nose, but Luke is most familiar with Ben's scent. Maybe one of them can sniff it out."

"I'll let Val know what we're doing," said Ms. Anne. She walked toward his front porch as he stepped outside with Molly.

"Hi," he said with a bright smile. "We're going on a walk. Want to come?"

"No, thanks. We're searching for Ben's cell phone. It might be in your yard. Do you mind if we look?"

Something odd passed over his face, a vague sense of annoyance. "Sure, but I have lots of flower beds in the yard, and you wouldn't be able to see them. Someone could trip and break something. I'll help."

I didn't know if he meant we could trip and break a bone or break something in his yard. I had a feeling it might be the second one. Ms. Anne seemed to get that feeling, too. She narrowed her eyes at him.

"We don't want to bother you."

He shot a glance at his watch. "No bother," he said with a smile, but the smile didn't quite reach his eyes.

They headed to the side of the house, being careful to avoid Viking Val's invisible flower beds. "Wow. Is your owner anal or something?" asked Jackson. "He's protective of his flower beds. I have the cure for that."

He squatted to take a poo. "Jackson," said Gracie. "Mind your manners."

"Hey, when you've got to go, you've got to go. Am I right, Capone?"

Suddenly, I had to go, too, but I decided to hold it until we got back to our yard. Jackson's poo looked so tiny it almost seemed cute. Mine was not.

Molly came up to me, and I gave her a lick in greeting. She licked me back but seemed preoccupied.

"Is everything okay?" I asked.

"Yes," she said, but she sounded a bit unsure. She seemed worried, too. "Capone, can I talk with you a second?"

"Sure."

We hung back while the others headed closer to the hedge dividing our property from Viking Val's. "Something strange is going on here," she said. "My human is acting very oddly. Even worse than usual."

I eyed Viking Val. He didn't seem any different to me. "What do you mean? Is he usually odd?" I asked. "Because I always thought he was a stand-up guy, and he makes awesomely buttery garlic bread."

As if on cue, my stomach growled. Loudly.

Curse my obsession with all things buttery and delicious.

Molly smiled. "He's a talented cook, and he's always been a great master, but..." She paused. "You're going to think I've gone crazy in my old age."

"You're not old, Molly."

She laughed. "Ah, but yes, I am, Capone. And that's why I hesitated to say anything to you. If anything happened to my person, what would happen to me? I could end up in the shelter. Or worse. No one wants a twelve-year-old Labrador with arthritis in her hips and bad eyesight."

"You have bad eyesight?"

"I do, but I didn't bring it up because I want your pity. I need to explain why I've done what I've done."

Her words chilled my heart. "What have you done, Molly?"

"I guess it's not so much what I've done. It's what I didn't do. I should have been more honest with you, but I was terrified. I was selfish. I see that now, which is why I need to tell you the truth." She glanced over her shoulder at Viking Val. "My human isn't right in the head. I don't understand half of what he says when he talks to me, but I can tell he's not in a happy place. He has a problem with obsessive behavior, as you probably guessed."

"The flower beds were a clue."

"Yes," she said with a smile. "He has to keep everything in its place, too, but now the problem is bigger."

"What is it?"

"My owner is up to something. I hate to say this, but I have to because it involves you."

"It involves me?"

"Not you personally," she said. "It's about your—"

"Capone. Come here," said Ms. Anne.

I wanted to hear what Molly had to say, but I could not ignore Ms. Anne. If she needed me, I had to help. "Give me a second," I said to Molly, then hustled to Ms. Anne.

She grabbed my face in her mittened hands and stared into my eyes. "We need to find Ben's phone. Can you help us, boy?"

Could I help her? Of course, I could. It would be my honor. I couldn't say that, though, so I wagged my tail instead. I swished it so hard that my body ended up wagging, too.

"At least he's enthusiastic," said Reporter Rob with a laugh.

"But will he have any clue what you're asking him to do?" asked Policeman Pat raising one eyebrow skeptically.

I barked at Policeman Pat. How dare he doubt my sniffer?

He held up both his hands. "Fine. I apologize. Get to work, doggie."

I set to work, searching through the snow with gusto. When I caught what I thought might be a whiff of Mr. Ben, I dove in.

"Don't let him dig up my flower beds...oh, geesh."

The warning came too late. I may have taken out one of Viking Val's prize rosebushes in my enthusiasm.

Why did it always have to be rosebushes? When I'd had to locate missing inventory in the backyard of Bartleby's Books, those had been hidden beneath roses. And now Mr. Ben's phone? It rested right in Viking Val's rose bed.

Note to self: Roses suck.

Luckily, I didn't get pricked by any thorns. And although the snow was deep, I found the phone and managed to pull it out. Ms. Anne seemed impressed. She gave me a big hug. Policeman Pat and Reporter Rob seemed impressed, too. They didn't hug me, but they did pat me on the head.

The only person who didn't act impressed? Viking Val.

"Capone. You are a menace. This rose came from a clipping from my grandmother Betty," he said, pulling up bits of the decimated rose bush with his gloved hand. He let out a sigh. "But I have others, and at least you found the phone. Great job, puppy."

I wagged my tail. I was proud of myself.

As Viking Val saw to what remained of his roses, the rest of us walked back to the house. "This is great," said Ms. Anne, holding the phone in her hands. "But how does it help us find Ben?"

Policeman Pat took it from her. "It may or it may not. Worst case, we'll know who he called last and if he got any text messages or not. Best case, it could give us some clues about what's going on here. Let's charge it and see."

THIRTY-THREE

What to do if someone goes missing:

1. Make sure they're actually missing and not just incommunicado.
2. Contact the police.
3. Hire a private investigator.
4. Get in touch with the media.
5. Enlist the aid of a doggo with an exceptional sniffer.

We went back into the house, and Ms. Anne quickly plugged Mr. Ben's phone into a wall charger near the door. "Hopefully, this will work," she said. She sat on a chair next to the phone, watching it and waiting for some sign of life. When a red battery mark appeared, she squealed. "It's charging. We should find out something soon."

The other humans were careful to wipe their feet on the mat by the front door as they came inside to wait with her. The new floors gleamed. The light fixtures sparkled. What had been a ruin was turning into a beautiful home. Viking

Val frowned, however. He didn't seem as impressed as the others with the transformation.

"Oh, no. The original hardware is gone from the front door. It was beautiful. It had the letter 'B' on it and the Boussard family crest."

"The crest?" asked Ms. Anne, her eyes still on the phone.

"A thistle and a Labrador."

"Like the one carved into the fireplace mantle?" she asked.

"Exactly. The Boussards were originally Canadian. They came from the Labrador region."

"Wait. That's a place?" I asked. "That's so cool."

Curse my lack of knowledge about Canadian geography. And Canadians. And also, geography.

"And you're on their crest," said Jackson, nudging me. "That's the one that looks like you, Capone. It's almost like a sign."

A shiver went over me. "You're right. Freaky."

Viking Val shook his head sadly, mourning the loss of the hardware. "I'd better go. Best of luck today. I hope you have news soon."

He left, and we watched him go. Contractor Carl must have overheard Viking Val's comment about the hardware. He gave a disgusted shake of his head.

"That guy doesn't have any idea what he's talking about. The hardware on that door was rusted all the way through and falling apart. What we installed is a reproduction, but it's period appropriate."

"It seems fine to me," said Ms. Anne.

"Ben understands restorations. He learned from the best. You don't want rusted-out hardware on any exterior door, especially the front door. It's a safety issue. And since things have been disappearing from this place on an almost hourly basis at this point, I'd say safety measures are necessary."

"Did you file a report?" asked Policeman Pat.

Contractor Carl sighed. "Not yet, Paddy. At first, I thought maybe it was my imagination or that things had been misplaced in the confusion. We had many people coming in and going out the last few days. But now the permits are gone. I'd planned to put them on the window once we finished with the hardware. They were right on this table. I swear I only left them there a few minutes when I went upstairs to help with the sink installation. I came back, and they were gone. If I didn't know any better, I'd say this place was haunted." Contractor Carl let out a laugh, but it died in his throat when the people in the room didn't laugh with him. "What? Are you telling me this place *is* haunted?"

Ms. Anne bit her lip. "That is the rumor," she said. "Not that I believe in that sort of thing personally, but there have been some strange things going on here. I will say that much."

"What kinds of strange things?" asked Reporter Rob.

"Ben had some things go missing, too. And we're pretty sure someone messed with his ladder. Thank goodness he used it in the house. If he'd been outside and higher up, he could have been hurt."

"And have your guys seen anything weird?" asked Reporter Rob, directing his question to Contractor Carl.

"We've only been here a couple of days, but this place is weird. We've heard some strange noises, like the sound of doors closing when there was no one else in the house. Oh, and we keep finding open windows. I've closed that window in the basement three times already. I got a lock to put on it, but guess what?"

"The lock went missing?" asked Reporter Rob.

"Bingo."

Ms. Anne frowned. "The window was open the other night. It woke Ben up."

"Yeah, the window wasn't installed properly, and it's old, like everything else in this place. We have a new one on order, but it's a special size, so it'll be ages before we get it." He shook his head. "And at this rate, it'll be months before we finish here. Haunted or not, I need to find those permits, or I'll have to stop construction."

"Are you planning to file a report on the missing items?" asked Policeman Pat.

Contractor Carl scratched his beard. "I wanted to wait until Ben comes back. Speaking of which, have you heard from him?"

Ms. Anne shook her head. "No, but we did find his cell phone, though." She pointed to the phone charging next to her. "It was in Val's yard."

"Why would it be over there?" asked Contractor Carl.

"And why did Val tell you he saw Ben drive away when Ben's truck hasn't been moved since last Friday?" asked Reporter Rob.

"Good questions," said Ms. Anne. She jumped when Mr. Ben's phone lit up. "It's working."

Contractor Carl leaned over, nearly spilling his drink on it. "What are you doing?" asked Policeman Pat with a frown.

Contractor Carl backed up a step. "Sorry. I hoped there might be a message for me on there."

"We don't know anything yet. Be patient."

"You're right. I'd better get back to work. We're already behind as it is. Good luck, you guys."

Contractor Carl left, and Policeman Pat turned to Ms. Anne. He held out his hand for the phone. "Let me see it."

Ms. Anne clutched it to her chest, eyes wide. "No."

He frowned at her. "What's the matter, Annie? You've been acting weird since I got here."

"It's because—"

Reporter Rob interrupted. "It's because we need to get this phone to the police station as soon as we can and file a missing person's report."

"Yes," Ms. Anne said, nodding her head vigorously. "We need to file a missing person's report. Now."

Policeman Pat sighed. "Fine but remember what I said." He paused. "I know when you're lying to me, Annie."

She lifted her chin in the air. "And I know when you're lying to me, Pat."

POLICEMAN PAT, Reporter Rob, Ms. Anne, and I met at the police station. Located on the main street of Beaver, it was right between the waffle shop and Grandpa Joe's Candy Shop, both great establishments.

Ms. Anne decided that although she could leave the other dogs and Rocco at home, I "could not be trusted." Her words, not mine. Which was how I ended up in the police station for the first time in my young life.

"Al Capone here in the flesh!" said Officer Stahl. He and I went way back. I wagged my tail at him.

It seemed ironic that a dog named Al Capone would be in the police station. Maybe I had more in common with my namesake than I realized. I mean, we both loved Italian food, we had weak impulse control, and we made unfortunate decisions. The difference was I felt guilty about my choices. Al Capone most likely had not.

As those thoughts swirled around in my head, the humans discussed the phone and how best to handle it. Ms. Anne sat at Officer Stahl's desk and filled out paperwork for a missing person's report. Her face looked pale but determined. She seemed better now that she was proactively doing something to find Mr. Ben, although she still acted worried sick about him.

Policeman Pat came up to the desk with Reporter Rob as Officer Stahl opened his laptop. "First, we're going to check Ben's calls and texts."

"There will be a lot from me on there," said Ms. Anne with a wry smile. "And Carl."

"The contractor?" asked Officer Stahl.

"Yes, he's been having issues with the renovation," said Policeman Pat. "He thinks someone may be sabotaging the project."

Reporter Rob jotted something on his notepad. "Carl said that?"

Policeman Pat shook his head. "I inferred it from our conversation."

Officer Stahl nodded. "Carl is not the type to misplace anything as important as a building permit. And he needs it for the garage next to the carriage house that Josie and Nate are building in the back."

"I forgot they were building a garage," said Ms. Anne.

"I only know that because Nate asked me some questions about property lines," said Officer Stahl. "They'll have to dig up part of the backyard to wire it for electricity and to install plumbing, but he wanted to have heat and a doggie bathing area in the garage, too. I'm guessing that's for you, Capone." He patted me on the head.

Heat sounded enjoyable, but a doggie bathing area? No, thank you. Then again, it might be necessary. Ms. Josie and I had been banned from the local pet salon.

I sighed at the memory. The groomer, located inside one of those big, chain pet supply shops, didn't accept appointments. It ended up being kind of a crapshoot. You might be the only dog getting groomed, or you might be in a tiny, noisy, room with, say, three Shih Tzus, a white, fluffy Poodle with bladder control issues, an elderly Golden Retriever who was blind and possibly senile, and a mixed breed so scared he vibrated.

That's what happened to me—the perfect storm.

The Shih Tzus were bass poles. Let's get that straight right now. And the Poodle seemed neurotic. The mixed breed shivered so badly the grooming table shook. Throw me into the mix, and things got ugly quickly.

I barked up a storm. Ms. Josie had brought me in only to put me on the waiting list. She planned to take me right back out. But the groomers, who looked very busy, ignored her when she came in. The ignoring was definitely on purpose because (as I said) I barked my head off. Also, Ms. Josie partially sat on me to keep me from bothering the Shih Tzus. It's hard to ignore a woman in a skirt straddling a giant, hyperactive, barking puppy.

I suspected they were irritated because I'd already made all the other dogs upset, as was my custom. The dogs had all been pretty quiet and calm until I entered that room. I caused a bit of a kerfuffle. I tended to do that. It was my thing. Mostly because my energy levels were off the chart, and the other dogs sensed it.

As soon as I barked, the Shih Tzus barked. The old,

blind Golden Retriever howled. The shivery dog tried to jump off the table, and the Poodle peed. This happened all at once. And I chose that moment to attempt to steal a bottle of organic mango doggie shampoo from the shelf inside the grooming area.

Not my proudest moment. I had no idea why I did it, but the theft was what finally got the groomer's attention.

"You'll have to buy that," she said over the noise. "He made teeth marks in it."

"No problem," said Ms. Josie, yanking the shampoo out of my mouth. "I want to get him groomed. When can you squeeze him in?"

She refused to meet Ms. Josie's gaze. "We can't. We're booked."

As Ms. Josie struggled to keep me from eating the shampoo, she heard the groomer's comment and blinked in surprise. "But I thought your sign said walk-ins only. Should I wait?"

Grumpy Groomer shook her head. "Nope. You should go. Now."

Oh, calamity. Public humiliation at the doggie salon.

And so, we went. I felt sorry for Ms. Josie. It hurt her feelings, and because of the punctures, the shampoo leaked all over the floor of her car. But, I mean, a car smelling like mangoes is not the worst thing in the world, right?

Note to self: Mango shampoo does not taste like mangos. Fun fact.

"I am never shopping there again," said Ms. Josie, with tears in her eyes. Not from sadness. Oh, no. She cried due to anger and shame. And also, because now she had to figure out where to get my grooming done.

We ended up calling a place Ms. Anne recommended called Soggy Doggy in Beaver. It was the perfect spot. A nice woman named Mistress Missy got me in right away, and she was awesome. She loved me and she was so kind and gentle. She said I was a good dog, took my picture, and she even gave me cookies.

Cookies. It was the best day ever.

I left smelling like roses (not fake mangoes), so it ended on a good note. And the moral of this story is...hmmm. I didn't know the moral of the story. Stay away from grumpy groomers? Don't shoplift? Shih Tzus are cute, little instigators of chaos? Mr. Knightley would never have found himself in a situation like that. But it did explain Ms. Josie's desire for a doggie bathing area in her new home.

But Ms. Anne wasn't concerned about doggie bathing areas at the moment. She worried about one thing only. Mr. Ben.

"What do we do now?" she asked Officer Stahl and Policeman Pat.

Officer Stahl scratched his chin. "We'll print out a list of his texts and calls and go over it carefully, but for now, let's see where he went on the day he disappeared."

He pulled up a map of Beaver on his laptop and attached Mr. Ben's phone to it using a cable. Then he entered something onto his computer and waited. It took only a few minutes, but they all leaned closer to see when the process finished. I wiggled in and put my paws on Officer Stahl's lap. I wanted to see, too. He patted my head.

"The last location," said Officer Stahl, pointing to a red dot on the screen. "I assume this was where you found the phone?"

Ms. Anne nodded. "Yes. In my next-door neighbor's yard."

"And this?" asked Officer Stahl, pointing to another dot.

"The carriage house."

"And this?" he asked, pointing to a dot a few blocks away from our address.

Ms. Anne frowned. "No idea."

He squinted at the screen. "It's 120 Bank Street," said Officer Stahl, with a frown. "Isn't that your mom's house, Pat? Where you're living right now?"

"It is," said Policeman Pat. "Ben came to my house?"

"It sure looks like it. The question is, why was Ben there the morning he disappeared?" asked Officer Stahl. "And why didn't you know about it?"

THIRTY-FOUR

What not to say to a person who is dying:

1. I understand how you feel.
2. Everything happens for a reason.
3. You'll be fine.
4. Did you kidnap the stepson of your late brother?

While Officer Stahl and Reporter Rob searched through the phone call log, Ms. Anne and Policeman Pat drove with me to 120 Bank Street. Pat's mom's house. They were silent the whole time. Ms. Anne's face was tight, and she had lines of worry around her eyes. When they pulled up in front of the pretty Dutch colonial with gray siding and white trim, Policeman Pat let out a sigh.

"I didn't realize he'd come to my house, Anne. Please believe me."

She opened the door of the car without glancing his way. "Let's see what your mom has to say."

We walked up the brick steps and into the quiet house.

There was an odd stillness here, and I sensed something I'd never experienced before. It was the deep, heavy quiet of a person living their last days.

"Don't be shocked when you see her," said Policeman Pat, keeping his voice low. "She's been sick for a while. She didn't let me know how bad it had gotten, or I would have come home much sooner."

Ms. Anne nodded and appeared to steel herself mentally as Policeman Pat led her to the back of the house. There was a lovely sunroom there, bathed in light, with views of the snowy backyard. In the sunroom sat a giant hospital bed with a tiny woman on it. She had her face turned toward the window and appeared to be sleeping. A nurse sat in a chair next to her bed. An IV dripped fluid down a tube, and the only sound in the room was the woman's slow, labored breathing.

I went straight to the bed and put my face on top of the crisp, white sheets to lick the woman's hand. She didn't have much time left on this earth.

Oh, calamity. I felt it as only a doggie could.

Ms. Anne seemed to sense it, too. When the old lady opened her eyes, Ms. Anne gave her a teary smile. "Hi, Mrs. Cavanaugh."

"Annie?" she asked, her voice soft. "Annie Weston?"

"That's me," said Ms. Anne, sitting in a chair next to her bed.

"It's so lovely to see you," said Mrs. Cavanaugh. She glanced down at me, and I realized she had the same blue eyes as Policeman Pat. I continued licking her hand, being ever so gentle, and she smiled. "And who is this?"

"This is Capone," said Ms. Anne.

"Oh, a mobster," said Mrs. Cavanaugh. "Like my brother."

Note to self: I needed to change my stupid name.

She laughed, and it soon morphed into coughing. The nurse got up to give her some water. After a few moments, she could speak again.

"Sorry. I shouldn't speak ill of the dead, but since I'm dying, I get a pass."

"Mom. Don't talk like that," said Policeman Pat, his voice full of emotion.

She sent him a sweet smile. "I'm sorry, dear, but it's true. And I'm okay with it. I've had a long life, and I've tried to be a decent person, so I'm not scared. Not really. Death comes to all of us, eventually. I told Ben that when he came to visit."

"Ben was here?" asked Policeman Pat.

She nodded. "I thought he died, so when I saw him standing in the middle of my room, I assumed I'd died, too. It gave me a start, but when Nurse Karen talked to him, I realized he was here and not a figment of my imagination. Silly me."

She laughed at the memory but didn't cough this time. I snuggled closer, putting my nose under her hand so she could pet me. She stroked my ears. "He's so soft. Like velvet. And so calm, too. What a charming puppy."

Ms. Anne and Policeman Pat exchanged a look, and Policeman Pat chuckled. "If you say so, Mom. But we need to ask you something important. Why was Ben here?"

She seemed confused. "He wanted to say goodbye, of course. The dear boy carried around so much guilt over what happened."

"Guilt over what?" asked Policeman Pat.

"Your uncle," she said. "Even though none of that was his fault. Sam made his own choices."

Policeman Pat nodded. "True."

"I loved him despite it all. Sam was a great brother, but his moral compass didn't always work correctly. I saw it, and I never deceived myself, but I chose to see the good in him along with the bad. I saw it in my other brothers, too. They were all kind to me, probably because I was the only girl. They doted on me, in fact."

Ms. Anne smiled. "How many brothers did you have?"

"Three, but there's only one left. My youngest brother. The baby of the family. He went into the same business as Sam." She sighed. "I loved them all, including Sam, but he did some vile things. I told Ben none of it was his fault. We had a lovely chat. I always liked that boy."

"Did he say anything else?" asked Ms. Anne.

Mrs. Cavanaugh nodded. "He told me about his life and his travels, and he told me about you, Annie. He shared how grateful he was for this second chance he'd been given to have a future with you. We don't all get a second chance to make things right. I told him that the last time I visited my brother, Sam had said the same. He wished he'd had a second chance. He says he would have done better. Been better. But who knows? We're all human in the end. He was flawed and imperfect. Unlike Labs. Labs are the real angels among us."

I licked her hand in gratitude. I officially loved Mrs. Cavanagh.

Ms. Anne laughed. "Capone might be an angel, but his halo is a bit crooked."

Mrs. Cavanaugh stared straight into my eyes, and it was like she saw my very soul. "All the best angels start out with crooked halos. Don't worry, puppy. You'll figure it out. You'll figure it all out. I promise."

WE LEFT the house in silence once again. My thoughts were full of Mrs. Cavanaugh's final words to me.

Curse my self-doubt. Would I figure this out? And, most importantly, could I do it in time?

The longer it took, the more danger it posed for Mr. Ben. I needed to get a move on.

This time Ms. Anne broke the silence. "I'm sorry, Pat," she said, practically blurting the words as we walked down the brick path toward the police car.

"For what?" he asked.

"For your mom. For everything."

He tilted his head and studied her face. "You thought I had something to do with Ben's disappearance, didn't you?" When her cheeks got red, Policeman Pat sighed. "I was still mad at him for disappearing all those years ago. Why would I make him disappear again when we just got him back?"

She bit her lip. "Because of your uncle and your inheritance."

We stood next to Policeman Pat's car. He opened the door to let us in and walked around to the driver's side to get in himself. I sat in the back, behind the partition in Policeman Pat's police mobile, a good place for a dog named Al Capone, but it didn't bother me so much this time. My head was too full of other things.

Policeman Pat's head must have been full, too. It wasn't until he started the engine and cranked up the heat that he spoke.

"I loved my uncle, but my mom is right. He did a lot of terrible things. I've worked hard to forgive him, mostly for my mom's sake, but it isn't always easy. Why do you think I became a cop, Annie? I wanted to make a difference, but I also wanted to break the cycle. My whole family was involved in this stuff at some point. Well, everyone except my mom." He shook his head sadly. "She always said the one thing a man can do is his duty if he is resolved to do it. I tried to follow her advice."

He'd just paraphrased a quote by Mr. Knightley. It was a sign, and it made me love Mrs. Cavanaugh even more. She must have been a Janeite, too.

I let out a bark of encouragement. It was a soft bark because I didn't want to hurt their ears in the confined space. Policeman Pat seemed to get it.

"Capone believes me."

"Pat, I believe you, too, but—"

He lifted a finger to stop Ms. Anne in mid-sentence. "I'm not quite done yet, Annie. You also asked about the inheritance. How would it look if a cop inherited money from a mobster—even a dead mobster? Uncle Sam had been a wealthy man, and he took care of my mom and me when my dad died. My dad worked for him, too. Did you know that?"

"I didn't."

"Yet another reason I became a cop. My dad died when he was my age during a botched robbery. My mom took the money from Uncle Sam, invested it wisely, and did everything she could to keep Ben and me away from that life. She thought of him as a second son, and I love my mom more than anything in this world. What would it have done to her if I hurt Ben? If you believe nothing else I said, do you at least understand that I would never do anything to cause my mother additional pain?"

He got choked up, and Ms. Anne put a hand on his arm. "I'm so sorry, Pat. I mean it. Please accept my apology."

With a nod, he swallowed hard. "Of course, I do. You're one of my oldest and dearest friends, and so is Ben, which is why this is so important. We need to find him."

"I agree."

"Good. Now that we've gotten that out of the way let's go back to the station. I want to see if they found anything in those phone records."

As we drove back to the station, my mind was in a jumble. It seemed like Policeman Pat told the truth, but humans were tricky creatures and skilled liars. Also, he had those strange, husky eyes. They still freaked me out.

Policeman Pat called Officer Stahl and told him about Ben visiting his mom. "We're on our way back. We'll be there in a few minutes. I wanted to warn you about something." He paused, and Ms. Anne eyed him curiously.

"What?" asked Officer Stahl.

Policeman Pat cracked a smile. "I have Al Capone in my squad car. Who'd have thought?"

I let out a whine, earning a giggle from Ms. Anne. It was beautiful to hear her laugh, even at my expense, but I saw the worry in her eyes. I felt worried, too.

I plopped down in the seat, wondering how many times the real Al Capone had ridden in a police car. It had likely been a lot of times. Was his heart ever as heavy as mine? Probably not. It seemed like there were two kinds of dangerous people—the sociopaths, like the ones I'd learned about on that PBS special, and those lacking a proper moral compass.

Sam Goodman had been a corrupt man, but he loved his family, and he seemed to have experienced guilt over what he'd done. But not every criminal was like that since some never felt anything at all. It was a lot to ponder.

We arrived at the station as the snow started to fall once again. I shivered. It got colder by the minute. If Mr. Ben stayed outside in this, he could quickly die from exposure.

That thought made me shiver, too. We didn't have

much time. I sensed it the same way I sensed it when someone was about to open a cheese wrapper. I may have been psychic.

Since time was of the essence, I ran up the steps to the police station at a full gallop, pulling Ms. Anne along with me. It was fortunate she didn't wear heels today.

"Whoa, Capone. Slow down," she said, but she didn't understand. We needed to figure this out now.

When we walked up to Officer Stahl's desk, he and Reporter Rob were listening to something. It sounded like muffled voices. I could make out Mr. Ben's voice, but not the other ones.

"Is that Ben?" asked Ms. Anne. She acted like she might be about to blubber again. I leaned against her as a means of comforting her. She seemed to appreciate it. She steadied herself and patted my head.

"It is," said Officer Stahl. "It seems like he recorded this before he went missing. It's muffled, though. I can't make out who is talking."

We listened carefully, and my chest tightened when I heard something the humans didn't seem to notice. They focused on the voices of the people talking, but I focused on something else entirely.

A single bark.

And it was my bosom buddy, Molly.

THIRTY-FIVE

A list of places known for animal hauntings:

1. The Whaley House Museum (San Diego, California). Thomas and Anna Whaley made the mistake of building their house on the spot where someone was hung only a few years earlier. Soon afterward, his ghost started appearing at their house, including that of the family dog. This place is so creepy the U.S. Commerce Department classified it as haunted.

2. The Stewards House at Montpelier Hill (County Dublin, Ireland). The scariest place in Ireland, it is said to be haunted by a giant black cat. Some say it's a demon. Others say it's the ghost of a cat that had been covered in whiskey and set ablaze by its owner. Either way, it's terrifying.

3. Airth Castle (Airth by Falkirk, Scotland). A Scottish castle sounds so lovely and romantic, but not if it's haunted by the spirits of two

children and their nanny. Supposedly, there is also a ghost dog roaming the hallways, and he's searching for ankles to bite. I suspect it must be a ghostly Chihuahua. What could be scarier?

4. All the inns in Cape May, New Jersey. People have spotted ghost cats throughout this town, and some even reported feeling a feline tail brush against their faces in the middle of the night. Cape May also has a ghost dog. If you visit Higbee Beach, they say you can sometimes see a large, black dog running along the sand before he vanishes into thin air.

5. The Farnam Mansion (Oneida, New York). Guests have reported many unusual events, from flickering lights to unexplained footsteps to phantom cats. Once the current owner decided to hold a midnight séance (always a stupid idea), and a white ghost cat appeared. Freaky.

6. Arundel Castle (Arundel, England). If you thought being haunted by ghost dogs and phantom cats was scary, this place is said to be haunted by owls. Even worse, if you see one, it's said to be a harbinger of death.

7. Bell's Witch Cave (Adams, Tennessee). A man named John Bell and his family started seeing weird-looking animals hanging around. One of them was a dog with the head of a rabbit. I mean, with ears and everything.

8. The Boussard Mansion (Beaver, Pennsylvania). A modern-day residence haunted by a single dog named Boo.

After hearing Molly's bark recorded on Mr. Ben's cell phone, I was eager to get home. Ms. Anne seemed eager as well. Officer Stahl and Policeman Pat followed her back to search the entire property to find clues. Reporter Rob said he had to research something at the library, but he'd be at the house as soon as possible. I hardly thought this was the time to visit the library, although I adored the library and books in general, but Reporter Rob was insistent.

"There is something I need to check out," he said.

Ms. Anne pulled him aside before he left. "I don't think Pat has anything to do with this. I may be wrong, but that's what my gut is telling me."

"Same," he said, shooting a glance to the side of the house where Policeman Pat and Officer Stahl had blocked off the area with police tape. Several other officers had arrived, and that made me happy. First of all, I liked police people. Secondly, it meant we'd have a better chance of finding Mr. Ben. And I had a team of my own.

"Listen up, guys," I said as I gathered my friends. "The humans are looking for Mr. Ben, but they need our help."

"Oh, here we go again," said Rocco, with a long stretch. "I'm going to have to save the day and nearly die. Then, Capone, the douche canoe, will get all the credit."

"Hey," I said, surprised. "Douche canoe? Really? Why do you keep calling me that?"

He shrugged. "I can't help it. It fits."

"Enough, feline," said Faraday, standing next to me in canine solidarity. "Let Capone speak."

"Thank you," I said. Life was so much easier now that Faraday liked me. "Here is the deal. We need to talk to Molly."

I explained about the recording on Mr. Ben's phone.

"She must have been there when it happened," said Gracie. "Maybe she saw who did it."

"*If* someone did it," said Jackson. "We don't know what happened. Maybe he fell in the river. Or got hurt and couldn't make it back inside. Or—"

"No," said Luke, his voice firm. "That's not what happened."

I tilted my head to study him. "What did happen, Luke?"

He let out a whine. "I'm not sure. I heard my human arguing with someone. He said something about a gun. I barked, and that's when he told me to leave. He said, 'Get out of here, Luke. Now.' He used his serious voice, so I listened, but I shouldn't have listened. I should have helped him."

The expression on Luke's face gutted me. "You can't blame yourself. You did the right thing, Luke. You listened to your master. But how did you get out of the yard?"

"Someone had left the front gate open."

"One of the workers?"

Luke shook his head. "I have no idea. I'm sorry I can't be more help. It scared me, and I panicked. It's all kind of a blur, but I know I took off like a big scaredy-cat. No offense, Rocco."

"None taken, fleabag."

Hearing that made me itchy. I scratched behind my ear. "Enough with the insults, Rocco. You love Mr. Ben, too."

He glared at me for a long moment before grudgingly admitting the truth. "I do."

"So, let's work together. We need to talk to Molly." My stomach growled. "And it's dinner time. That means she'll be out back in a few minutes. She always goes out right after breakfast and dinner. This is our chance."

We ran to the back door and started barking. Ms. Anne frowned. "What is up with you guys?" she asked, letting us out. "Bunch of weirdos."

We were a bunch of weirdos. Misfits. Strays. An obnoxious cat. A warped pair of Pugs. But together, we became something more. Together, we turned into a team—a family. And we would find a way to fix this.

After we peed, we sniffed around, found the right spot, and did our business. A path had been shoveled to the carriage house, and a small area had been cleared for the little dogs. Luke and I were big enough we could go anywhere. And Rocco didn't go outside.

"Savages," he muttered under his breath, but he waited on the steps near the kitchen door. When Molly came out, at last, he was the first one who heard her. "She's out, doggos. Hurry up."

We ran to the fence separating our yards. It was a chain link, but a hedge blocked the view. We had to bark to get her attention. I wiggled into the hedge until my nose touched the fence and called out to her.

"Molly. Come here. We need to talk. It's urgent."

Molly's hearing wasn't great, and her eyesight seemed even worse. It took her a few tries to find me. "Capone. Thank goodness. I've wanted to talk to you, too, but you were gone all day."

"I'm sorry. But right before we found Mr. Ben's phone, you told me you had to share something with me. Was it about Mr. Ben's disappearance?"

"I'm not sure," she said, her tone woebegone. "But my owner may have done something awful, and I couldn't stop him. I'm so sorry."

"Is he..." I gulped. "Is Mr. Ben okay?"

"I don't know," she said softly. "I saw my owner arguing

with him. Something about your house. I wasn't paying attention, but I'm pretty certain of one thing."

"What?"

"Two men went into your house. Only one came out. My master. Which can only mean—"

"Mr. Ben is somewhere in the house," I said, the wheels turning in my head. "But where?"

"I have no idea, puppy. I'm sorry."

A door opened, and Viking Val stuck out his head. "Molly. Time to come in. What are you doing over there?" He let out an exasperated huff. "You're as naughty as Capone. Why are you in my flower bed?"

Curse my rotten reputation. Even a bad guy thought I was naughty.

Viking Val came down the steps, so handsome and perfect. He seemed like such a gentleman, but I'd learned a lot in my relatively short life. One important lesson? Being a gentleman had nothing to do with someone's appearance. It was only about how they acted.

My own Mr. Nate wore old jeans and ripped-up T-shirts, but he was a gentleman. Like Mr. Darcy.

Mr. Ben didn't own a single cravat, and yet he was a gentleman, too. Like Mr. Knightley.

But Viking Val? As much as he looked like a walking advertisement for all things gentlemanly, maybe he wasn't a gentleman at all. I began to suspect he might be a bad guy, a Frank Churchill. He may have even been as deceitful, in a way, as my namesake, Al Capone.

But, with Al Capone, at least his scarred exterior hinted at his gruesome interior. Such was not the case with Viking Val. A pretty package did not always indicate a lovely gift.

It scared me. Viking Val had been so friendly when we'd met him. Maybe too nice. Had it all been an act? I couldn't tell since I did not have a degree in criminal psychology. Being named after a criminal gave me some street cred, enough that I could ascertain one thing—Viking Val was not at all what he appeared. Maybe the name I'd given him should have been a clue. I'd called him Viking Val because of his blond, striking looks. Perhaps he was a Viking in more of the pillaging sense. That would be terrible.

Note to self: Be careful with nicknames. Sometimes people live up to them.

"Come on, girl," said Viking Val, getting annoyed. "You can't stay out here all night."

Molly let out a whine. "You'd better go, Capone. I don't want him to see you. But remember one thing when you find Ben." She glanced over her shoulder, wagging her tail at her master before turning back to me. "Even if he's a bad person, he's my person, and he needs help. Please help him, Capone. Please help all of us."

With that, she strode slowly over to Viking Val. I slipped out of the bushes, but not before I saw Viking Val give Molly a gentle pat on the head. "Come on, girl. Time for a treat."

It confused me. Viking Val treated his dog so kindly, but he may have hurt Mr. Ben. He cooked incredible lasagna and treated Ms. Anne with the utmost respect, but he also lied to her face without a hint of guile.

When a dog is guilty, you know it. They duck their head and act ashamed. But a human? Sometimes it's hard to tell.

"WHAT SHOULD WE DO?" asked Luke once we went back inside. Ms. Anne fed us dinner, but I was so upset I barely enjoyed it. I still ate, mind you, but without the usual joy I got from my kibble.

"I'm not sure," I said. "This house is big, but it's not that big."

Jackson finished his meal, let out a loud belch, and plopped down onto the ground. "We're missing something."

"Missing?" asked Faraday. "Oh, my gosh. I may have figured something out."

He got so excited he peed. Rocco groaned. "What is wrong with you? You just tinkled outside."

He sent Rocco a scathing glare. "When I went outside, that was a normal pee. This was a happy-and-yet-nervous pee. They are quite different. Also, I have a small bladder. At least I don't pee in a box, furball."

"Enough," said Gracie, with a yippy bark. "Faraday, what did you figure out?"

The small Pug stepped away from his pee. "The things that went missing. What if Val took them?"

"It's possible, I guess," said Gracie. "But it doesn't mean anything."

"Oh, yes, it does," said Faraday, hopping up and down like he had small springs in his feet. "What went missing? What were the most important items?"

"My bully stick," said Jackson.

Faraday rolled his Puggy eyes. "Capone ate your bully stick, Jackson."

Gracie spun in a circle like she always did when she got excited. "My special doggie bed went missing. The pink one with sparkles."

I thought Faraday might lose his mind, but he remained

calm. "It's still at our old house, Gracie. We didn't bring it after the fire."

"Oh," said Gracie. "And my pink collar?"

"At the house."

"And my pink snow booties?"

"At. The. House."

Faraday spoke through clenched teeth, so I decided to intervene. "Lots of things went missing," I said, considering his question. "But the two most important things were the original plans for the house and the keys."

He got so excited he peed again, but only a few drops this time. "Exactly, Capone. Why would Val take those? He must know something we do not."

"Like what?" I asked, genuinely perplexed.

"Like there is a secret room in this house somewhere."

We all said, "Ooooooooooh," in unison. Well, everyone except Rocco. The fluffy cat narrowed his eyes at Faraday.

"And how can we find this secret room, Puglet? Especially if the humans don't realize it exists?"

I got so excited I fell over. I couldn't help it. Faraday peed when excited, and I became clumsier than usual. It may have been a Lab thing.

"I've got it," I said. "I know where the room is, which means I also know where Mr. Ben might be right now."

"Where?" asked Luke. He didn't trip or pee when he got nervous, but his ears went down, and his eyes got bigger.

"Think about it," I said, letting out an excited bark. "Viking Val kept asking about finishing the basement. He seemed obsessed with the drywall. What if there was a reason for that? What if he knew about the secret room? If so, he could have made Mr. Ben go inside. He could have locked him up. And maybe he's hoping when the drywall is installed, it'll mean..."

I couldn't say the words. Luke did it for me. "My owner will be sealed in there. Buried alive. Like a tomb."

Since I'd watched a special about the ancient Egyptians on PBS once, I understood that would not be a great way to go. "Exactly," I said.

"We need to save him," said Gracie. "We need to make a plan."

Faraday agreed with her. "But I'm wondering one thing," he said. "Why would Val do it?"

I'd wondered the same thing myself. "I have no idea, but that's not the only thing that worries me. We've figured out Viking Val is not a good guy, but Ms. Anne has not. She might have some suspicions about him, but I doubt she has any idea that he's dangerous. And I don't know how we can warn her."

We turned to stare at Ms. Anne, who sat on a chair by the fire with a worried frown on her pretty face. When she caught all of us staring at her, the frown deepened. "What is it?" she asked as the doorbell rang.

Oh, calamity. It was Viking Val. With Molly.

And before we could find a way to tell her what was going on, Ms. Anne invited them in for a cup of tea.

THIRTY-SIX

Ways to distract a potentially dangerous person:

1. Bark at them until it gets uncomfortable.
2. Make growly noises.
3. Knock over their tea.
4. Stare at nothing and make them think you've
   seen a ghost.

I probably should have thought this through. I'm not skilled at improvising, which was why we stared at Viking Val in shock when he came into the house. Our lack of reaction caused Ms. Anne to stare at us in confusion.

"Why isn't he barking?" she asked, perplexed.

With that, the floodgates opened. We all started barking, except for Luke. He growled at Viking Val. I had to nudge him to get him to stop.

"She doesn't understand," I said. "We can't let him know that we know. Get it?"

"Yes," he said, containing his growl but still showing his teeth.

"Are you missing a tooth?" I asked.

He narrowed his eyes at me. "Yes. Why?"

"No reason. I never noticed it before."

"I lost it in a fight with another dog," he said. He'd startled me, which must have been apparent from the expression on my face, and he rolled his eyes. "It's no big deal. I always forget how sheltered you are, Capone."

"Hey, I've been in fights," I said, showing him my ear. "A German Shepard named Hans bit part of my ear off in doggie daycare once. I was super brave. Mostly because I didn't feel it, but I was still super brave."

"Impressive. Hans at doggie daycare, huh? He sounds terrifying."

"He was," I said, but before I could explain, Viking Val tilted his head to indicate the policemen outside.

"You've got the entire Beaver police force here, Anne. You'll find him soon."

"I hope so," she said, chewing on her fingernail. She showed him into the kitchen. They sat at a table drinking tea, bizarre since it seemed like Viking Val might be responsible for what had happened. Not that I could share this information with Ms. Anne, sadly enough.

Curse my inability to communicate effectively with those of the human persuasion.

"What are we going to do?" I asked. "She could be in danger."

"I doubt it," said Faraday. "As the tall and abnormally good-looking human observed, the property is crawling with police officers. As long as they are here, all will be well."

Policeman Pat stuck his head in the door. "Annie, I need to check on my mom again, and the other guys will start a search by the river. We won't be long. Are you okay on your own?"

"I'm fine," she said. "Val's here."

Oh, calamity. This might be the worst-case scenario.

"Pssst, Capone," said Molly. "Come here. I need to talk with you."

"What is it?" The other dogs came, too. Rocco perched on his favorite chair and scowled down at us.

She eyed the humans in the kitchen. "Last night, I saw something strange. My owner left the house in the middle of the night. He came over to your house and climbed in through a window to the basement."

"Are you sure?"

"I am. And this isn't the first time. I've seen him do it before."

I remembered the footprints in the snow in the basement the night Mr. Ben and I found the open window, and I gasped. Had Viking Val been down there with us? "Oh, no. That's where Mr. Ben is. He's in the basement. We need to go down there, but we have to be discrete. We can't let Viking Val realize we're onto him."

"How will we do that?" asked Gracie.

"We need a distraction. Molly, can you handle that?"

She nodded. "Sure. I know what to do. My owner already believes this place is haunted. I'll stare at nothing and growl. It'll freak him out. Watch."

She did as she said. She jumped up, knocking over Viking Val's tea, and went into the kitchen. Once she got there, she stared at the wall and growled. Viking Val and Ms. Anne followed her. The sound of her growl made my hackles go up. It made Viking Val's hackles go up, too. "What is it, girl?" he asked, dabbing distractedly at his tea-stained trousers. "This is so strange. They say dogs are attuned to the spirit world."

When Molly started barking, we took advantage of the

opportunity and shot downstairs. We needed to find Mr. Ben quickly.

The basement was cold and dark and seemed empty. "What should we do?" I asked.

Faraday glanced up at me, his buggy Pug eyes glowing eerily in the darkness. "Use your nose, Capone. You've got this."

He spoke with absolute conviction. Faraday believed in me.

"The little dog is right," said Rocco. "You have a nose like no other. Do what you were born to do, pup. Follow the trail. Find Ben."

"Okay," I said, straightening up. "I can do this."

Closing my eyes, I tried to channel Mr. Knightley, the most sensible of all of Austen's heroes. He would know what to do in a situation like this. I also remembered all the lessons my late uncle Clancy had taught me. His job had been finding lost people. He was a K-9 search and rescue dog, one of the best, and his blood ran through my veins.

I sniffed around, getting acquainted with all the different scents in the basement. The other dogs watched me, quiet and still. Yet I felt their support and their trust. The problem? So many smells in the basement competed for my attention. Chemicals. Alcohol. Cleaning supplies. Mold. Old things. And the basement was huge, which also proved to be a problem.

"If only someone could point me in the right direction."

A dark shape appeared in front of me. About my size, it seemed to be made of shadows, but it had glowing yellow eyes and a tail.

I gazed at it in shock. "Boo?"

"Boo who?" asked Luke. "Who is Capone talking to?"

"It must be Boo, the ghost dog," said Faraday. "Capone can see him. Oh, my gosh. He's here. This is so scary."

Faraday tinkled again behind me, one scent among so many others, but I ignored him. This was important. Boo didn't wish to hurt me. He wanted to help. I sensed it, and I'd learned to trust my doggie intuition. It had never led me astray before.

Well, not often.

Boo tilted his head to indicate a long, dark hallway before he faded away. I went over and sniffed the spot where I'd seen him. Had he really been there? I thought so. Was I scared? Yes. Would I pee myself like Faraday? No. Because there had to be a reason he appeared, the answer seemed to be down this hallway.

I walked along the hallway, sniffing the whole way. When we reached a pile of boxes at the end, I froze. I smelled something, but what was it?

I peeked behind the boxes and found something extraordinary. "The missing keys," I said. "Thank you, Boo."

Was it my imagination again, or did I hear a faint, ghostly bark?

Jackson must have heard it, too. "What was that?" he asked, sounding worried. "Are you okay, Capone?"

I popped my head out from behind the boxes. "I'm fine. The keys are here. And the plans. And a bunch of tools."

"But where is Ben?" asked Luke.

"He must be down here somewhere," I said. "We have to search for clues."

"How do we know it's a clue?" he asked since he was new to all this mystery-solving stuff.

"It has to be something that stands out. Something that doesn't belong here or that seems out of place."

"Like that big piece of brand-new drywall over there?" he asked.

He was right. It stood out. And I didn't remember it being there the last time we were in the basement.

"The question is, what's behind that drywall?" asked Faraday. "We need to move it."

The doorbell rang upstairs. I heard the clunk of Contractor Carl's heavy boots. Thank goodness. At least Ms. Anne wasn't alone with Viking Val anymore. Things were looking up.

"Let's move this. Now," I said.

After making sure all the little dogs and Rocco stayed out of the way, Luke and I stuck our noses behind the large panel of drywall and pushed. It didn't take a lot of effort. It was pretty light and landed with a soft *thunk*.

We paused, but the conversation continued upstairs. They hadn't heard us.

"There is nothing there," said Gracie, prancing closer. As she pranced, her nails suddenly made a clinking sound. I stared at her in surprise. The floor of the basement was dirt. Why did it sound like she stood on something metal?

The piece of drywall hadn't been hiding something on the wall. It had been hiding something on the floor.

"Is that a door?" asked Jackson.

It was a full-sized door with a small, metal handle. And all around the door, it smelled like Mr. Ben. "This is it," I said. "He must be down there."

"Open it, Capone," said Luke. "Hurry."

I tried grabbing the handle with my teeth to lift it but to no avail. I wasn't strong enough.

Note to self: I need to work out more.

"It's no use. We should get Ms. Anne," I said, heading toward the steps.

"Wait," said Rocco. "Mr. Tall Blond and Crazy is still up there. We can't risk it."

"But what should we do?" I asked, letting out a whine.

"Work together," said Rocco. "We can figure this out."

"The feline is correct," said Faraday, eyes scanning the basement. "We need a rope."

"Like this?" asked Jackson, pulling a long piece of rope from a rickety metal storage shelf. When we stared at him in surprise, he laughed. "Puggy eyes. They give us excellent peripheral vision, don't they, Faraday?"

"Truth," he said. "Let's do this."

Faraday pulled the rope to the handle. He threaded one end of the rope through the handle and pulled until both sides seemed even.

"Does anyone know how to tie a knot?" he asked.

We stared at him, dumbfounded. Rocco let out a sigh. "Oh, for Pete's sake. I do. Follow my instructions."

With Rocco's help, we managed to get two solid knots on the end of each rope. "How did you know how to do that?" I asked.

He snorted. "You aren't the only one who watches PBS, dummy."

I had turned Rocco, the cat, into a PBS fan. That thought filled my doggie heart with joy. "You are amazing," I said.

"I am. Now get to work. The Pug has a plan. And since he is the smartest one amongst you, I strongly suggest you listen."

"The cat is correct," said Faraday. "And I'm going to need all of you to help."

"Definitely. What should we do?" I asked.

"Jackson and Luke need to take one end, and you and Gracie have to take the other. You're going to grab the rope in your mouths and pull it as soon as I say so. The knots will help you hold on. Got it?"

Gracie stared at the rope in disgust. "In my mouth?"

Jackson nudged her. "You've had worse things in your mouth."

She gaped at him. "And what do you mean by that exactly?"

Jackson's eyes widened in panic. "I meant that time you thought Faraday's poo was a dog treat."

Gracie made a gagging noise. "That was terrible. Why did you have to bring it up?"

"Because compared to that, this rope isn't so nasty," he said. "Come on, baby. You've got this."

She let out a huff but grabbed on as instructed. She and Jackson held the knots toward the end of the ropes. Luke and I grabbed onto the knots closer to the door.

"On the count of three pull with all your might, okay? As soon as the door lifts high enough, Rocco and I will push this box over to hold it open. Got it?"

He tilted his head to indicate an empty wooden crate near the metal door. Rocco muttered a curse. "Of course, you're giving me the most dangerous job. It figures."

"We'll do it together. According to my calculations, it's light enough we can move it but heavy enough to hold the door up. Are you in?"

"Do I have a choice?"

"No," we all said at once.

"Fine. Then I'm in."

"Is everyone ready?" asked Faraday, making eye contact with each of us. "On the count of three. One. Two. Three. Heave. Ho. Heave. Ho."

I'm not sure what the heaving and ho-ing was about, but we pulled with all our might. Gracie's feet skittered on the dirt floor, but she didn't give up. Jackson used his Pug bulk, all 38.5lbs, to serve as an anchor. Luke and I gave it everything we had.

When I thought it might be hopeless, the door lifted a crack. I got so excited I nearly dropped the rope but managed to keep it in my mouth. We pulled and pulled, straining with the effort. At last, it was high enough that Rocco and Faraday could slide the wooden box into place.

"Now, let it down slowly," said Faraday.

We did as instructed, and to my surprise, it worked. The box held the door open. We peeked inside.

"Stairs?" asked Gracie. "The basement has a basement?"

"A super creepy hell hole," said Luke with a shiver. "And it's cold down there, too. And dark."

"It's okay, Luke. Smell it."

He took a long whiff. "My human. He's down there."

"Exactly. Let's go."

Squeezing carefully under the door, I led the way. The others followed. It took a few minutes for our eyes to adjust, and when I saw what was down there, I groaned.

"Is this some kind of dungeon?" I asked.

We saw three doors in front of us. All of them looked old, and all of them had ancient padlocks on them.

"This is super creepy," said Jackson. "Those Boussards were freaks."

"No, they were brewers," said Faraday, indicating some barrels in the corner. "This was likely their cold storage."

I didn't think a family of beer brewers needed a dungeon with padlocked cells, but maybe Faraday was right. He'd been right about everything so far.

Eying the padlocks, a thought occurred to me. "We need the keys. I'll go and get them."

Running up the steps, I carefully slipped through the opening and grabbed the keys. I found the other dogs studying the doors when I brought them back.

"I can smell him," said Luke. "He's close. But behind which door?"

An excellent question. I glanced up and noticed a ledge and a tiny gap between the door frame and the ceiling.

"Rocco?" I asked, indicating the ledge. "Maybe you can see inside from there."

He called me something that was not an endearment, but he scampered up the steps. From the top, he could carefully crawl across the narrow ledge.

"You owe me for this one, Capone," he said. "I expect catnip tonight. I don't care how you get it. And why do humans always have to hide things in basements? I don't understand the point. Why not hide something in the attic, maybe? Or, better yet, next to the fireplace?"

When he got to the first door, he paused. "Can you see anything?" I asked.

"No," he said. "It's a small room with nothing but barrels in it."

He crawled to the next door. That was empty, too. When he reached the third door, I held my breath.

"Is he in there?"

"I can't tell," said Rocco. "Wait, I see something—"

The rest of his sentence was lost in a frantic meow as Rocco fell off the ledge and disappeared from view. Oh, calamity. Had I killed my kitty cat?

"Rocco? Rocco?"

To my relief, a few seconds later, I heard Rocco's snarky voice. "Five. I'm down to five lives now, Capone. I blame you."

"Oh, thank goodness. Is Mr. Ben in there? Is he okay?"

There was a pause. "He's here, and he's alive, but he's freezing. He needs help."

"What are we going to do?" I asked. Automatically, I turned to Faraday for guidance.

"We're going to unlock the door," he said. "Obviously."

But before we could attempt it, the door above us swung open and bathed the area where we stood in light. When I saw Ms. Anne there, I started barking happily, but she didn't seem glad to see me. She appeared frightened. She walked carefully down the steps, with Viking Val and Molly behind her. I let out a low growl, but then I realized someone stood behind them—someone holding a gun.

It was my buddy, Contractor Carl.

THIRTY-SEVEN

Rules of being part of a family of gangsters:

1. Demonstrate complete obedience and loyalty to the boss.
2. Follow a code of silence.
3. Avenge any attacks on family members.
4. Avoid contact with authorities.

"He's dangerous," said Molly, her eyes full of worry. "Be careful. Don't make any noise. Don't draw any attention to yourself. Be as safe as you can." She sauntered toward us, head bowed, and joined us in front of the door.

"I'm scared, Molly," I said.

"Me, too, puppy. Me, too."

Ms. Anne seemed frightened, too, but she also acted ticked off. "Why are you doing this?"

"Snitches get stitches," said Contractor Carl. He had his usual cheery smile on his face, but there was something cold and dark in his eyes.

Curse my lack of street smarts.

The irony that a dog named Al Capone could not recognize an actual bad guy was not lost on me. I needed to encourage Ms. Josie to remember to call me Alphonse. Or even Al. But it may be too late. I had a feeling I might be stuck with this name forever.

Not that I'd live forever. Judging by the way things were going, I might not survive the night.

Ms. Anne followed Contractor Carl's gaze to the third door, comprehension dawning on her face. "Ben? Oh, my God. Ben? Are you in there?"

She lurched forward as if planning to run to the door. Viking Val held her back. Were they working together? Viking Val and Contractor Carl?

Oh, calamity. Why hadn't I seen this coming?

"Sit on the keys, Jackson," said Faraday as we huddled in front of the door. "You have a big butt."

"Excuse me?" asked Jackson, acting offended.

"He's right," said Gracie. "Do it."

Luke shivered next to me. "What are we going to do?"

"I'm not sure, buddy," I said. "But it'll take a miracle to get out of this one."

Policeman Pat appeared at the top of the steps. He stared down at us in confusion. "Uncle Carl?"

"The plot thickens," said Jackson. "What a surprise."

"Indeed," said Faraday. "It all makes sense now. Carl is a Goodman."

"Uh, no. He's a bad man," said Luke, confused.

"You're both right," I said, a chill in my heart. "He's a Goodman and a bad man."

"What do you mean?" asked Luke.

I swallowed hard. "Contractor Carl is Sam Goodman's younger brother."

The burly contractor glanced up at Policeman Pat in

surprise. "What are you doing here, Paddy? You were supposed to be at your mom's house. This isn't how it's supposed to play out."

When Policeman Pat edged his way down the steps, Contractor Carl raised his gun. Policeman Pat studied his face. "Are you seriously going to shoot me, Uncle Carl? We're family."

"There is family, and then there is *family*, and we both know where my loyalties lie. I took an oath the day I turned eighteen and never broke it. Not once."

"But you left that life," said Policeman Pat, making his way slowly toward his uncle. "You've been a model citizen since the day you got out of jail ten years ago. Don't mess that up, now."

"I have no choice," he said. "As soon as I saw Ben's face, I realized what I had to do."

"You killed him?" he asked, and Ms. Anne let out a sob, but Contractor Carl shook his head.

"No, but he's going to die of natural causes soon. If he hasn't already."

Ms. Anne struggled in Viking Val's grip. He tried to calm her. "He has a gun, Anne. And he's not stable."

"He's right," said Molly. "I thought my owner was nuts for being obsessed with this house, but that guy is certifiable. He's looney tunes."

Contractor Carl let out a laugh. He did seem looney tunes. He had his back to the second door. Ms. Anne and Viking Val stood on his left. Policeman Pat was on his right. He waved his gun back and forth at them. "I'm not stable?" he asked. "That's rich coming from you, Dr. Val. I'm not the one sneaking into houses and stealing things."

Viking Val's face got red. "I didn't steal anything. I did, however, borrow a few items, but only because I needed them to locate something that should have been rightfully mine in the first place. I planned to return them. I swear."

"What are you talking about?" asked Ms. Anne.

Contractor Carl filled her in. "I caught him down here, trying to get into these rooms. I made him leave the keys behind and opened the doors after he left."

"Oh, my," I said. "Viking Val was in the wrong, too. Vanity working on a weak head produces every sort of mischief."

I gave my friends a sidelong glance, but they didn't chastise me for quoting Austen again. Jackson agreed with me. "Truer words were never spoken, pup."

Ms. Anne seemed momentarily stunned by Contractor Carl's revelation about our gentlemanly next-door neighbor. "You're the one who took the keys and the plans?" she asked, glaring up at Viking Val in disgust. "Did you sabotage the ladder, too?"

He had the decency to look ashamed. "When I saw Ben had the plans, I realized they might hold a clue. I had to delay the project. I was so close."

"Close to what?"

"To finding the treasure of the Boussards," he said. "My grandmother was the daughter of Peter Boussard, conceived right before he went to war. He and my great-grandmother planned to marry, but Peter died two weeks after he left. Then Henry killed himself." Viking Val stared at the dank, dark walls of the basement. "Down here. After killing Peter's dog, Boo. He didn't want Boo to be on his own, but he had no idea my great-grandmother was pregnant. No one did."

"Sad story," said Contractor Carl. "I have one, too. The best man I ever knew, my brother, died in jail because some ungrateful kid ratted on him. But that kid supposedly died.

He drowned in the river. Imagine my surprise when I show up for work this week, and he's here, alive and well." He shook his head. "I understood exactly what I had to do. Honor is everything. Family is too. I thought you understood, Pat. Even though you turned your back on all of us when you started wearing that." He waved his gun to indicate Policeman Pat's uniform.

"I never turned my back on you, Uncle Carl. Who visited you in jail every week? Who helped you when you got out? You can't go back to jail. Your kids need you. They're only in high school."

Contractor Carl's face hardened. "And unless I do this, they'll have no inheritance. Neither will you. It'll all go to him." He tilted his head to indicate the third door.

"Psst." I heard a sound above us. It was Rocco, climbing on the ledge. He glanced at me, then at Contractor Carl's bald head, then at me again. Once again, Rocco had a plan.

Note to self: Cats always have a plan.

Faraday understood Rocco's message, too. "Clever kitty cat. On the count of three, we attack."

"Wait. What?" asked Jackson, confused.

Faraday ignored him. "One, two—"

Before he could say three, Rocco flew off the ledge and landed on Contractor Carl's head, claws digging into his bald scalp. Faraday went after his ankles, biting down hard, and Gracie did the same. Jackson was late to the game. He walked up and kicked Contractor Carl, but at least it seemed like a solid kick. Molly stayed out of the way. She was an old lady, after all.

But then came the final blow. Luke and I acted as one, body slamming Contractor Carl and pushing him to the floor. Unfortunately, as we did so, his gun went off. The sound was deafening.

"Oh, no," said Ms. Anne. "Pat."

The bullet had struck Policeman Pat, sending him into a pile of old boxes. He sank to the floor, and Ms. Anne ran to help him. As she did so, Viking Val grabbed Contractor Carl's gun.

"Don't move," he said, but he needn't have worried. Contractor Carl had hit his head hard when we knocked him over. He was out cold. Viking Val smiled at us. "Great job, doggies."

"And cat," said Rocco, stepping away from Contractor Carl's bloodied head. "They never thank the cat, and it was all my idea."

Almost as if Viking Val understood him, he grinned at Rocco. "And cat. We know you're the real hero here."

Rocco rubbed against Viking Val's legs. "At last. An intelligent life form. I've finally found it."

As Ms. Anne called for help on Policeman Pat's phone, Viking Val grabbed the rope we'd used to open the door and tied up Contractor Carl. He went over to where Policeman Pat lay on the floor, blood seeping from his shoulder. He was unconscious.

"I'll take care of him," said Viking Val. "You get Ben out of there. He's probably suffering from hypothermia at this point."

"Okay," said Ms. Anne. "But how?"

I grabbed the keys and carried them to Ms. Anne. "My hero," she said, hugging me. "Don't worry, Ben. I'm coming."

Kneeling on the floor, she tried one key after another, groaning in frustration. There were a lot of keys.

"Hold on, Ben. I've got you," she said. "I promise."

I heard a faint tap coming from inside the room. Was it Mr. Ben?

Ms. Anne heard it, too. "That's right. I'm coming. Just a few minutes. I swear."

The keyring was huge. It had at least twenty keys on it. She tried each one patiently. Methodically. Until she slipped one inside and heard a magical click as the padlock sprang open. She took it off the latch and tossed it onto the floor before flinging the door wide open. Mr. Ben, who must have been leaning against the door, slumped to the ground.

"Annie," he rasped. "You saved me."

She wrapped her arms around his shivering, cold body, smiling through her tears. "I had help. Come on, guys. We need to warm him up."

We surrounded him in a cocoon of fur. He partially sat, partially leaned against Ms. Anne. "I didn't think you'd be able to find me," he said, teeth chattering. "I thought I'd die in there. I thought I'd never see your face again. Never get to tell you how much I love you."

"Shhh," she said, kissing his dirty, pale face. "I love you, too, and of course, I found you. Well, the animals found you. Capone brought me the key."

They both stared at me. "How...?" asked Mr. Ben, confused.

"No idea."

A shadow flickered past us on the wall. I glanced up at it, and this time I wasn't the only one to see it.

"Boo," said Luke, his brown eyes huge in his freckled face. "Thank you." The shadow disappeared, and Luke's eyes met mine. "And thank you, too, Capone. For everything."

"All in a day's work," I said, giving him a bow.

"Oh, brother," said Jackson. "Does this mean we're going to be in the paper again?

The police arrived, along with the EMTs and Reporter

Rob behind them. "I'd say that is a definite possibility," I said with a laugh, relief flooding through my body. That relief grew exponentially when I heard a voice I recognized.

"Capone? Jackson? Rocco?" Ms. Josie appeared at the top of the steps. I rushed up to meet her and nearly knocked her over in my enthusiasm. "Oh, puppy. My puppy. You've grown."

I did a happy, bouncy dance, licking her and loving her. My human was here at last. This had to be the best day ever —kind of. Ms. Josie had returned home, and Mr. Ben remained alive, but Policeman Pat seemed like he was in rough shape. They carried him up on a stretcher. Mr. Ben walked up next to Ms. Anne, but he wasn't in good condition. Viking Val, being a doctor, assisted them, but he must have realized I was worried. He patted me on the head.

"You did well, pup," he said. "They're going to be okay."

Ms. Anne gave Ms. Josie a quick hug. "Welcome home," she said. "Never a dull moment, right?"

Ms. Josie kissed her cheek. "Not with Capone around." I let out a whine of outrage, and they laughed. "Go with Ben. I'll take care of everything here."

We went upstairs to a room bustling with people. Officer Stahl was there, and Fireman Fetch. Mr. Nate, on crutches, grinned at us. "Hi, doggies. Hi, Rocco."

I made a move to leap toward him, but Ms. Josie, with her lightning-quick reflexes, held me back. "No way. You cannot tackle him the way you did me. The man just had surgery. Be gentle."

Mr. Nate moved to sit down on a chair. As soon as he lowered his crutches, we ran up to him, greeting him with the same enthusiasm as we had Ms. Josie but being respectful of his injured leg. "It's wonderful to see you guys, and it's so great to be home."

Ms. Josie and Mr. Nate looked suntanned and happy. Married life seemed to agree with them, broken bones, and all. The EMTs carried Policeman Pat outside. He was talking, which seemed like a promising sign. Ms. Anne followed Mr. Ben to the second waiting ambulance. He was bundled in blankets.

"Will they be okay?" asked Ms. Josie when she saw Viking Val. Even with blood on his hands and covered in dirt, he still looked like a perfect gentleman. Albeit a gentleman who'd broken into our house to find a long-lost treasure, but no gentleman was genuinely perfect. I may be living proof of that. And I realized Jane Austen had been right once again—how we act defines us, not how we appear. And I did something good today. So had Viking Val.

"They'll both be fine," he said. He ducked into the powder room to wash his hands. He watched as the police led Contractor Carl away in handcuffs when he came out. "But I can't say the same about him. He'll be back in jail for a long time."

"And he deserves it," said Reporter Rob.

"Where have you been, big brother?" asked Fireman Fetch. "You disappeared."

"I went to the library," he said. "Researching this guy." He lifted his thumb to Viking Val.

"Me?"

"Your family history."

Ms. Josie frowned. "What are you talking about?"

"Val is the last of the Boussards," he said. "And I thought you were the bad guy. First, I thought it had to be Pat who was causing trouble. Then I thought it was you."

"I thought the same," I said.

"Me, too," said Molly. "I was so afraid my owner had done something awful. I mean, not that sneaking into a house to steal treasure isn't deplorable, but at least it isn't homicide or kidnapping."

"Silver linings," said Faraday.

"How did you figure it out?" asked Viking Val.

"I had a hunch when you got so upset about the hardware for the front door. And your ring was also a clue." He pointed to the ring on Viking Val's hand. "I recognized the Boussard crest."

Viking Val held up his hand, admiring the gold ring. "Peter Boussard gave it to my great-grandmother the day he left for war. A promise ring. It was all she had left of him."

"That's so sad," said Ms. Josie.

"Then I found this," said Reporter Rob. He held up a copy of an old photograph. Although black and white and grainy, it showed two men standing by the fireplace with a black Lab. The dog could have been my twin.

"Boo," I said softly.

"It has to be," said Jackson. "But take a gander at the humans."

"Oh, my," I said.

Viking Val was the image of Peter Boussard. He took the paper from Reporter Rob's hand. "I've never seen this," he said. "May I keep it?"

"Of course," said Reporter Rob. "But you have some explaining to do."

"I agree," said Viking Val. "But can it wait? I'd like to go check on both patients if you don't mind."

"I'll go with you," said Reporter Rob.

"Me, too," said Fireman Fetch.

"Let us know what's going on," said Ms. Josie. "Please."

"Will do," said Reporter Rob, giving her a salute. "Welcome home."

Ms. Josie and Mr. Nate laughed. "Quite the welcome," said Mr. Nate after everyone left.

"It was," said Ms. Josie, perching on the arm of his chair. "One can never have too large a party. But I have to say the house looks great."

"Oh, and speaking of rings..." He picked up their wedding rings from the small dish on the end table.

"Were we?" she asked, lifting one eyebrow, and extending her left hand.

"Not really, but I think it's time to make this officially official." He slipped the ring onto her finger. It sparkled there prettily, and she admired it a moment before putting the other ring on his finger and kissing him firmly on the lips.

"Let's not think about where these rings have been, okay?"

"Good idea. And I'm sorry I didn't carry you over the threshold," said Mr. Nate. "My bad."

"Plenty of time for that later, Mr. Murray."

"Sounds like a plan, Mrs. Murray. It's good to be home."

THIRTY-EIGHT

Why dogs are better than people:

1. We are always happy.
2. We're the best listeners.
3. We have pure hearts.
4. We don't judge.
5. We never lie.
6. We are excellent caregivers.
7. We are man's (and woman's) best friends—
   forever and always.

The following day, Mr. Ben got released from the hospital, and we went to visit him at Ms. Anne's house. She took excellent care of him. He rested on the couch, leaning back on a mountain of pillows, and covered in a blanket. Luke curled up on his lap. Mr. Nate sat on a chair with his foot propped up on an ottoman. Ms. Josie studied them with a smile.

"You two look the worse for wear," she said. "How are you, Ben?"

"I'm fine," he said. "Good as new."

"Other than being dehydrated and cold, he seems okay," said Ms. Anne, getting emotional once again as she sat next to him on the couch. "It's a miracle. When I think of you all alone in that basement, it breaks my heart."

She brushed a lock of hair out of his eyes and kissed his forehead. He smiled up at her. "I wasn't exactly alone."

"What do you mean?"

He gave her a crooked smile. "You're going to say I'm nuts."

She snorted. "I know you're nuts. But I don't understand why you say you weren't alone."

"There was a dog down there with me. I think it may have been Boo."

Ms. Anne covered her mouth in surprise. "Boo, the ghost dog?"

He nodded, acting a bit embarrassed. "I don't believe in that sort of thing, and maybe I hallucinated, but I swear I saw him. And there is something else." He paused. "He was searching for something."

"The treasure?" asked Ms. Anne.

"Yes. I think so."

"We should call Val," she said. "He'll want to hear this."

"You believe me?" he asked, taken aback.

"Of course, I do." She covered his hand with hers. He had bandages on his fingers and some cuts and scrapes from the altercation he must have had with Contractor Carl, but he did look pretty good.

"Tell us more about this ghost dog," said Ms. Josie. I barked in agreement, and she laughed. "We all want to know."

"There isn't a lot to tell. I saw this black shape. At first, I thought I had imagined it. Then I thought it had to be

Capone. I assumed I'd die down there, but the dog gave me hope. He didn't leave my side. I found an old tarp in the corner, enough to provide some warmth, but it was awful, though. If not for that dog, I might have given up."

"Boo the Ghost Dog, huh?" asked Ms. Anne.

"Yes, and when Rob came to see me at the hospital, he showed me a copy of the photo he'd found in the library."

"The one with Val's ancestors in it?" asked Mr. Nate.

"Exactly. I saw it, and everything clicked into place."

"What clicked into place?" asked Ms. Josie.

He smiled at them. "It might be easier to show you than to tell you."

WHEN MR. BEN felt well enough, he and Ms. Anne came to our house for dinner. Policeman Pat remained at the hospital, but he would be released in a few days. Contractor Carl was in jail, where he'd be for a very, very long time. Viking Val, Reporter Rob, and Fireman Fetch joined us. Mr. Ben said he had something important to share.

"What could it be?" asked Molly, curled up next to me on the rug.

"I have no idea."

It was beautiful to have all my friends together again. Of course, Jackson and Rocco were still with me, but Faraday, Gracie, and Luke now lived at Ms. Anne's house. I missed the days of all of us being together under one roof. Although we'd only been apart a few days, it seemed like much longer.

We frolicked and played, being careful not to hit Mr. Nate's bad leg or to knock into Mr. Ben. They were both in recovery mode, which was why, when Ms. Josie saw me revving up to do zoomies, she put a stop to it.

"Don't even think about it, Capone." To her surprise, I listened.

Ms. Anne laughed at the expression on her face. "He's grown up a lot the last few weeks," she said.

"Is he calmer?" asked Ms. Josie.

"Uh, no."

"Has he stopped stealing bras?"

"Definitely not."

"Has he stopped eating weird things?"

"Not at all."

"Does he still bark at the UPS truck?"

"Every day."

"Then how has he grown exactly?"

Ms. Anne shrugged. "He listens better now. I guess that's it. But we have to face facts. Labs don't ever calm down completely. He'll act like a puppy for years."

"She's got that right," said Molly. "I didn't calm down until I was ten. Even then, I still had my wild moments."

"Oh, well," said Ms. Josie, kissing my nose as she ruffled my ears. "I wouldn't want it any other way."

Ms. Anne walked over to Mr. Ben. "Are you ready?" she asked.

He nodded, and everyone grew quiet. "I know where the treasure might be hidden," he said. "It's in here." He pointed to the spot on the fireplace with the carving of a Lab on it.

"That's it?" asked Faraday. "No build-up? No suspense? No excitement?'

"Mr. Ben is a man of few words," I said, wanting to defend him, although I had to agree with Faraday. It was a bit anticlimactic. "A gentleman says what needs to be said. No more. No less."

"No fun," said Jackson. When I looked at him in shock, he rolled his Puggy eyes at me. "I'm kidding, Capone. Let's listen to the humans. I want to see the treasure."

"Without any further ado..." said Mr. Ben.

Faraday snorted. "He never had any ado to begin with." When I shot him a dirty glance, he apologized. "Sorry. I'll shut up. I love Ben. I'm teasing."

As we watched, Mr. Ben wiggled the carving of the dog. "I noticed this didn't fit right when I repaired the mantle. I thought it had been made that way by accident, but now I'm not so sure. May I?" he asked, holding up a small chisel.

"Please do," said Mr. Nate. "I'm dying to find out what is in there."

He wasn't the only one. Viking Val sat on the edge of his seat.

It took Mr. Ben a few minutes to pry it loose, but he had been right. There was something behind the carving of the Labrador—a small, velvet pouch.

"Let Val open it," said Mr. Nate. "It's his family."

I thought Viking Val might cry. "Thank you," he said, choked up with emotion. He opened the pouch carefully and dumped the contents in his hand. When the humans realized what he held, they laughed.

"Why are they laughing?" asked Faraday. "What is it? Can you see, Capone?"

I put my front legs on Viking Val's chair to get a look. When I saw what it was, I laughed, too.

"It's a dog tag," I said. "I can't believe it."

Viking Val held it up. The gold circle sparkled in the sunlight streaming in through the windows. He read the inscription. "Boo. The best dog ever, and the Boussard's treasure." He shook his head, reaching over to pet Molly. "I should have known. Our dogs are our greatest treasure. I'm sorry, old girl. I got so distracted I forgot to focus on what was most important. This life. This moment. And you. I was such an idiot."

Molly stared up at him adoringly. "I have no idea what you're yammering on about, but that's okay. I love you, my human, and I always will."

As I watched all my friends, old and new, enjoy this moment of camaraderie, it reminded me of another line from *Emma*. "It's such a happiness when fine people and fine doggies get together."

When I heard the faint sound of a dog barking, I glanced up in time to see Boo standing by the door, but this time he wasn't alone. A young man, who looked an awful lot like Viking Val, stood with him.

Boo smiled at me, his dog tag hung again on his ghostly neck. He'd found what he'd been searching for all these years. He'd been searching for his boy. Somehow, because of some magic or miracle I could never understand, as soon as Viking Val held the long-lost dog tag in his hand, Boo and his master were reunited at last.

As they slipped out the door and disappeared in a blaze of golden light, I realized I wouldn't see either of them again, but that was okay. Viking Val had been right. The key was to focus on this life. This moment. These people. These friends. And to realize I was lucky indeed.

Most of the time.

Ms. Anne spoke to Ms. Josie. "I've been meaning to ask, have you seen my pink, fluffy slippers? I haven't been able to find them."

Curse my obsession with female footwear.

I let out a belch, one that tasted like pink fluff and

happiness. Ms. Josie and Ms. Anne looked at me, identical expressions of concern on both their faces, as my stomach produced a strange gurgling sound.

Oh, calamity. When would I learn?

Both ladies grabbed their coats and put on their boots without saying a word. "Where are you going?" asked Mr. Nate.

"The vet," said Ms. Josie.

His eyes widened. "Oh, no. What did Capone eat this time?"

How the heck did he know it was me?

Note to self: I needed to make better choices. I also needed to stop eating non-food items.

But the truth was that life is too short not to enjoy it fully and taste a bit of everything.

Except for pink slippers. I probably should stop tasting those.

THIRTY-NINE

Reasons I love my family:

1. They support me in everything I do.
2. They love me even when I make lamentable decisions.
3. They take excellent care of me.
4. They don't judge me for my Jane Austen obsession.
5. They never stop surprising me.

After the snow melted and the ground thawed a month later, we found something remarkable. A simple stone stood in the corner of the backyard next to a giant oak tree. Etched on it were the words, "Here lies Boo. He was a good boy."

"Someone cared enough about him to give him a proper burial," said Ms. Anne, blinking away tears.

Mr. Ben kissed the top of her head. "And they were right. He was a good boy. He helped me when I needed it most. When I thought I might never see you again."

That brought on a fresh flood of tears. Ms. Josie, standing next to Ms. Anne, patted her back. Ms. Anne seemed very emotional, but she'd been through a lot. Now everything was perfect, though. Mr. Ben had made his home with her, in Beaver, and he was in the process of moving his business here, too. Even though Ms. Anne was teary today, she was also blissfully happy.

Women were a mystery. A beautiful, confusing mystery.

Viking Val pulled the dog tag we'd found in the fireplace out of his pocket and placed it on top of the stone. It felt right that the tag should remain with Boo, even if Boo was no longer here.

"It looks like you crossed everything off your list, Capone," said Jackson.

"What list?" I asked, then I remembered. I'd made a list of ways I would improve the lives of others, and I'd done it all.

1. I convinced Ms. Anne that Mr. Ben was her Mr. Knightley.
2. I helped Jackson and Gracie find a peaceful solution to their problems.
3. I earned Rocco's forgiveness by helping him out of the tree.
4. I made Luke feel safe and helped him understand he's part of the family now.
5. I gained Faraday's trust and showed him how to be a true friend.
6. I found a way to put the soul of Boo the Ghost Dog to rest at last.

"You're right. How did you know about my list?" I asked.

He snorted. "You told us. I thought you were nuts, but it turned out you made it happen after all. Nice job, pup."

Gracie let out a sniff. "But I'm still so sorry about Boo. It's such a sad story. No good came of it at all."

"There is nothing we can do about the past, Gracie," said Faraday. "Don't cry."

"I can't help it. I'm so emotional lately. I don't understand what's wrong with me."

When the humans went inside, we followed them. It turned out Ms. Anne and Mr. Ben had a rather important announcement. She held up her left hand to display a simple gold band.

"They got married?" I asked as everyone congratulated them. "But when? How?"

"At the courthouse this morning," said Gracie, her voice shaky. "So beautiful and romantic."

"Are you crying again?" asked Jackson. "What is wrong with you?"

"I don't know," she wailed. "I've been crying at everything lately."

Ms. Anne cried as well. "Sorry," she said. "I'm so happy. But there is something else we need to tell you. And it kind of explains why I've been weeping at the drop of a hat."

Her words sounded oddly like Gracie's. "What's going on?" I asked, but they silenced me.

"I want to hear her big announcement," said Molly. "Be quiet, puppy."

I did as Molly asked but had no idea what was happening. Not until Mr. Ben placed a gentle hand over Ms. Anne's belly.

"We're expecting," he said, his face bright with happiness.

There was a moment of stunned silence. Ms. Josie broke it by squealing. "When? How? I mean, I understand how, but this is a miracle. I'm so happy for both of you. No wonder you've been so emotional. Hormones will do it."

We stared at them in stunned silence. Then we turned to Gracie, who continued to sniff and cry next to Jackson. When she caught us staring at her, she frowned.

"What?"

"Um, your owner is expecting a litter," I said.

"Humans don't call it a litter, Capone," said Gracie. "It's a baby."

"Oh. My bad. Anyway, do you have something to tell us, Gracie?"

She blinked in surprise, comprehension dawning on her face. She glared at Jackson. "You said you were fixed."

Jackson seemed like he might faint. "I... I thought I was. You said you were fixed, too. How did this happen?"

Gracie started pacing. "I only went into heat that one time. I didn't think it was possible."

Rocco shook his head. "Jackson. You don't have the equipment necessary to reproduce."

Jackson shot a quick look between his legs. "Oh, thank goodness."

"Which can only mean one thing," said Rocco. "If Gracie is pregnant, you aren't the father."

"What?" asked Jackson. "Then who is?"

"Oh, my. We may have a Wickham in our midst," I said. "And Gracie is our Lydia."

"Gracie, you dirty dog. What have you done?"

Rocco made a funny noise, like a snort and a laugh mixed together. "The question is who has she done, Jackson. And the answer should be quite obvious. There are only three unneutered dogs in our group. Capone, Luke, and the Puglet. It had to be one of them."

"Oh, calamity," I said. Could it have been me? I had no idea.

Suddenly, I found it hard to breathe. Curse my lack of knowledge regarding the reproductive process. They never discussed this sort of thing on PBS.

I thought I might swoon. I sank onto the grass and stared at my friends in horror.

"I'm too young to be a father."

Note to self: It's going to be an interesting summer.

TO READ MORE *about Capone's adventures, get the first book in the series,* Love, Chocolate, and a Dog Named Al Capone. *Or follow him on Facebook at* Capone the Wonder Dog.

SIGN UP *for Abigail Drake's newsletter to get information about new releases, free content, and wonderful prizes!*

THANK YOU FOR READING! *If you enjoyed this book, please click here to give it an honest review: Books by Abigail Drake*

ABOUT THE AUTHOR

Abigail Drake is the award-winning author of seventeen novels, but she didn't start her career in writing. She majored in Japanese and economics in college, and spent years traveling the world, collecting stories wherever she visited. She collected a husband from Istanbul on her travels, too, and he is her favorite souvenir.

Abigail is a coffee addict, a puppy wrangler, and the mother of three adult sons. She writes contemporary romance, women's fiction, and young adult fiction, and has taught workshops for many different writing organizations. In her spare time, she blogs about her dog, Capone, and teaches writing classes for children at her local library. For more about Abigail, visit her website: https://www. abigaildrake.net.

ABOUT THE OTHER AUTHOR

Capone the Wonder Dog is a Labrador of impeccable grace and breeding. He enjoys walking in the meadow, chasing rabbits, and stealing butter wrappers from the garbage can. This is his debut novel, which he wrote with the help of his owner since he does not have thumbs and can't type. He dreams of one day becoming a bestselling author, and of catching the irritating robin that mocks him daily from the back patio.

ALSO BY ABIGAIL DRAKE

<u>Women's Fiction</u>

The Tink Holly Chronicles
Rebel Without a Clause

The South Side Stories
The Dragonsong Law Offices
The Hocus Pocus Magic Shop
The Enchanted Garden Cafe

Passports and Promises
Delayed Departure
Flying Solo
New Heights
Saying Goodbye

A Dog Named Al Capone
Hearts, Flowers, and a Dog Named Al Capone
Love, Chocolate, and a Dog Named Al Capone

Other
Lola Flannigan
Traveller

<u>Young Adult Fiction</u>

The Bodyguard

Starr Valentine

Tiger Lily

<u>Non-Fiction</u>

The Reformed Pantser's Guide to Plotting

For more about Abigail, visit her website:

https://www.abigaildrake.net

www.ingramcontent.com/pod-product-compliance
Lightning Source LLC
Chambersburg PA
CBHW020337010826
48970CB00012B/1350